ROYDEN LEPP

RUST™

SOUL IN THE MACHINE

Published by
ARCHAIA™

ROYDE

RU

SOUL IN TH

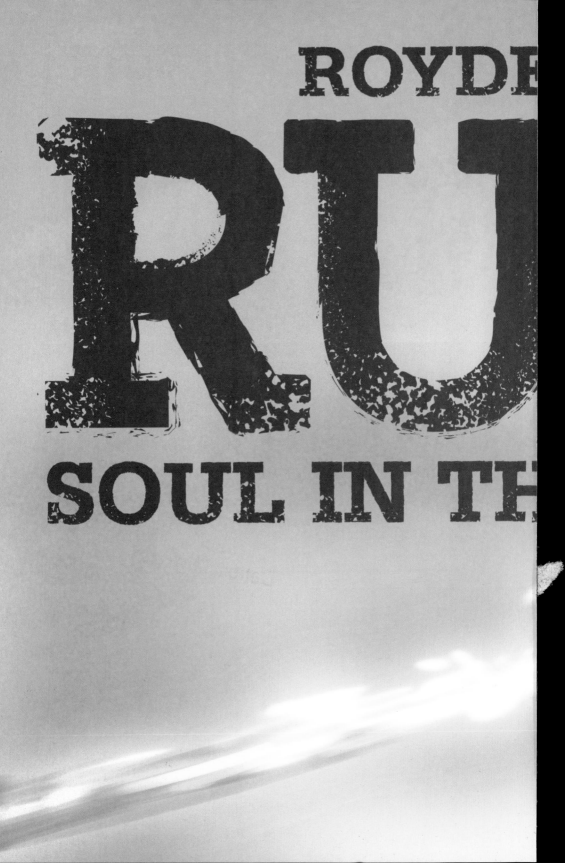

N LEPP

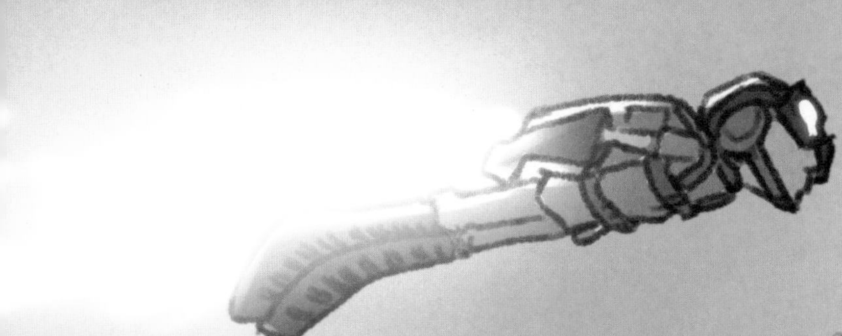

ST

E MACHINE

TM

ARCHAIA.

RUST VOLUME FOUR: SOUL IN THE MACHINE,
February 2018. Published by Archaia, a division of
Boom Entertainment, Inc. Rust is ™ and © 2018 Royden
Lepp. All Rights Reserved. "RUST: Day 23" was previously
published in MOUSE GUARD, LABYRINTH, AND OTHER
STORIES A FREE COMIC BOOK DAY HARDCOVER
ANTHOLOGY 2014. ™ & © 2014 Royden Lepp. All Rights
Reserved. Archaia™ and the Archaia logo are trademarks
of Boom Entertainment, Inc., registered in various
countries and categories. All characters, events, and
institutions depicted herein are fictional. Any similarity
between any of the names, characters, persons, events,
and/or institutions in this publication to actual names,
characters, and persons, whether living or dead,
events, and/or institutions is unintended and purely
coincidental.

BOOM! Studios, 5670 Wilshire Boulevard, Suite 450, Los
Angeles, CA 90036-5679. Printed in China. First Printing.

ISBN: 978-1-68415-162-2, eISBN: 978-1-61398-947-0

Written & Illustrated by
Royden Lepp

Logo Designed by
Fawn Lau

Flatted by
Nechama Frier

Designer
Scott Newman

Associate Editor
Cameron Chittock

Editor
Sierra Hahn

Special Thanks to
Rebecca Taylor

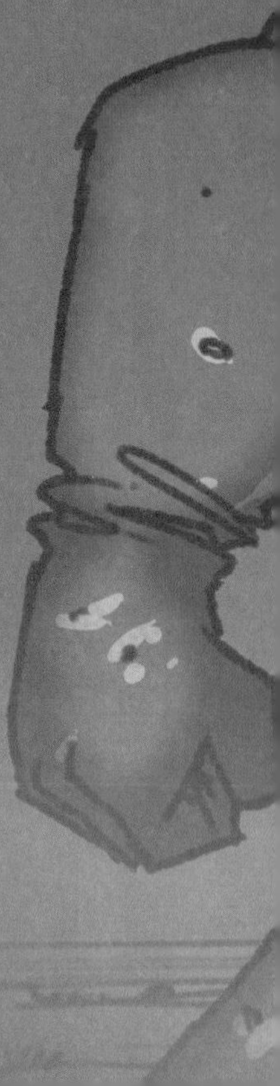

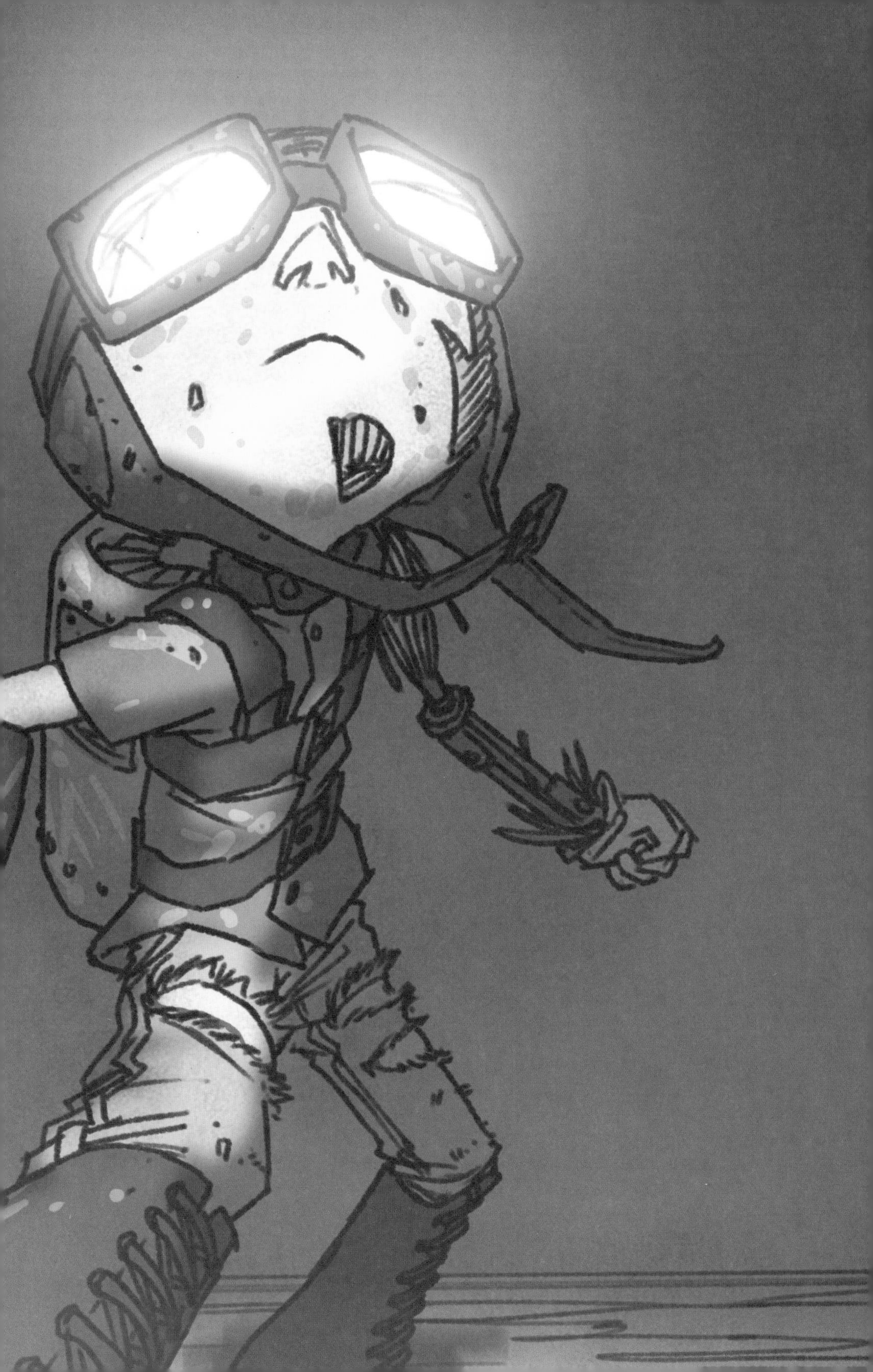

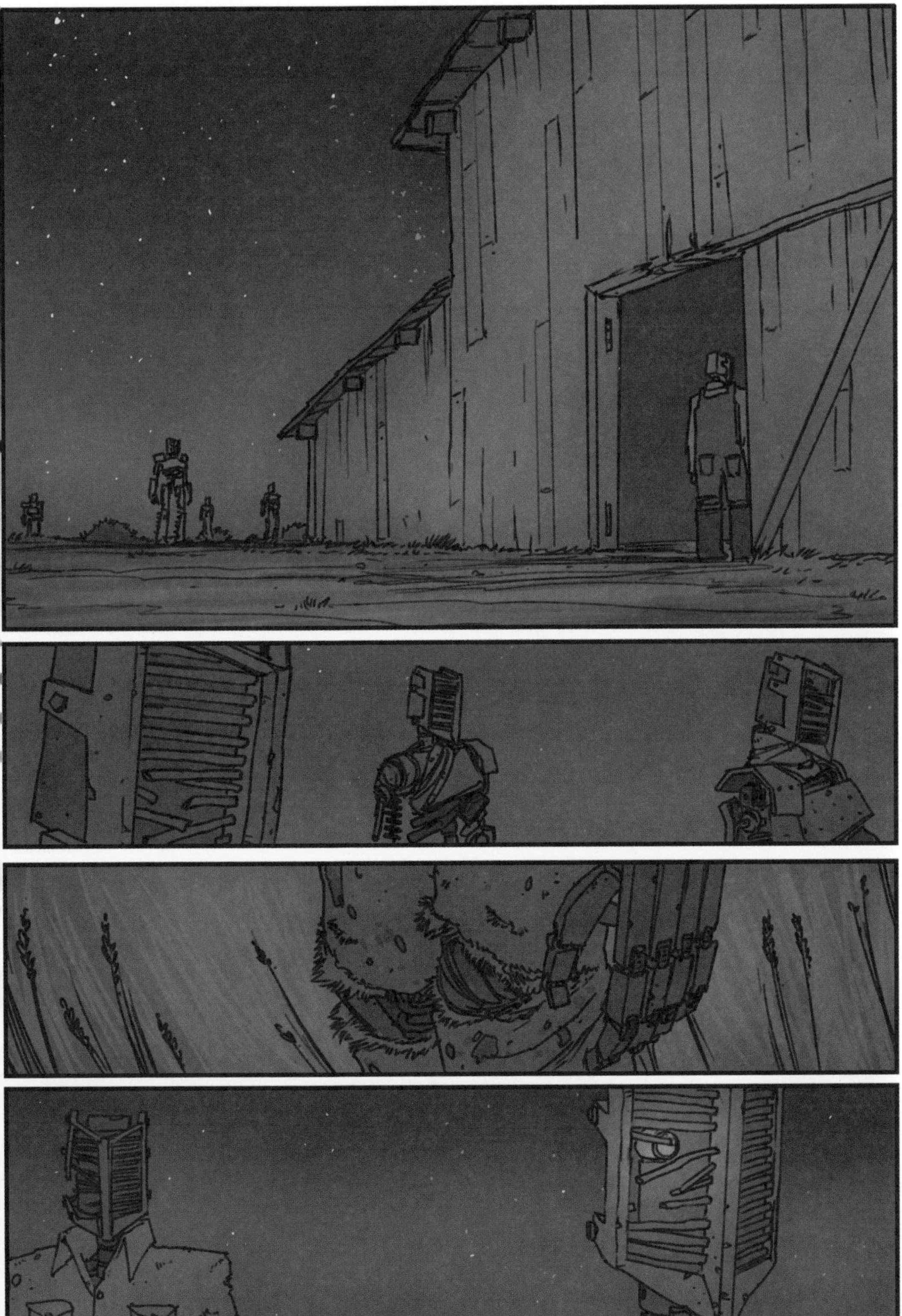

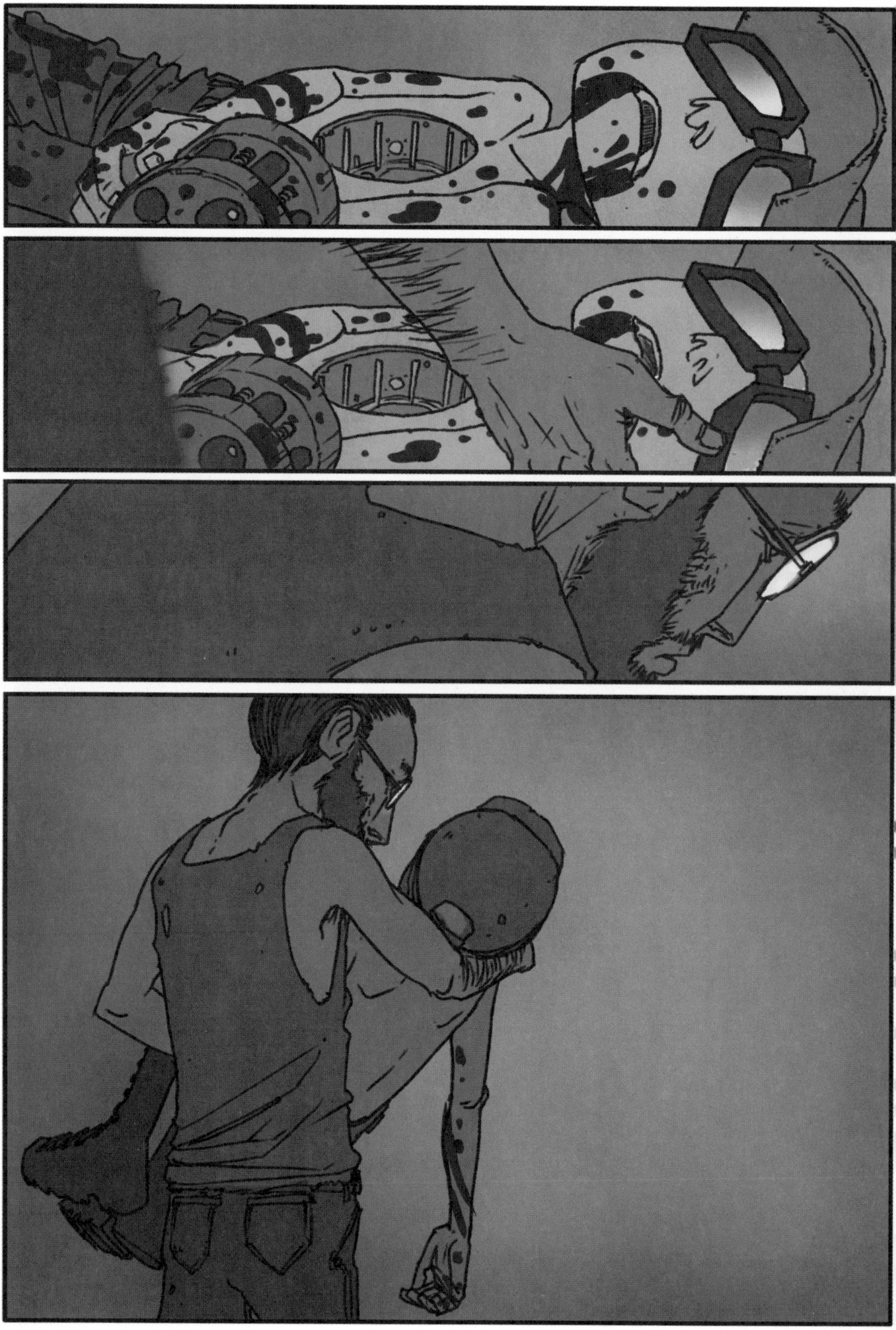

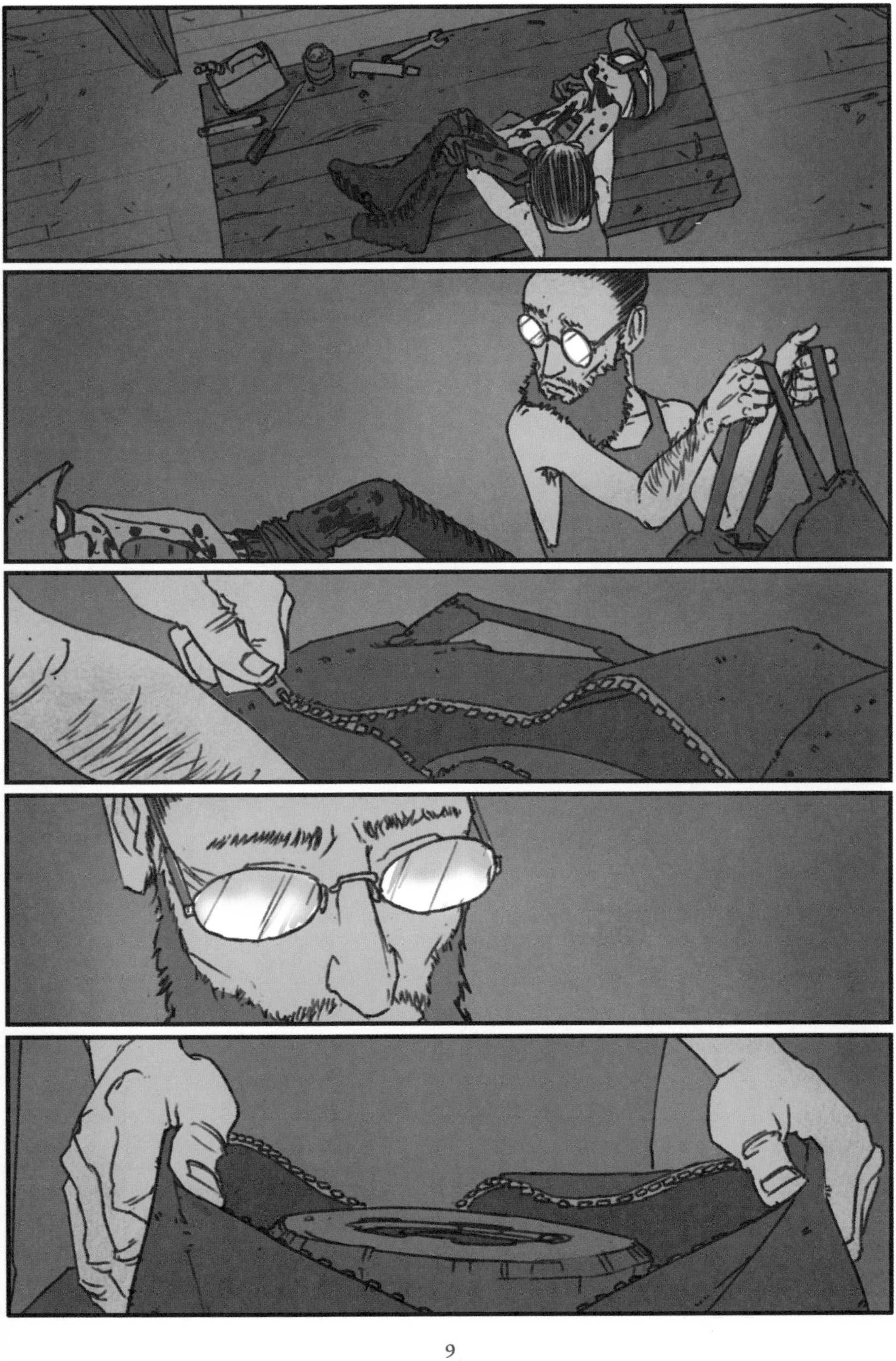

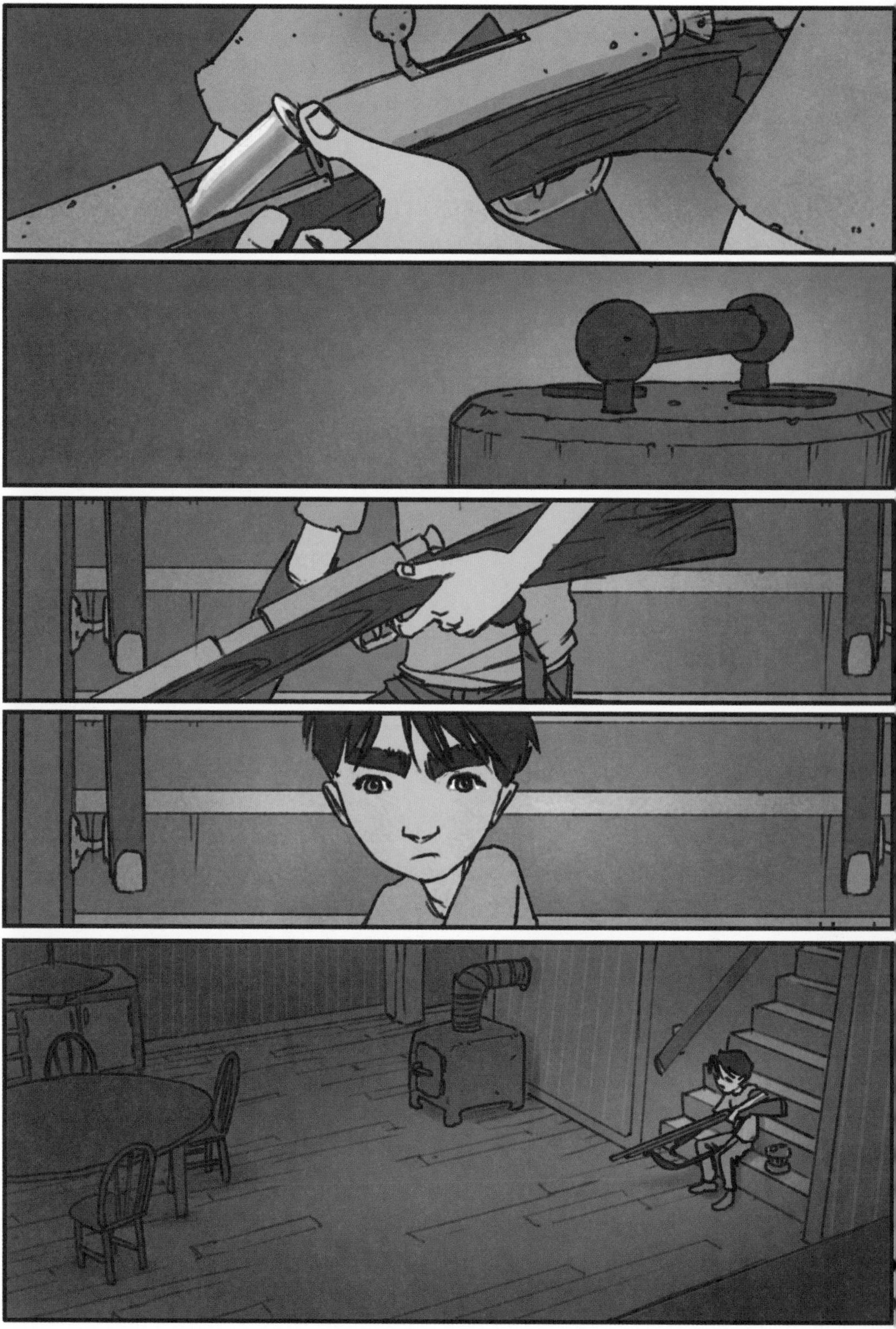

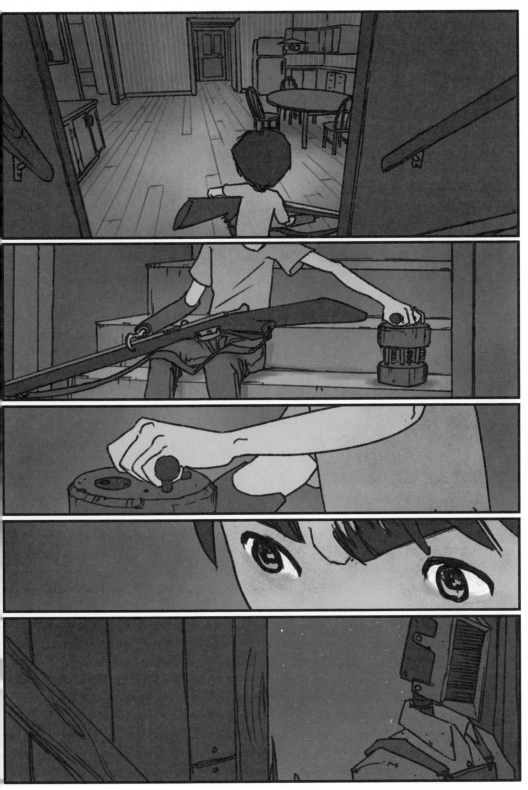

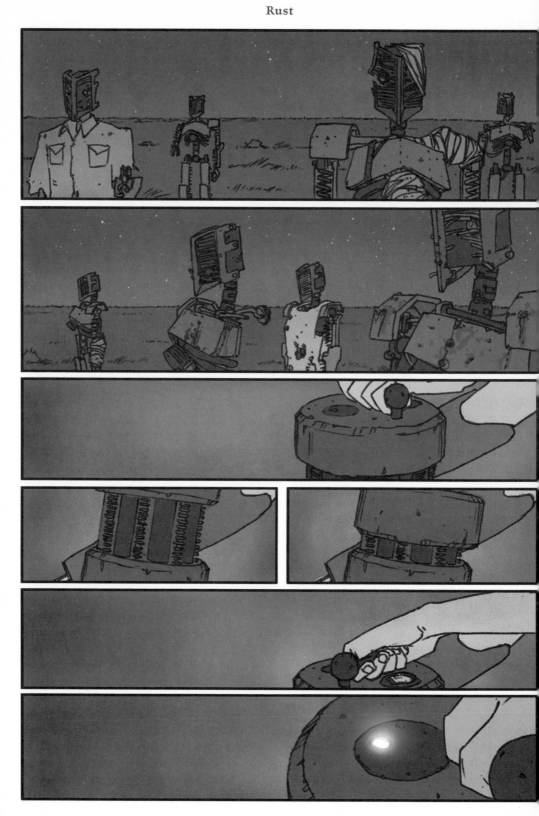

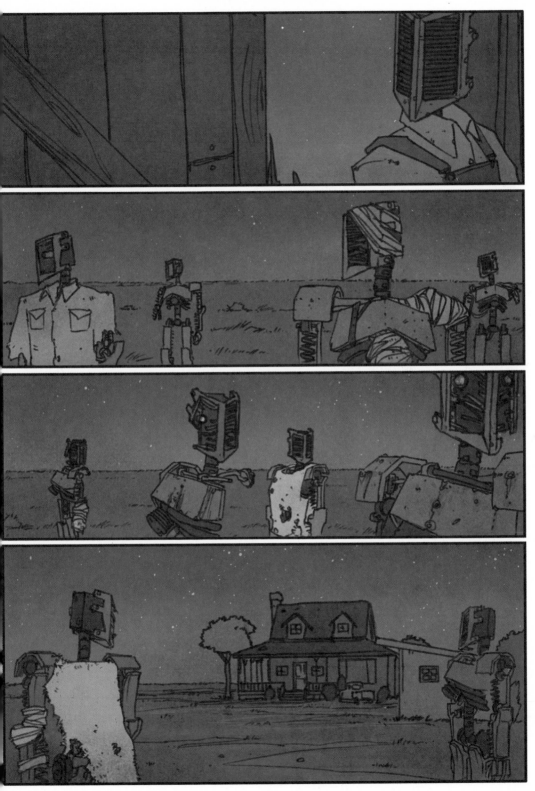

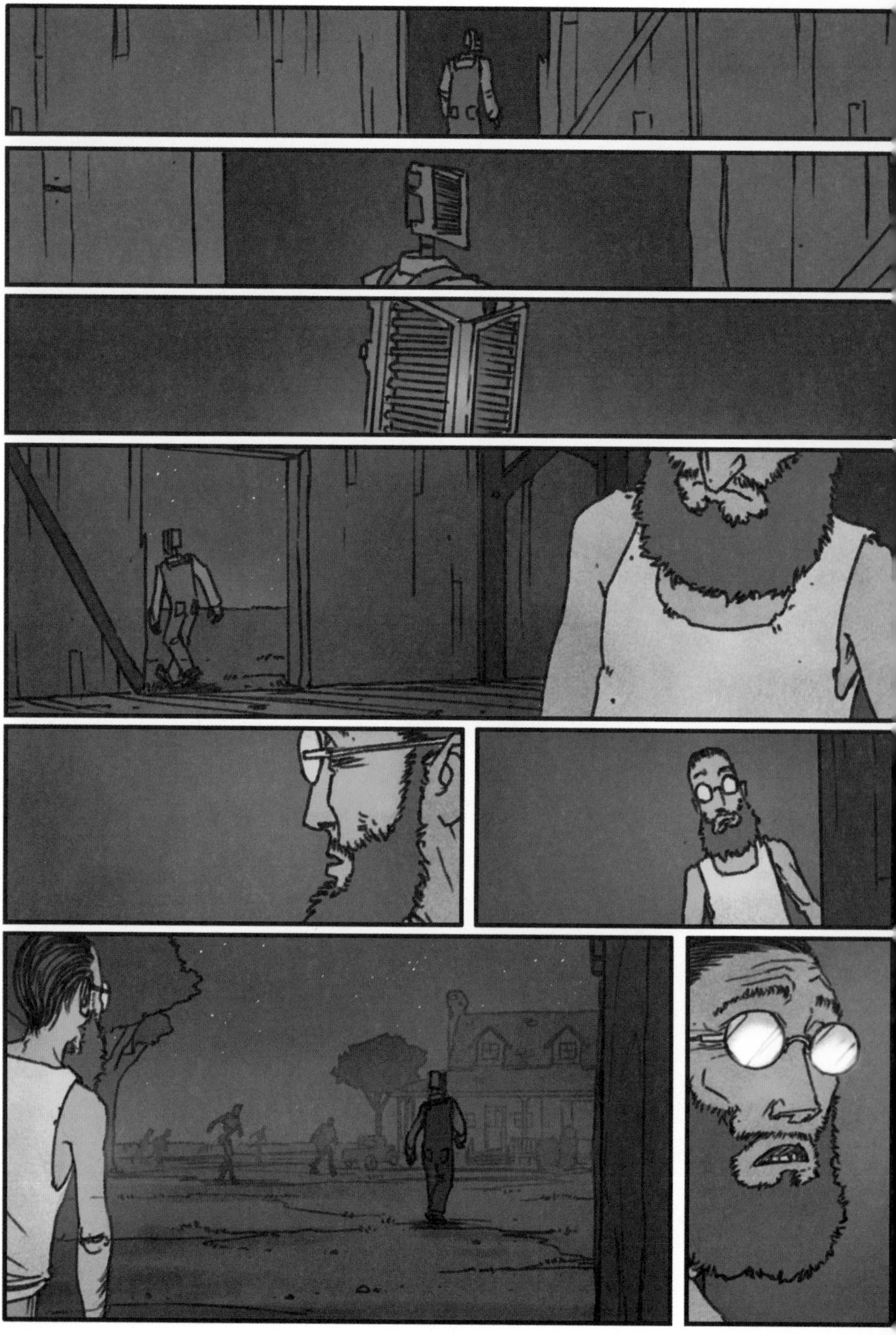

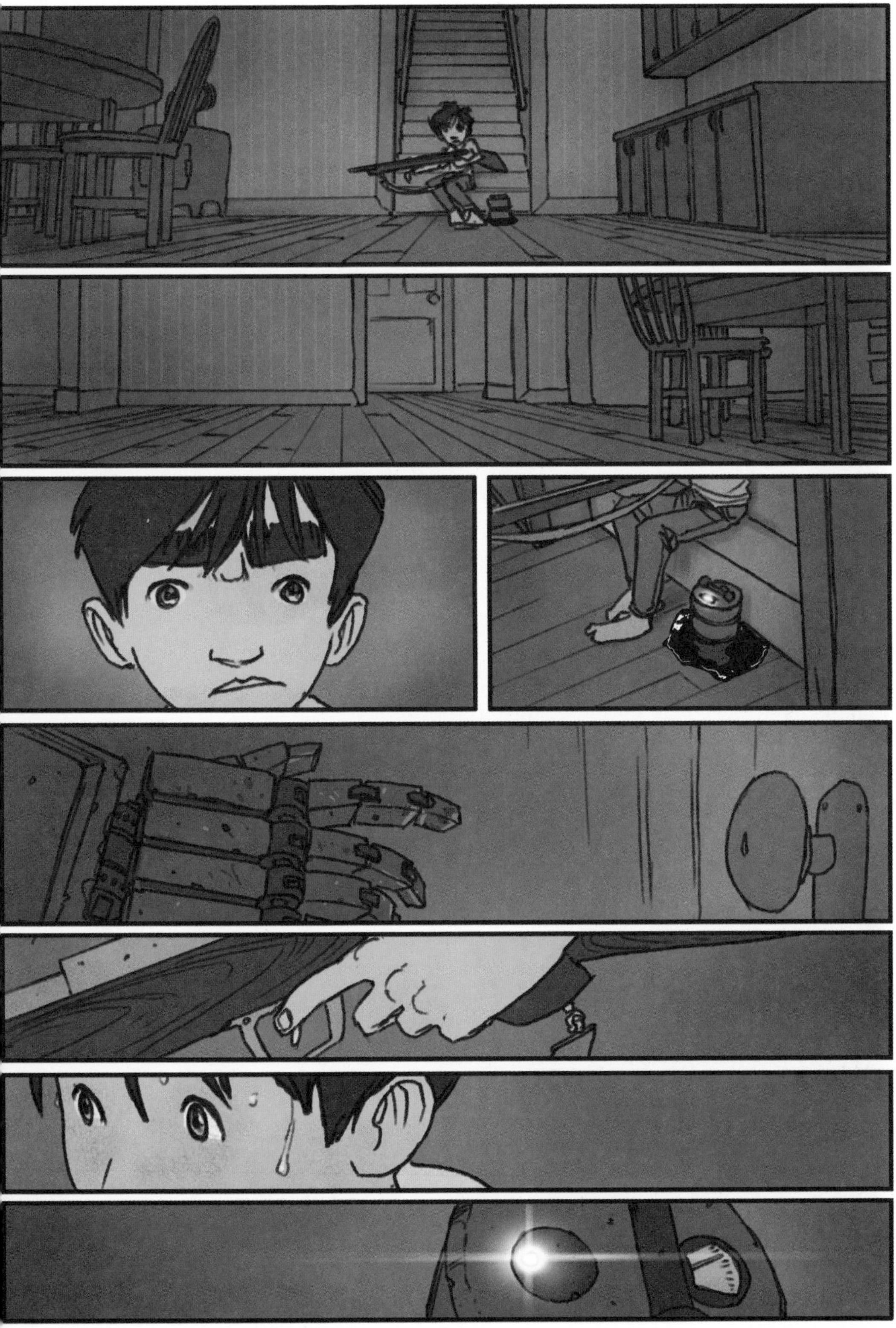

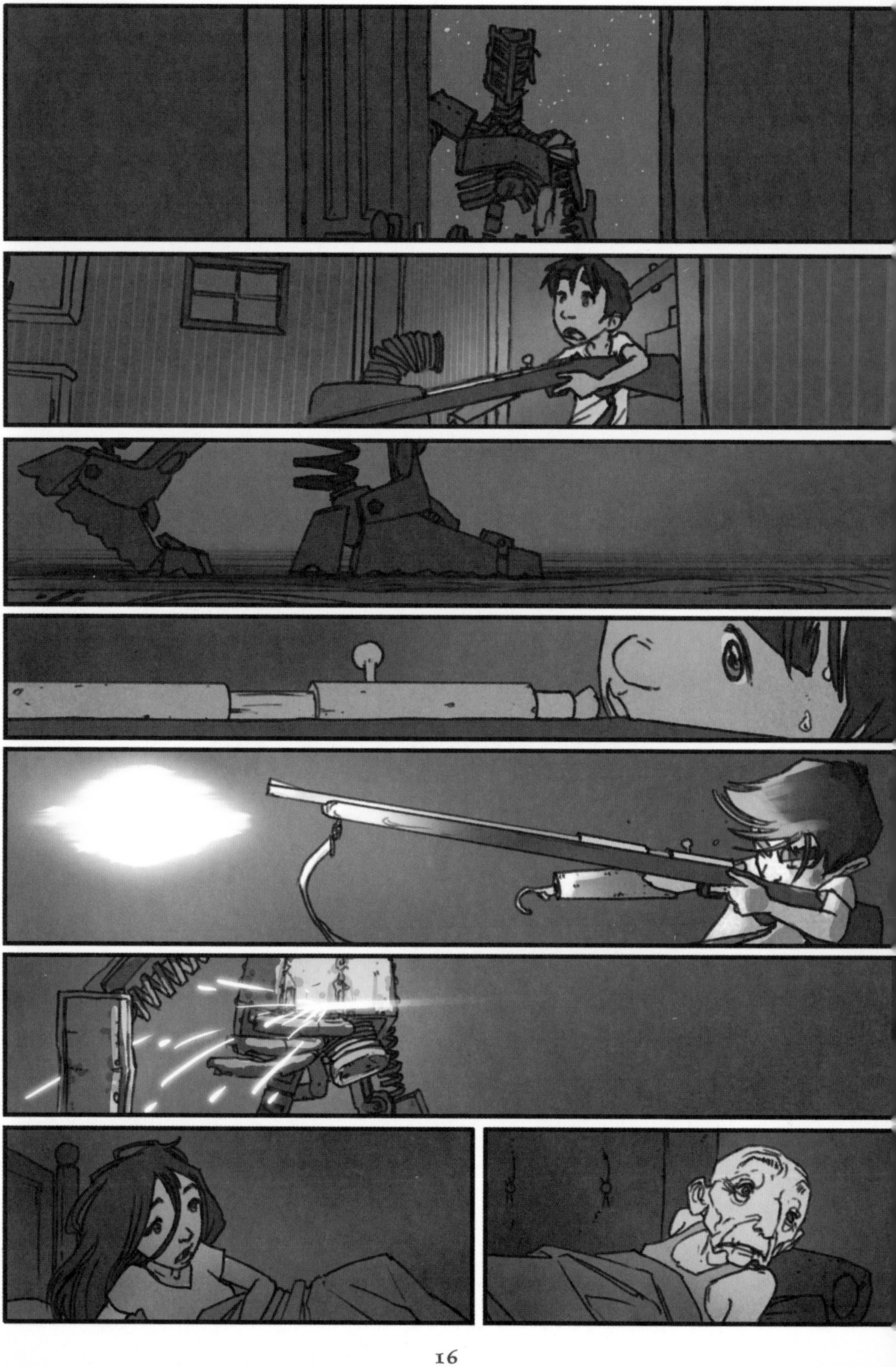

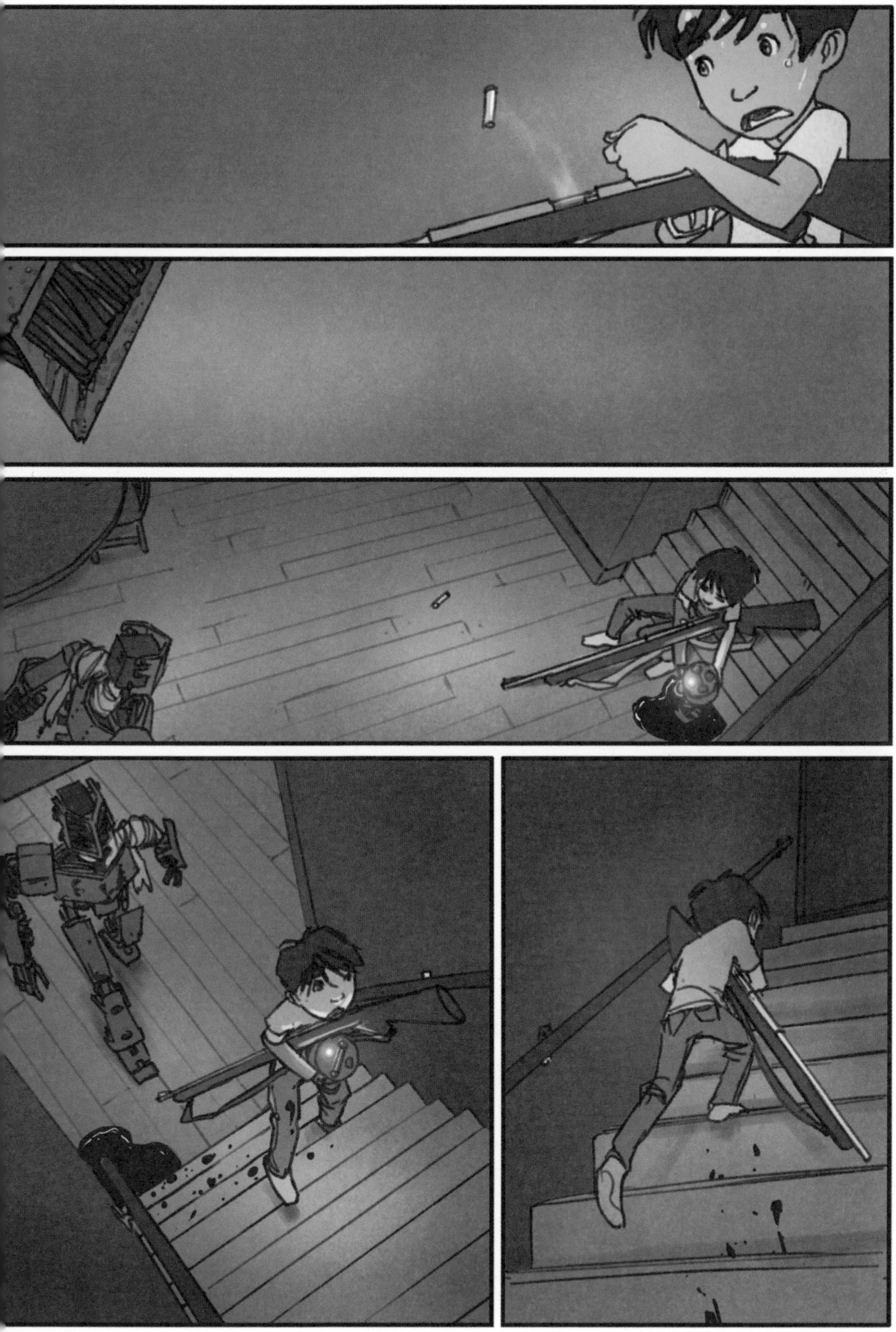

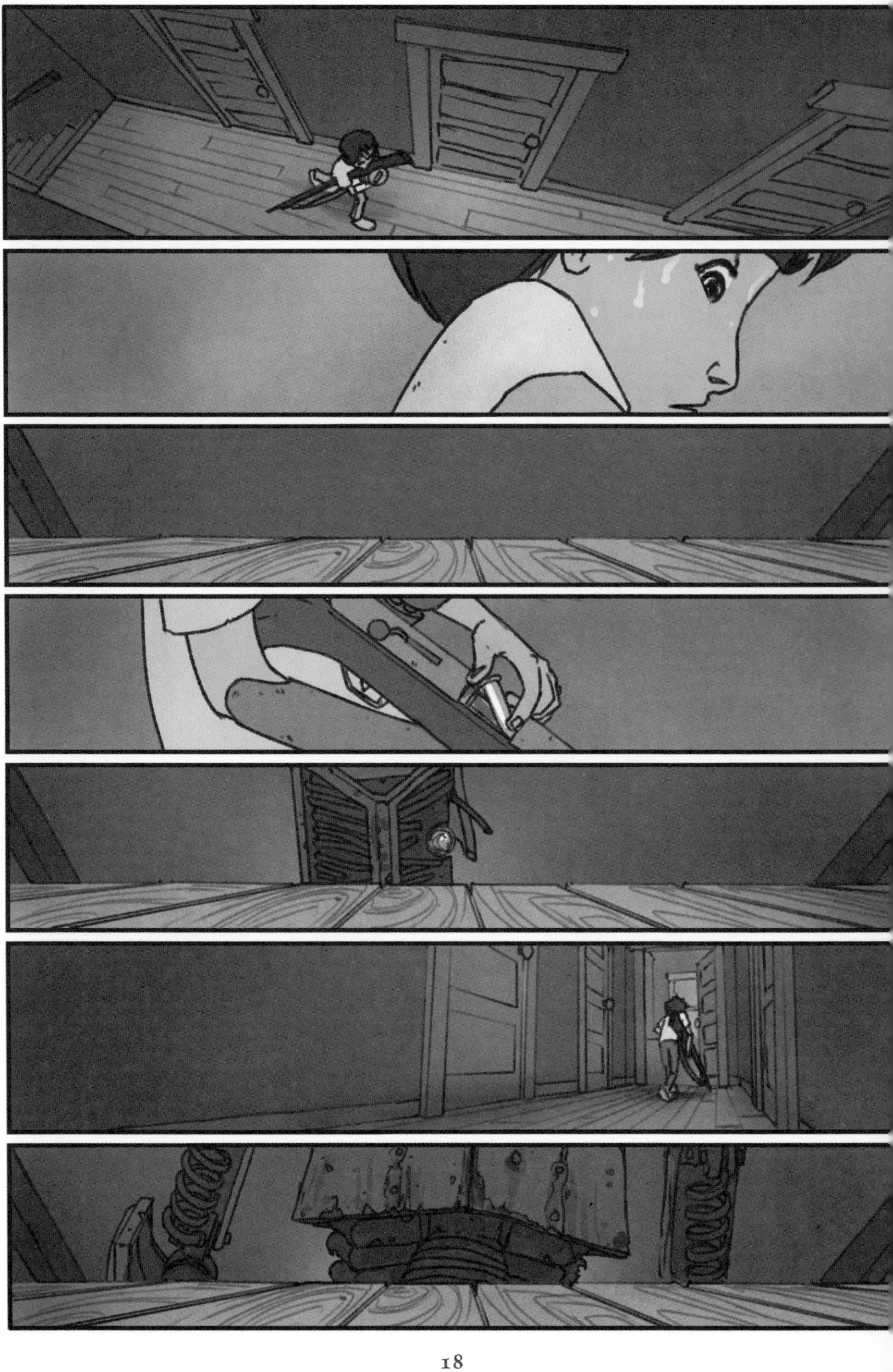

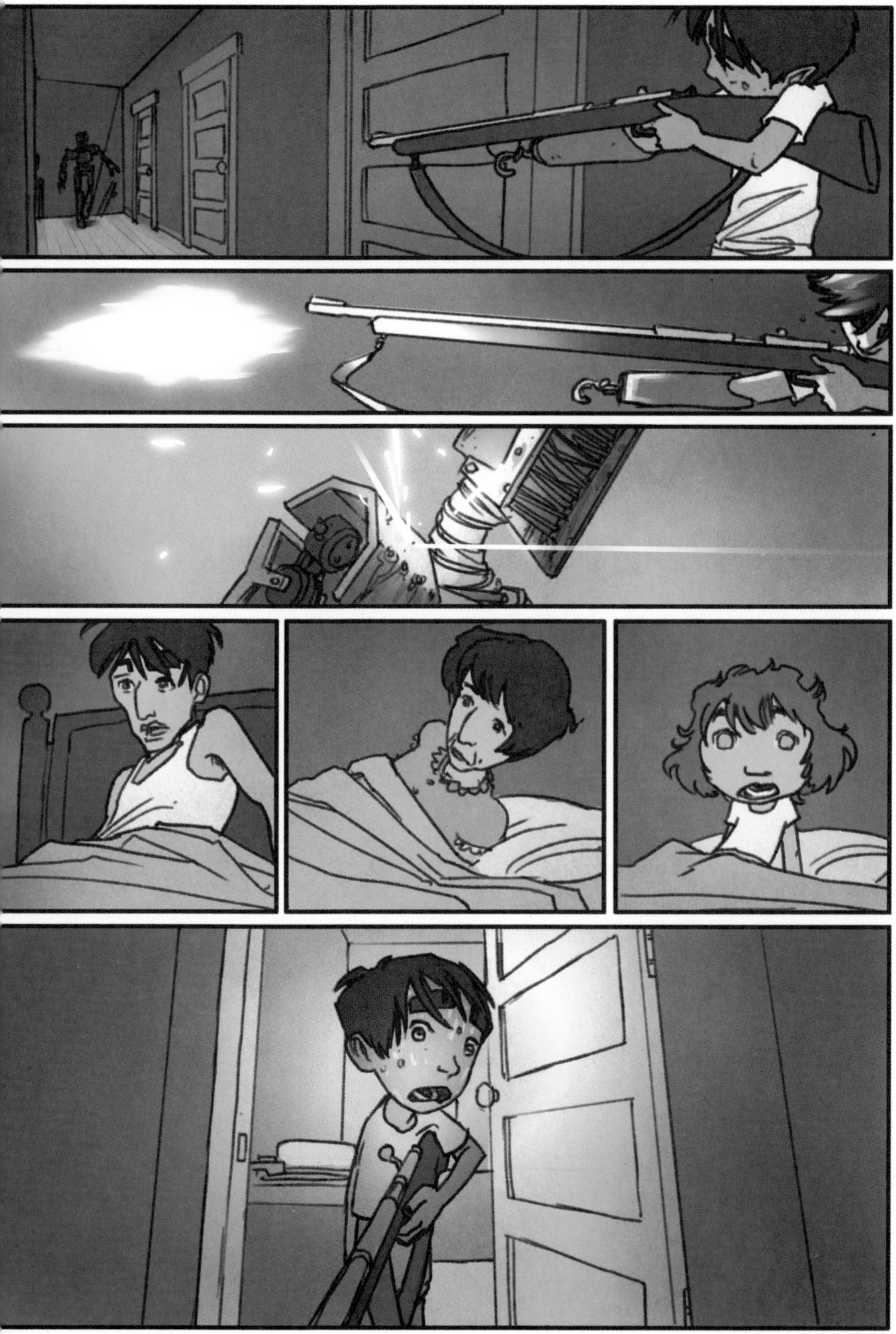

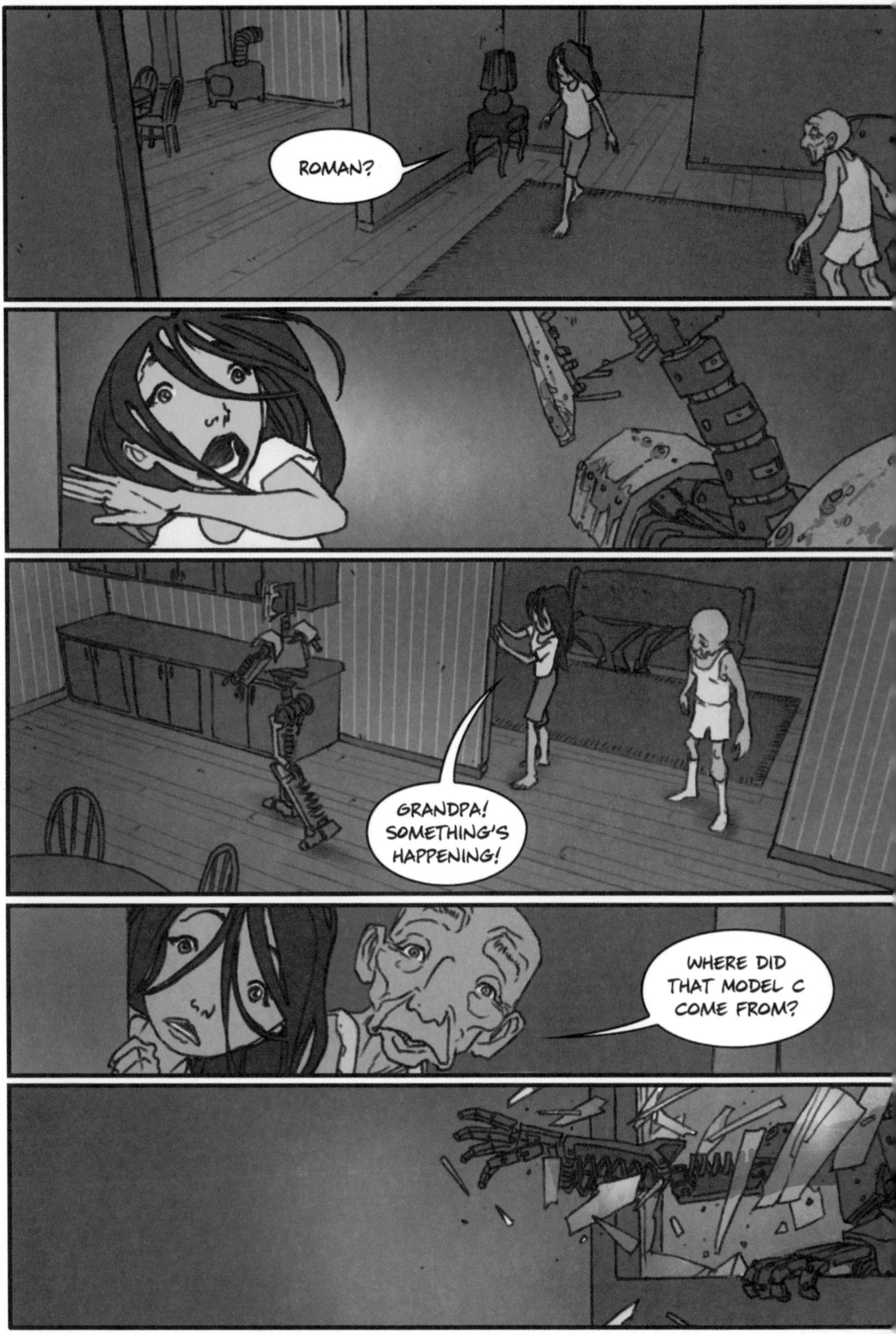
ROMAN?
GRANDPA! SOMETHING'S HAPPENING!
WHERE DID THAT MODEL C COME FROM?

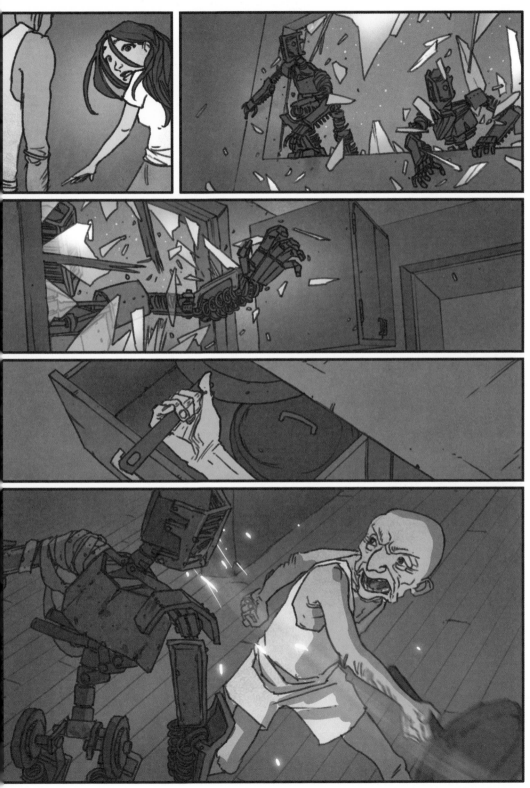

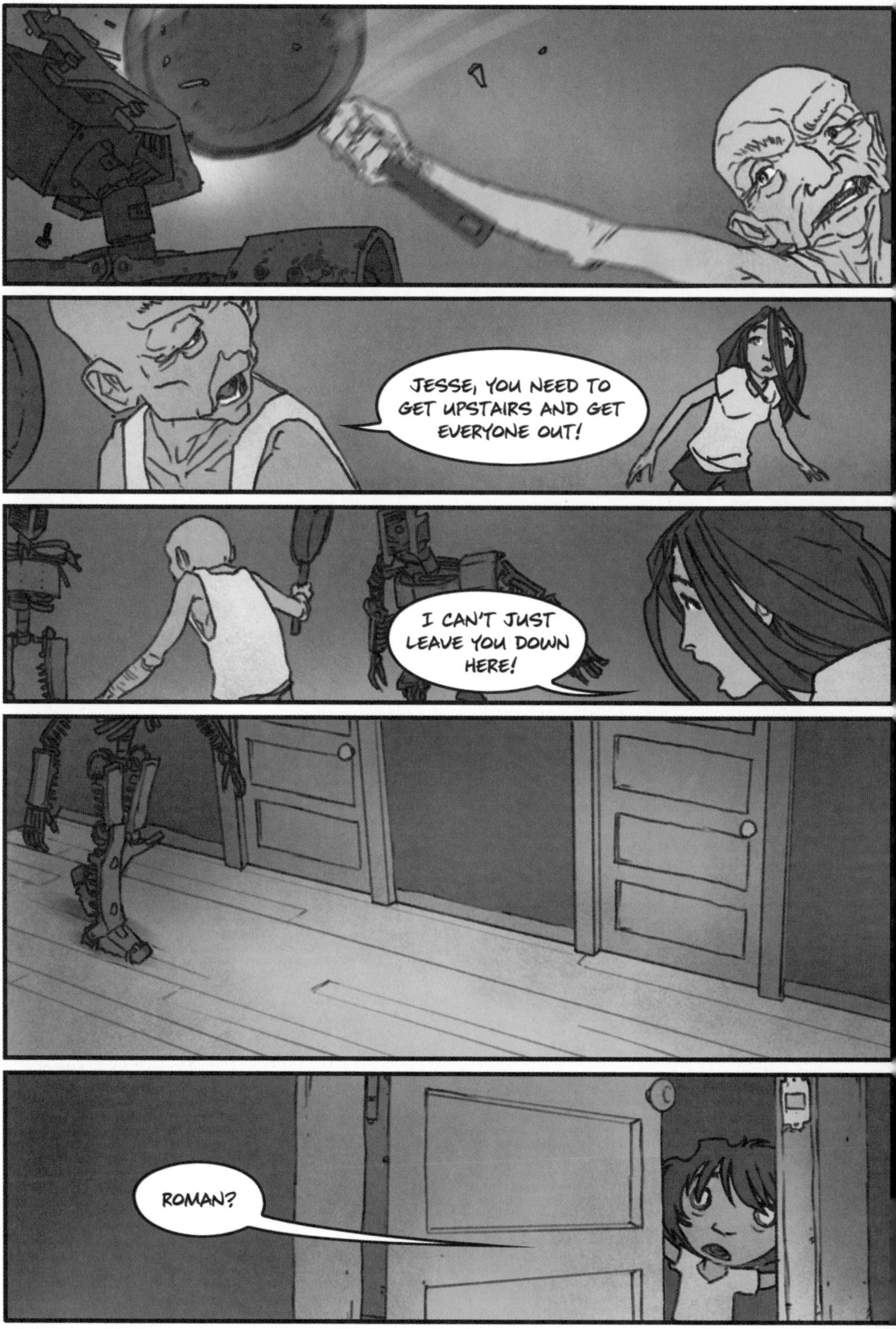
JESSE, YOU NEED TO GET UPSTAIRS AND GET EVERYONE OUT!
I CAN'T JUST LEAVE YOU DOWN HERE!
ROMAN?

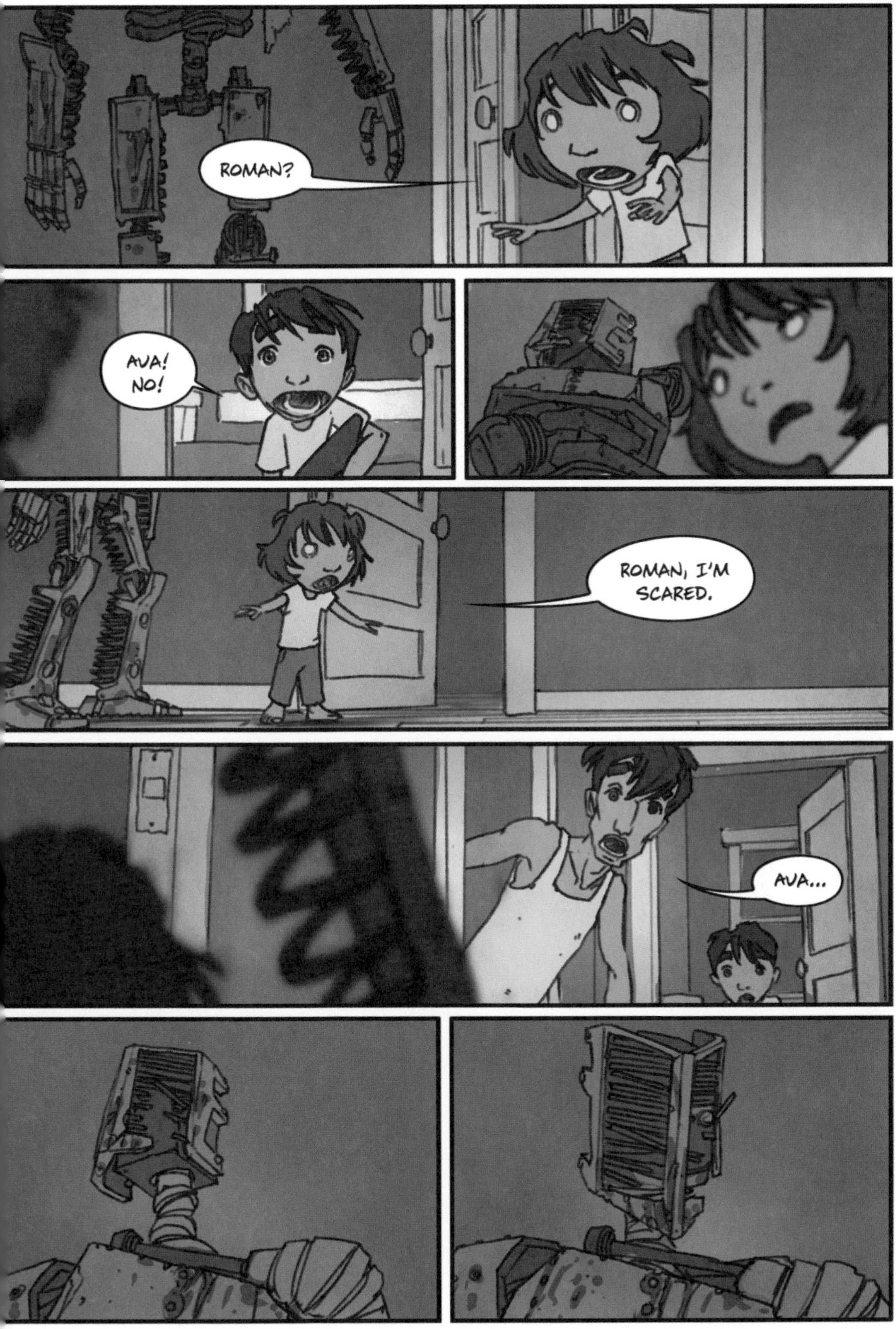
ROMAN?
AVA! NO!
ROMAN, I'M SCARED.
AVA...

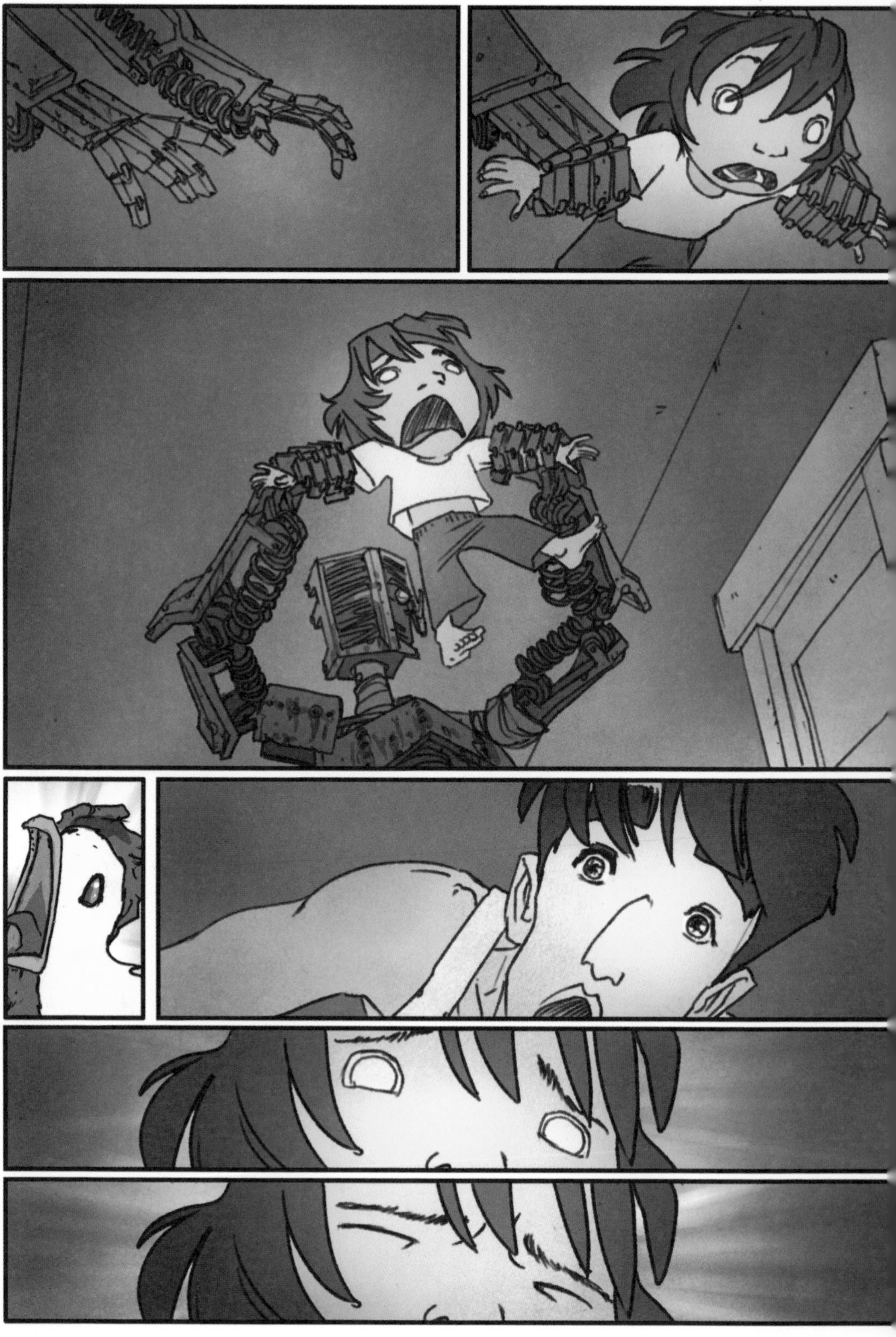

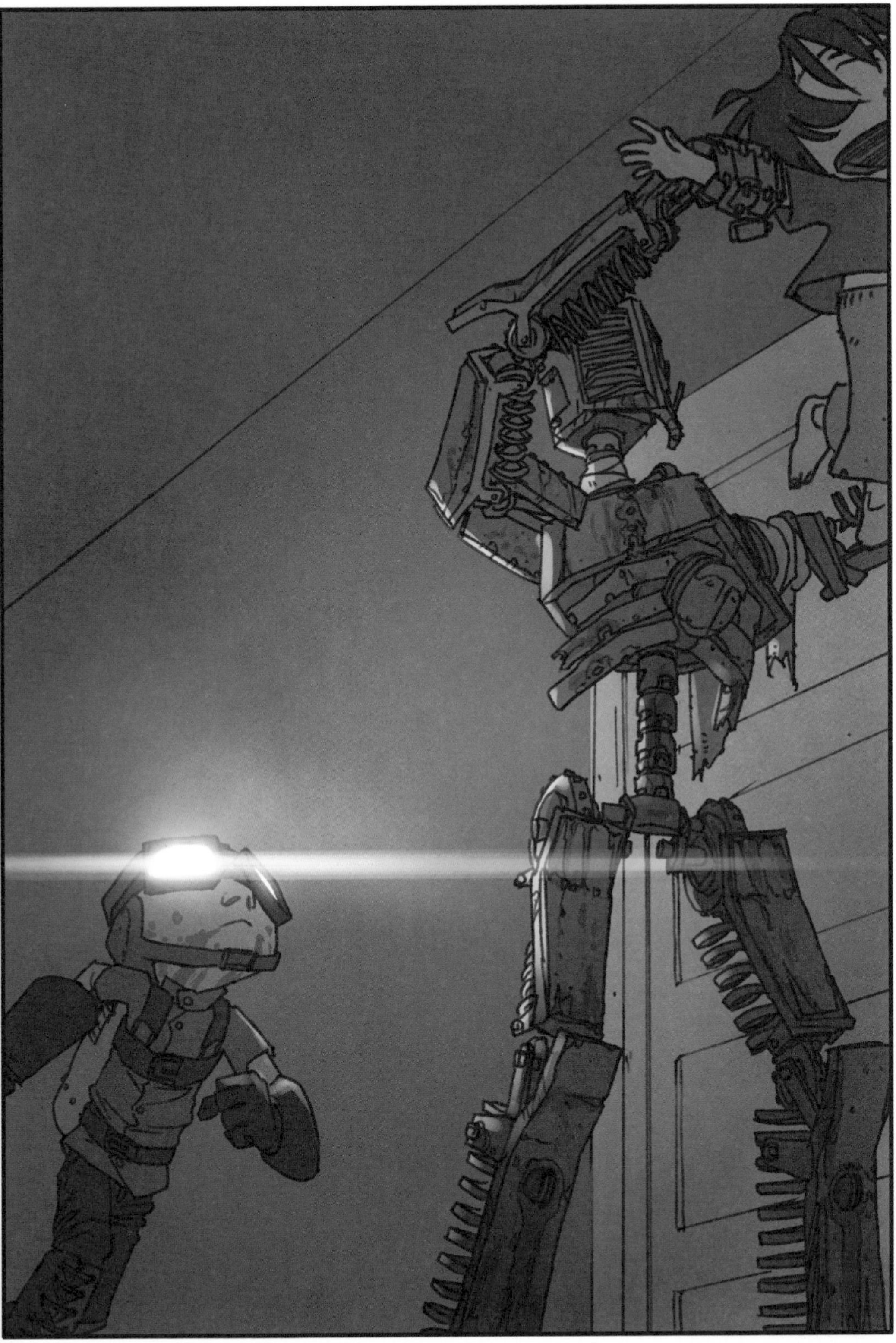

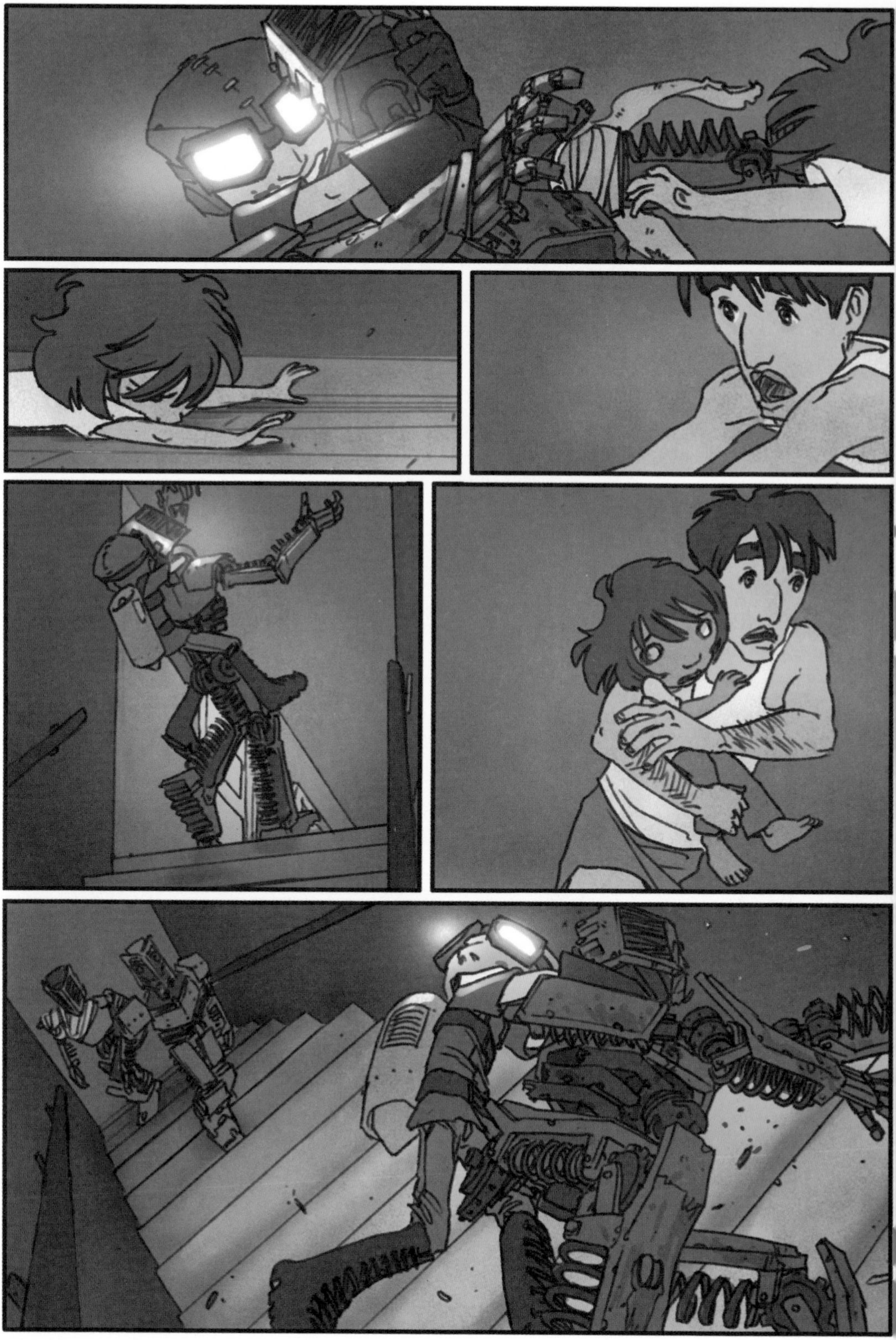

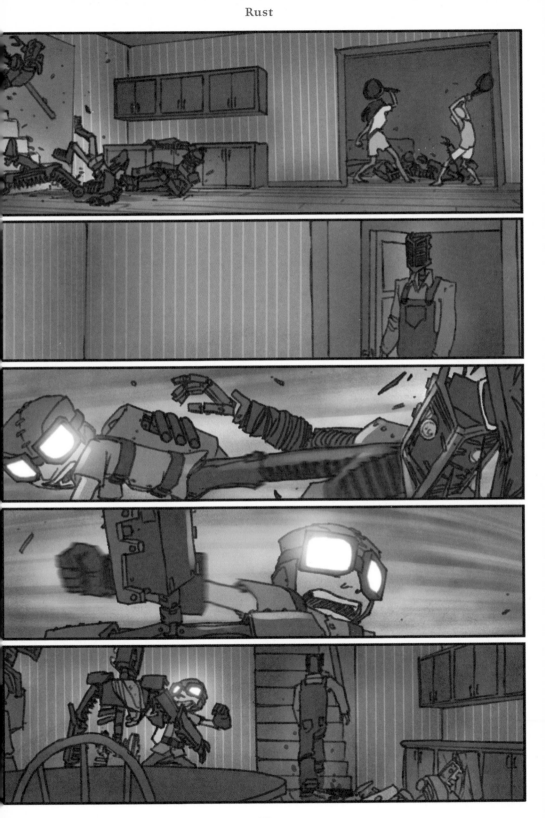

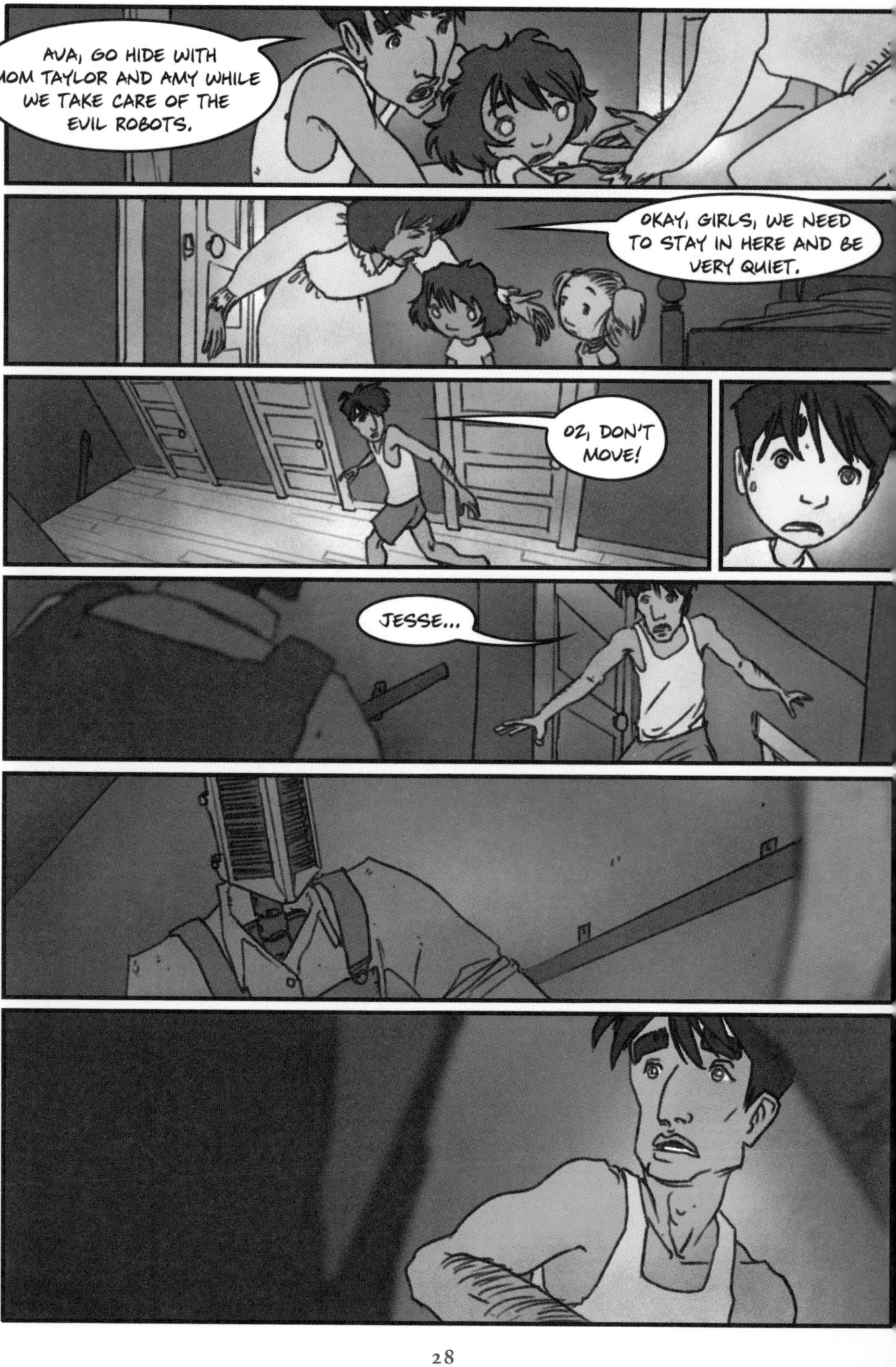
AVA, GO HIDE WITH MOM TAYLOR AND AMY WHILE WE TAKE CARE OF THE EVIL ROBOTS.
OKAY, GIRLS, WE NEED TO STAY IN HERE AND BE VERY QUIET.
OZ, DON'T MOVE!
JESSE...

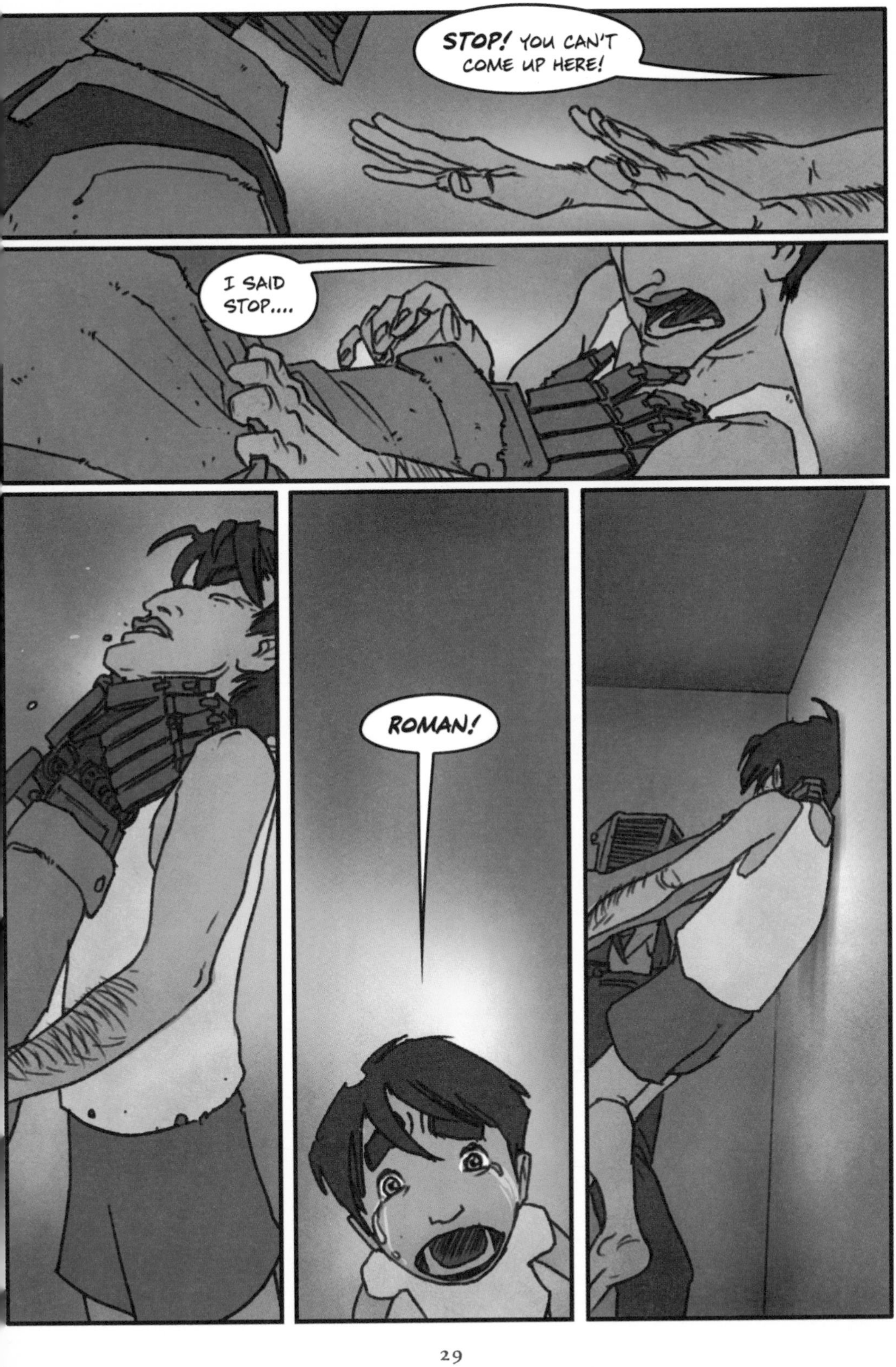
STOP! YOU CAN'T COME UP HERE!
I SAID STOP....
ROMAN!

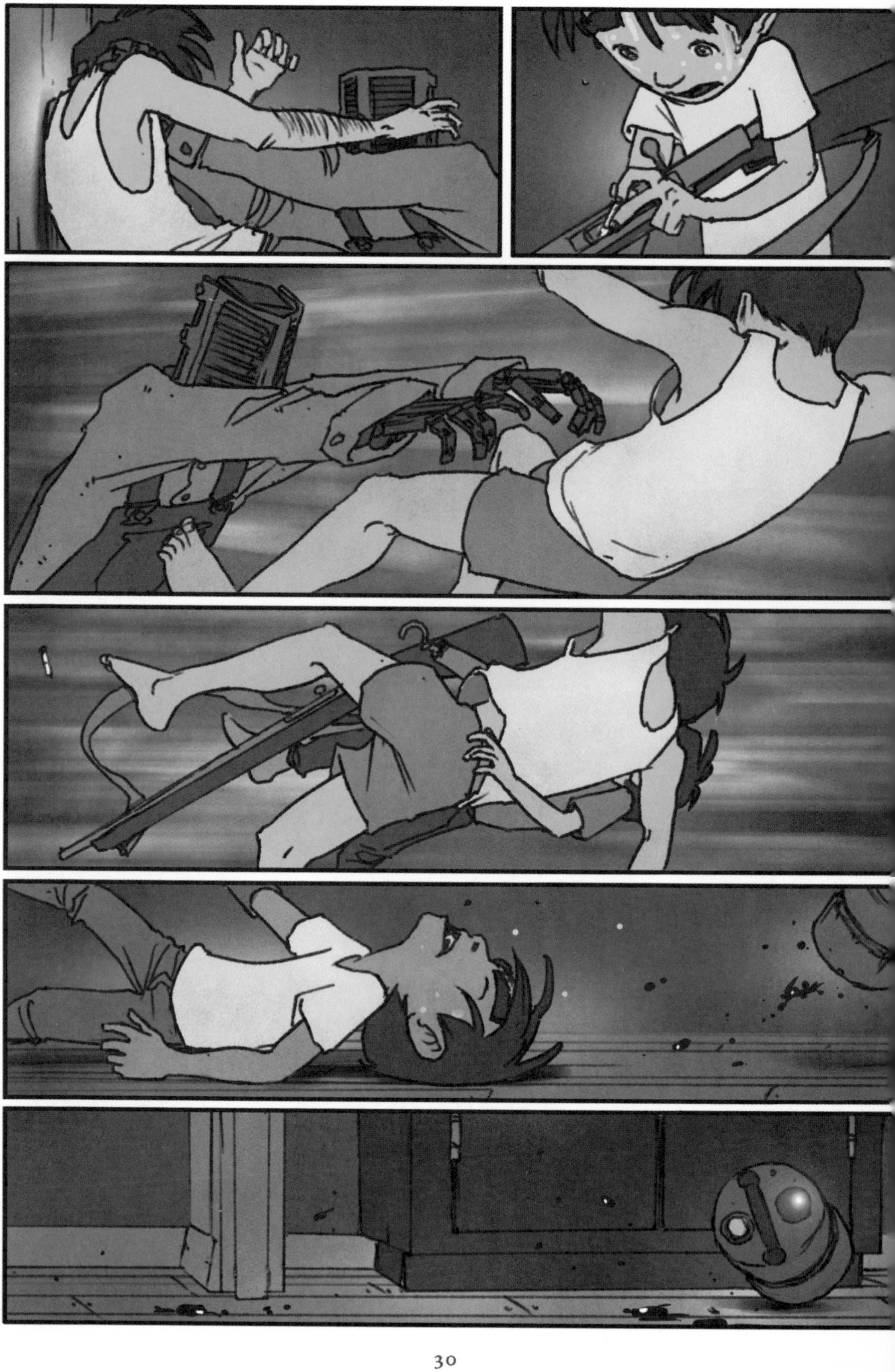

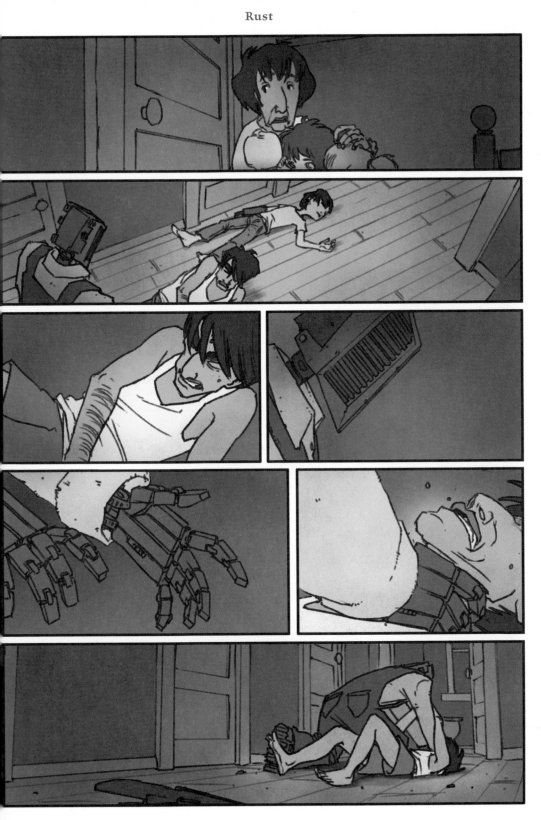

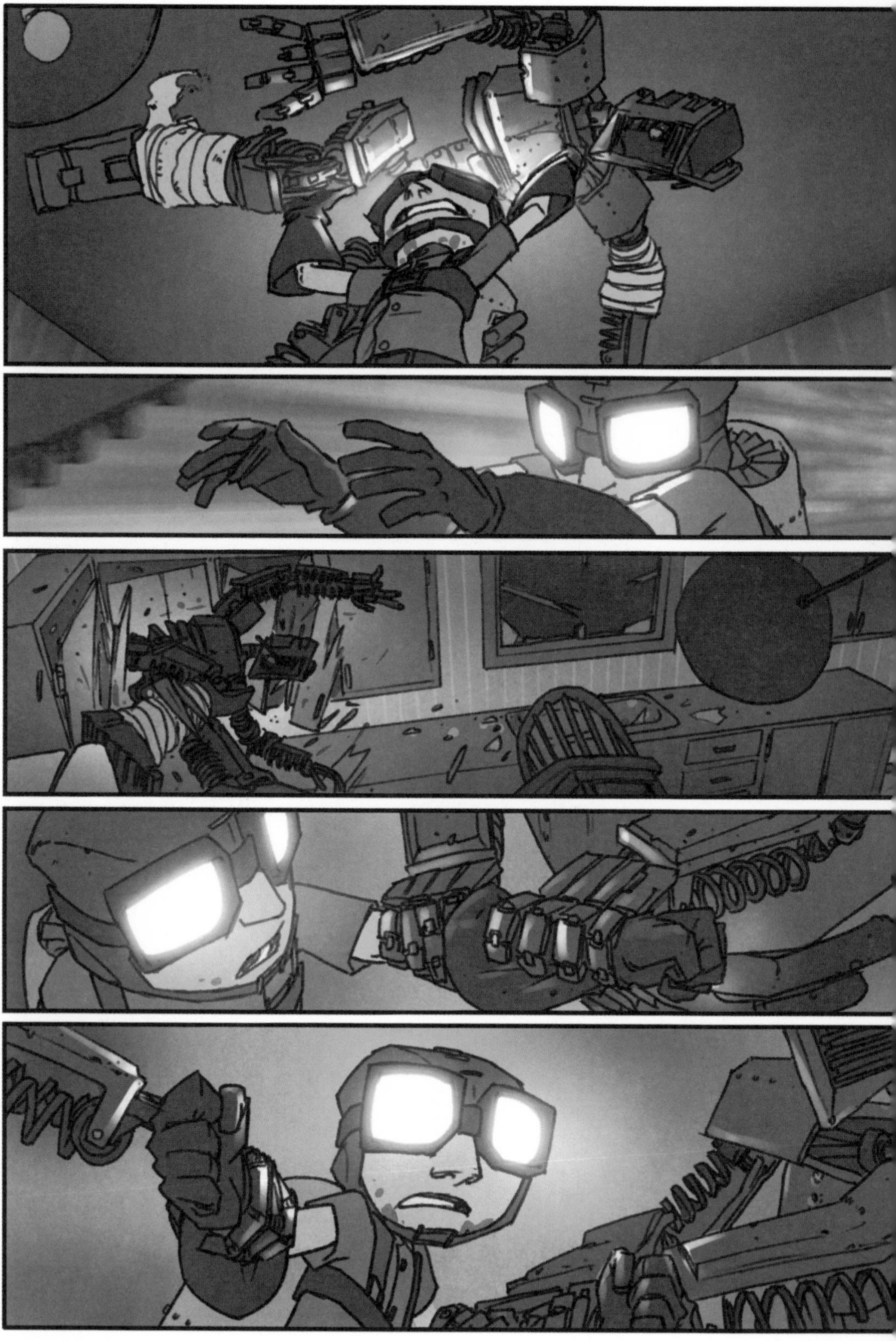

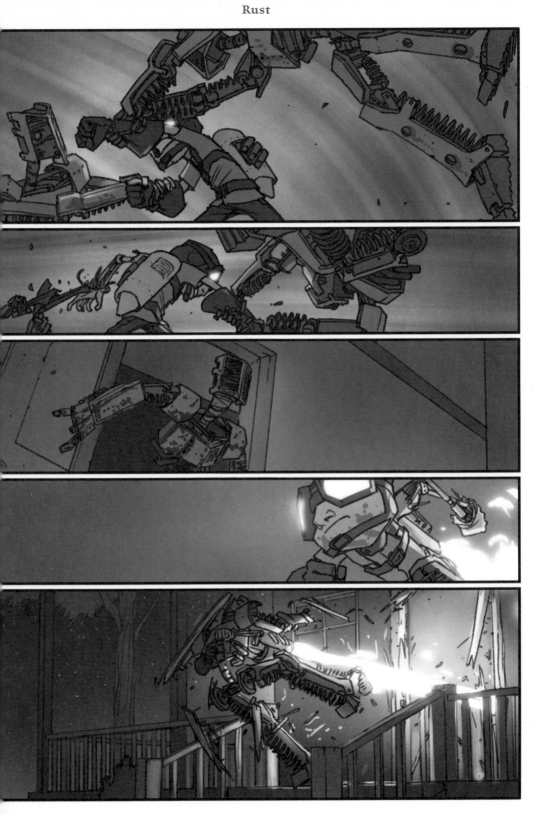

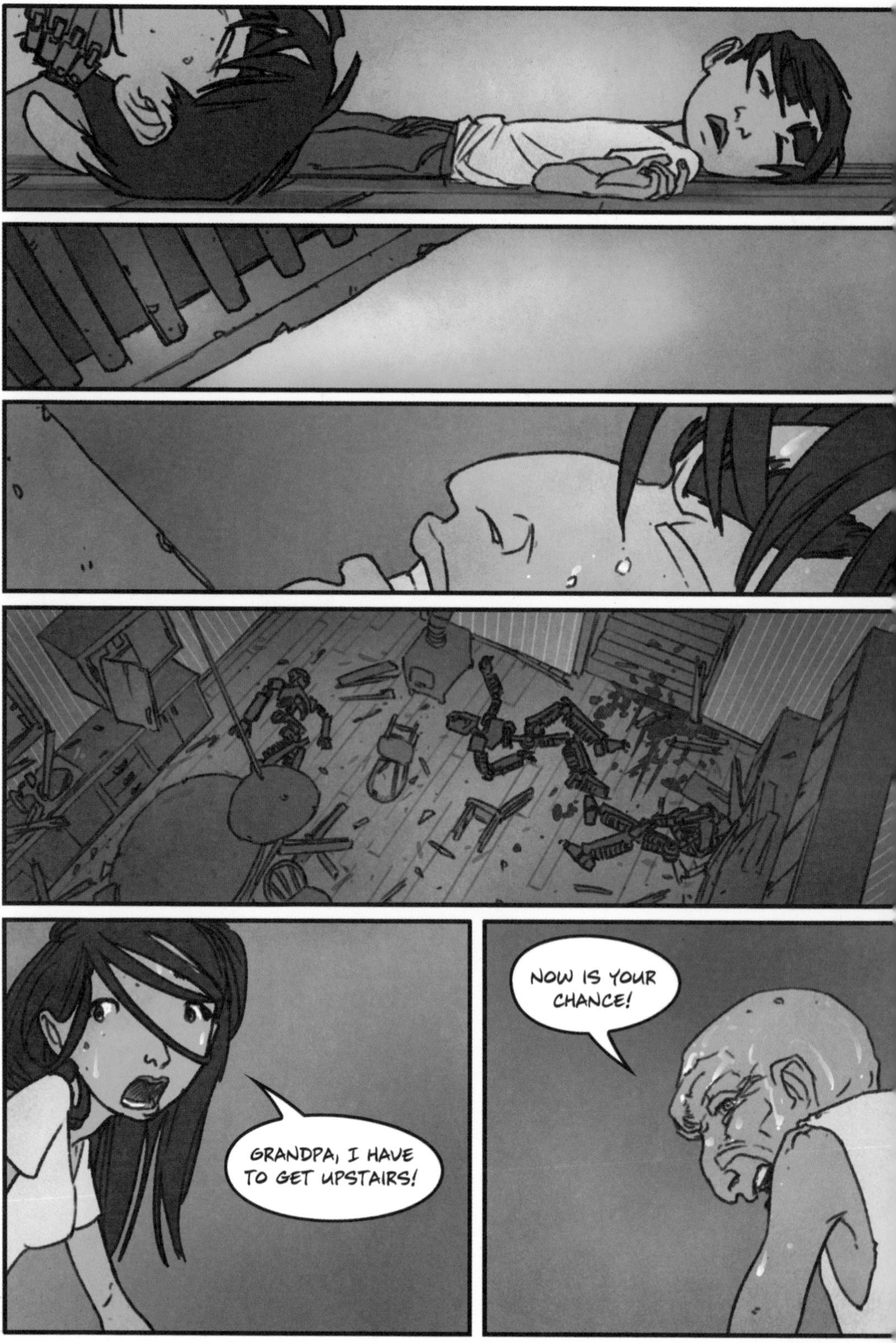
GRANDPA, I HAVE TO GET UPSTAIRS!
NOW IS YOUR CHANCE!

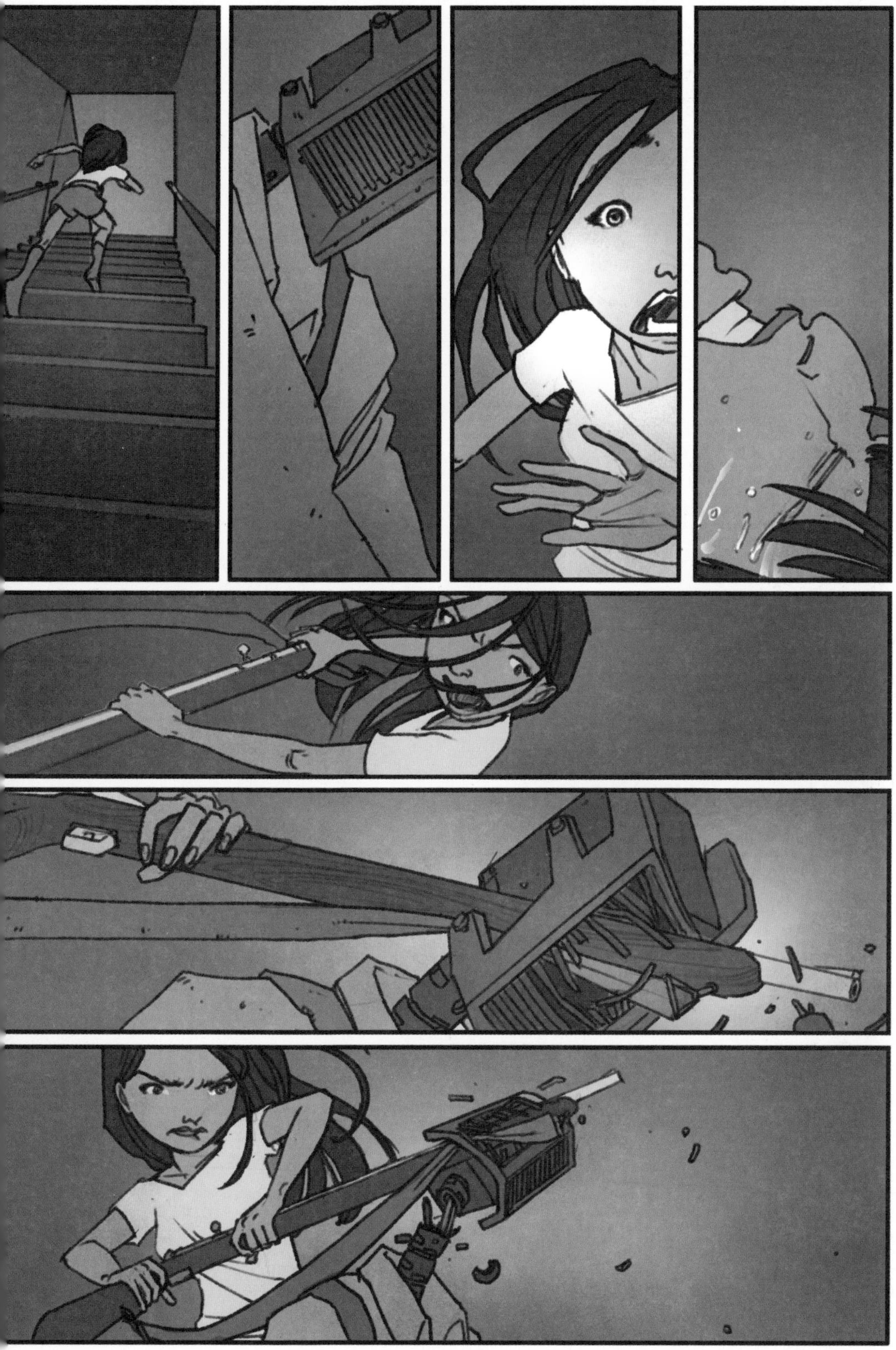

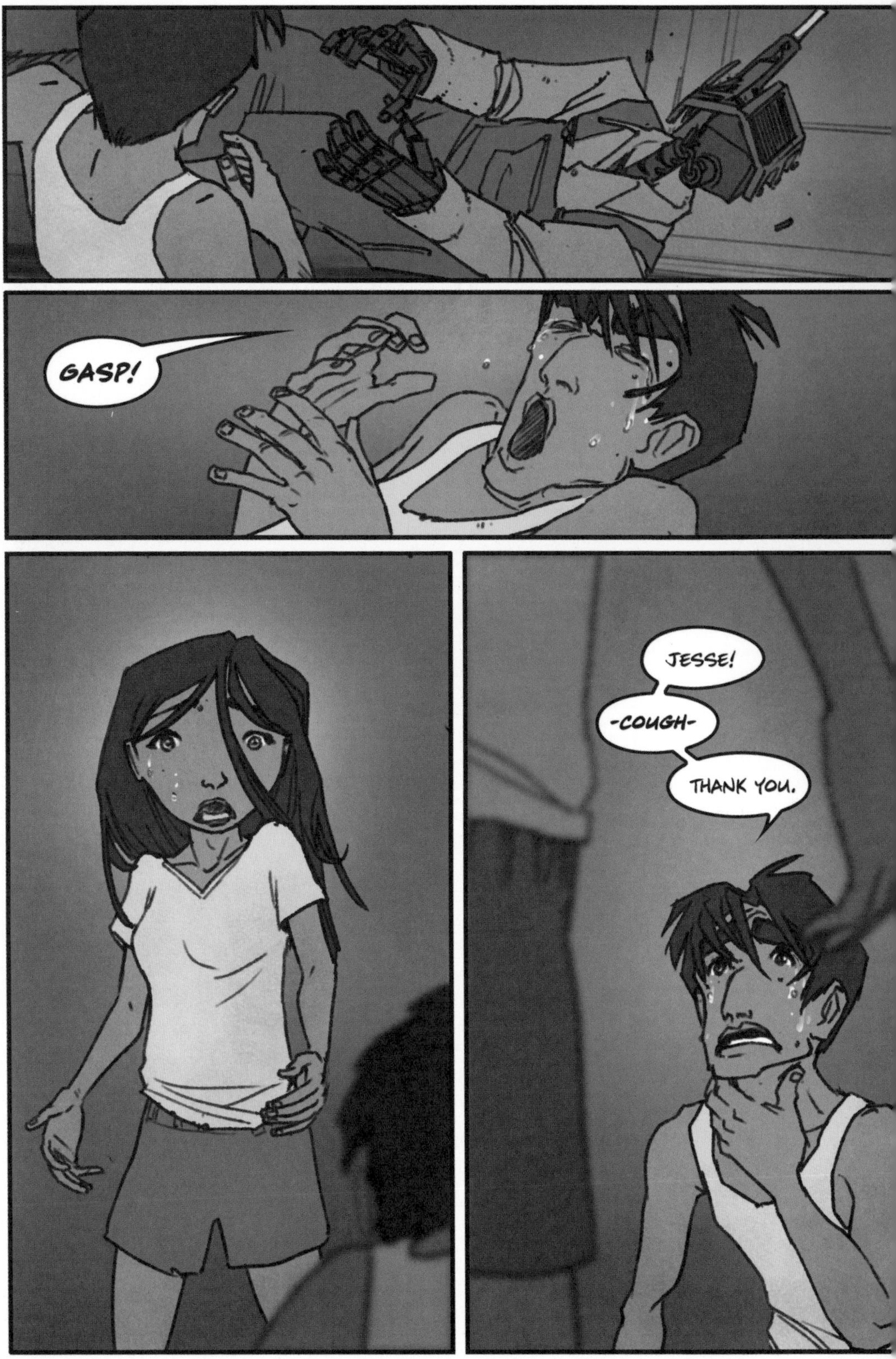
GASP!
JESSE!
-COUGH-
THANK YOU.

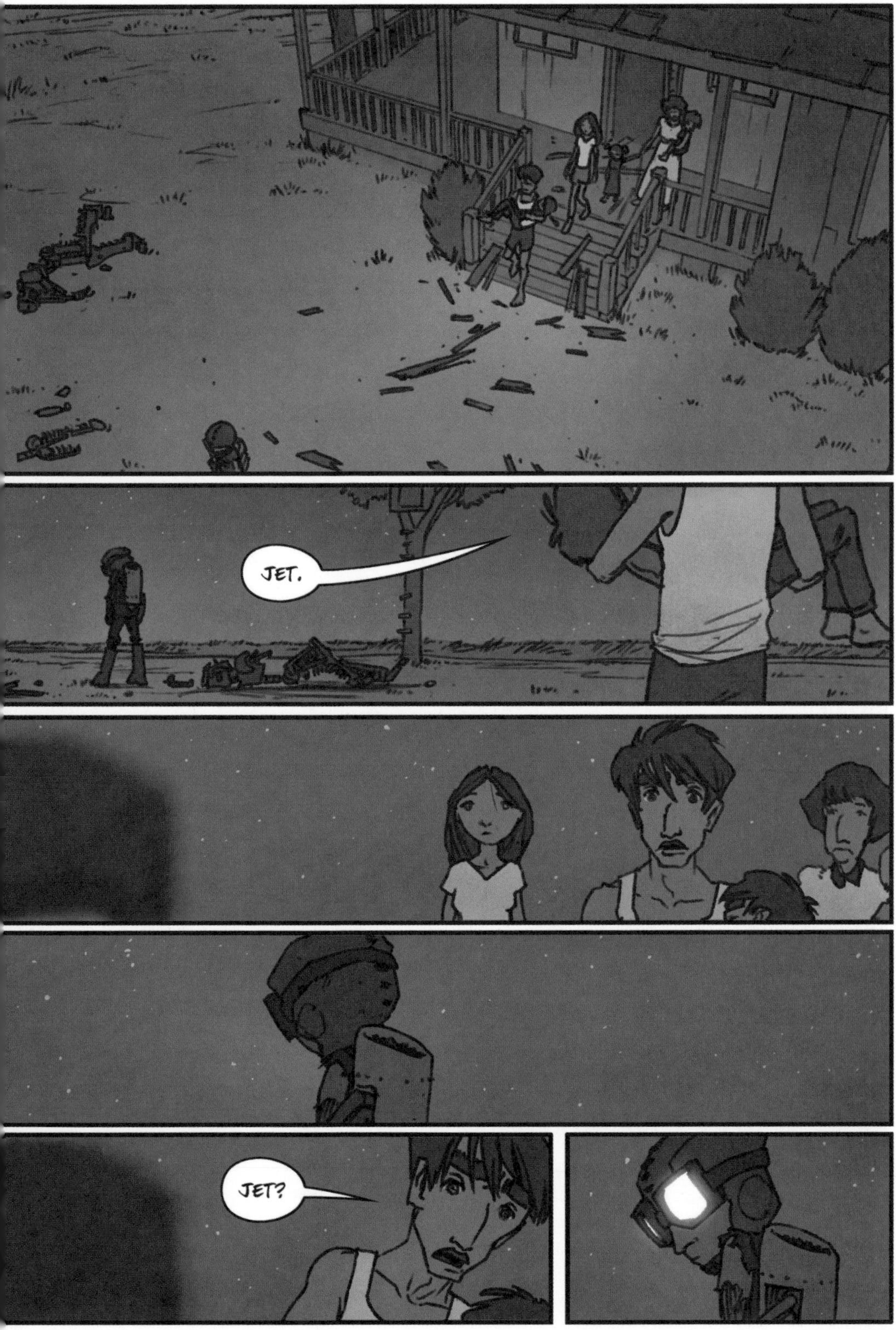
JET.
JET?

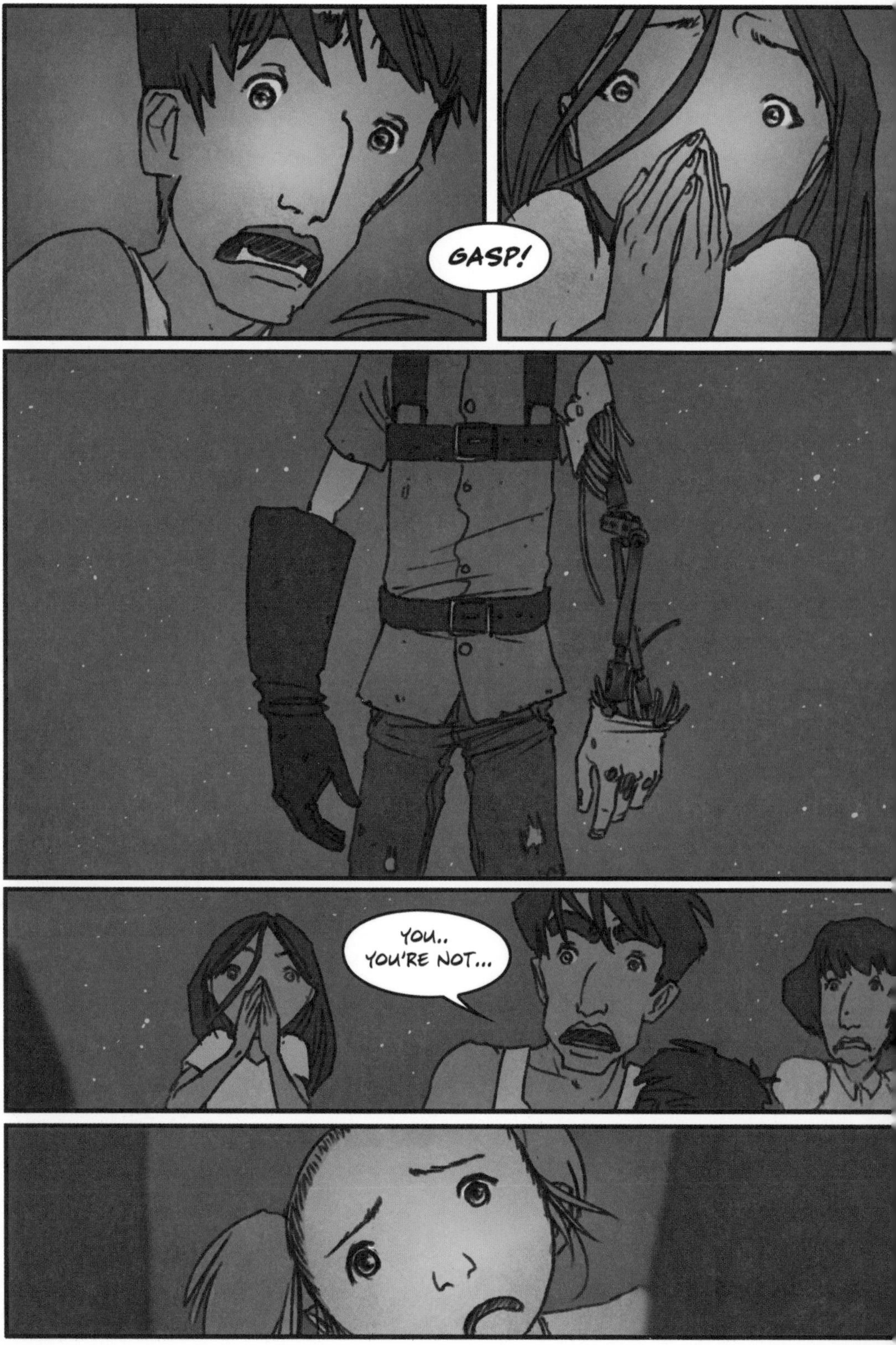
GASP!
YOU..
YOU'RE NOT...

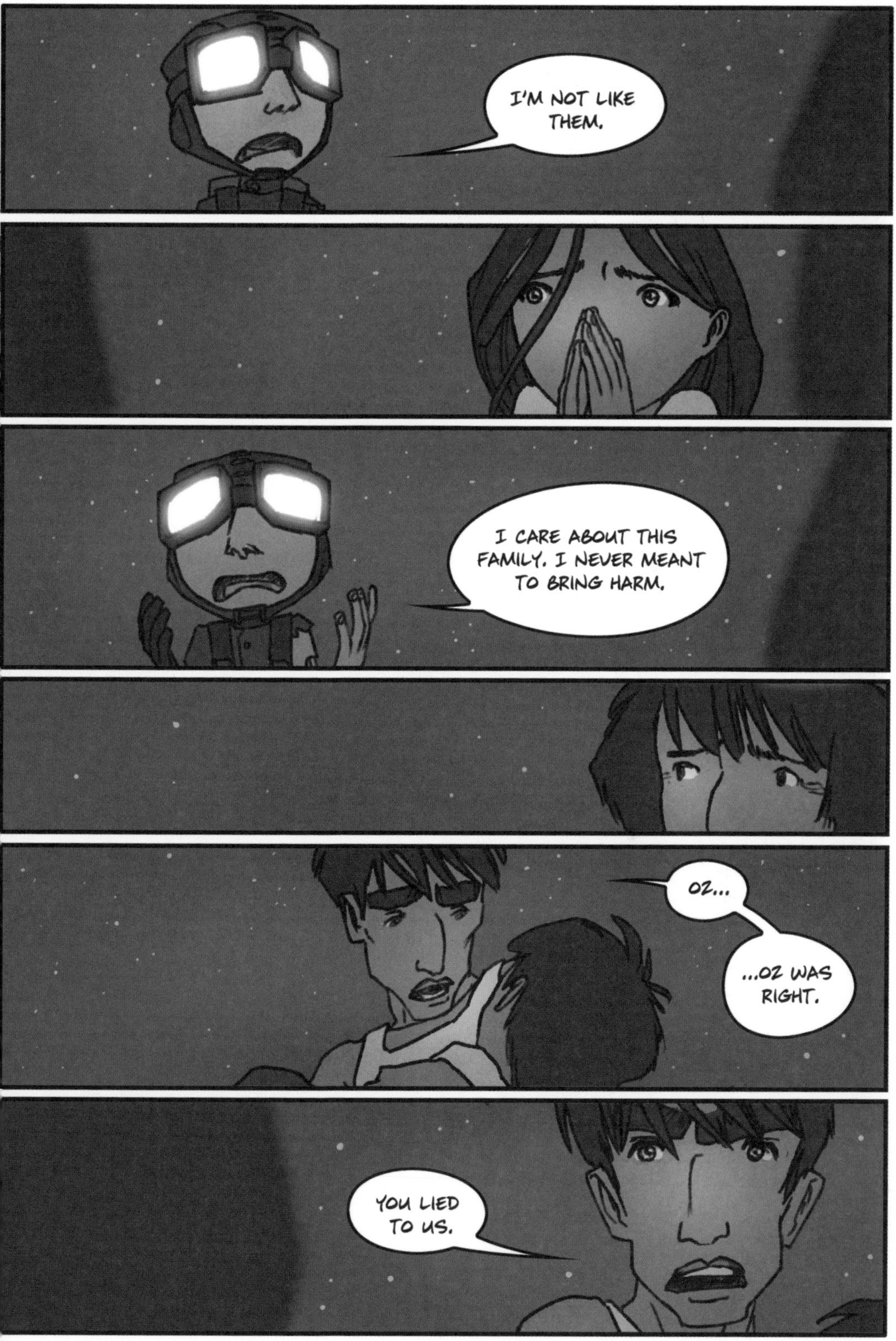
I'M NOT LIKE THEM.
I CARE ABOUT THIS FAMILY. I NEVER MEANT TO BRING HARM.
OZ...
...OZ WAS RIGHT.
YOU LIED TO US.

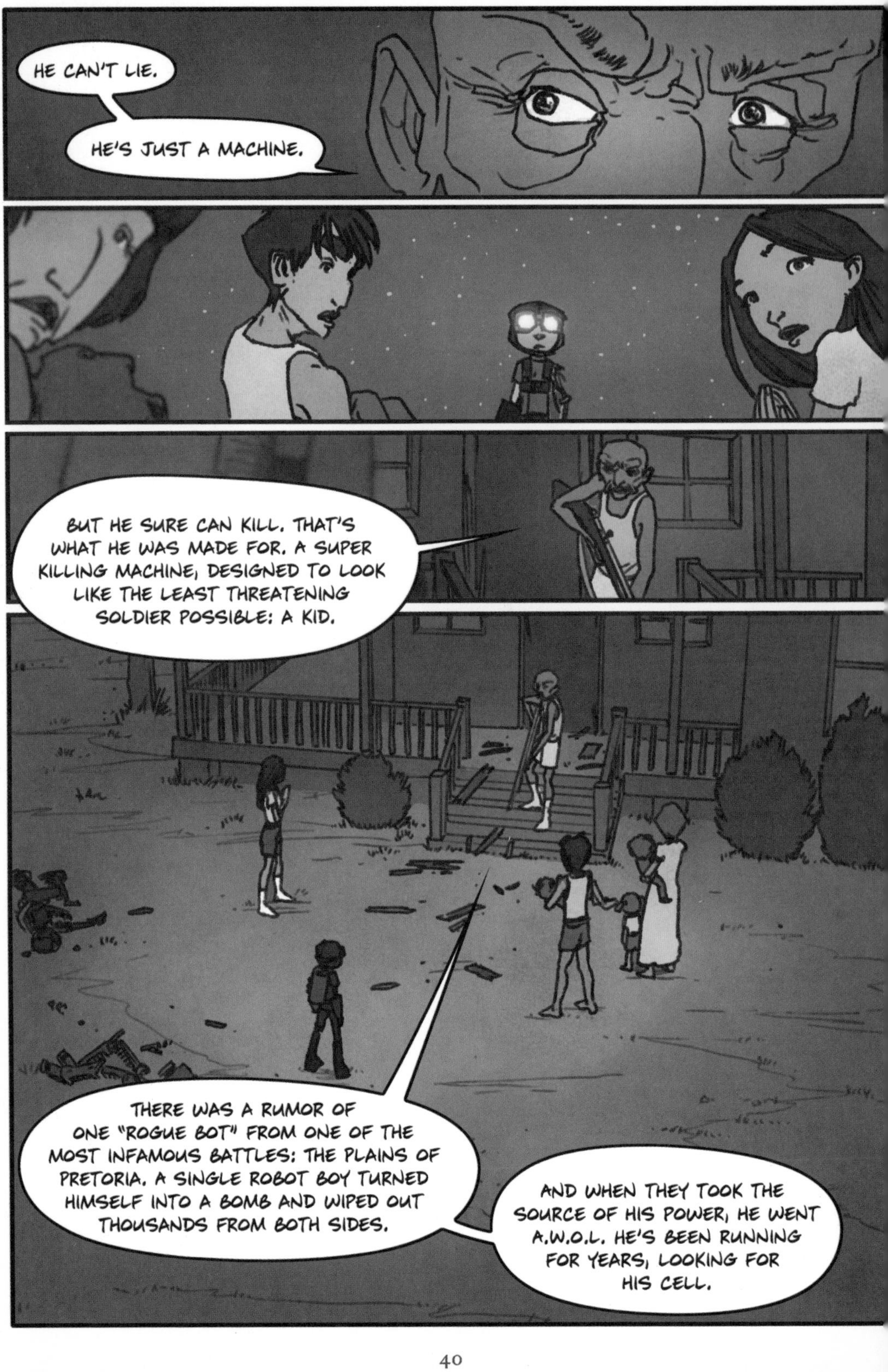
HE CAN'T LIE.
HE'S JUST A MACHINE.
BUT HE SURE CAN KILL. THAT'S WHAT HE WAS MADE FOR. A SUPER KILLING MACHINE, DESIGNED TO LOOK LIKE THE LEAST THREATENING SOLDIER POSSIBLE: A KID.
THERE WAS A RUMOR OF ONE "ROGUE BOT" FROM ONE OF THE MOST INFAMOUS BATTLES: THE PLAINS OF PRETORIA. A SINGLE ROBOT BOY TURNED HIMSELF INTO A BOMB AND WIPED OUT THOUSANDS FROM BOTH SIDES.
AND WHEN THEY TOOK THE SOURCE OF HIS POWER, HE WENT A.W.O.L. HE'S BEEN RUNNING FOR YEARS, LOOKING FOR HIS CELL.

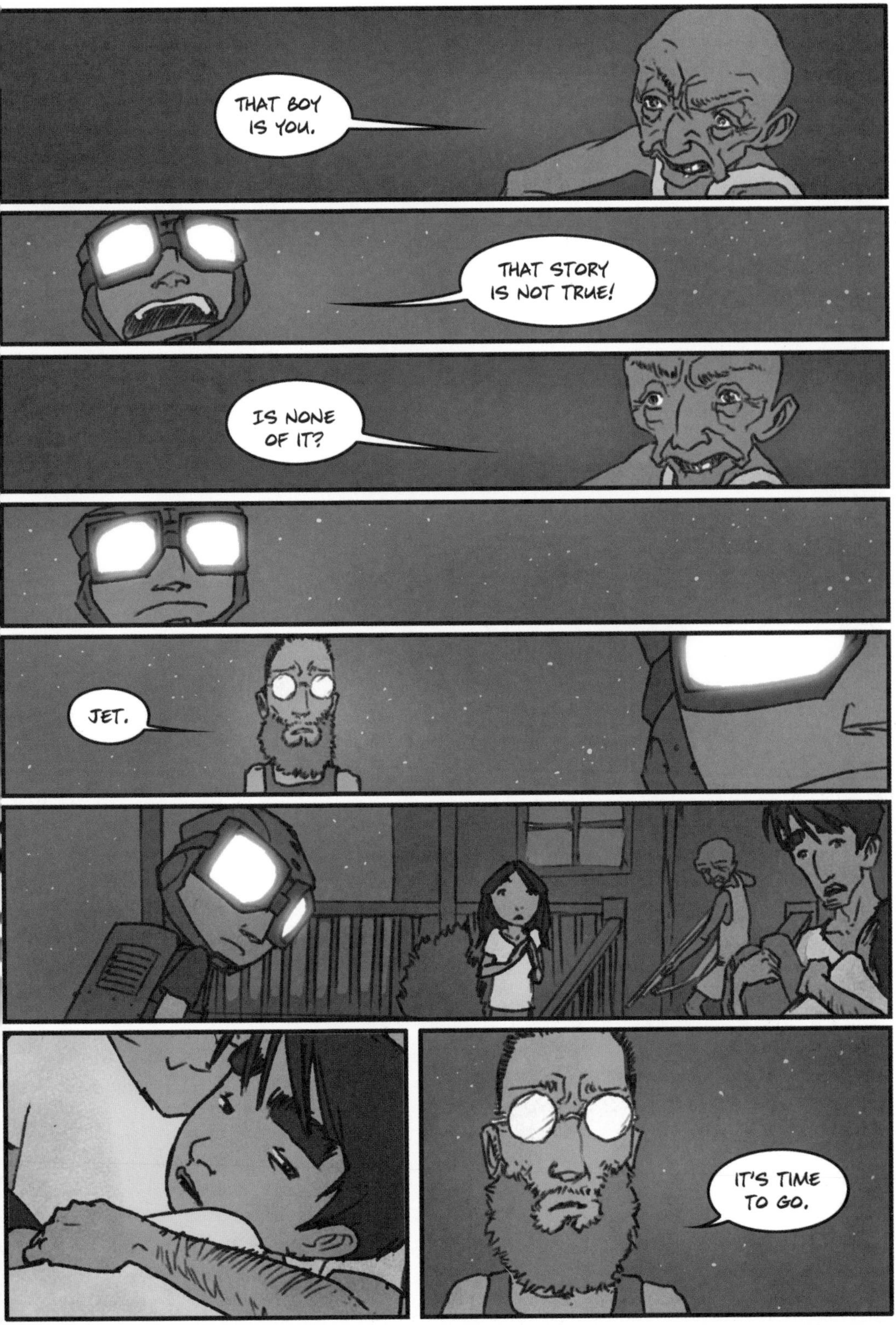
THAT BOY IS YOU.
THAT STORY IS NOT TRUE!
IS NONE OF IT?
JET.
IT'S TIME TO GO.

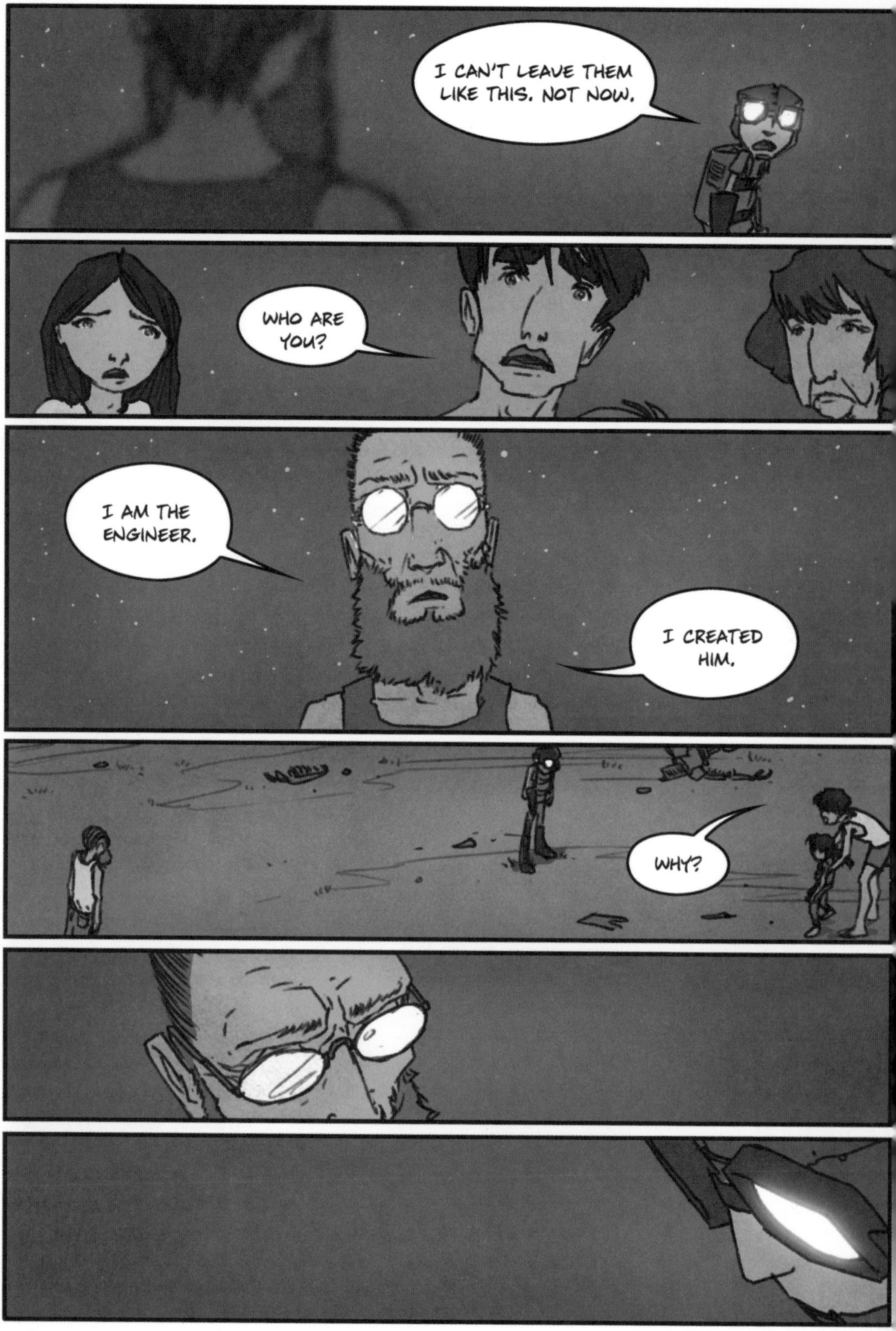
I CAN'T LEAVE THEM LIKE THIS. NOT NOW.
WHO ARE YOU?
I AM THE ENGINEER.
I CREATED HIM.
WHY?

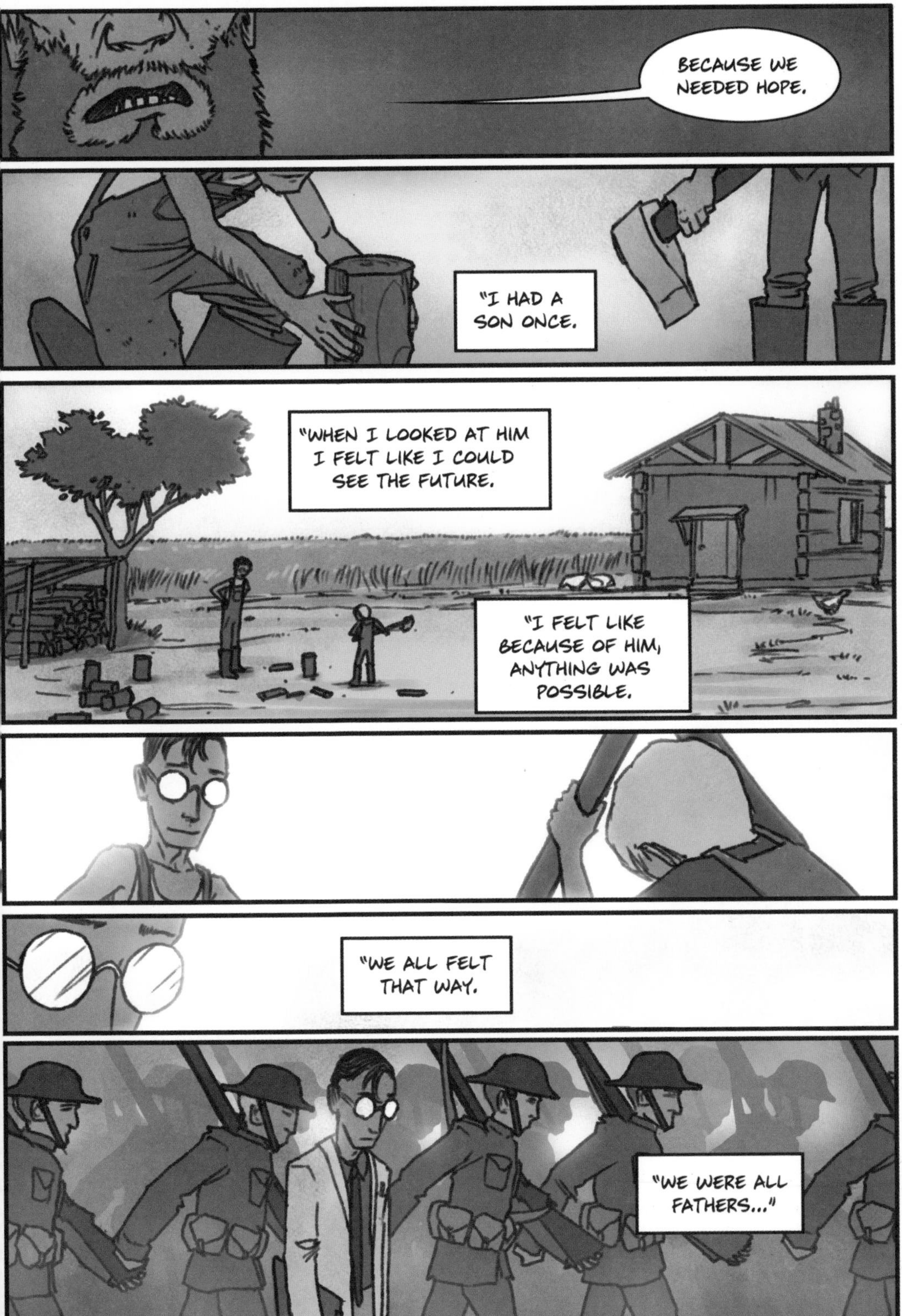
BECAUSE WE NEEDED HOPE.
"I HAD A SON ONCE.
"WHEN I LOOKED AT HIM I FELT LIKE I COULD SEE THE FUTURE.
"I FELT LIKE BECAUSE OF HIM, ANYTHING WAS POSSIBLE.
"WE ALL FELT THAT WAY.
"WE WERE ALL FATHERS..."

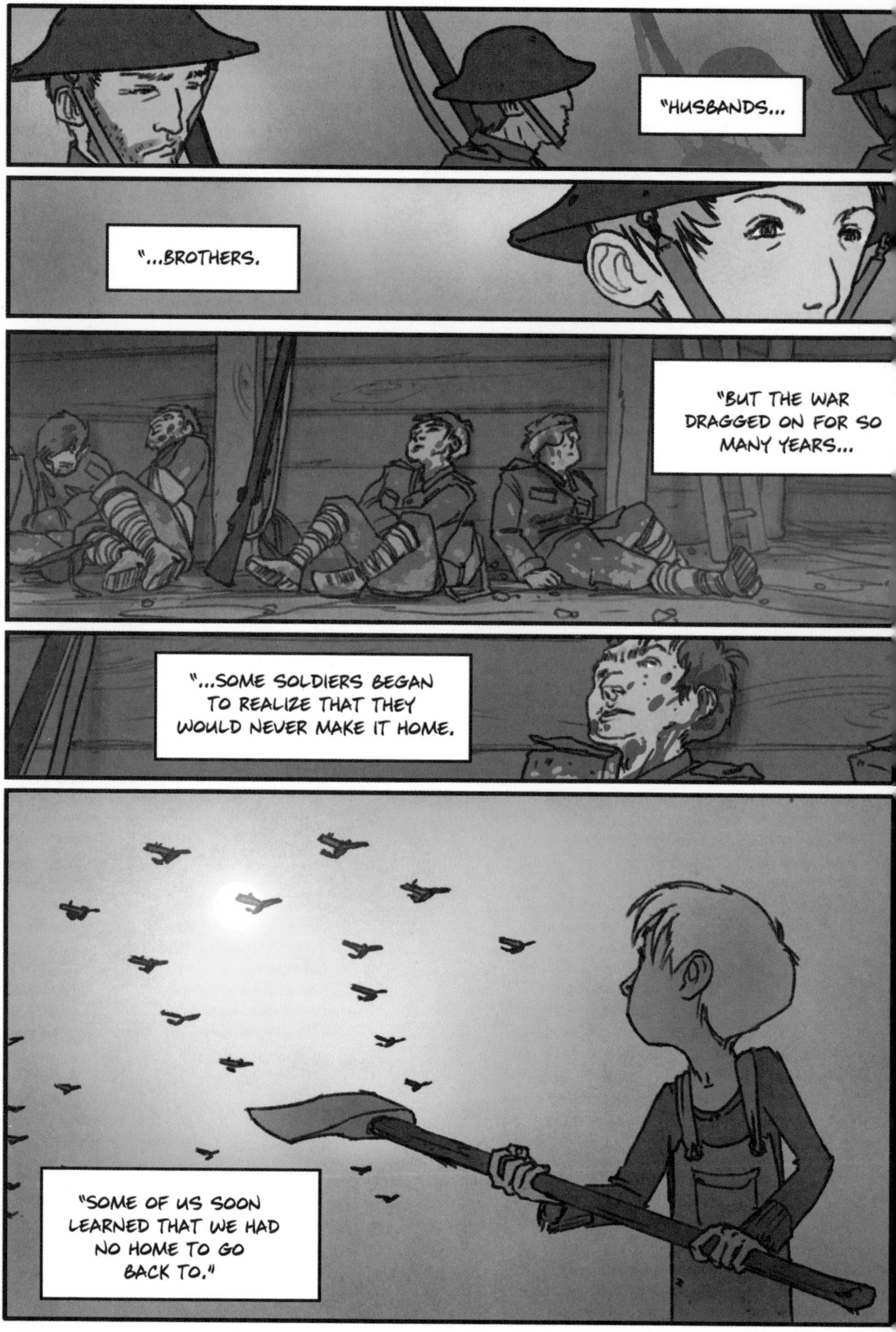
"HUSBANDS...
"...BROTHERS.
"BUT THE WAR DRAGGED ON FOR SO MANY YEARS...
"...SOME SOLDIERS BEGAN TO REALIZE THAT THEY WOULD NEVER MAKE IT HOME.
"SOME OF US SOON LEARNED THAT WE HAD NO HOME TO GO BACK TO."

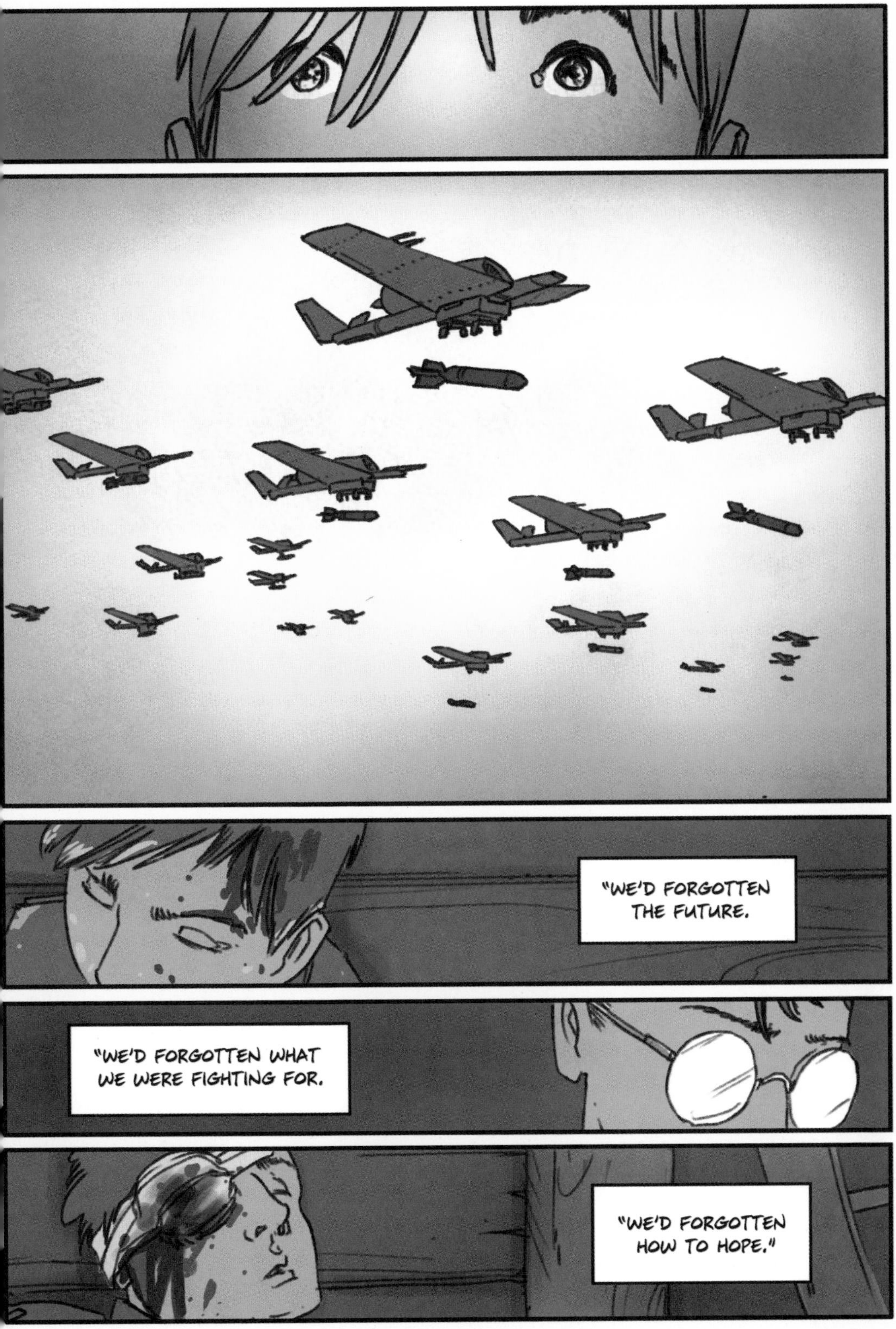
"WE'D FORGOTTEN THE FUTURE.
"WE'D FORGOTTEN WHAT WE WERE FIGHTING FOR.
"WE'D FORGOTTEN HOW TO HOPE."

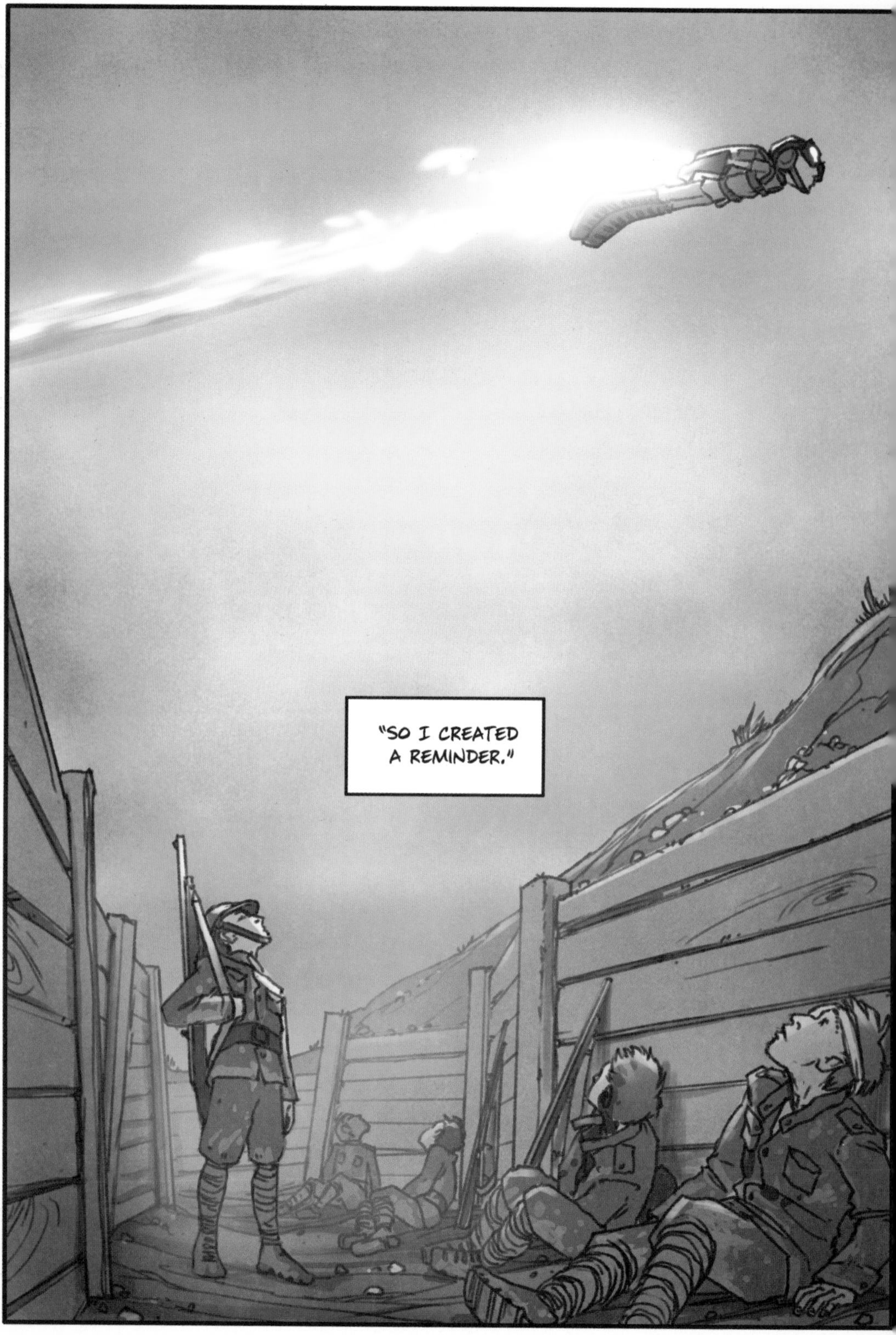
"SO I CREATED
A REMINDER."

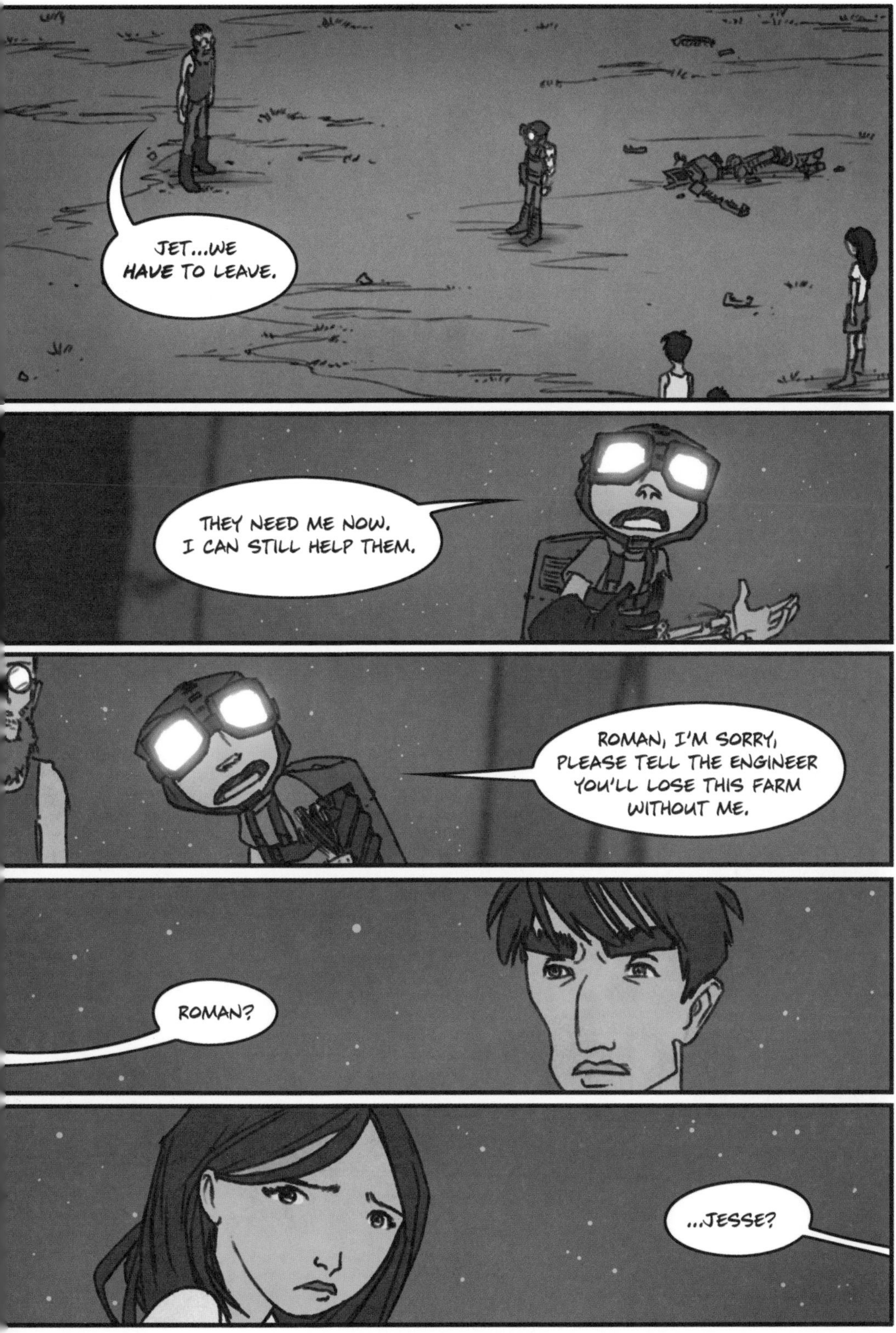
JET...WE HAVE TO LEAVE.
THEY NEED ME NOW. I CAN STILL HELP THEM.
ROMAN, I'M SORRY, PLEASE TELL THE ENGINEER YOU'LL LOSE THIS FARM WITHOUT ME.
ROMAN?
...JESSE?

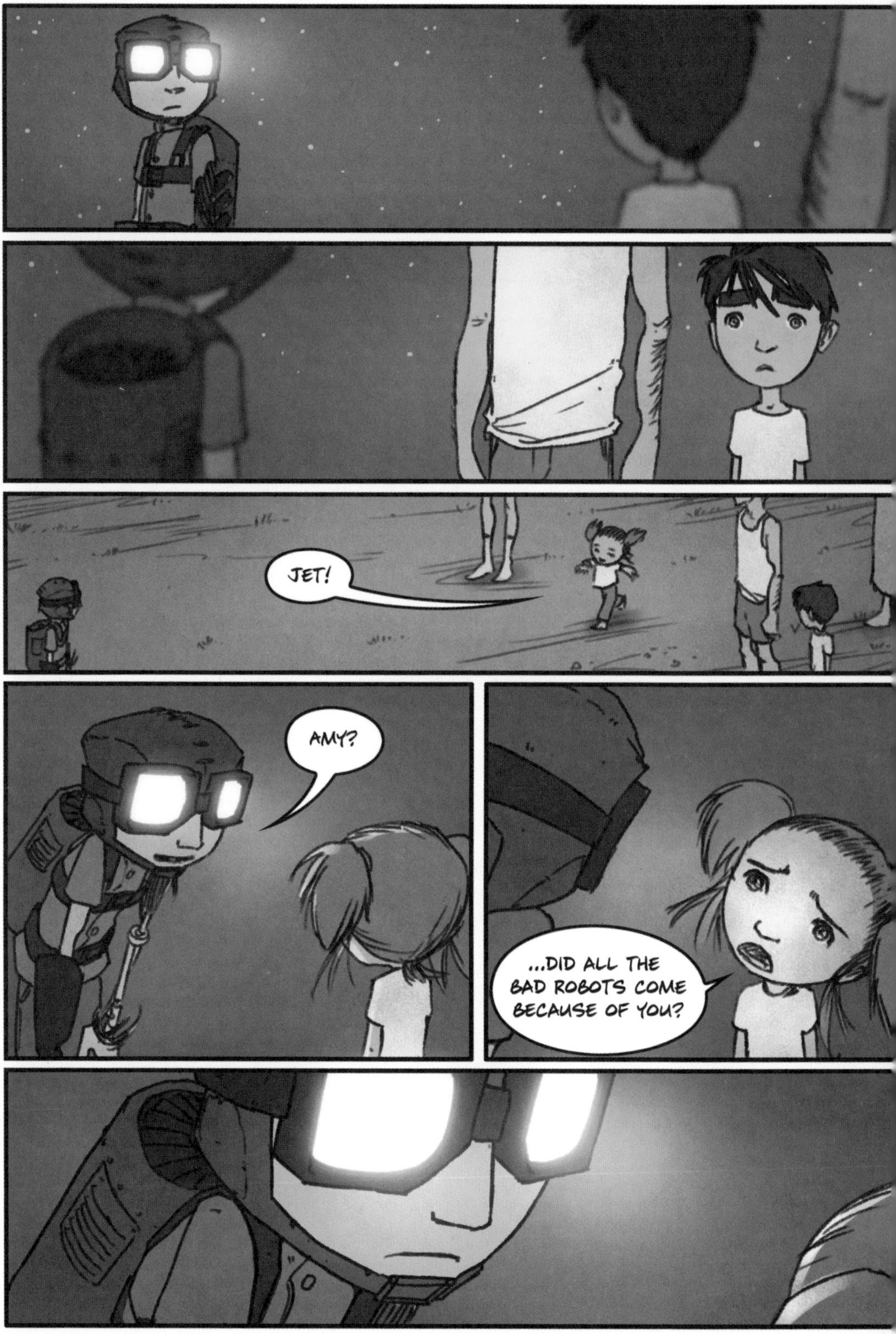
JET!
AMY?
...DID ALL THE BAD ROBOTS COME BECAUSE OF YOU?

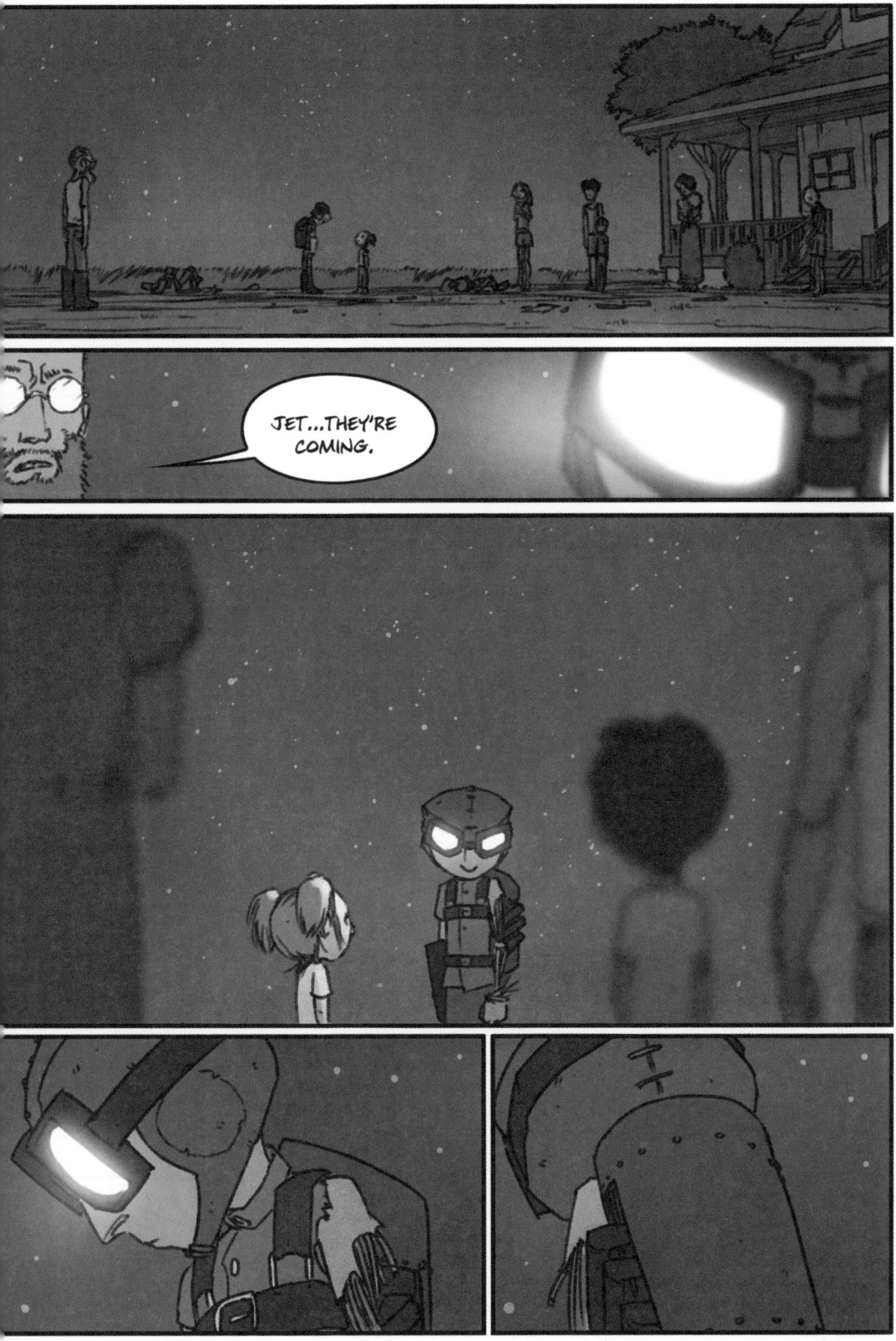
JET...THEY'RE COMING.

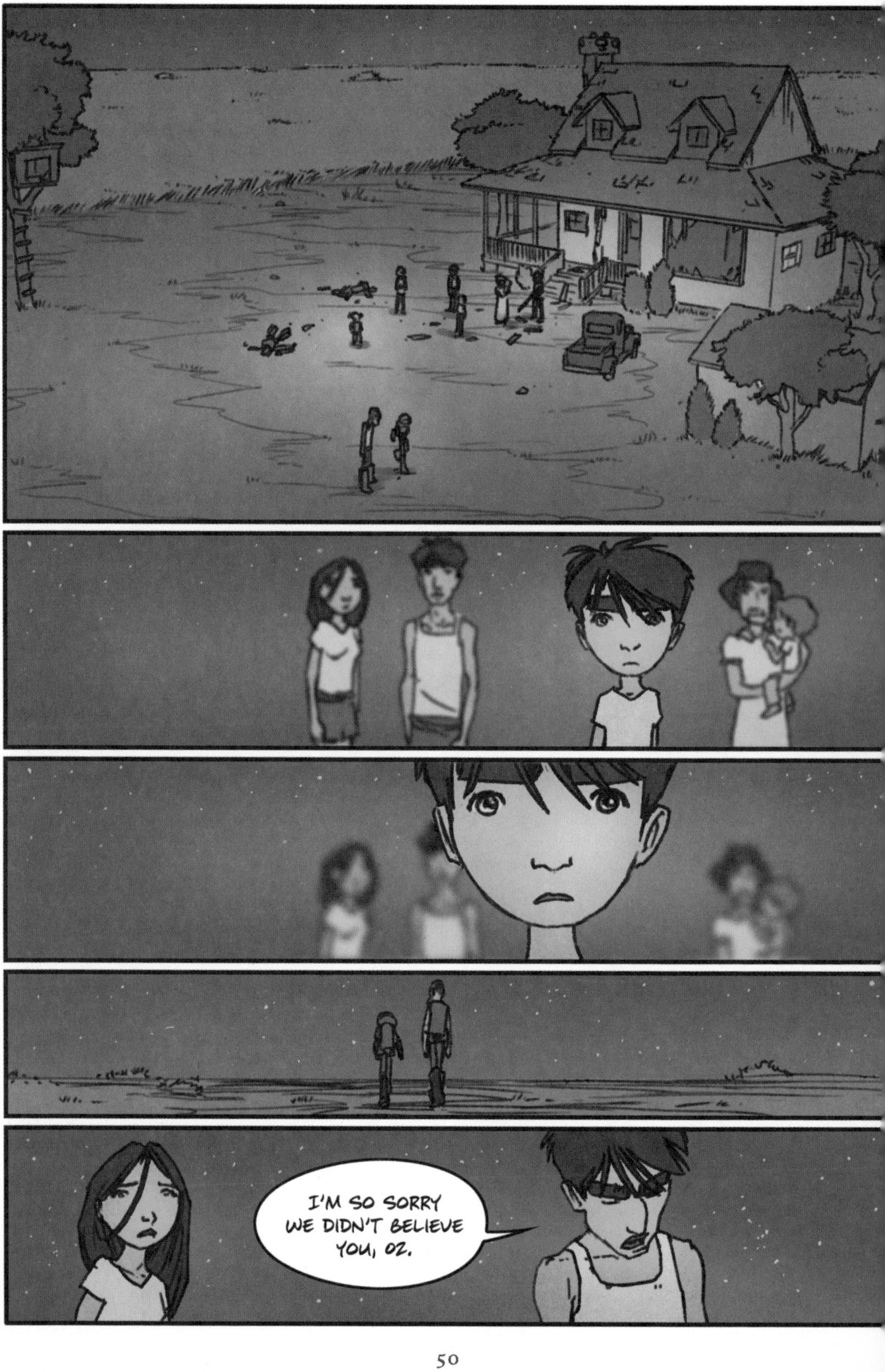
I'M SO SORRY
WE DIDN'T BELIEVE
YOU, OZ.

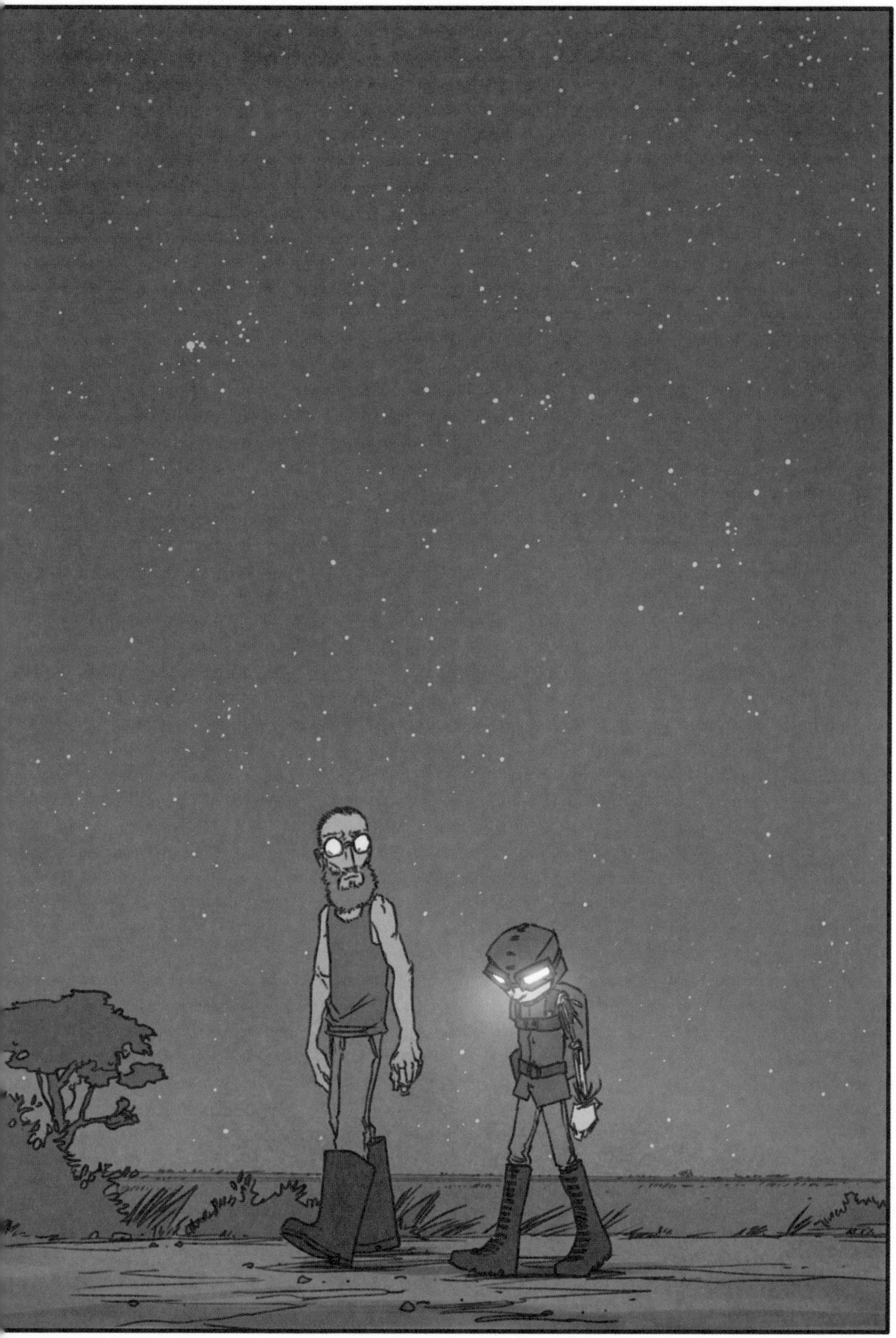

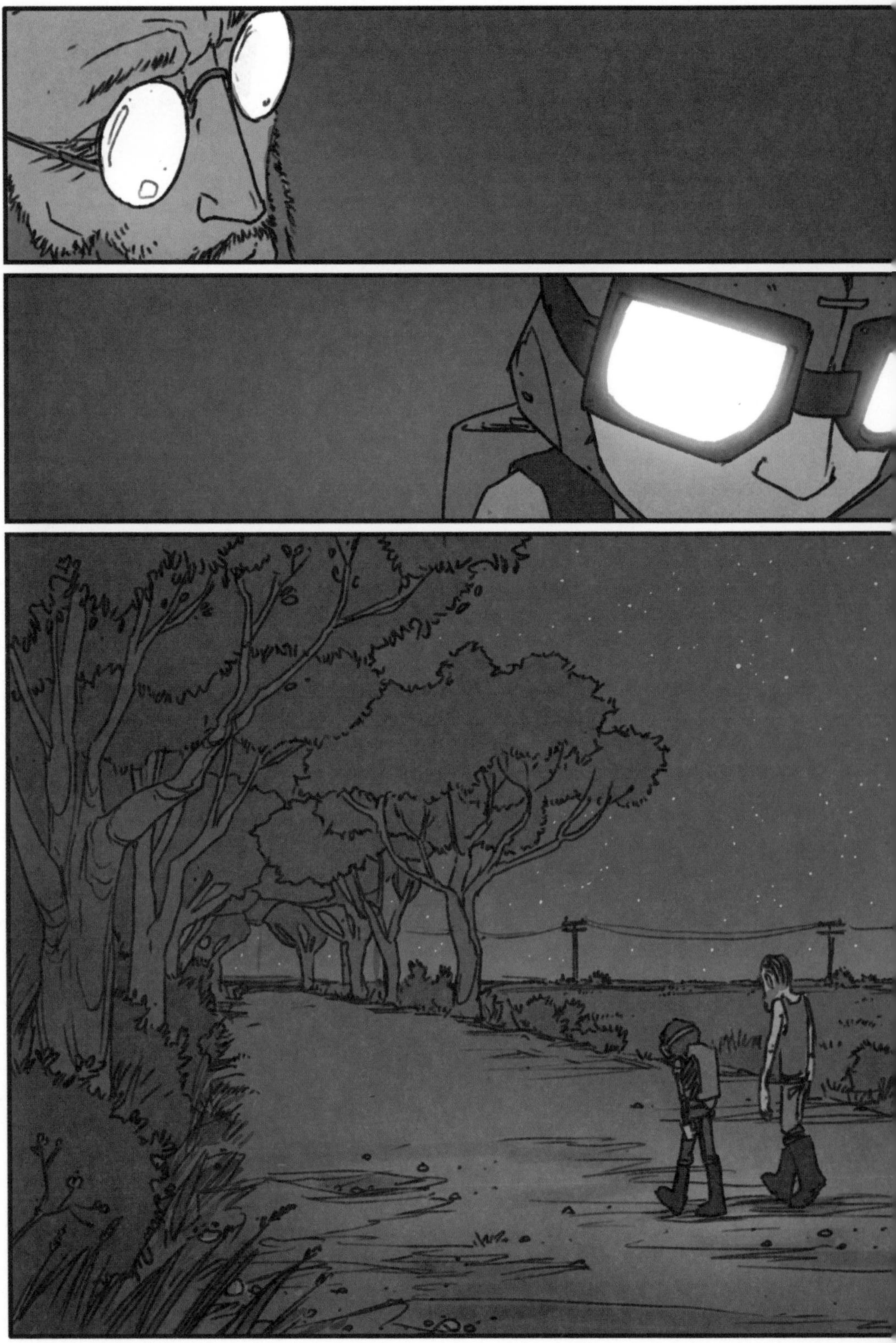

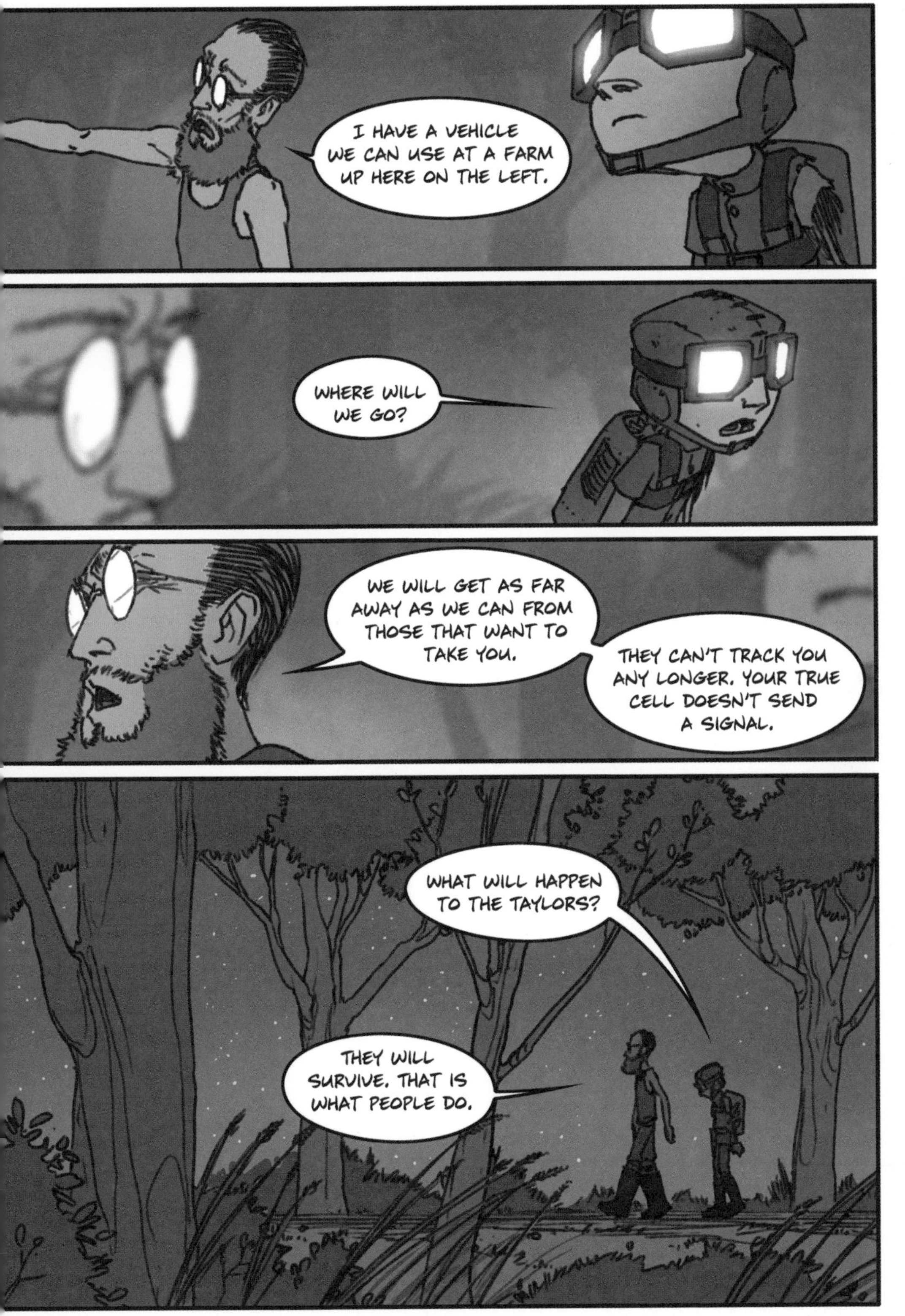
I HAVE A VEHICLE WE CAN USE AT A FARM UP HERE ON THE LEFT.
WHERE WILL WE GO?
WE WILL GET AS FAR AWAY AS WE CAN FROM THOSE THAT WANT TO TAKE YOU.
THEY CAN'T TRACK YOU ANY LONGER. YOUR TRUE CELL DOESN'T SEND A SIGNAL.
WHAT WILL HAPPEN TO THE TAYLORS?
THEY WILL SURVIVE. THAT IS WHAT PEOPLE DO.

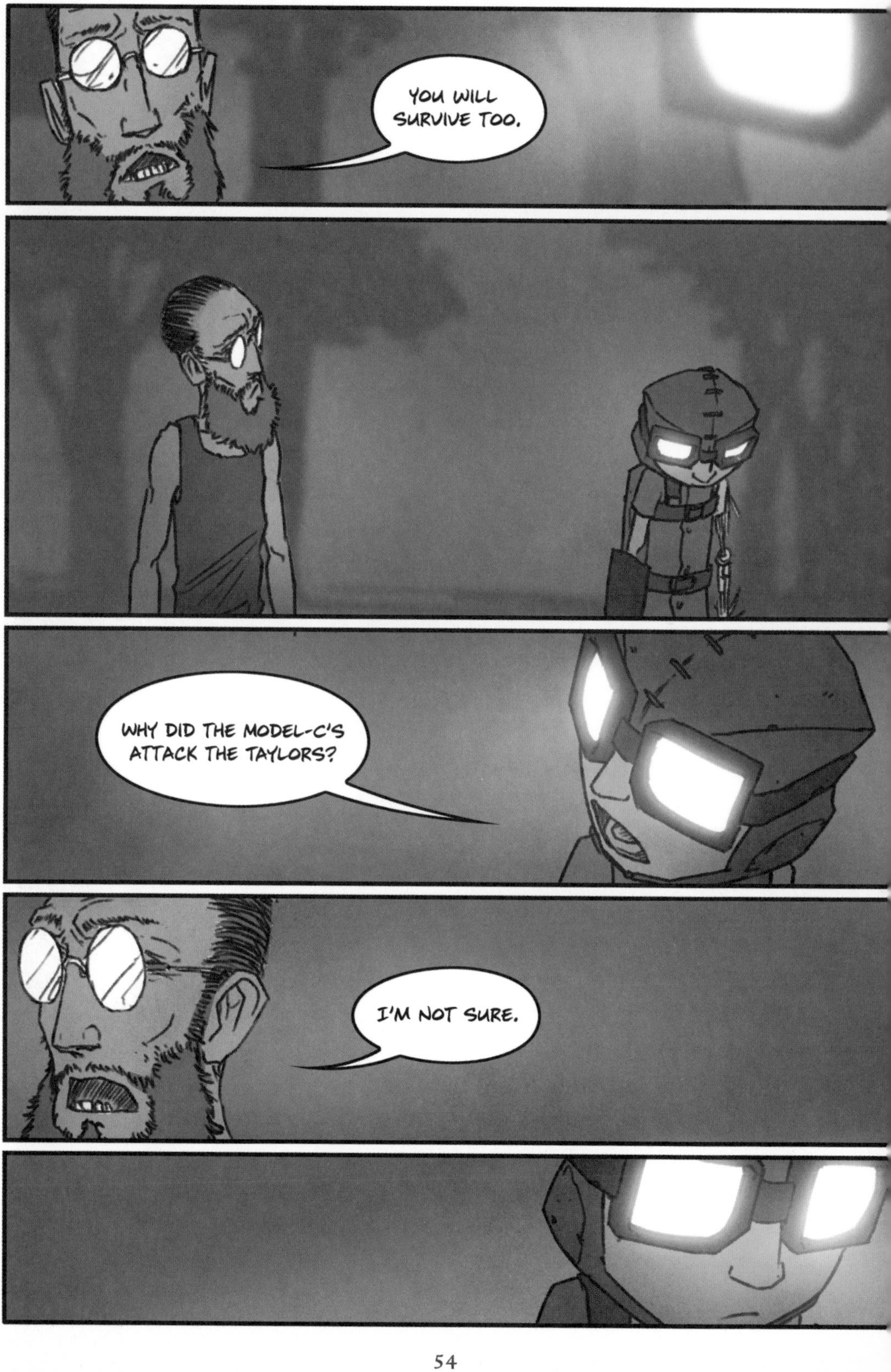
YOU WILL SURVIVE TOO.
WHY DID THE MODEL-C'S ATTACK THE TAYLORS?
I'M NOT SURE.

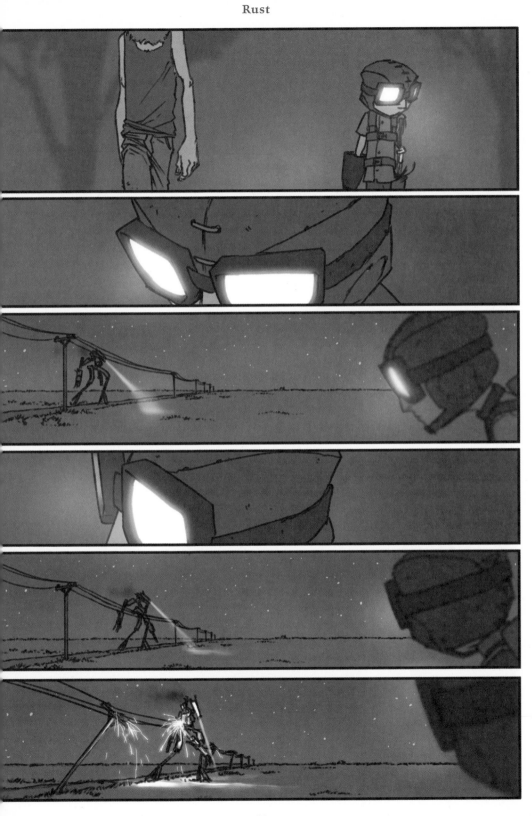

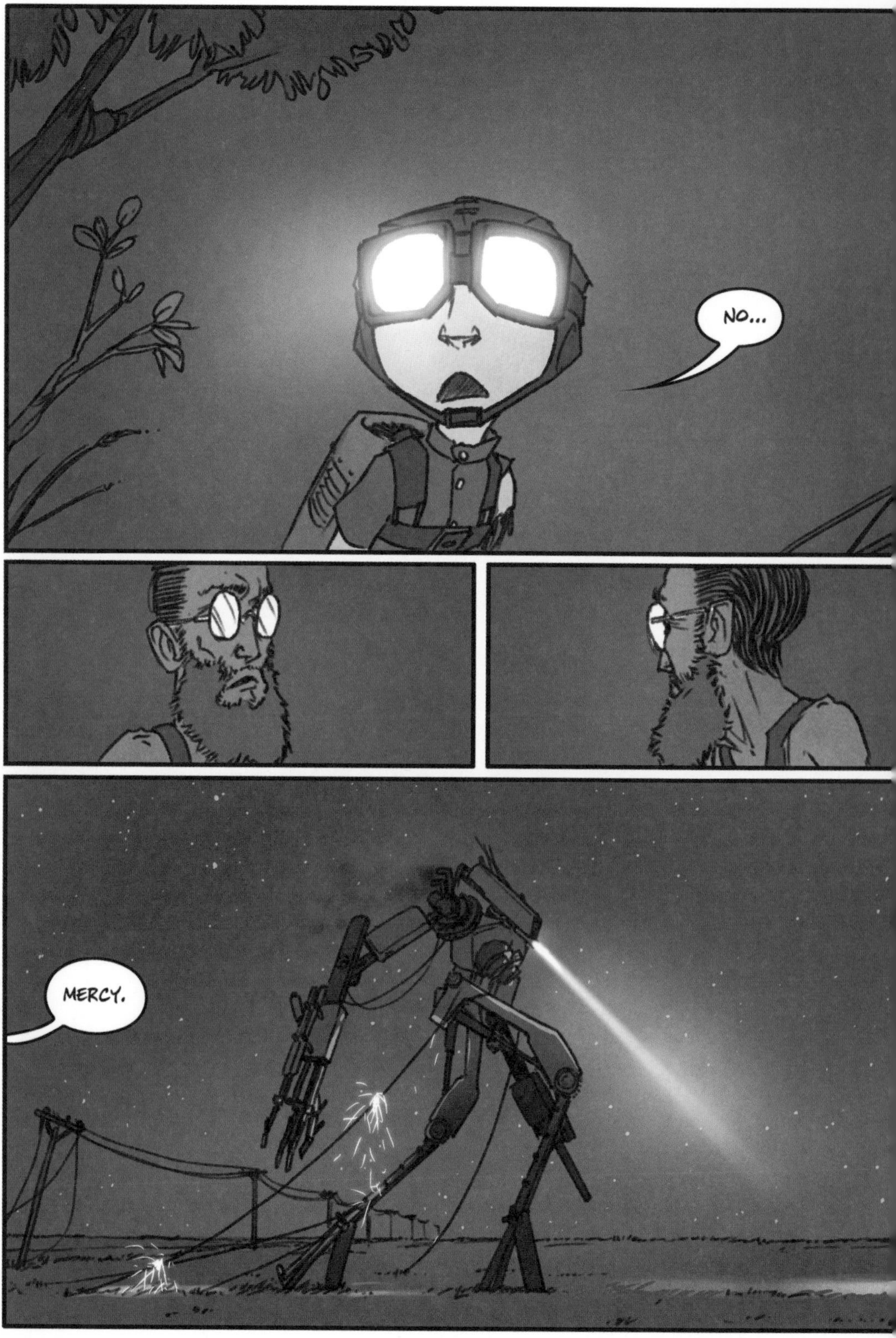
NO...
MERCY.

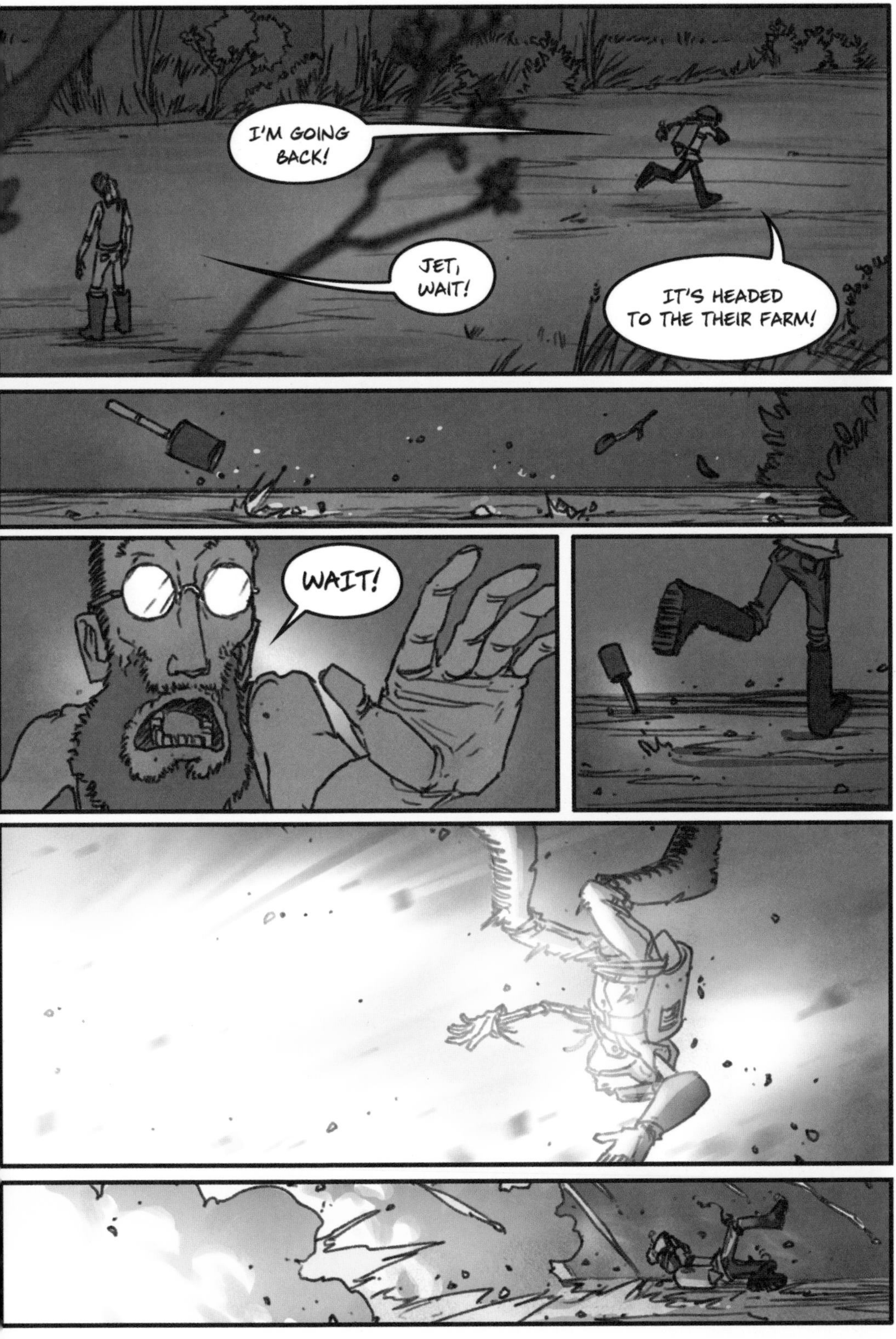
I'M GOING BACK!
JET, WAIT!
IT'S HEADED TO THE THEIR FARM!
WAIT!

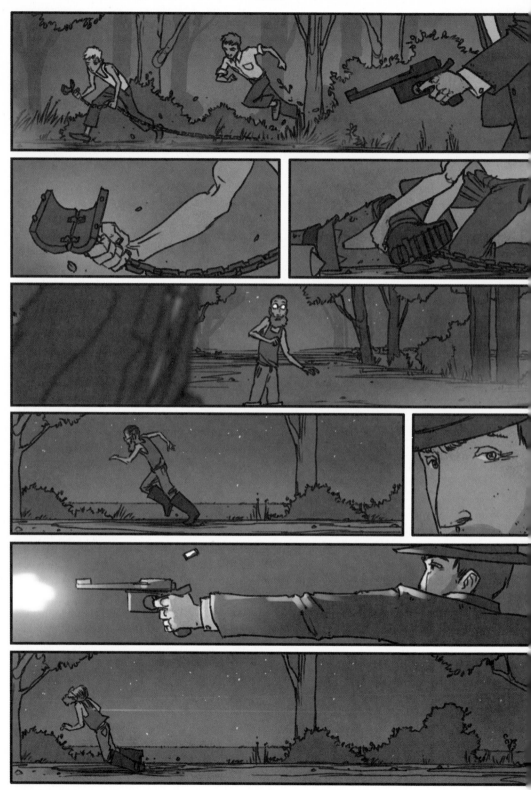

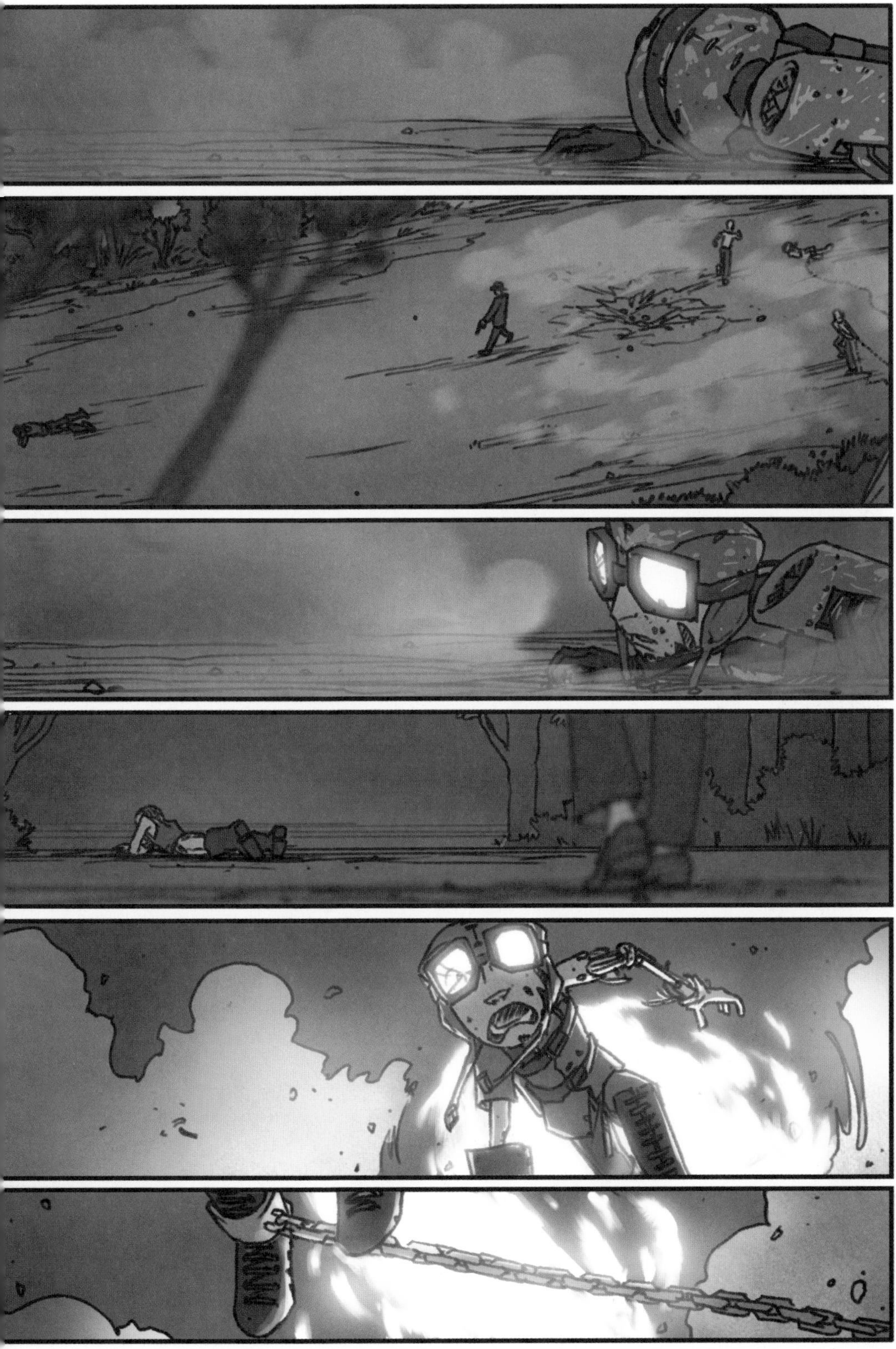

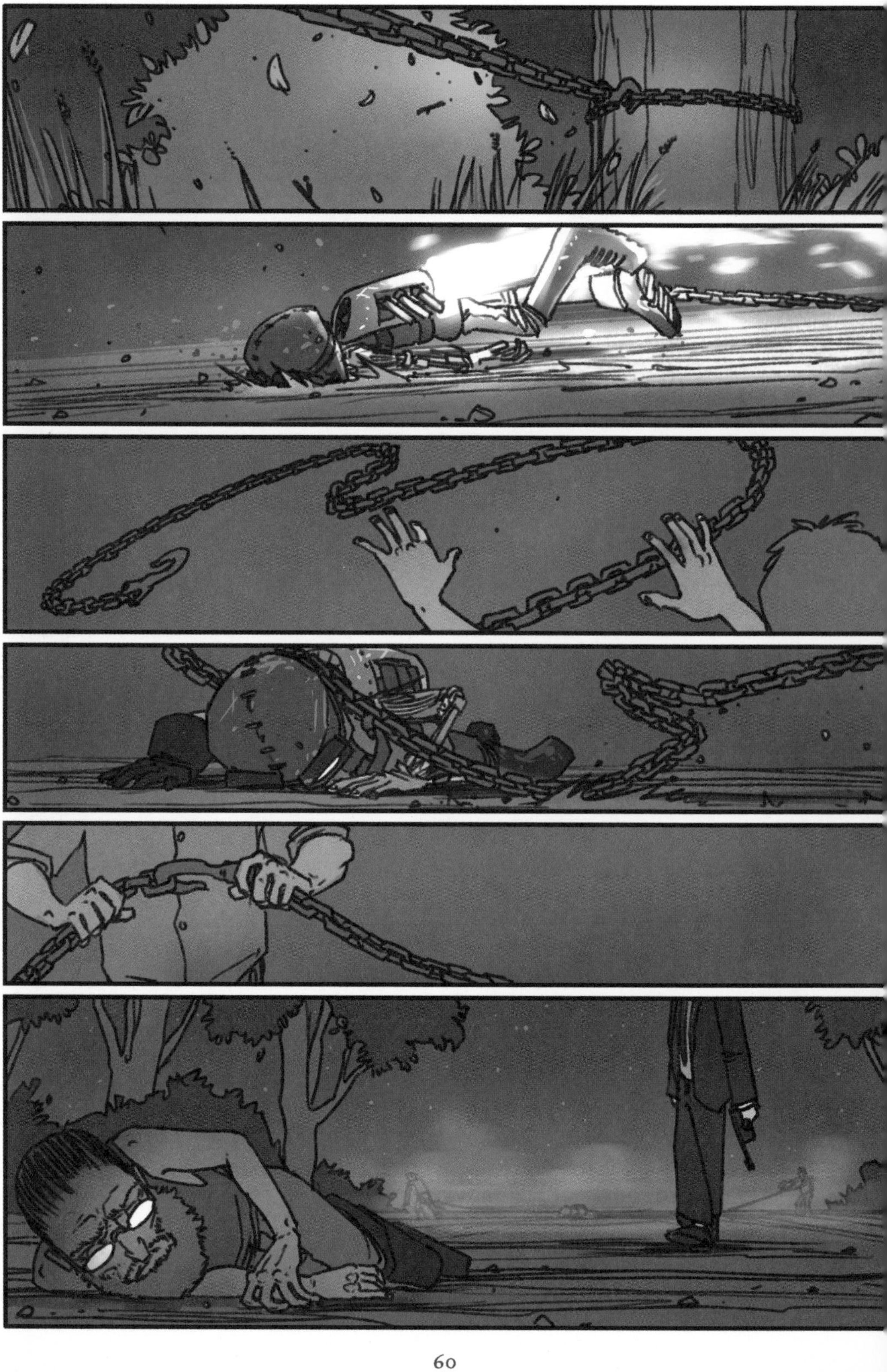

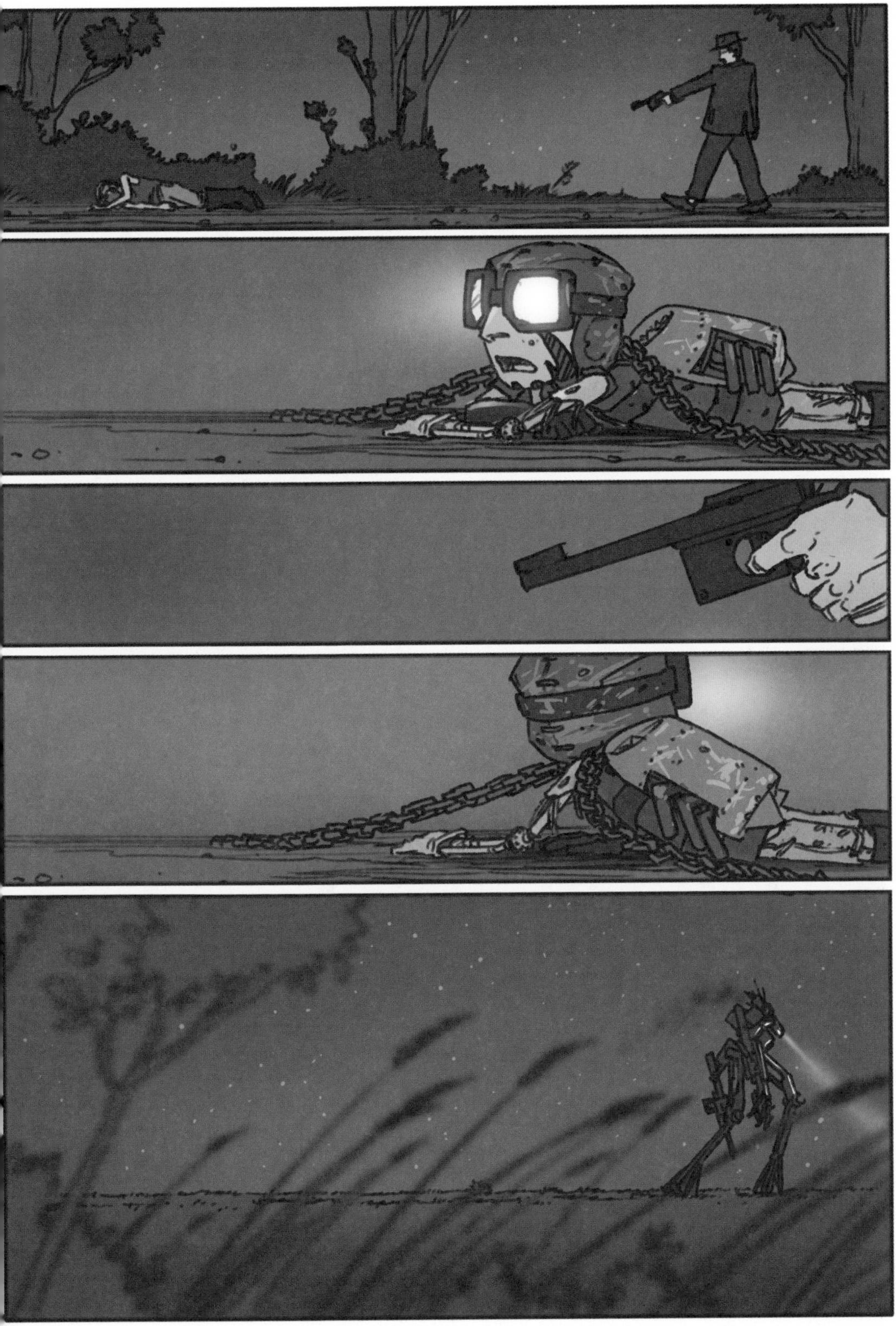

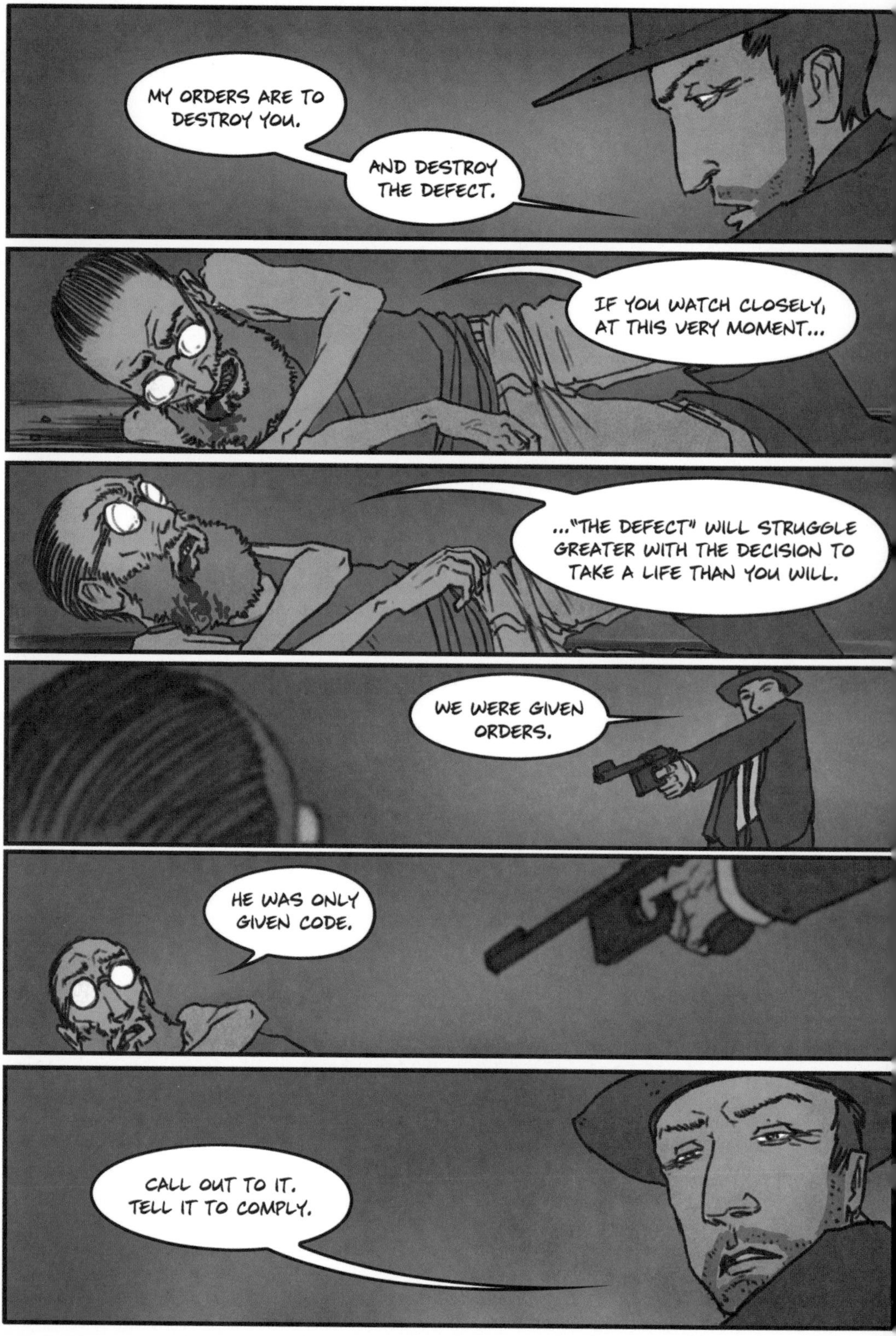
MY ORDERS ARE TO DESTROY YOU.
AND DESTROY THE DEFECT.
IF YOU WATCH CLOSELY, AT THIS VERY MOMENT...
..."THE DEFECT" WILL STRUGGLE GREATER WITH THE DECISION TO TAKE A LIFE THAN YOU WILL.
WE WERE GIVEN ORDERS.
HE WAS ONLY GIVEN CODE.
CALL OUT TO IT. TELL IT TO COMPLY.

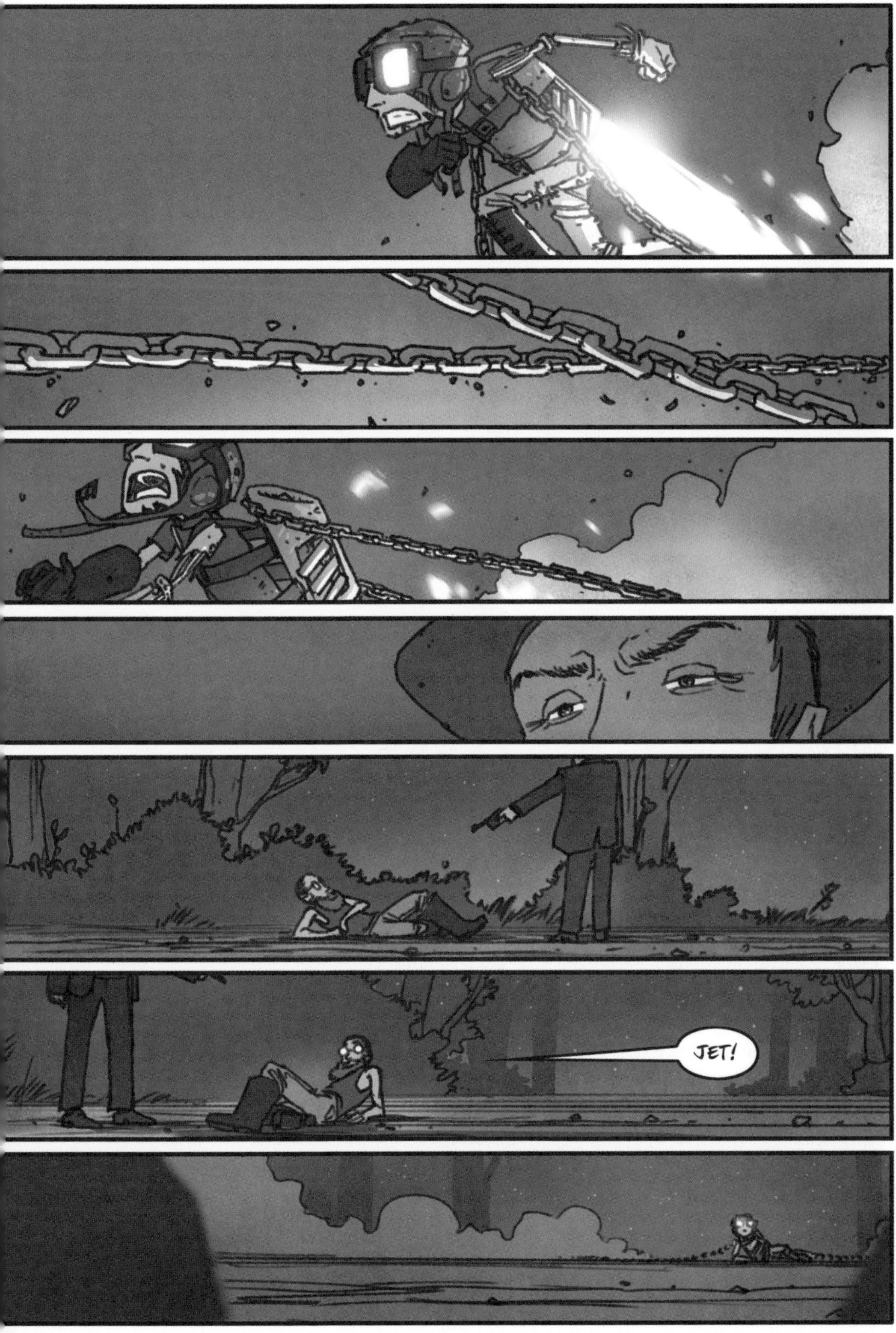
JET!

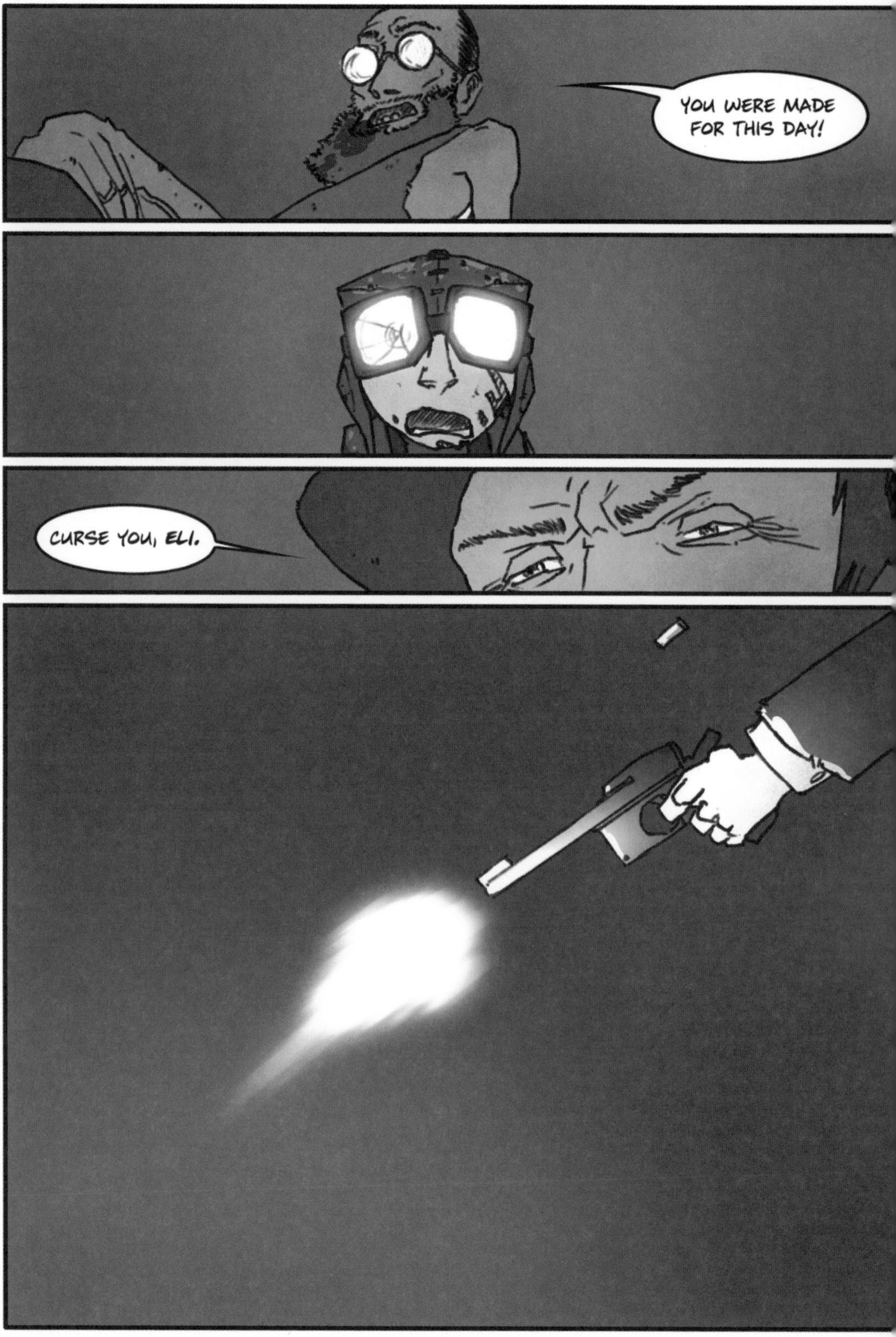
YOU WERE MADE FOR THIS DAY!
CURSE YOU, ELI.

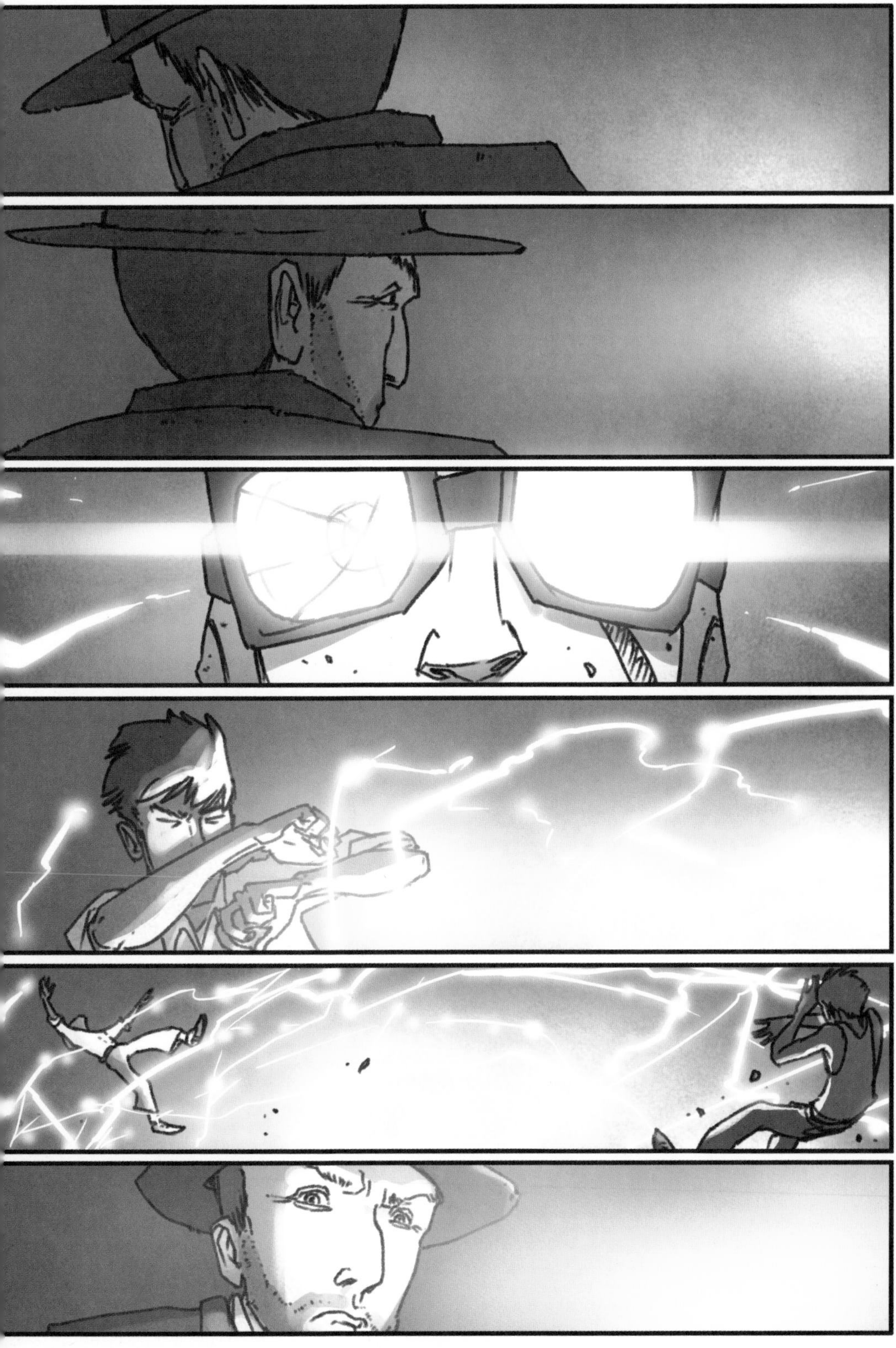

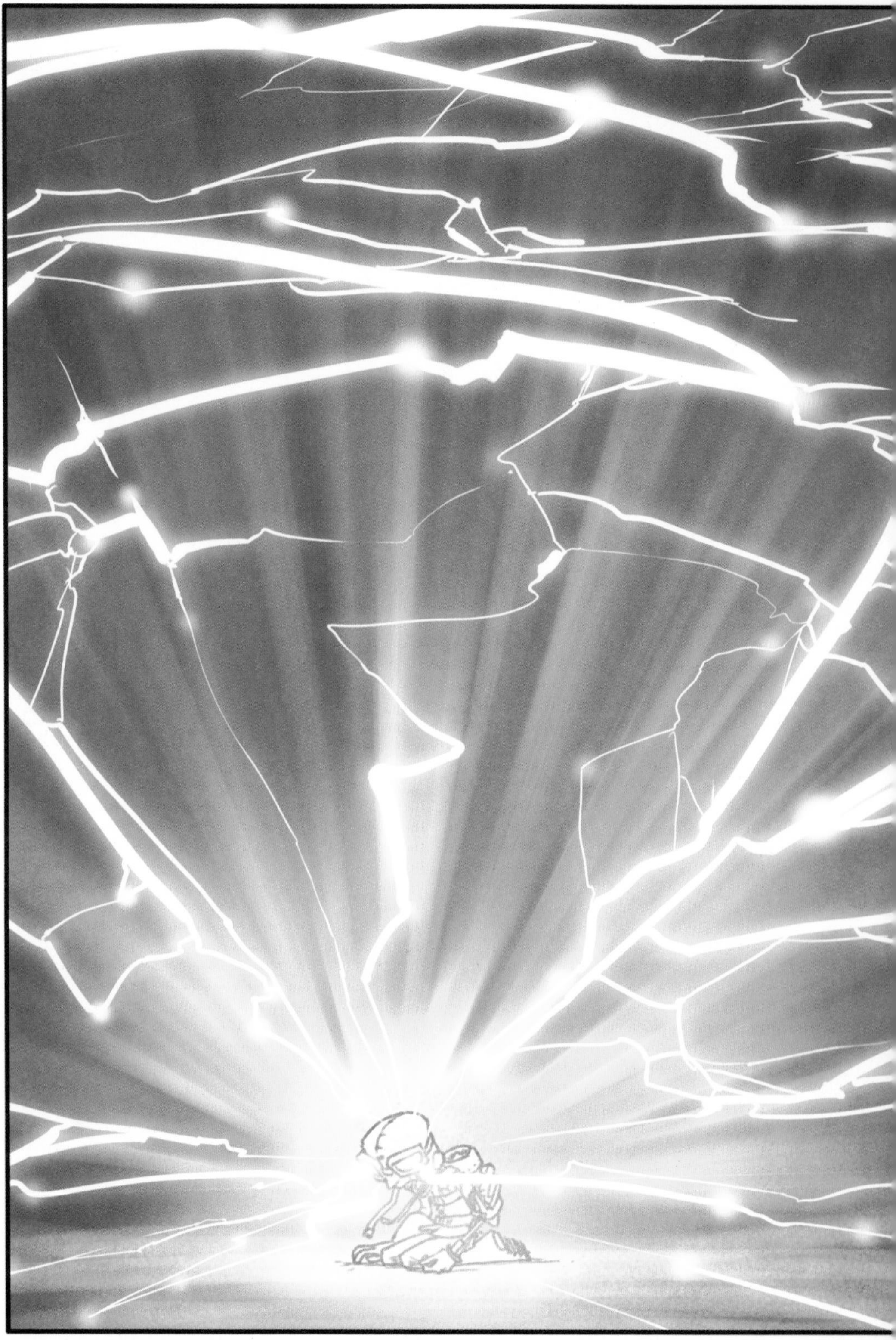

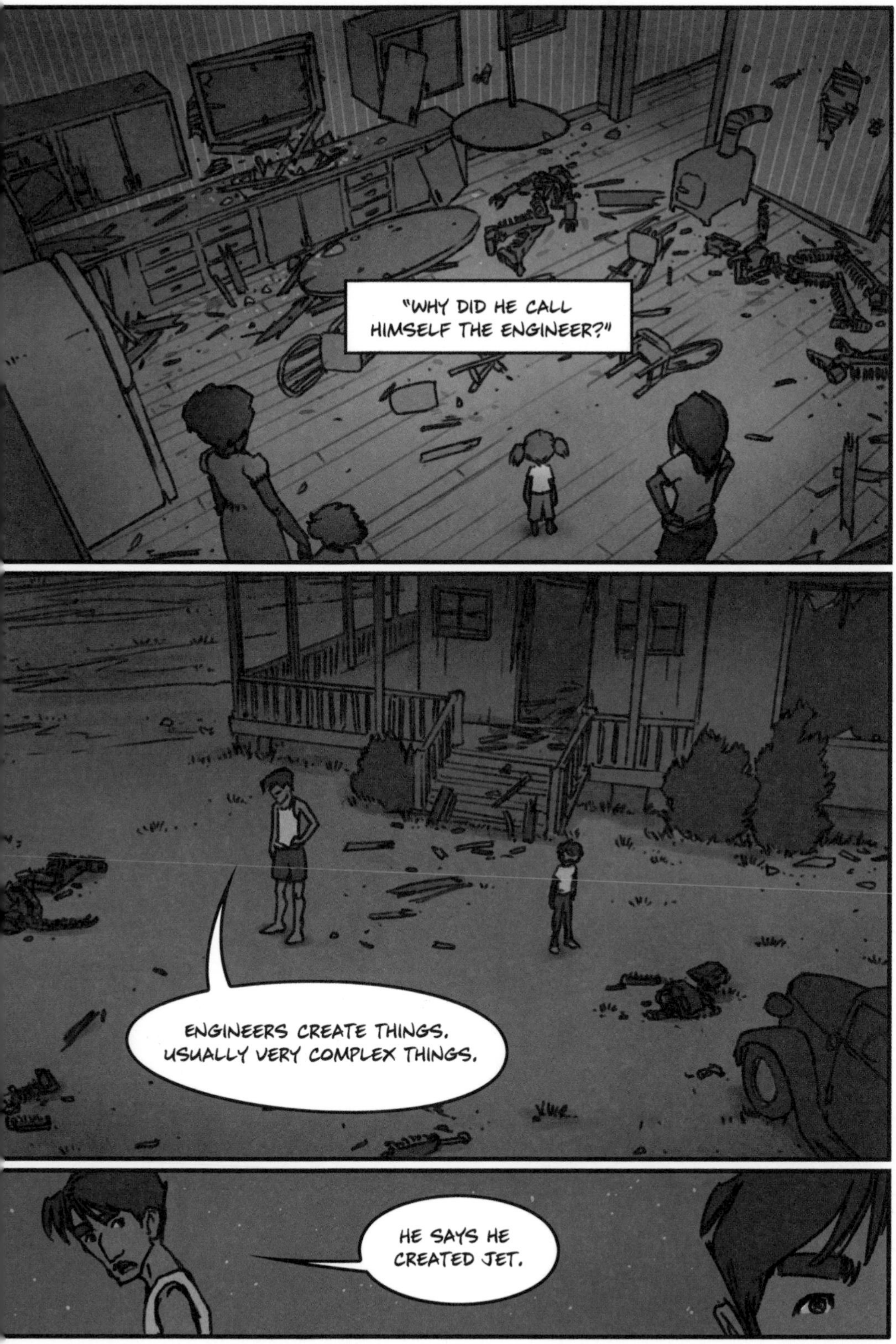
"WHY DID HE CALL HIMSELF THE ENGINEER?"
ENGINEERS CREATE THINGS. USUALLY VERY COMPLEX THINGS.
HE SAYS HE CREATED JET.

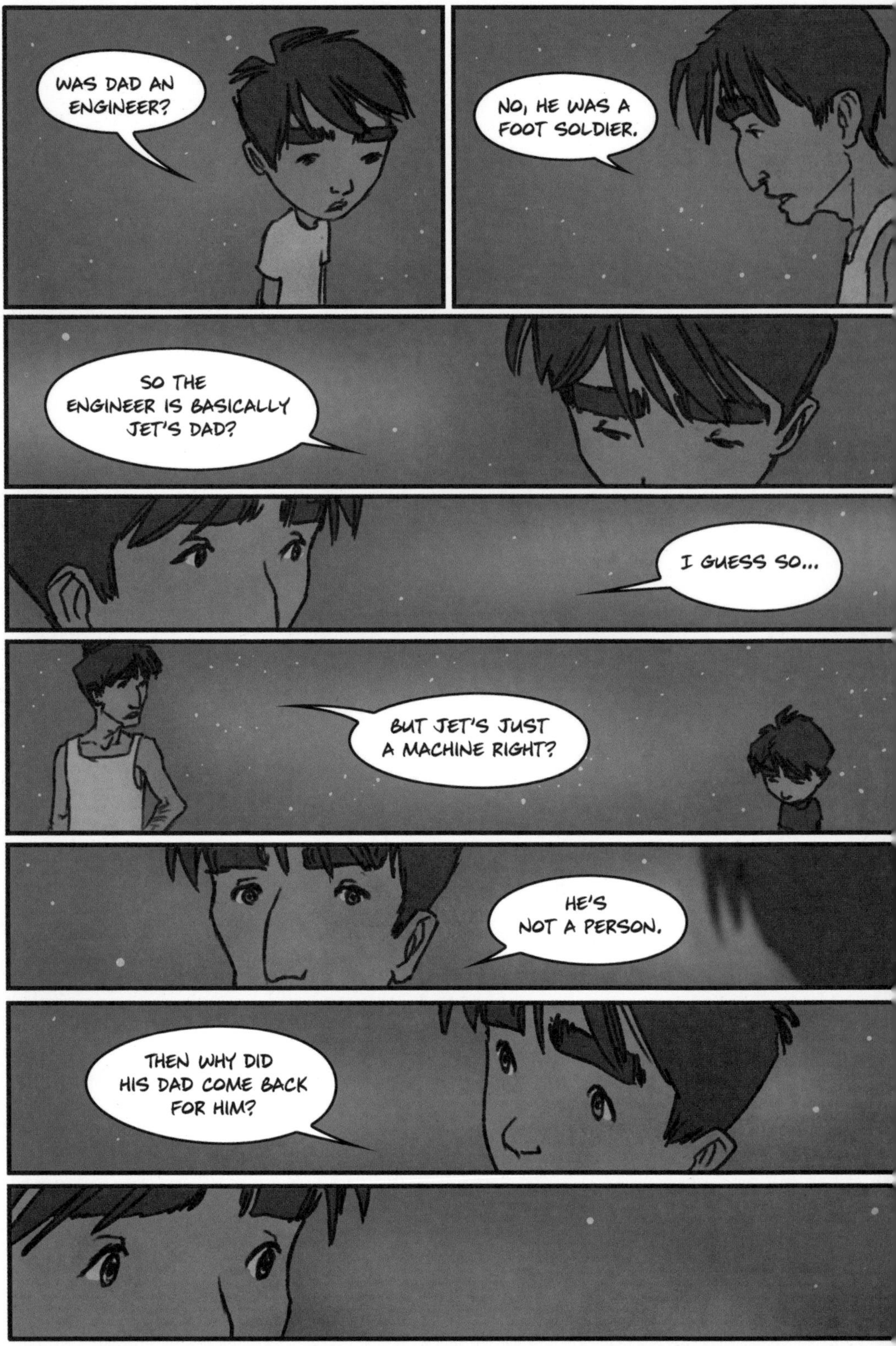
WAS DAD AN ENGINEER?
NO, HE WAS A FOOT SOLDIER.
SO THE ENGINEER IS BASICALLY JET'S DAD?
I GUESS SO...
BUT JET'S JUST A MACHINE RIGHT?
HE'S NOT A PERSON.
THEN WHY DID HIS DAD COME BACK FOR HIM?

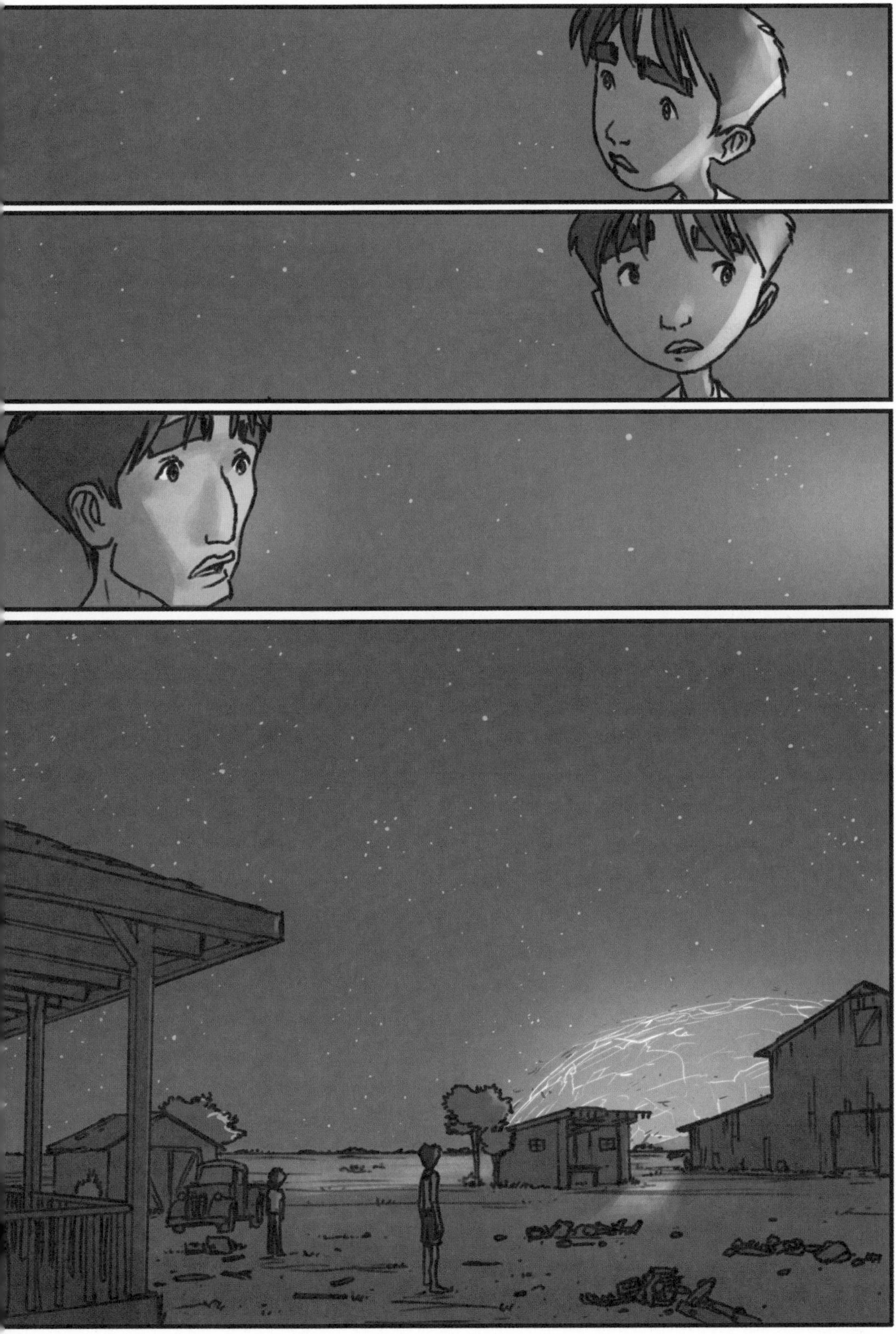

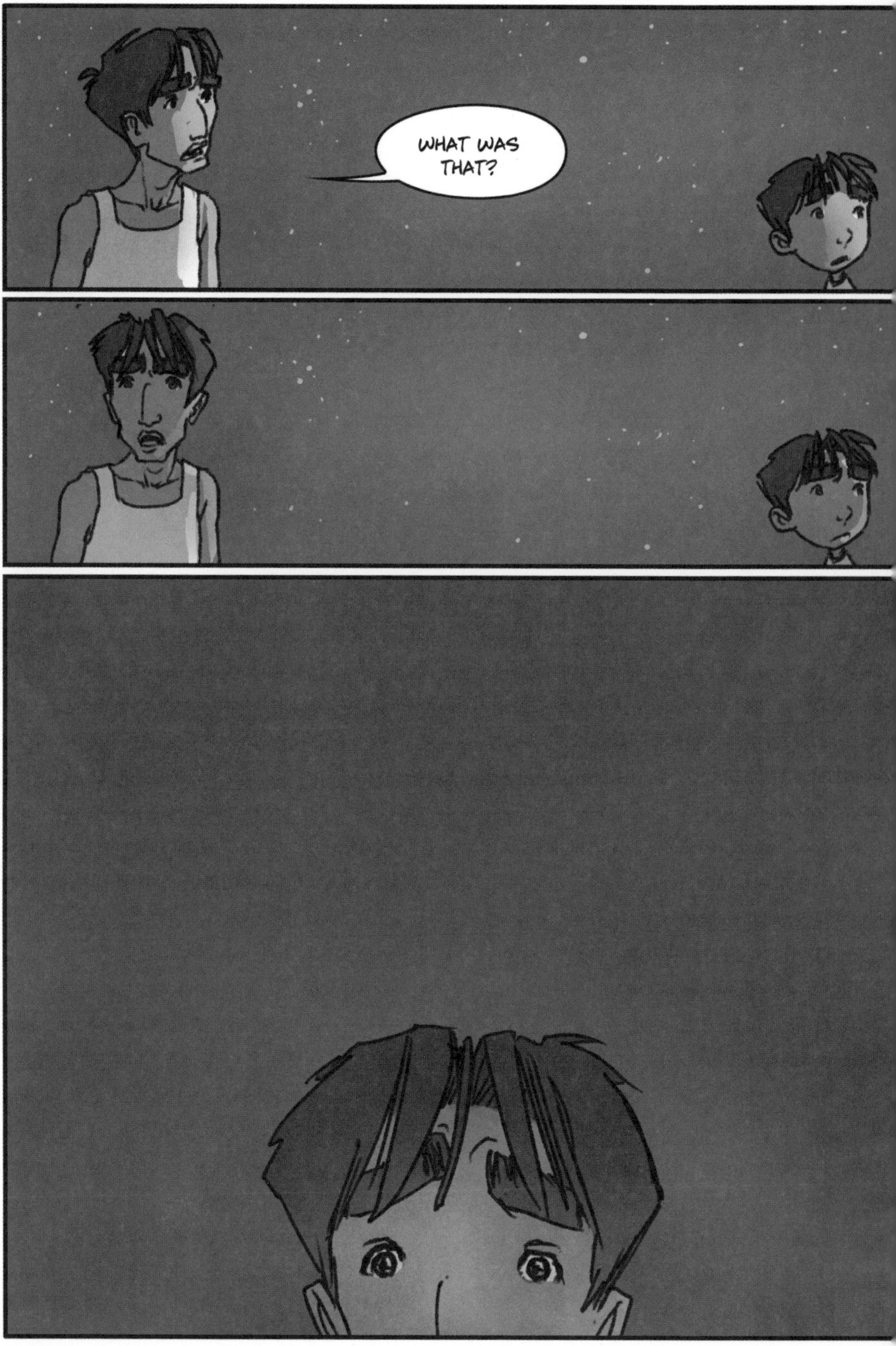
WHAT WAS THAT?

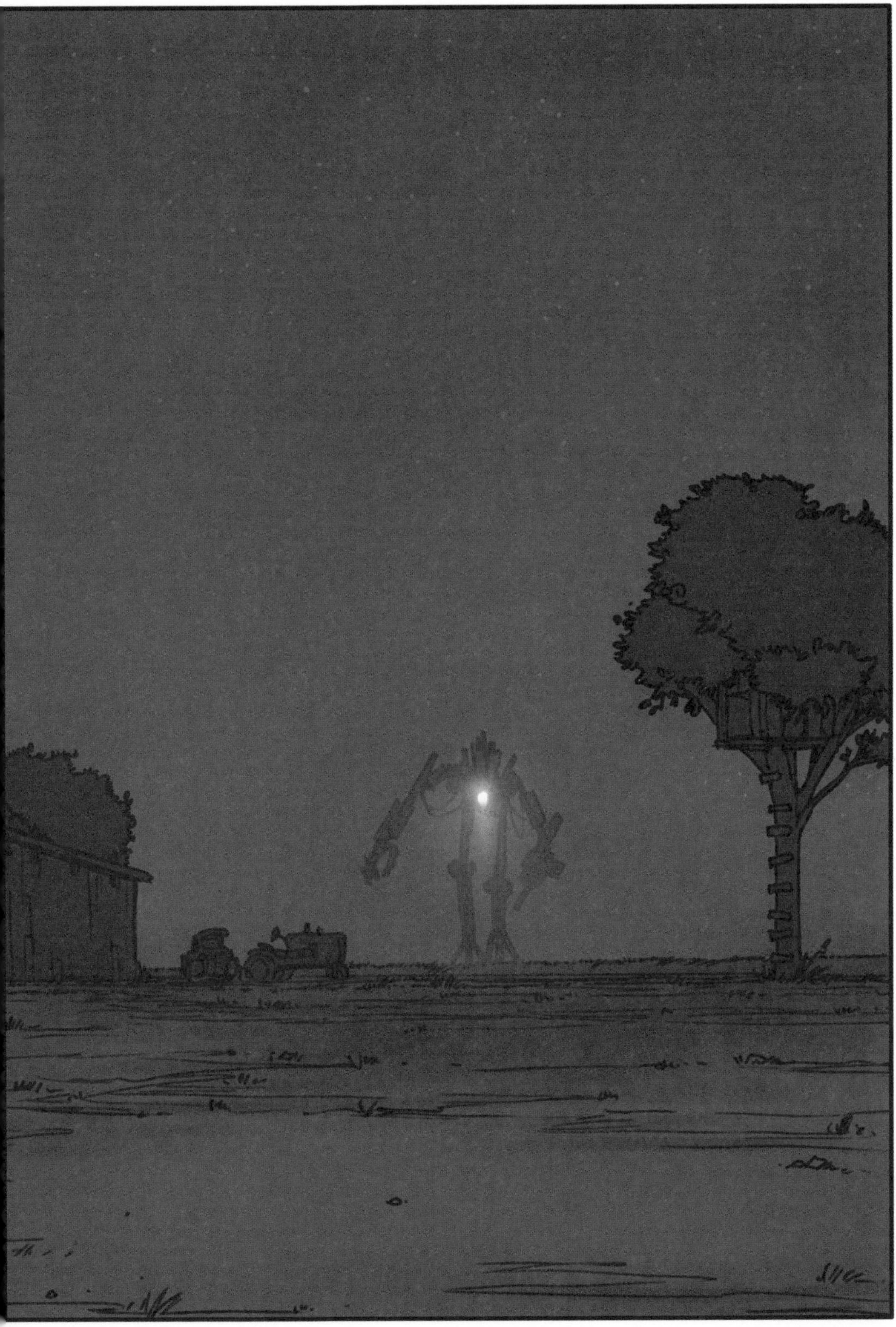

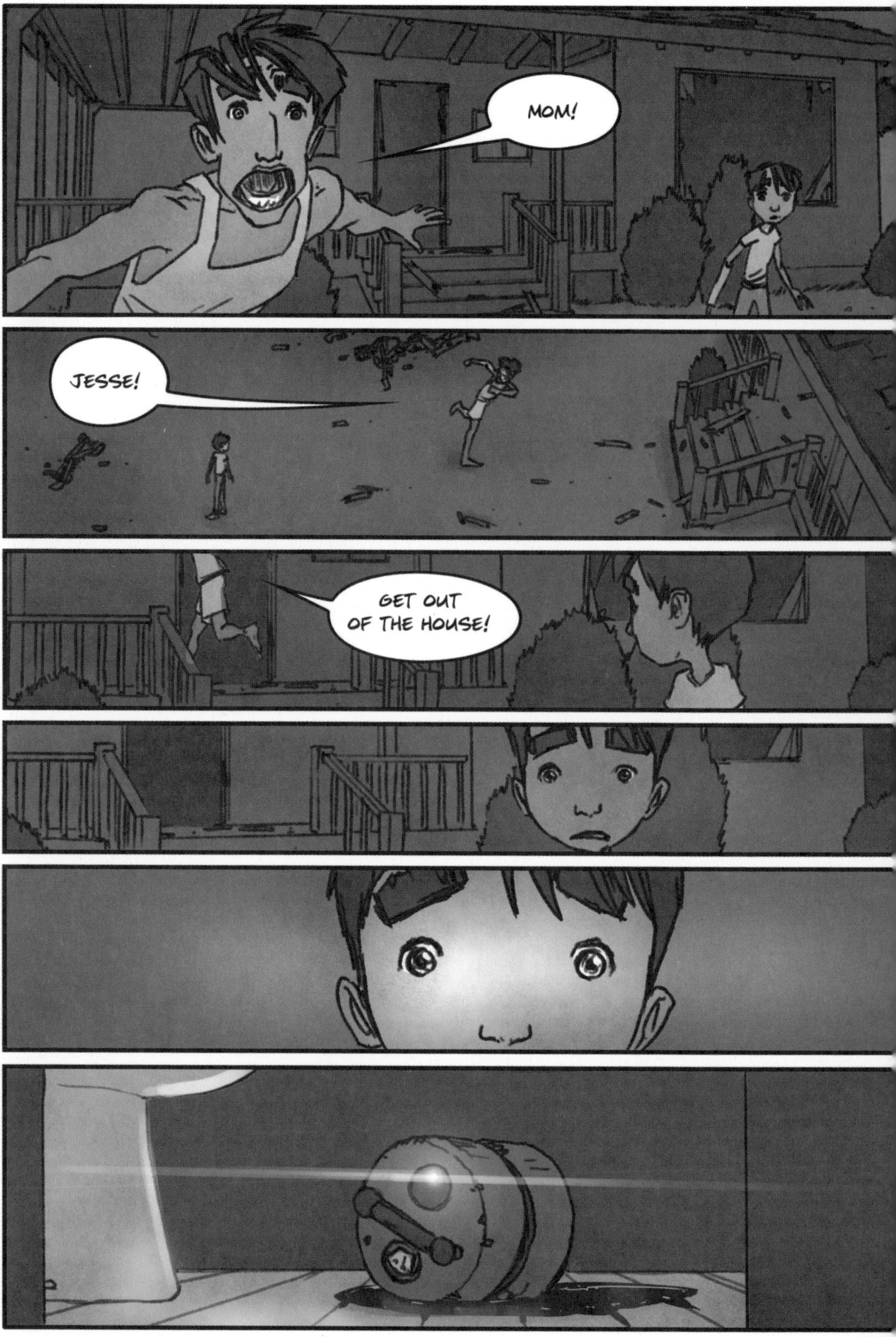
MOM!
JESSE!
GET OUT OF THE HOUSE!

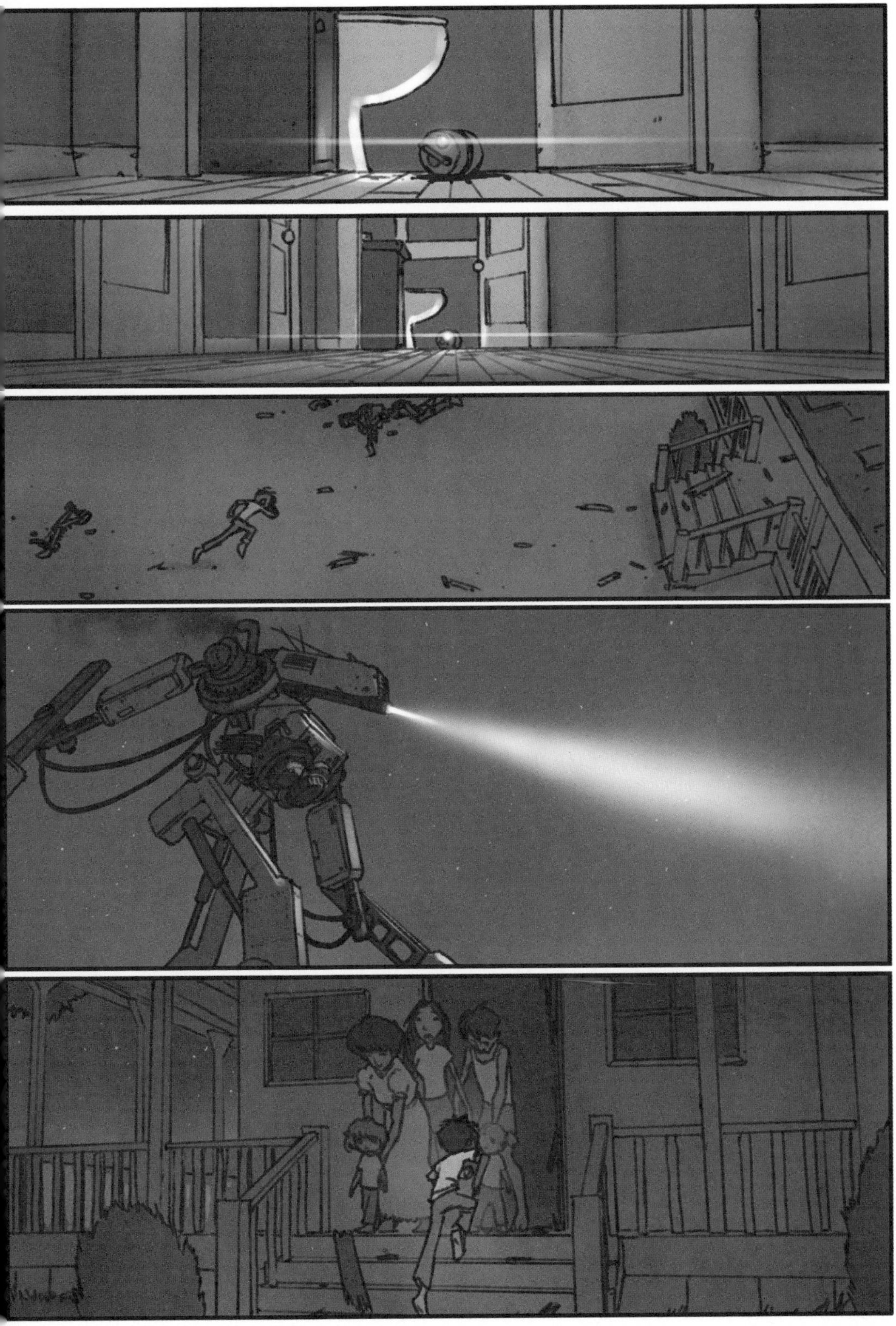

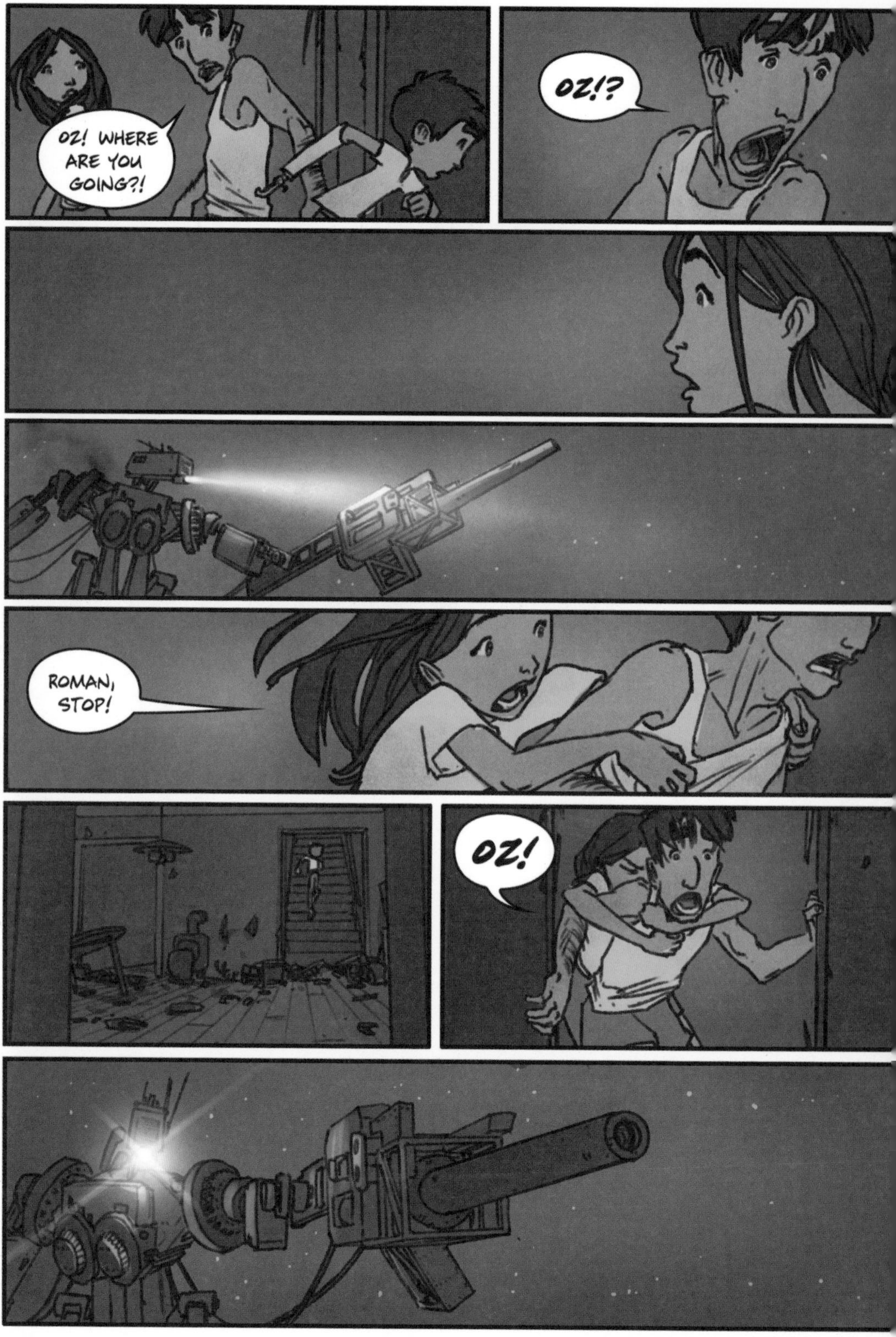
OZ! WHERE ARE YOU GOING?!
OZ!?
ROMAN, STOP!
OZ!

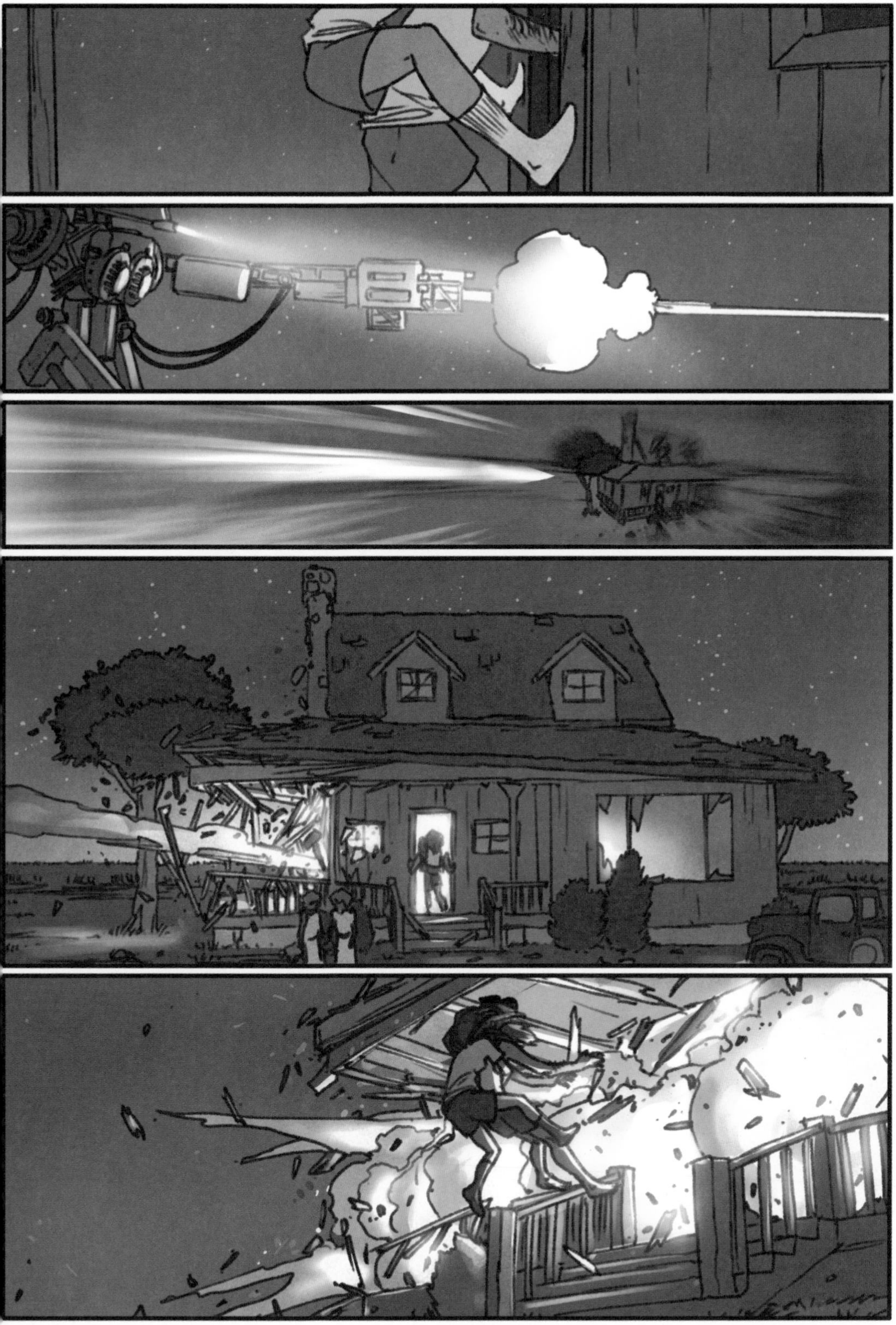

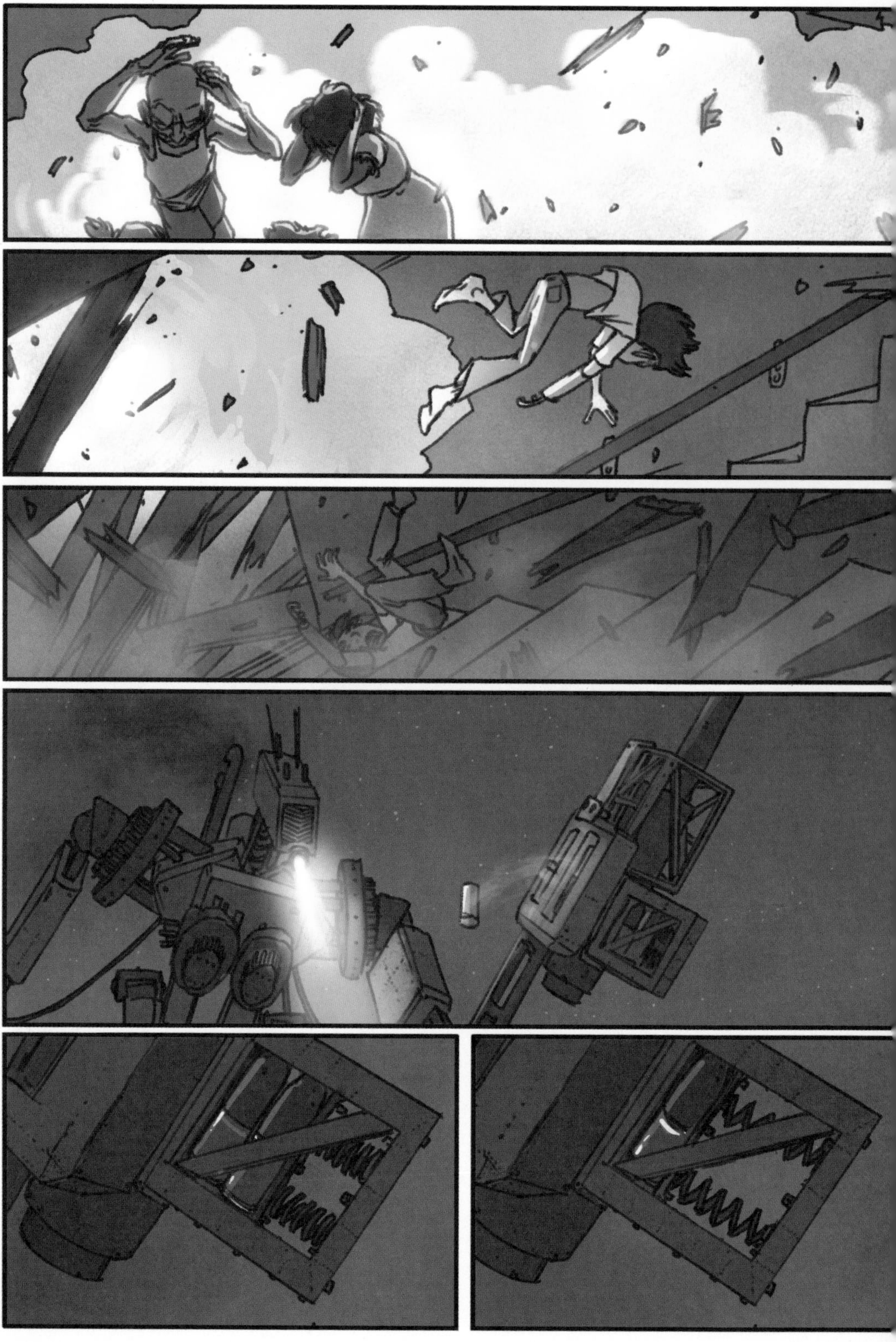

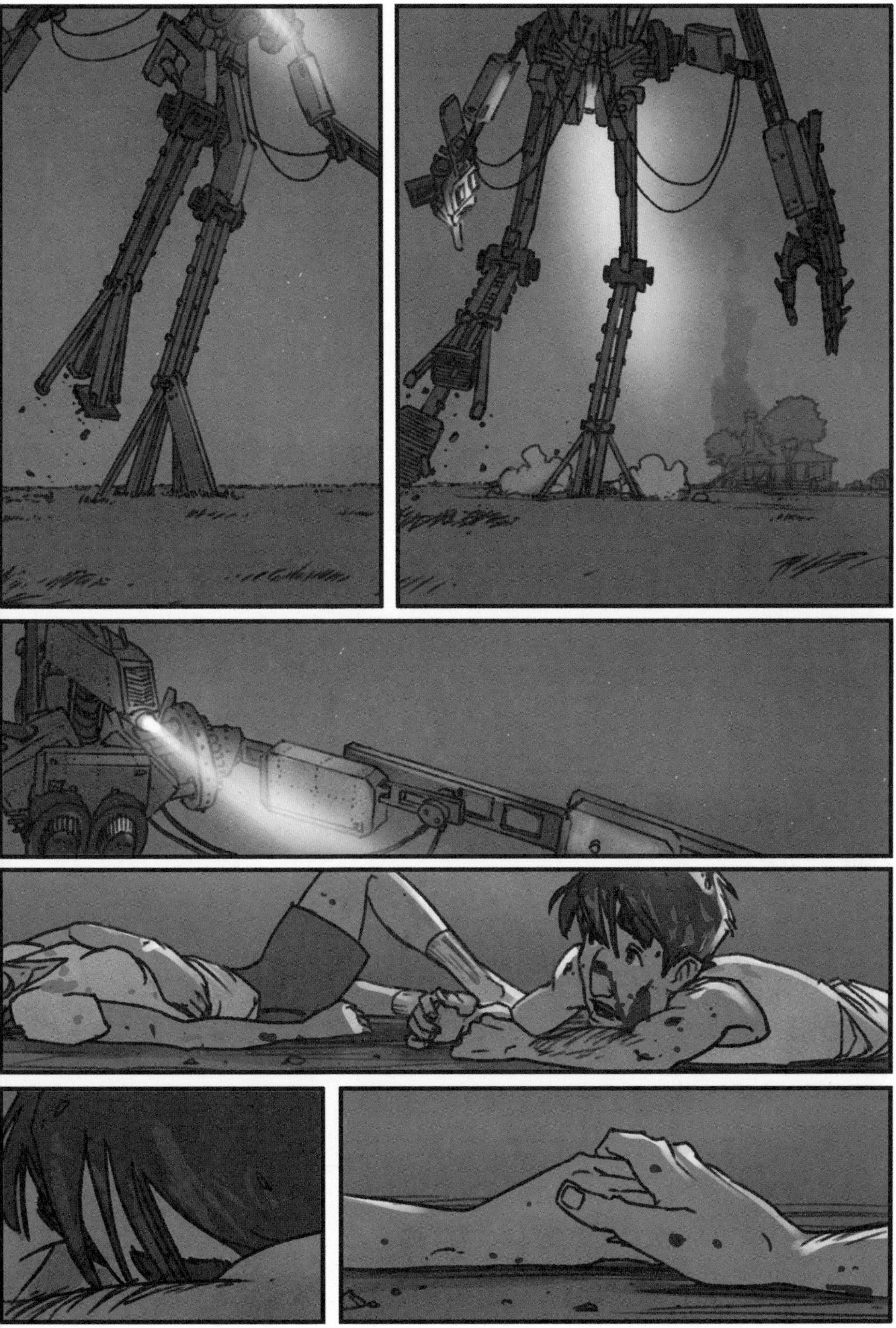

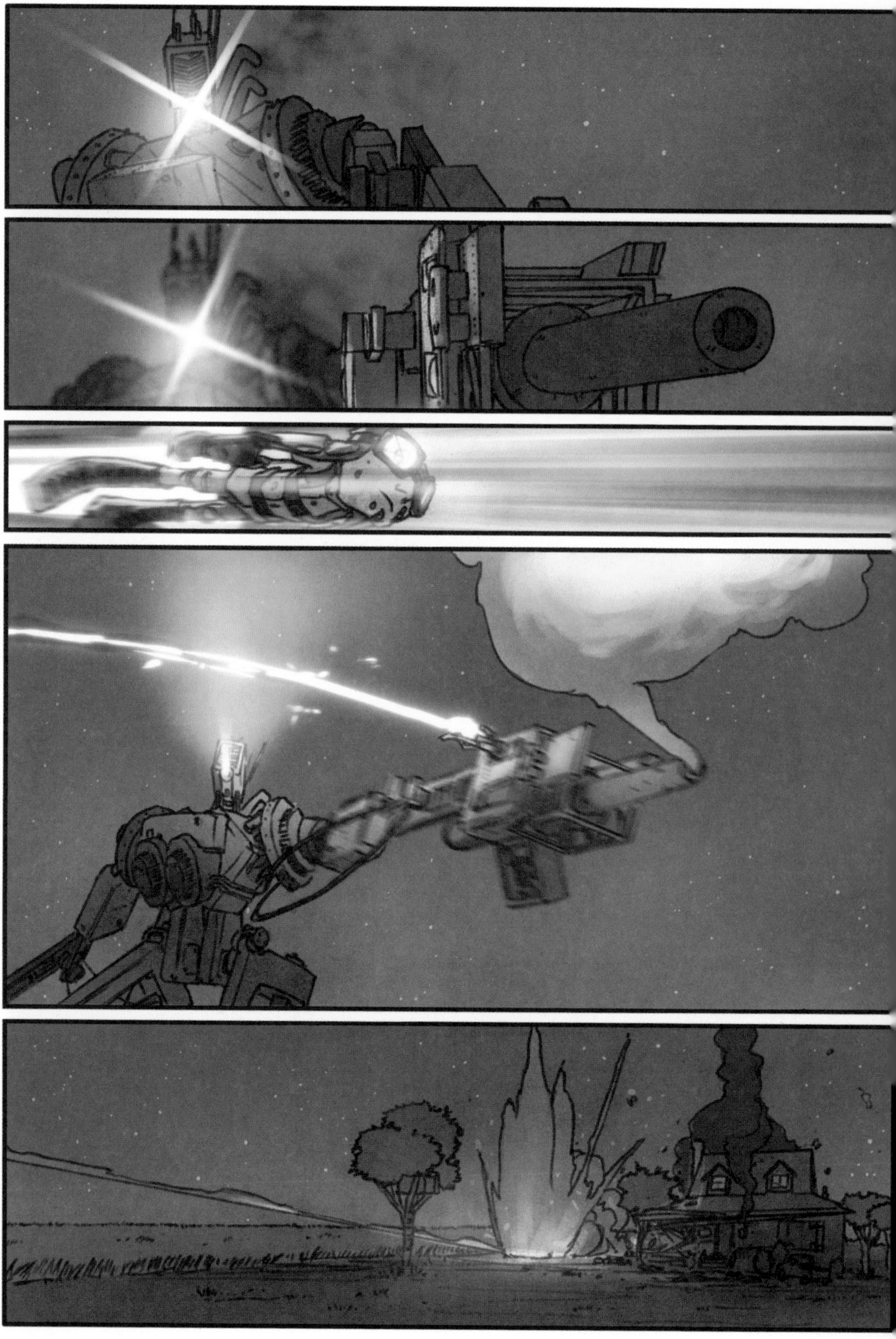

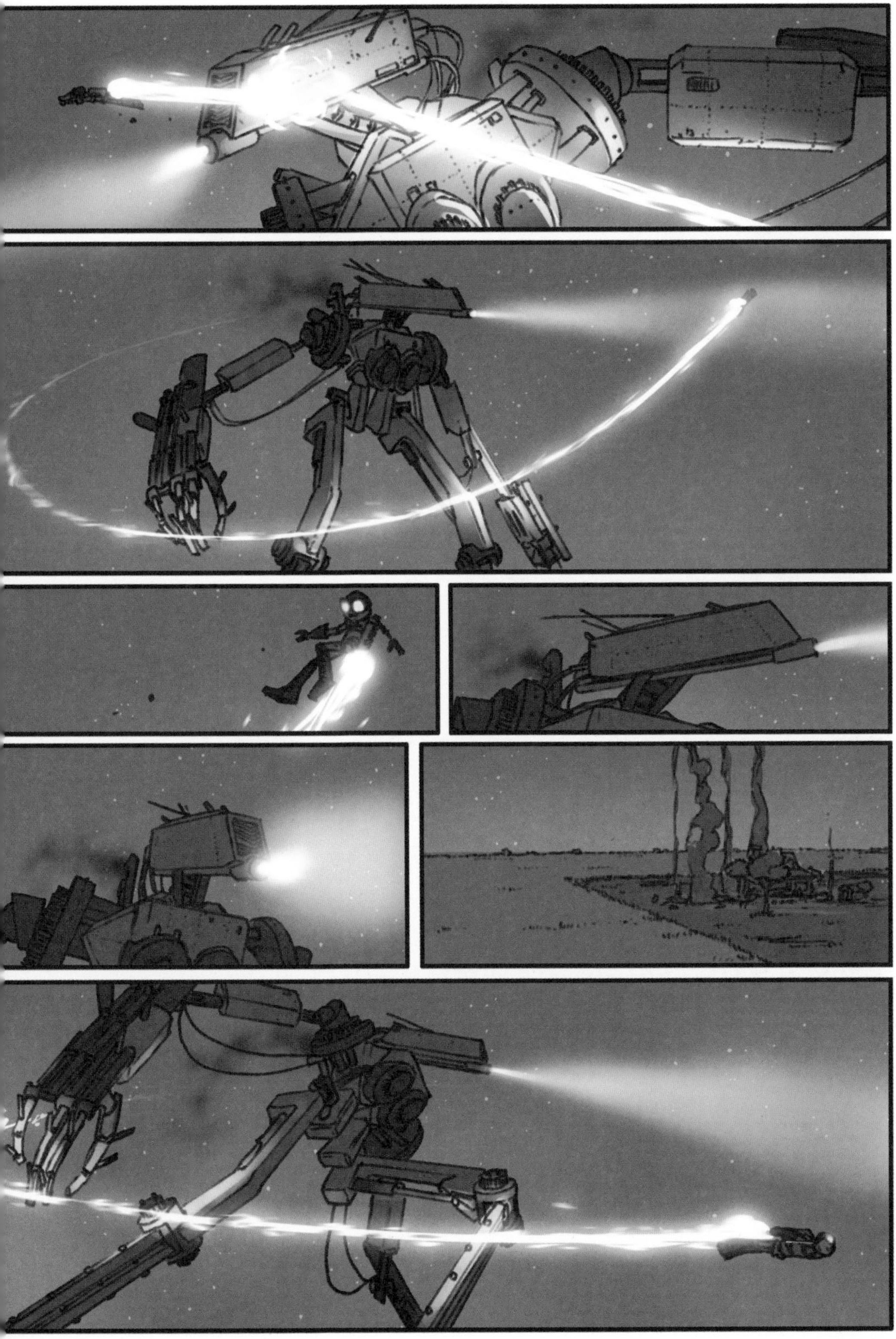

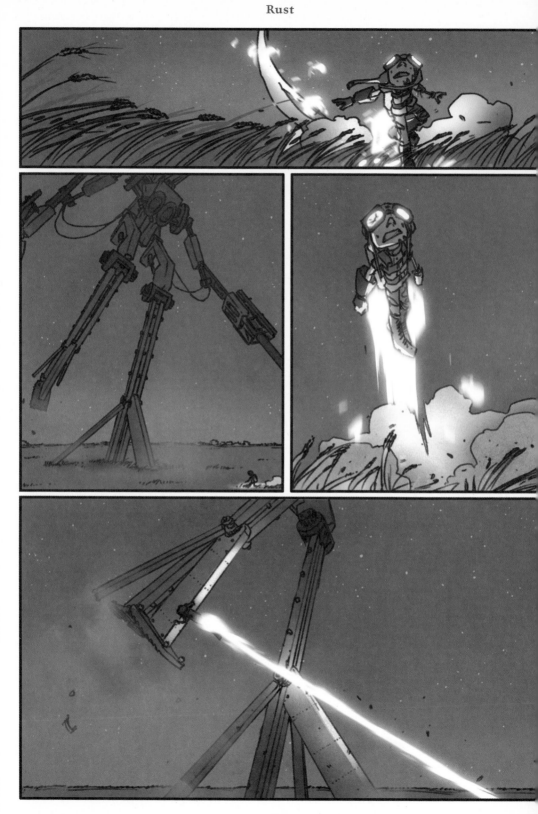

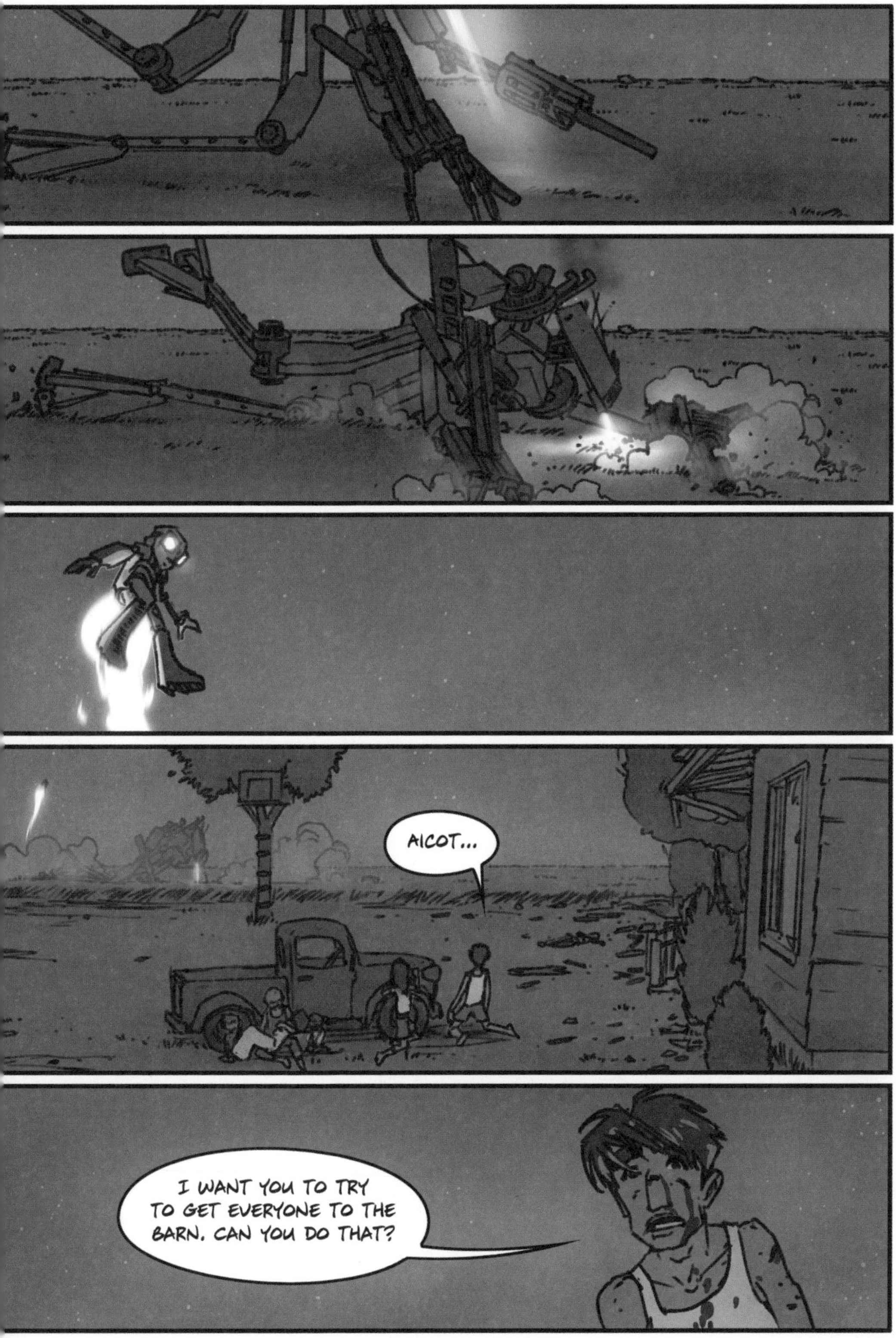
AICOT...
I WANT YOU TO TRY TO GET EVERYONE TO THE BARN. CAN YOU DO THAT?

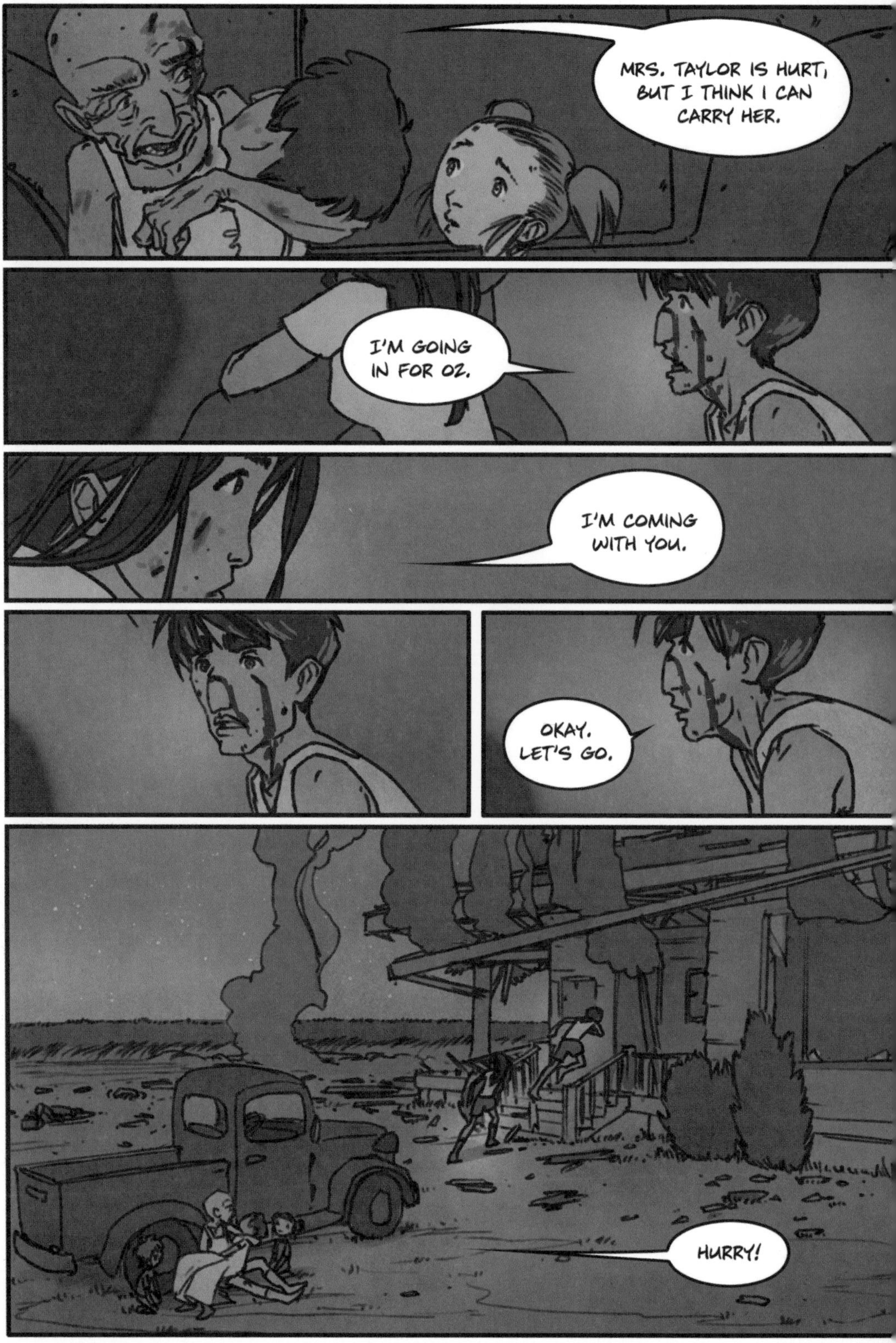
MRS. TAYLOR IS HURT, BUT I THINK I CAN CARRY HER.
I'M GOING IN FOR OZ.
I'M COMING WITH YOU.
OKAY. LET'S GO.
HURRY!

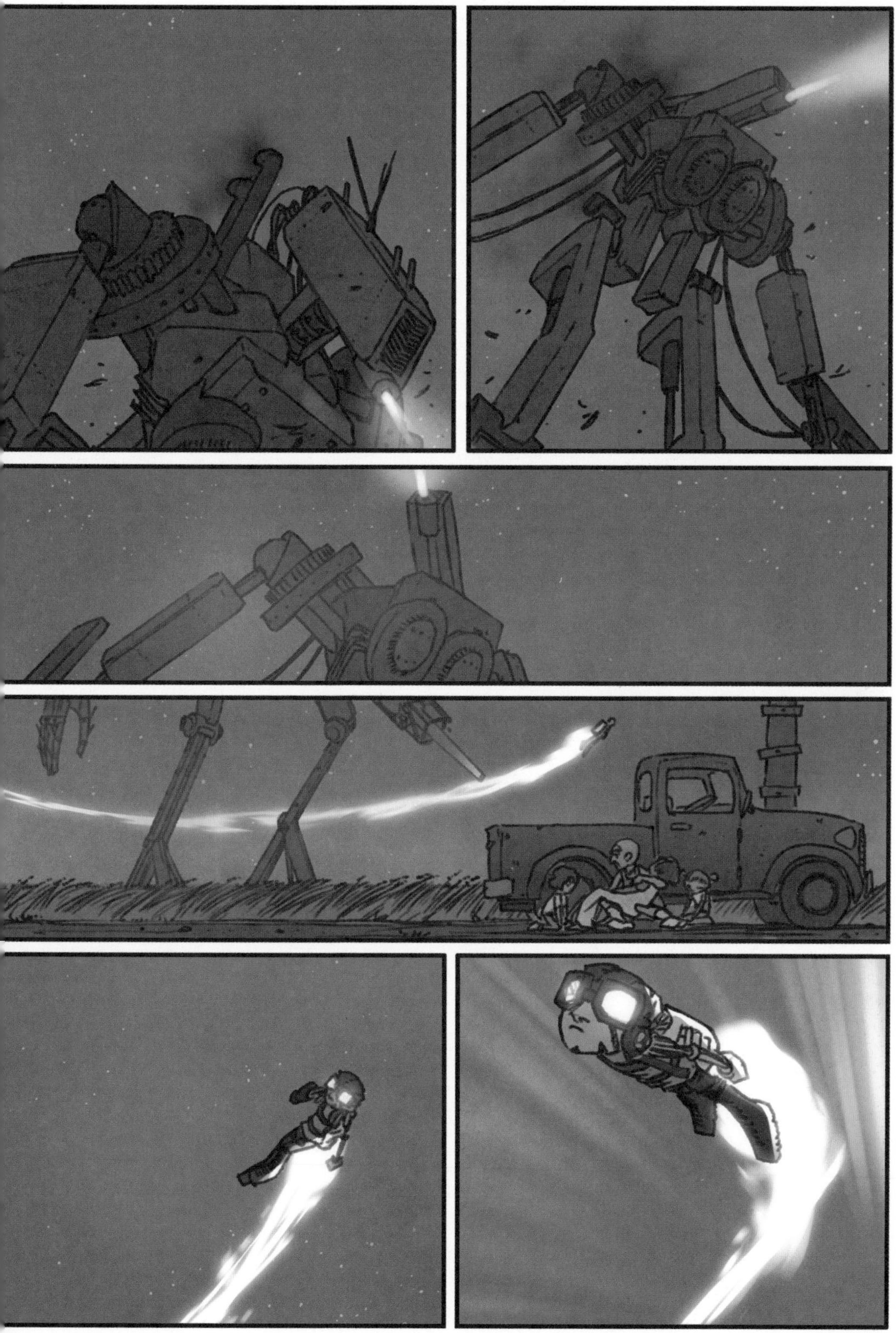

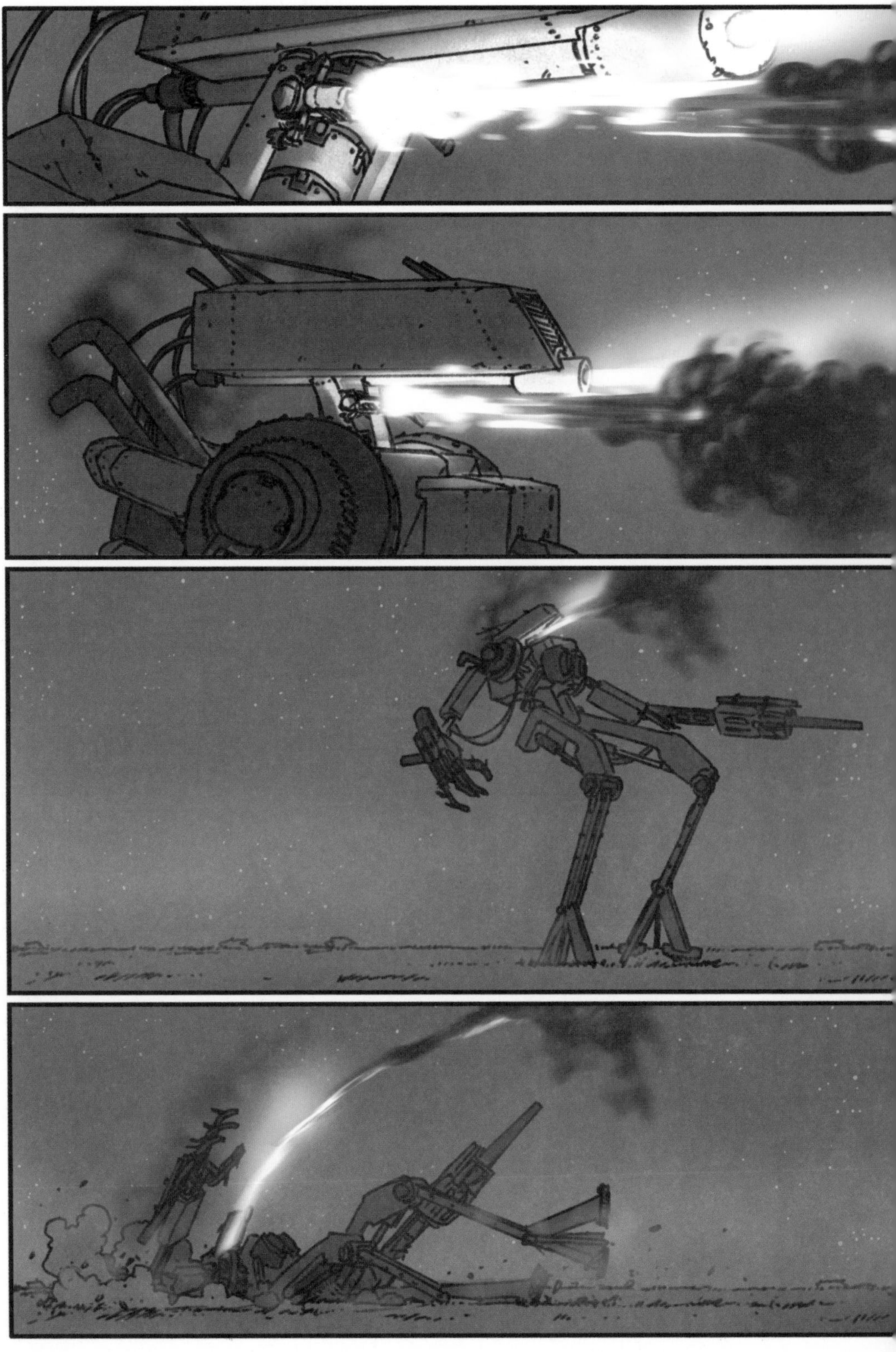

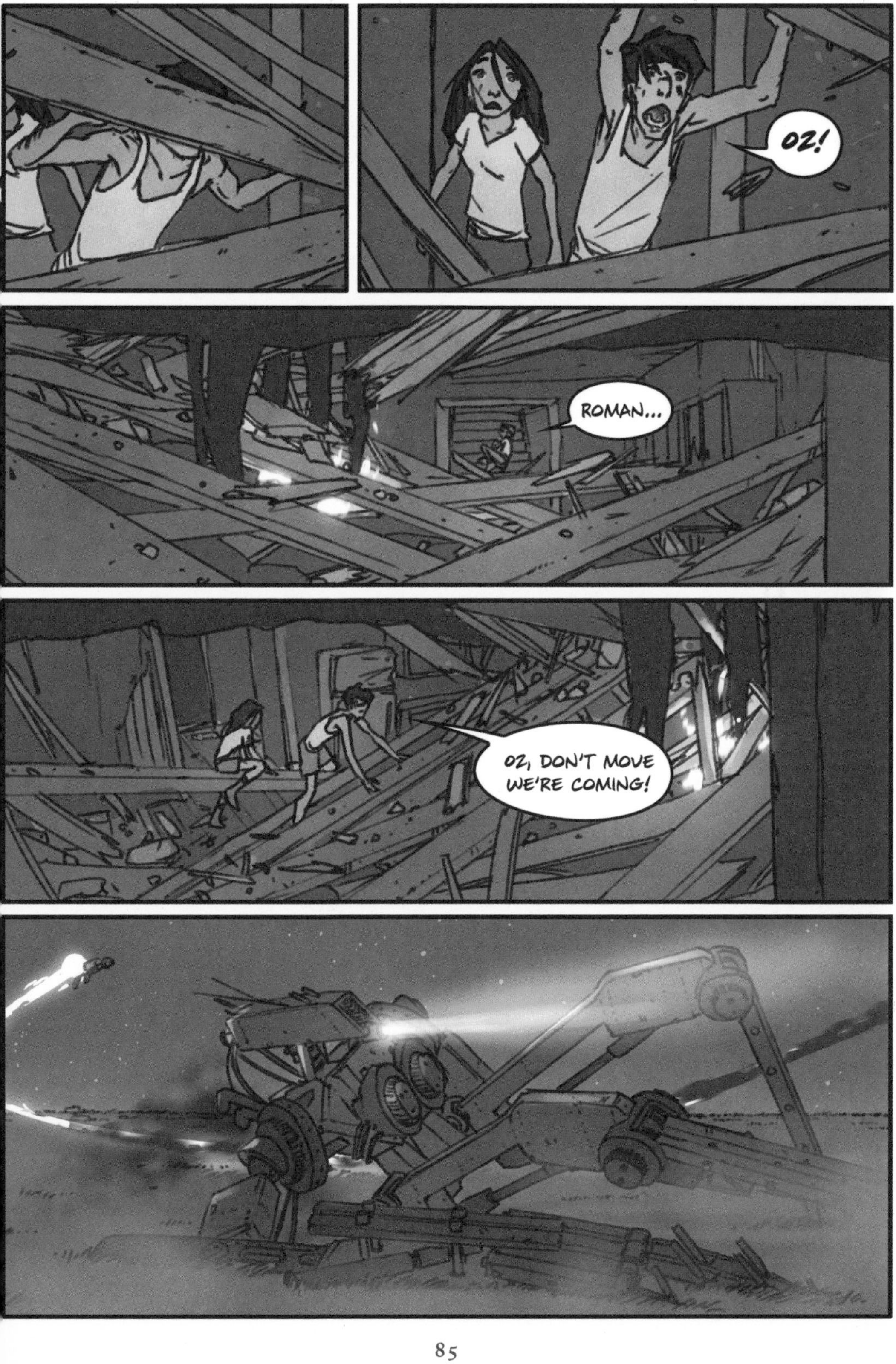
OZ!
ROMAN...
OZ, DON'T MOVE
WE'RE COMING!

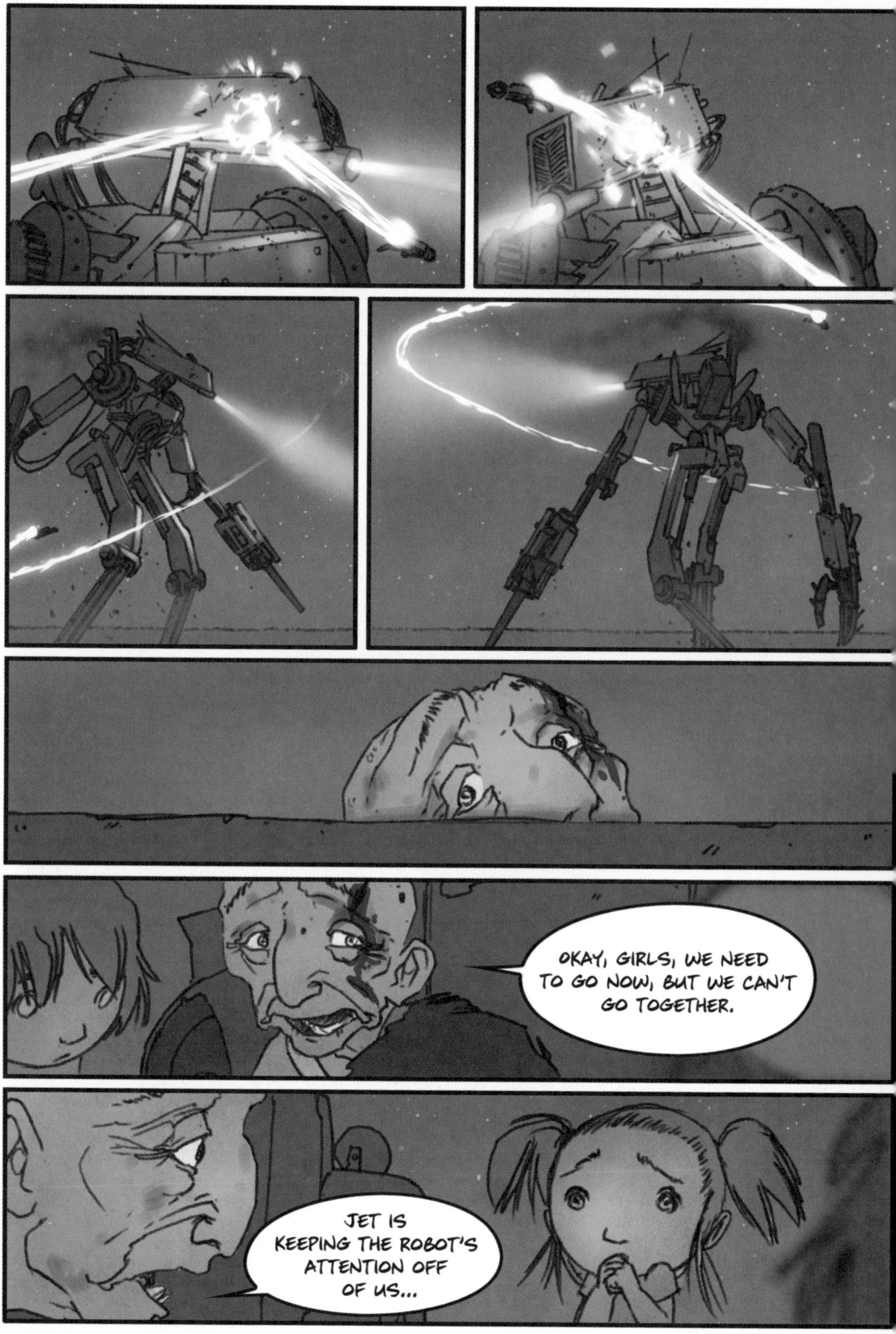
OKAY, GIRLS, WE NEED TO GO NOW, BUT WE CAN'T GO TOGETHER.
JET IS KEEPING THE ROBOT'S ATTENTION OFF OF US...

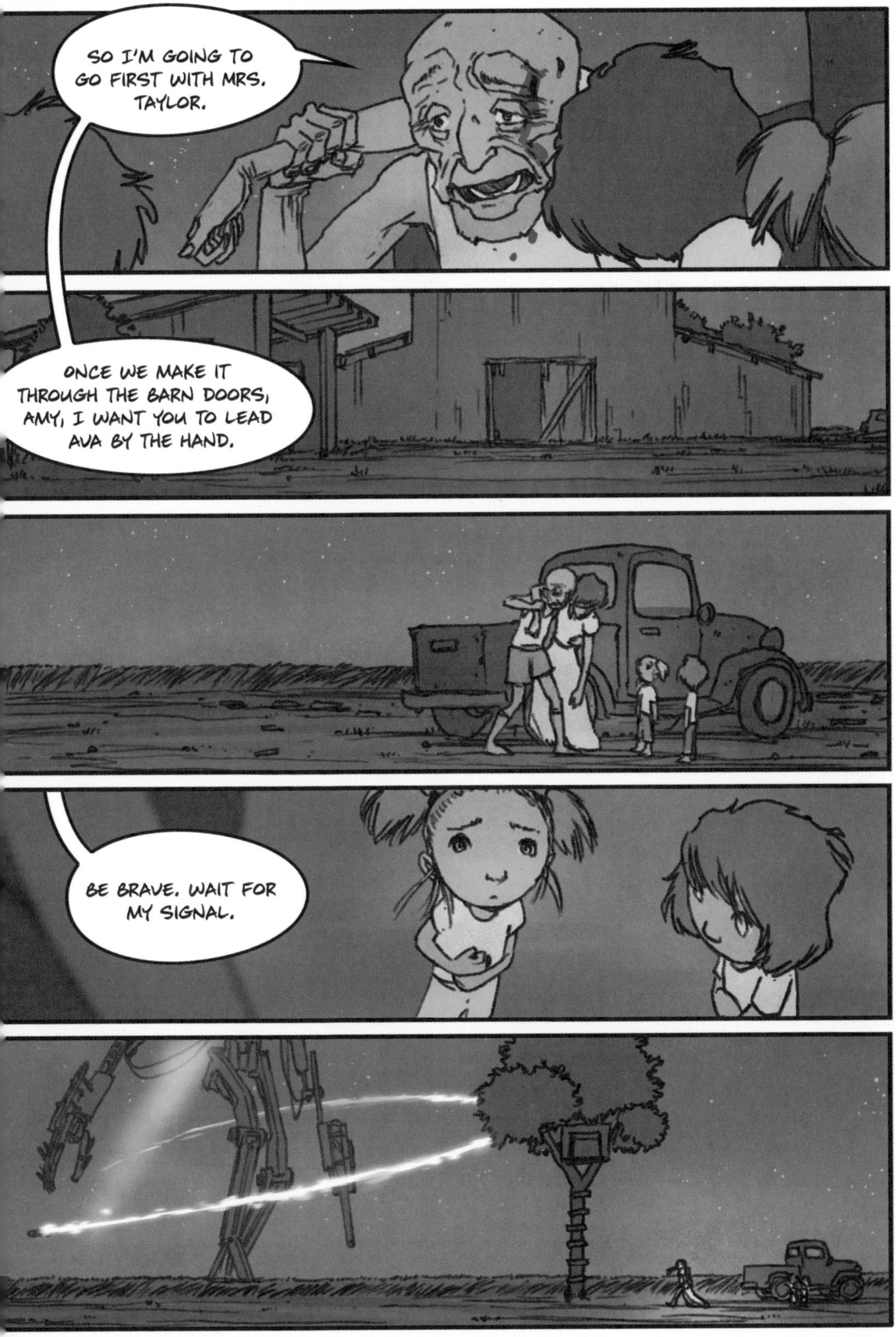
SO I'M GOING TO GO FIRST WITH MRS. TAYLOR.
ONCE WE MAKE IT THROUGH THE BARN DOORS, AMY, I WANT YOU TO LEAD AVA BY THE HAND.
BE BRAVE. WAIT FOR MY SIGNAL.

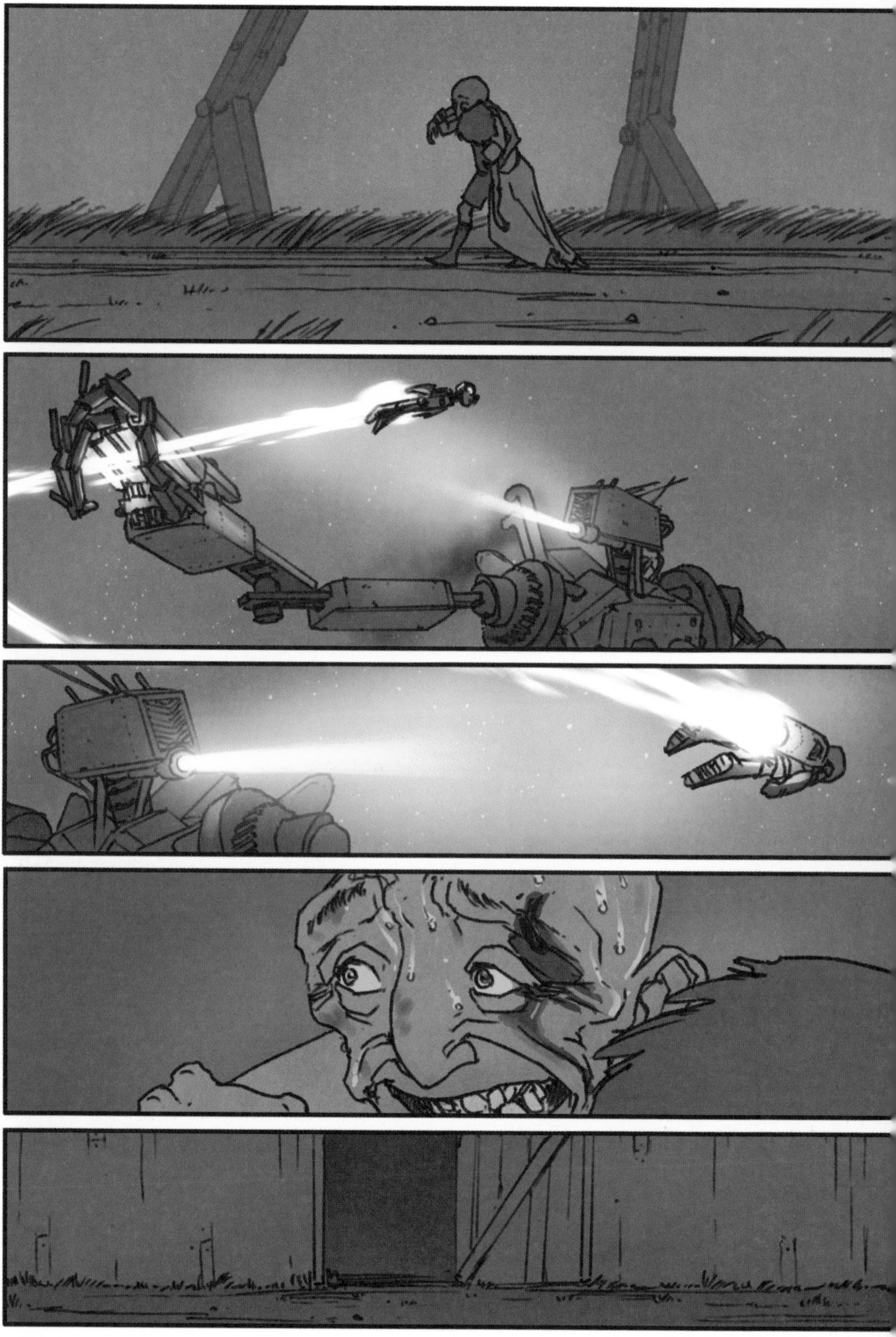

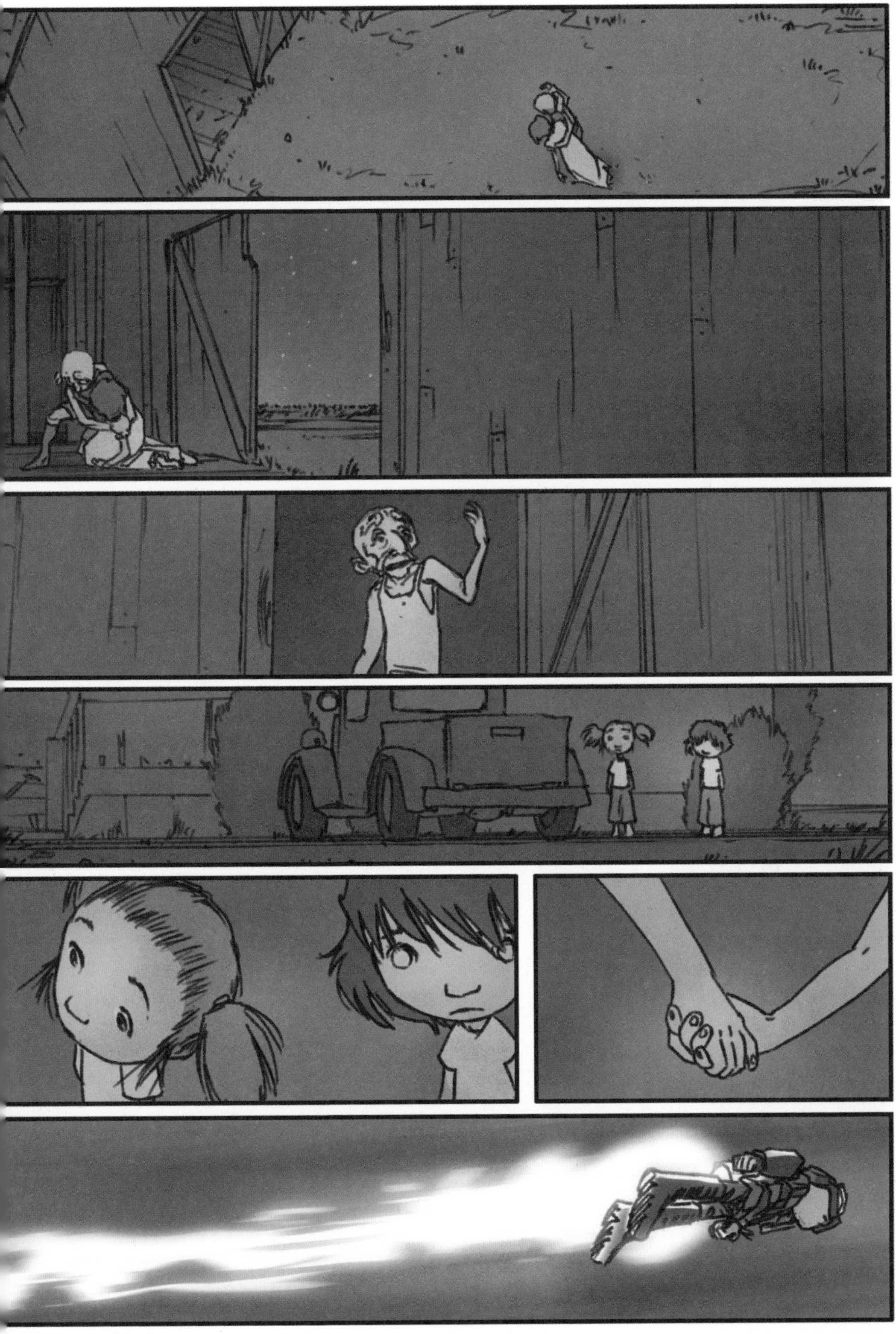

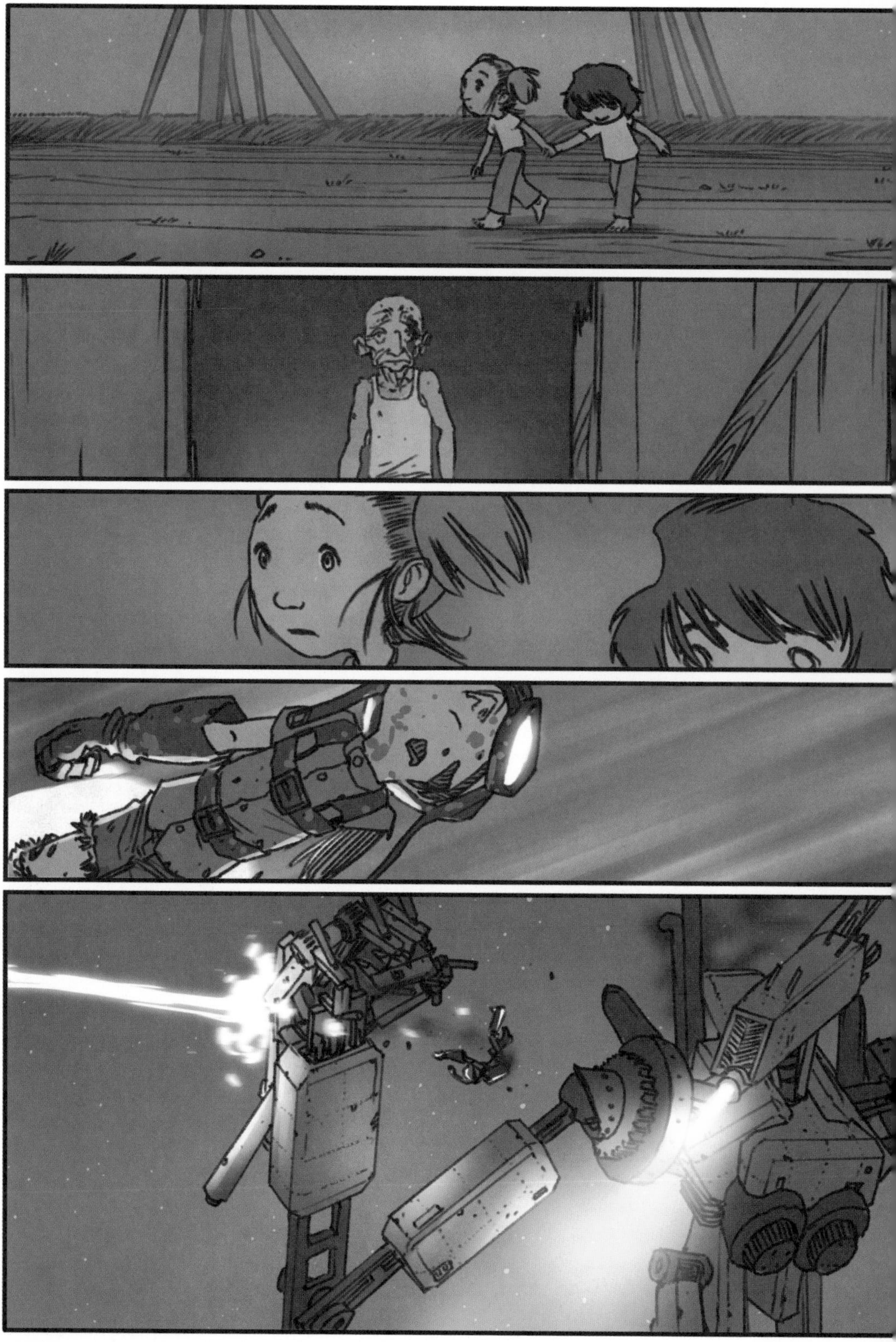

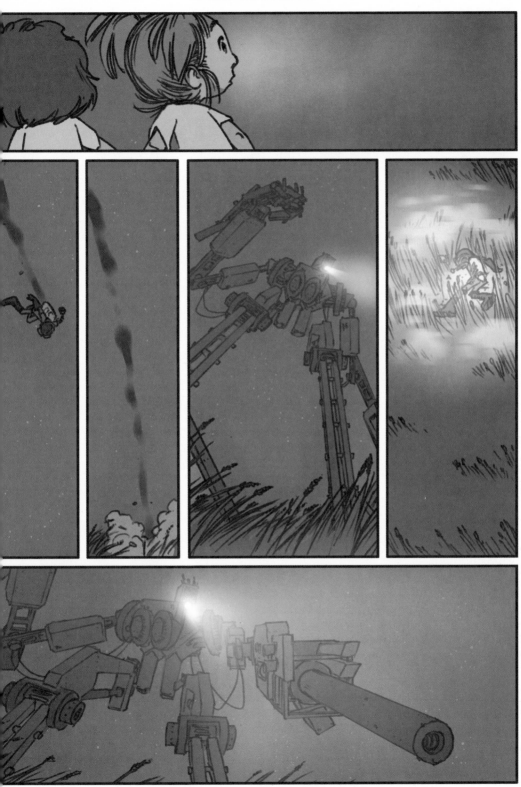

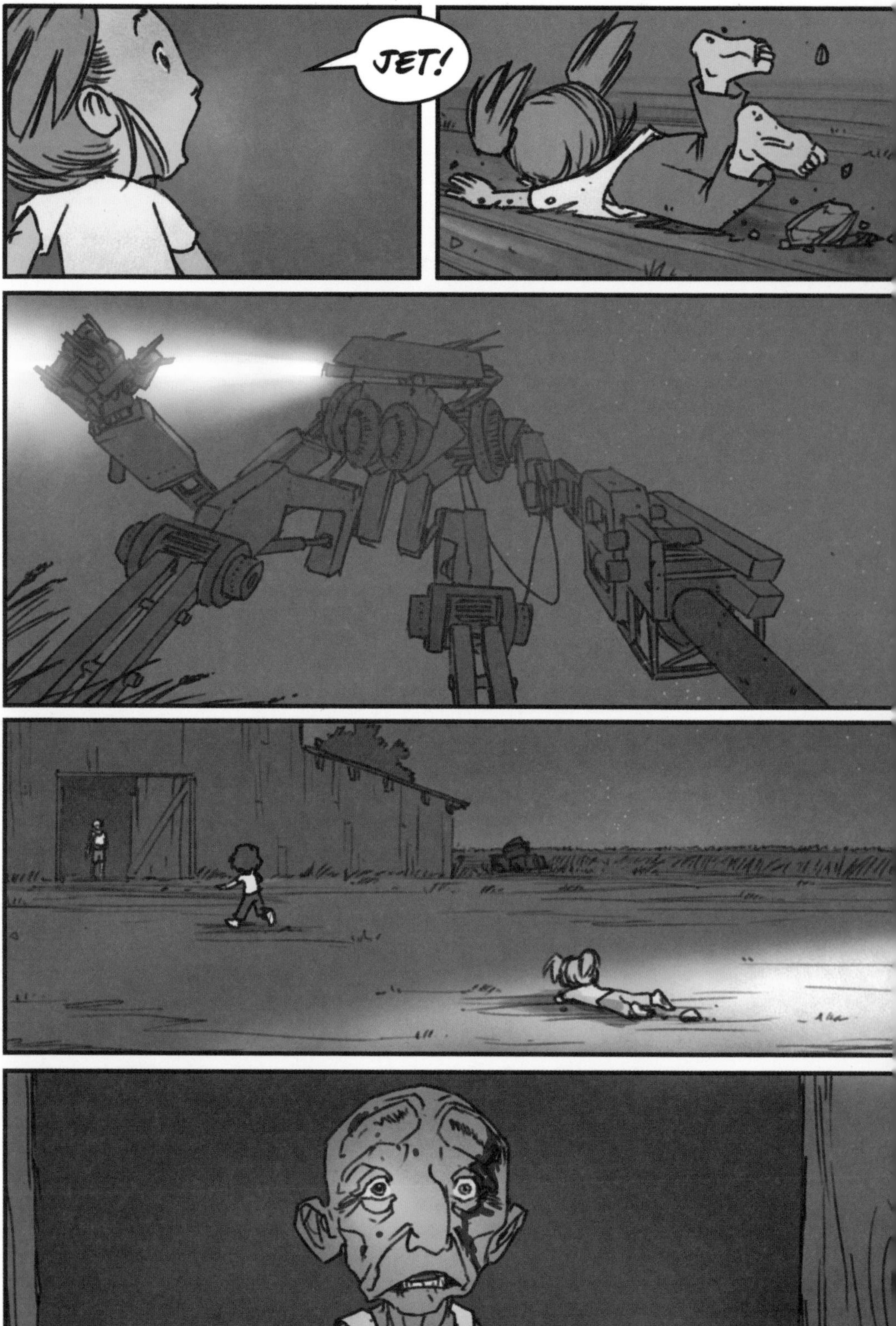
JET!

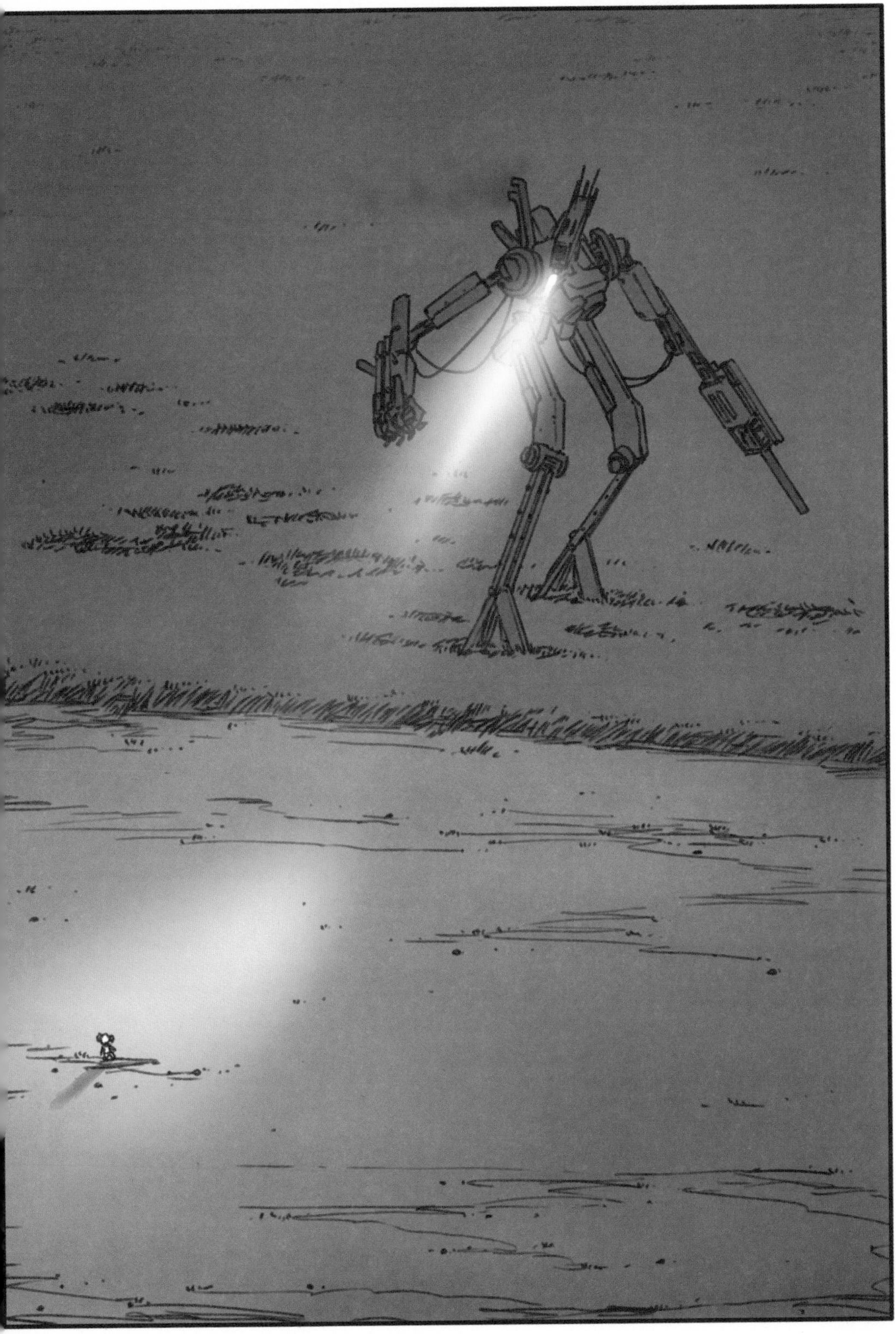

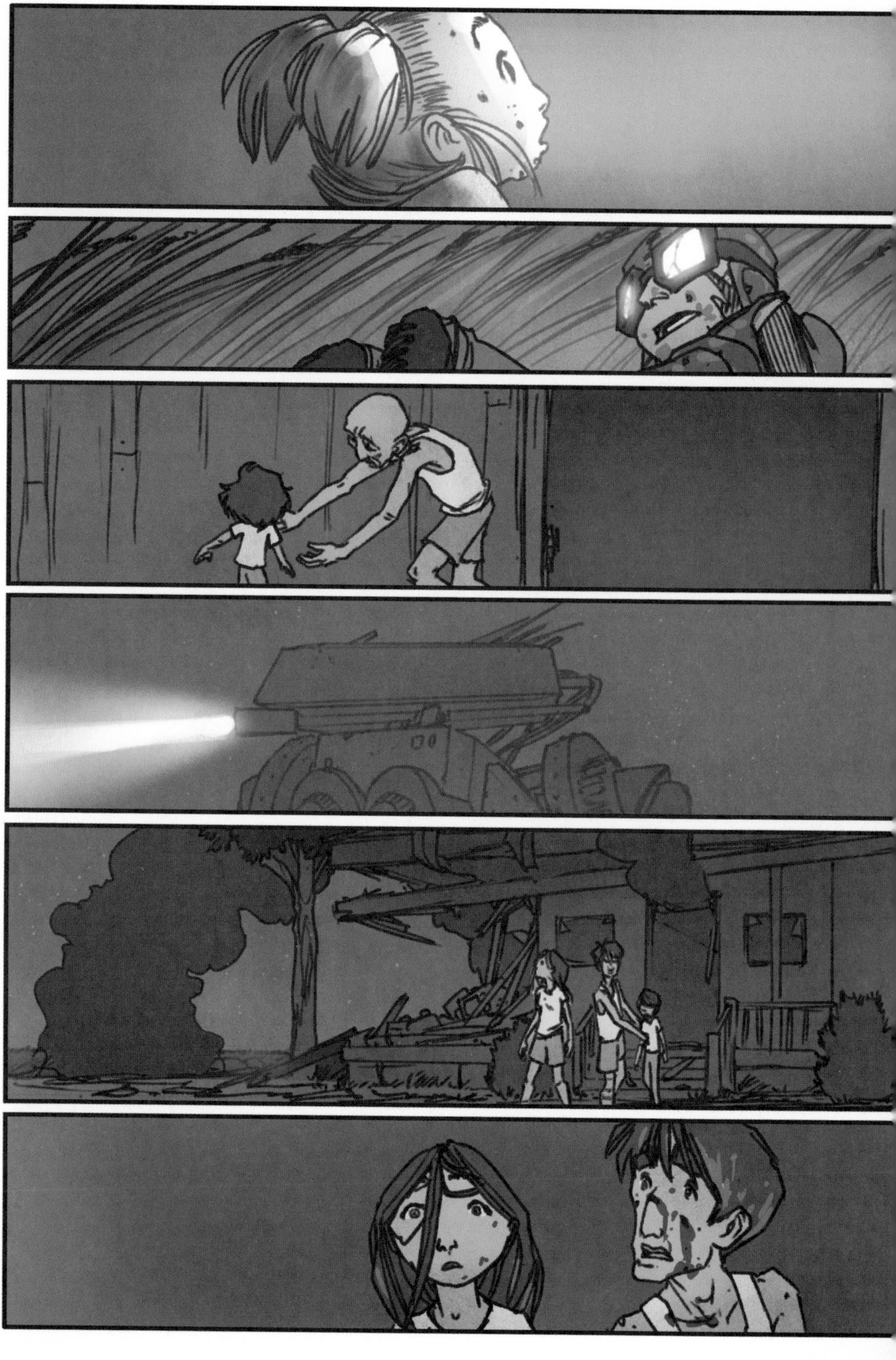

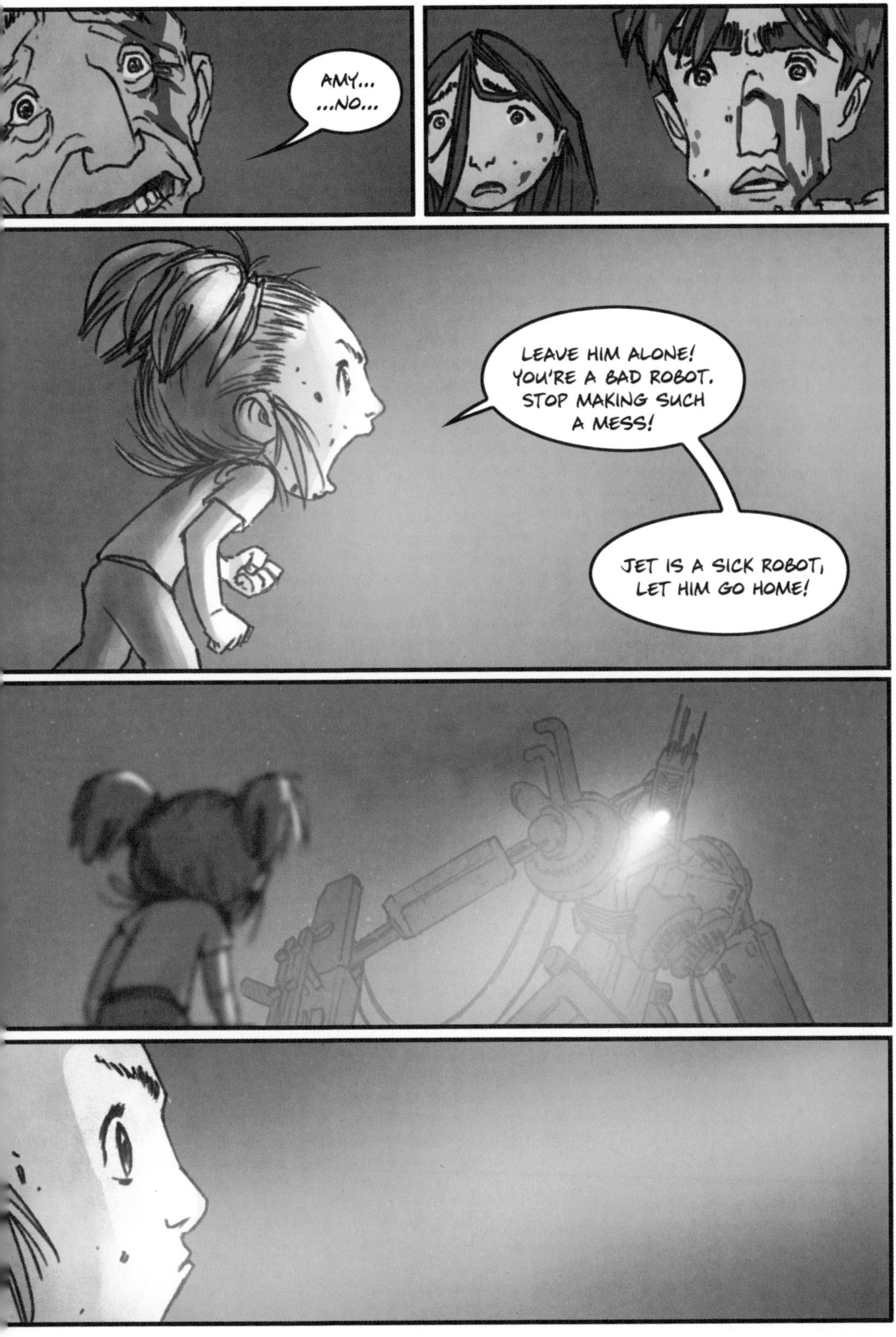
AMY...
...NO...
LEAVE HIM ALONE! YOU'RE A BAD ROBOT. STOP MAKING SUCH A MESS!
JET IS A SICK ROBOT, LET HIM GO HOME!

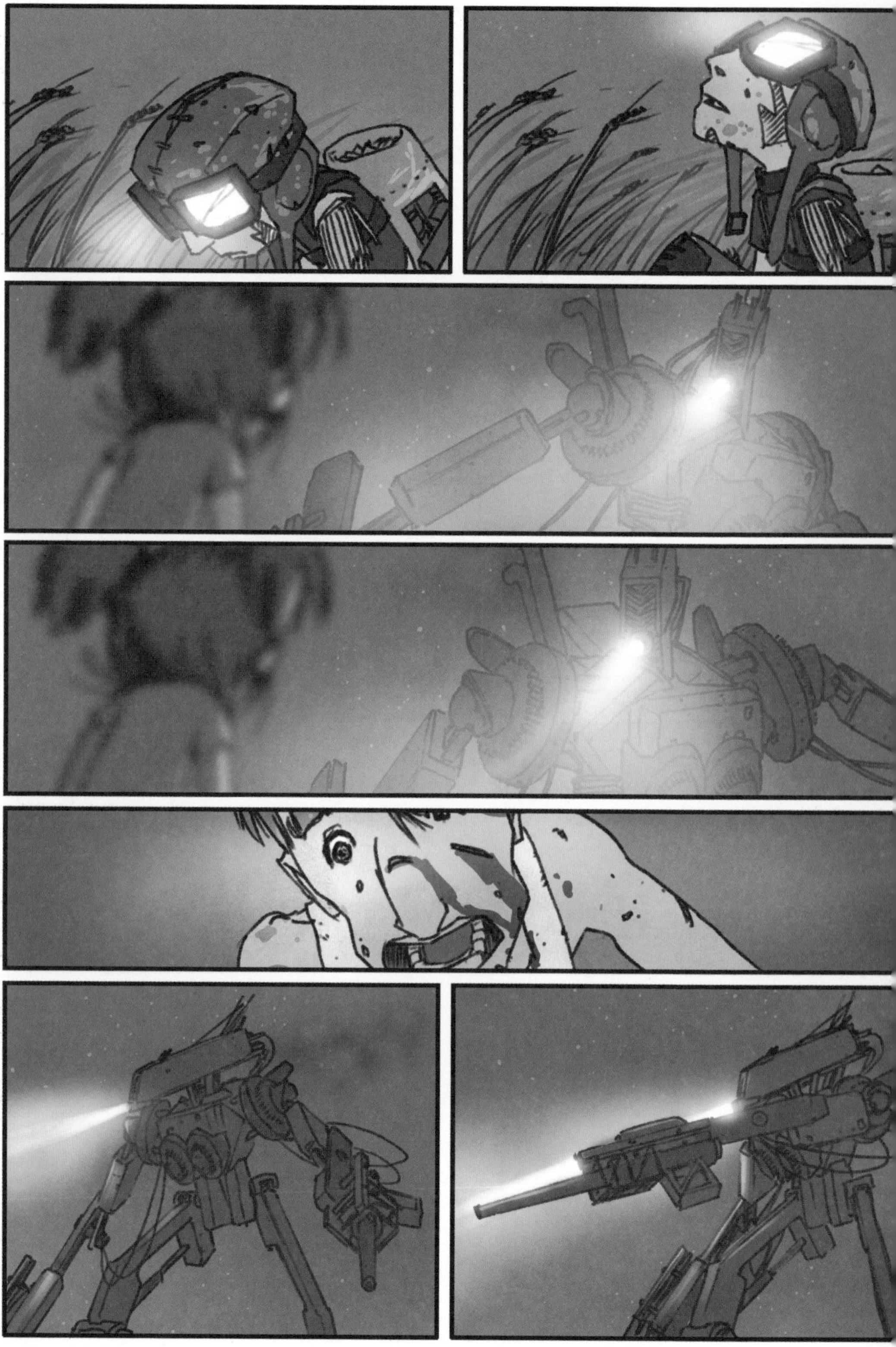

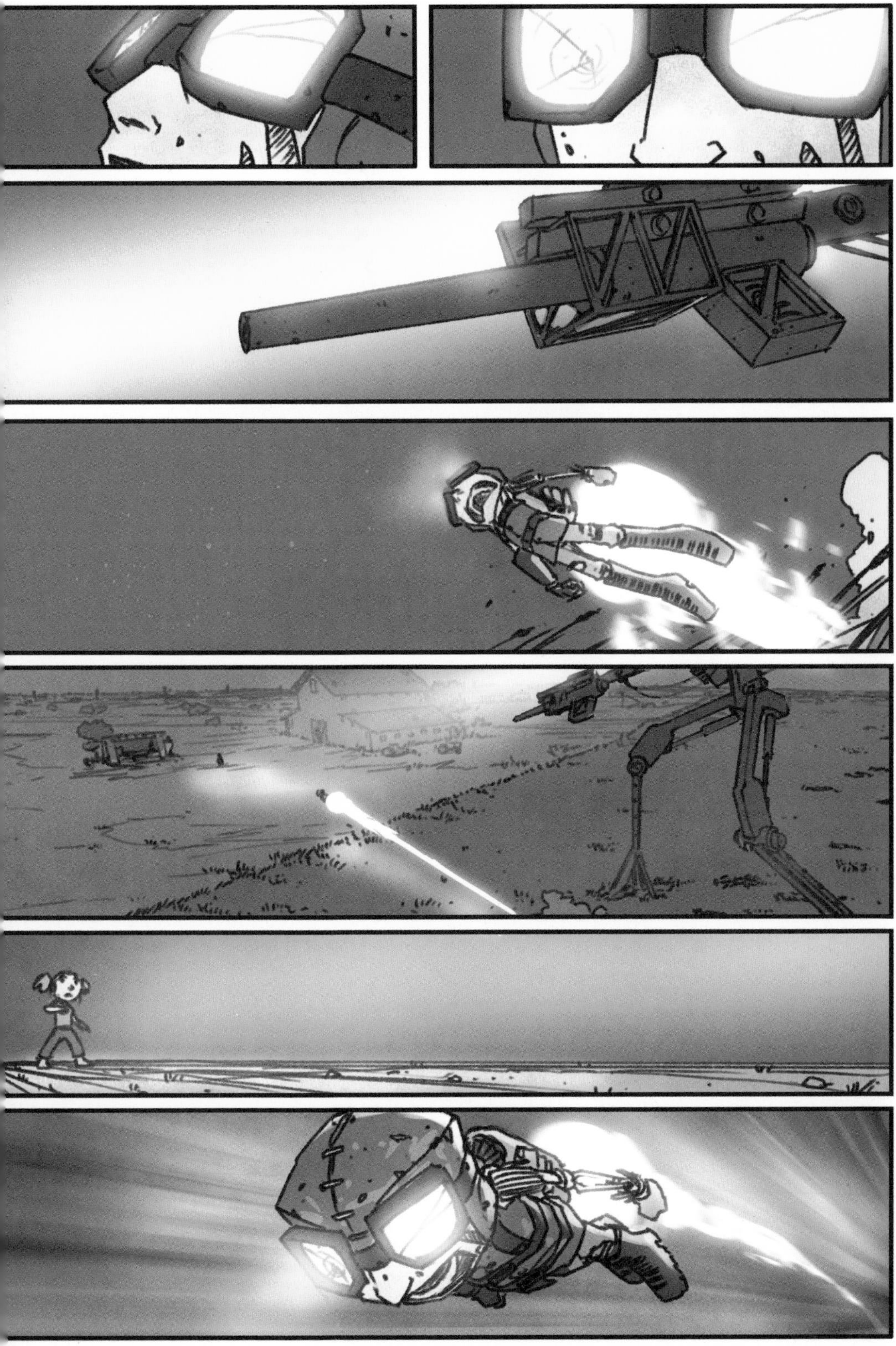

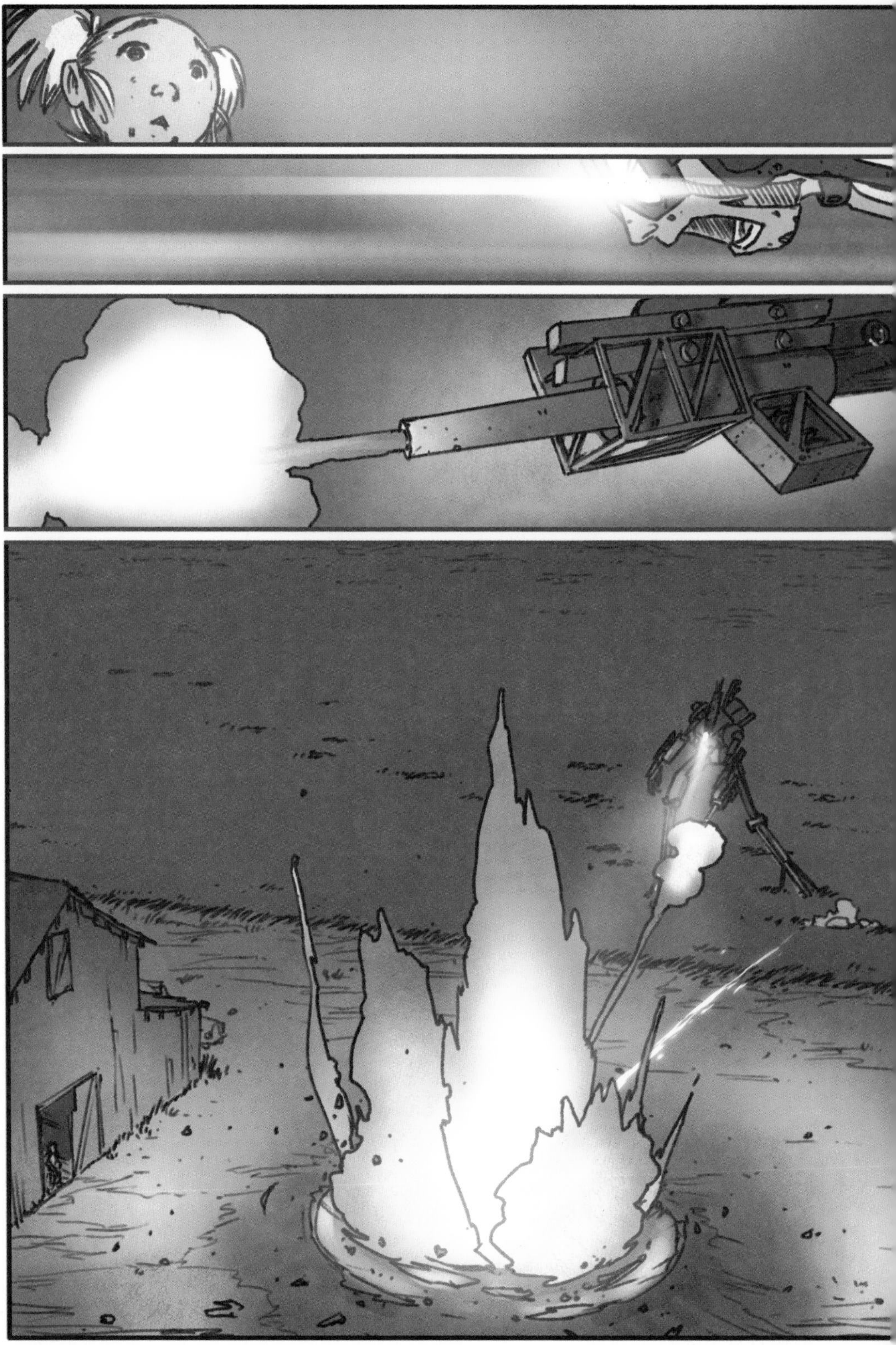

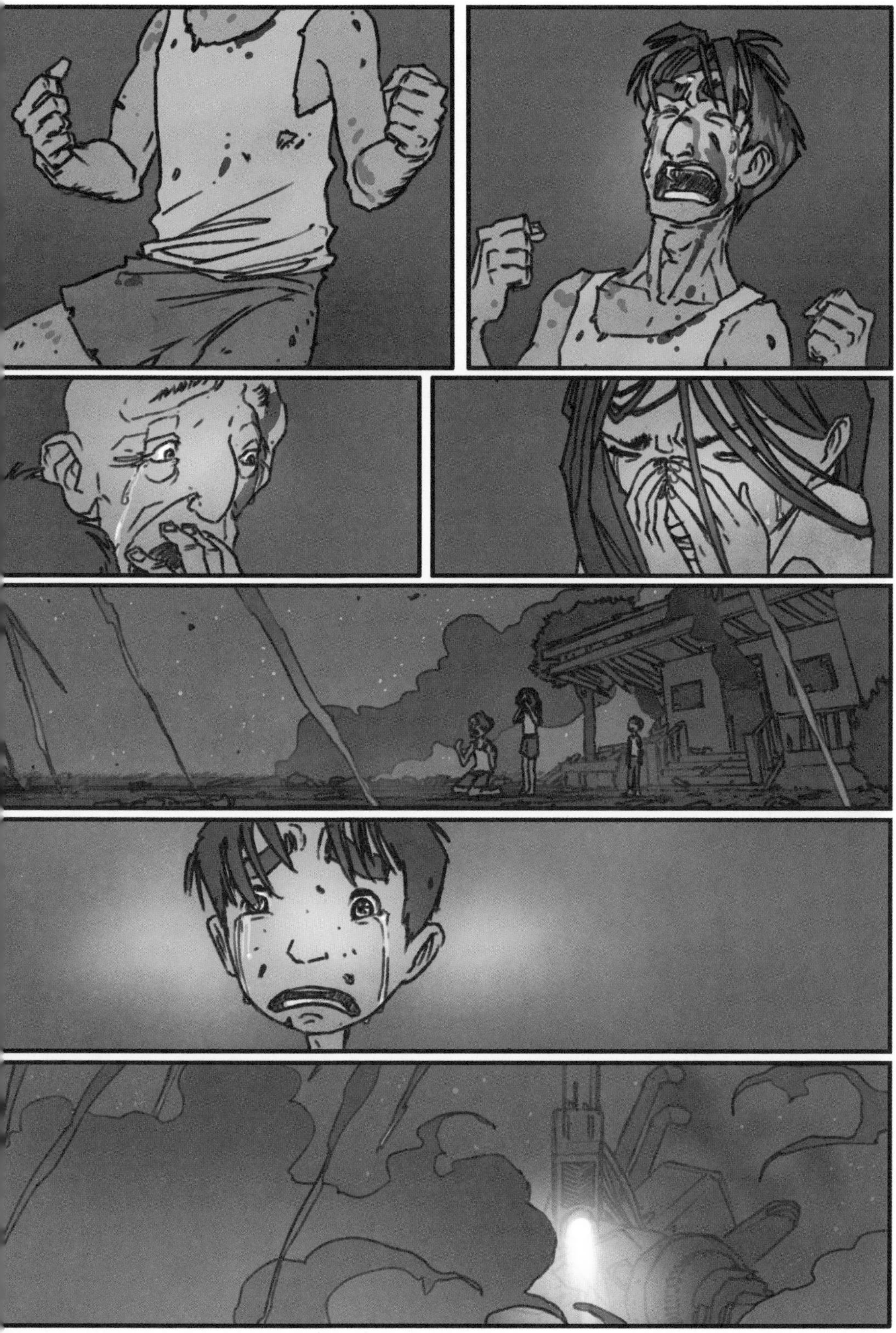

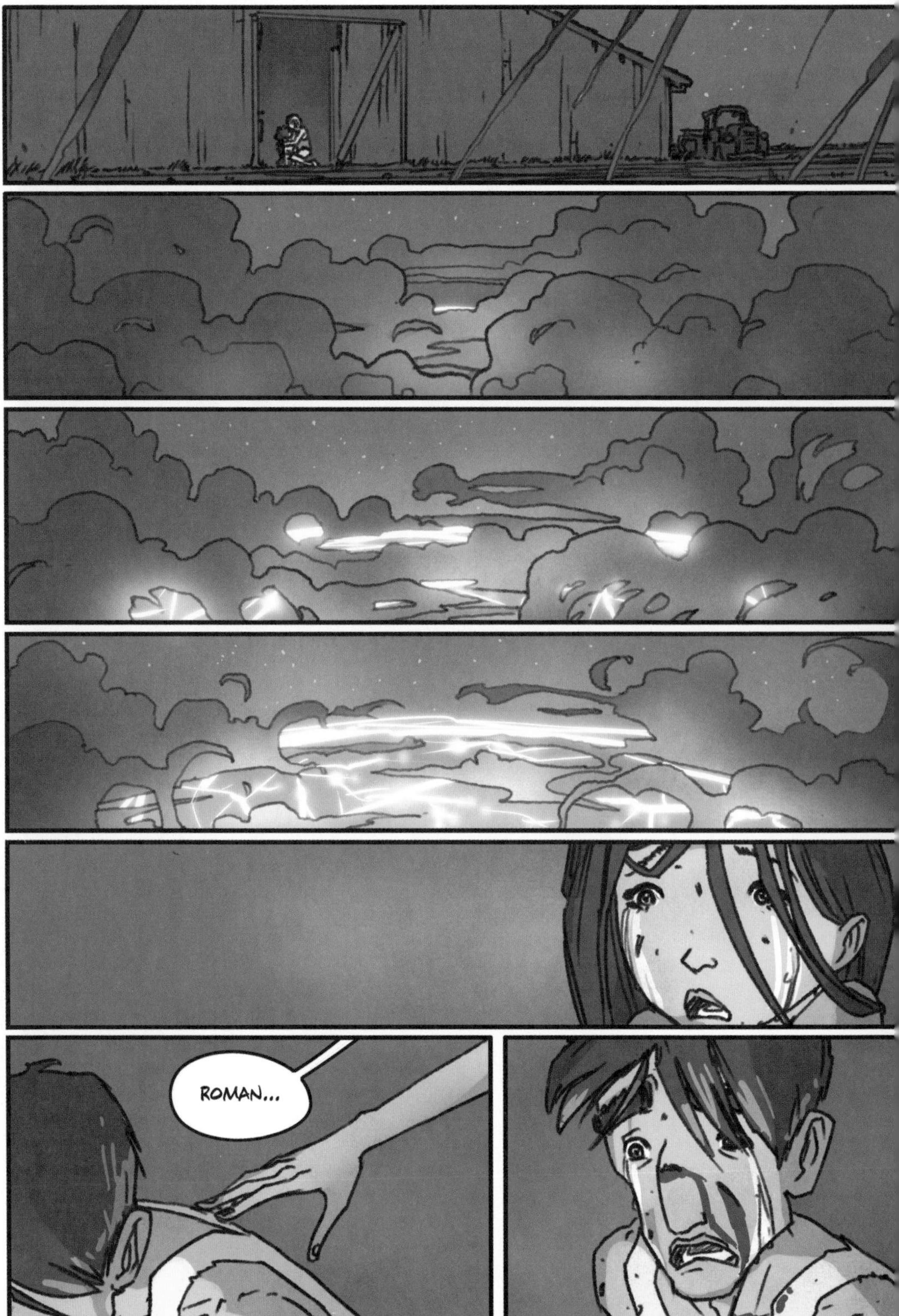
ROMAN...

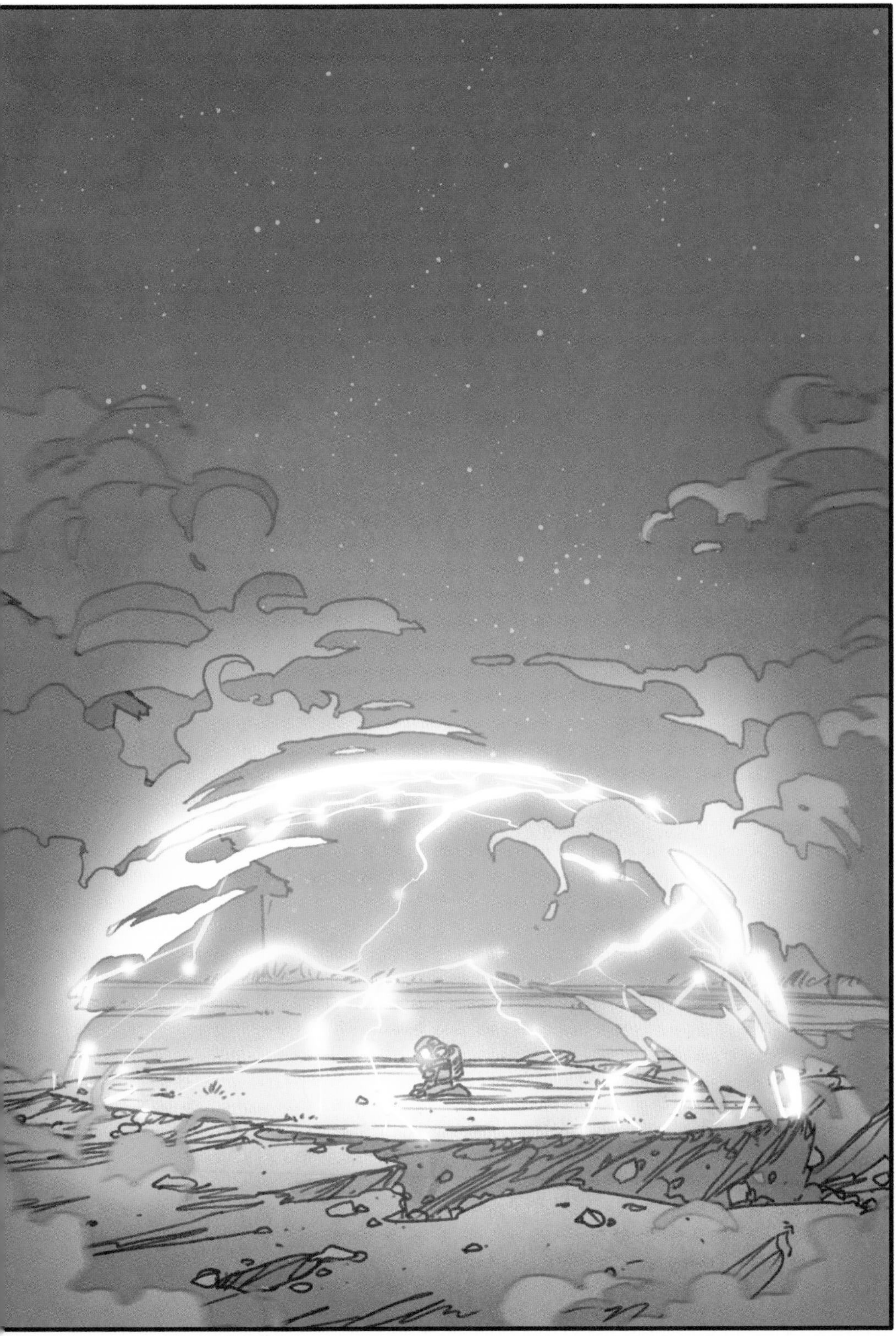

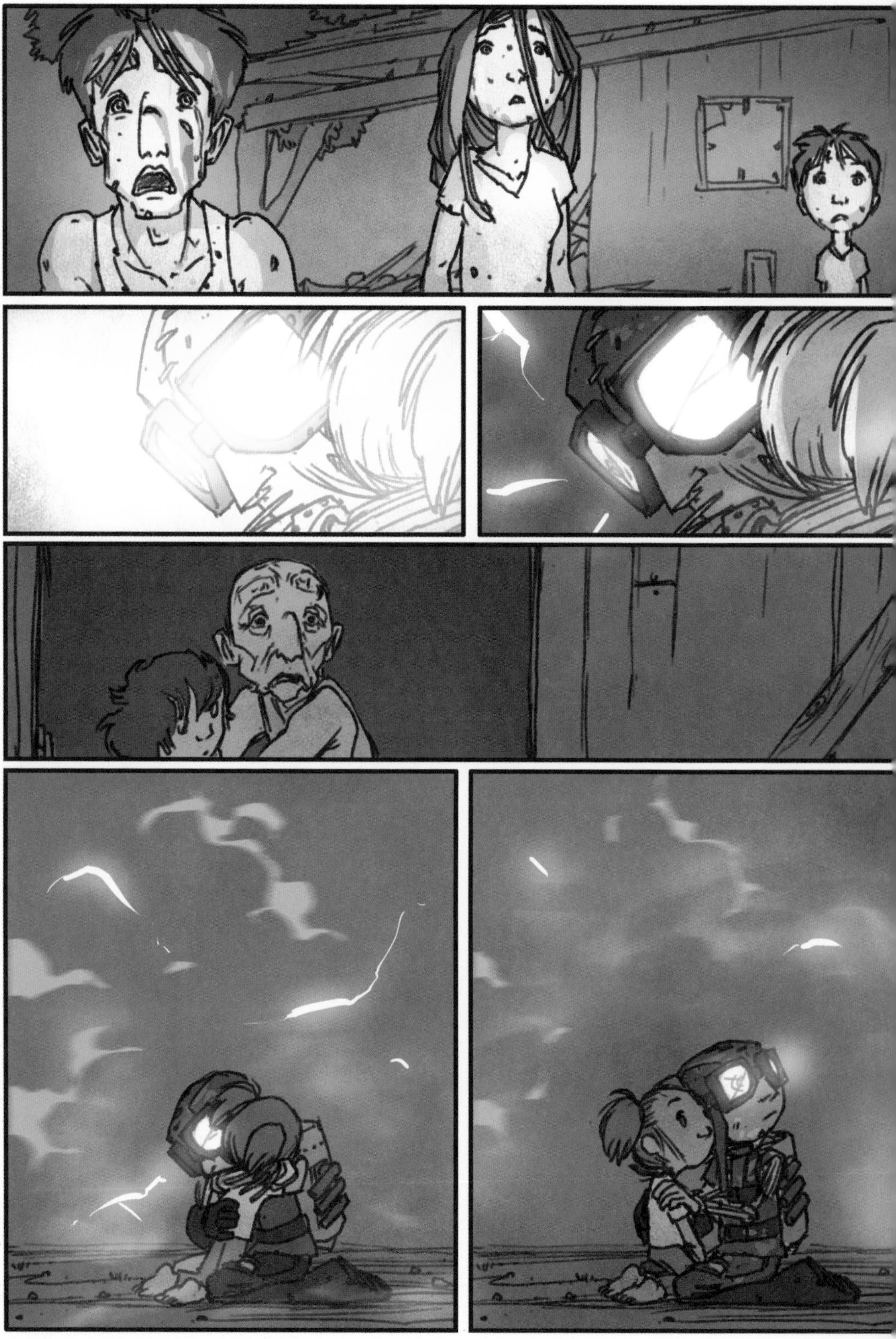

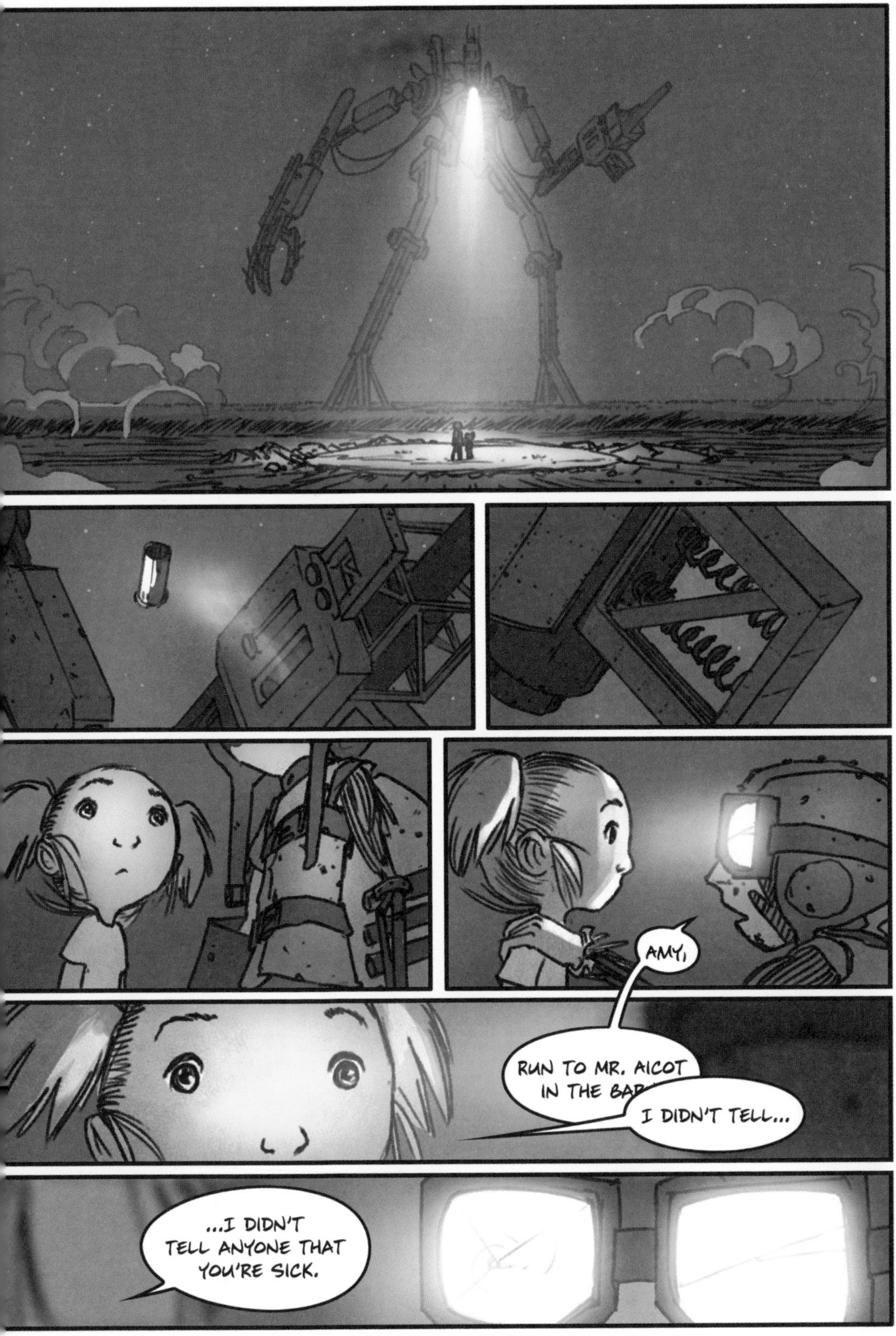
AMY,
RUN TO MR. AICOT IN THE
I DIDN'T TELL...
...I DIDN'T TELL ANYONE THAT YOU'RE SICK.

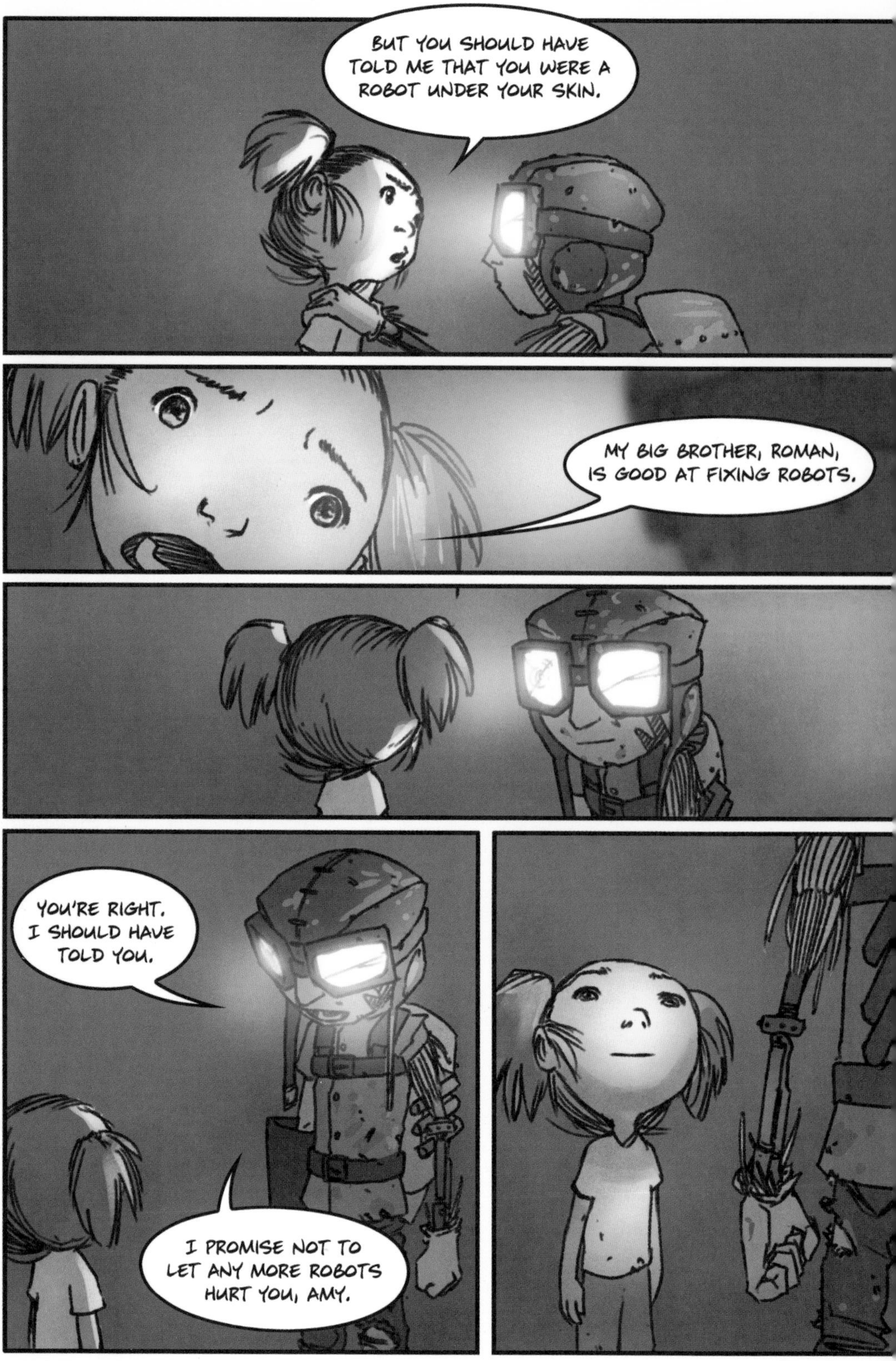
BUT YOU SHOULD HAVE TOLD ME THAT YOU WERE A ROBOT UNDER YOUR SKIN.
MY BIG BROTHER, ROMAN, IS GOOD AT FIXING ROBOTS.
YOU'RE RIGHT. I SHOULD HAVE TOLD YOU.
I PROMISE NOT TO LET ANY MORE ROBOTS HURT YOU, AMY.

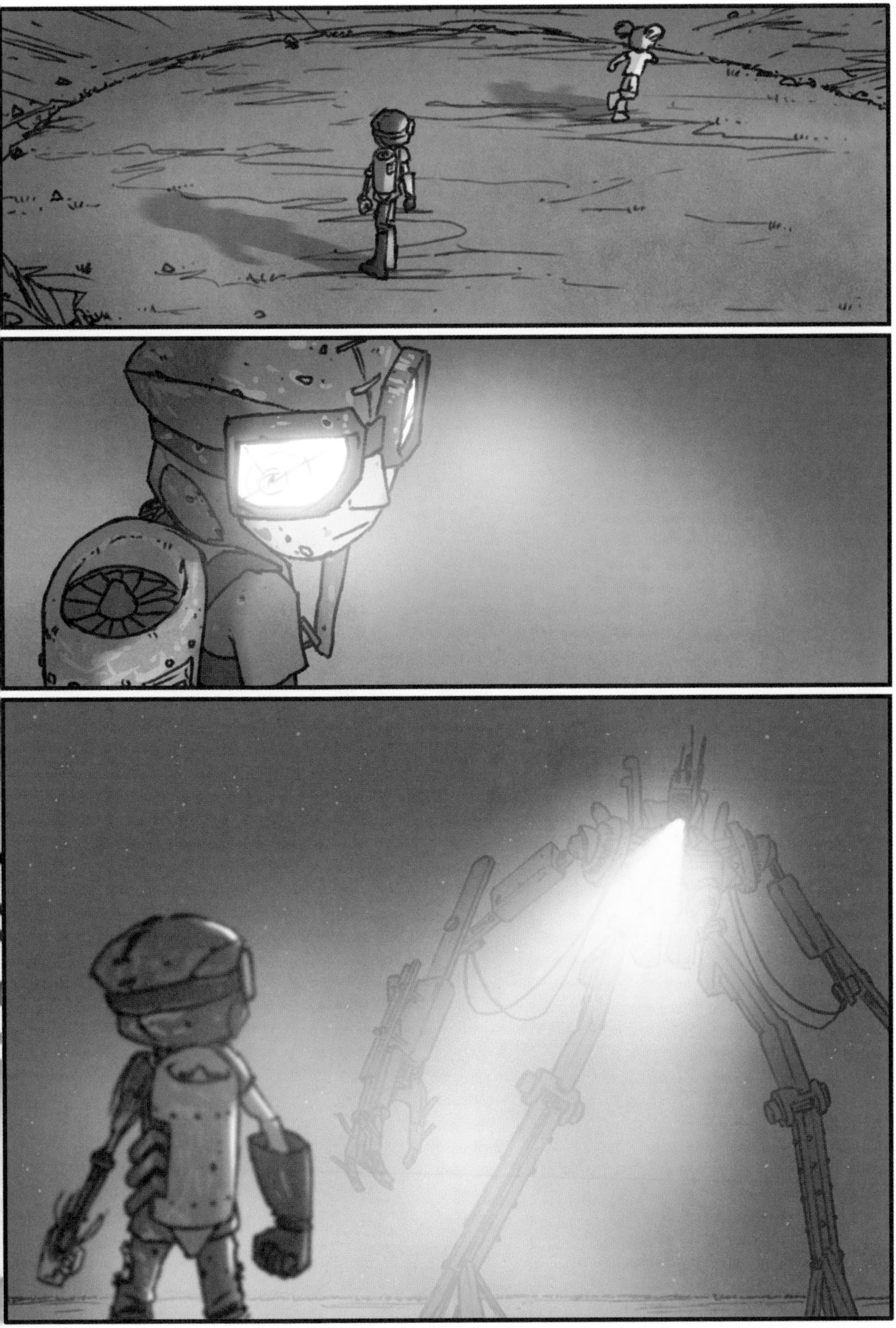

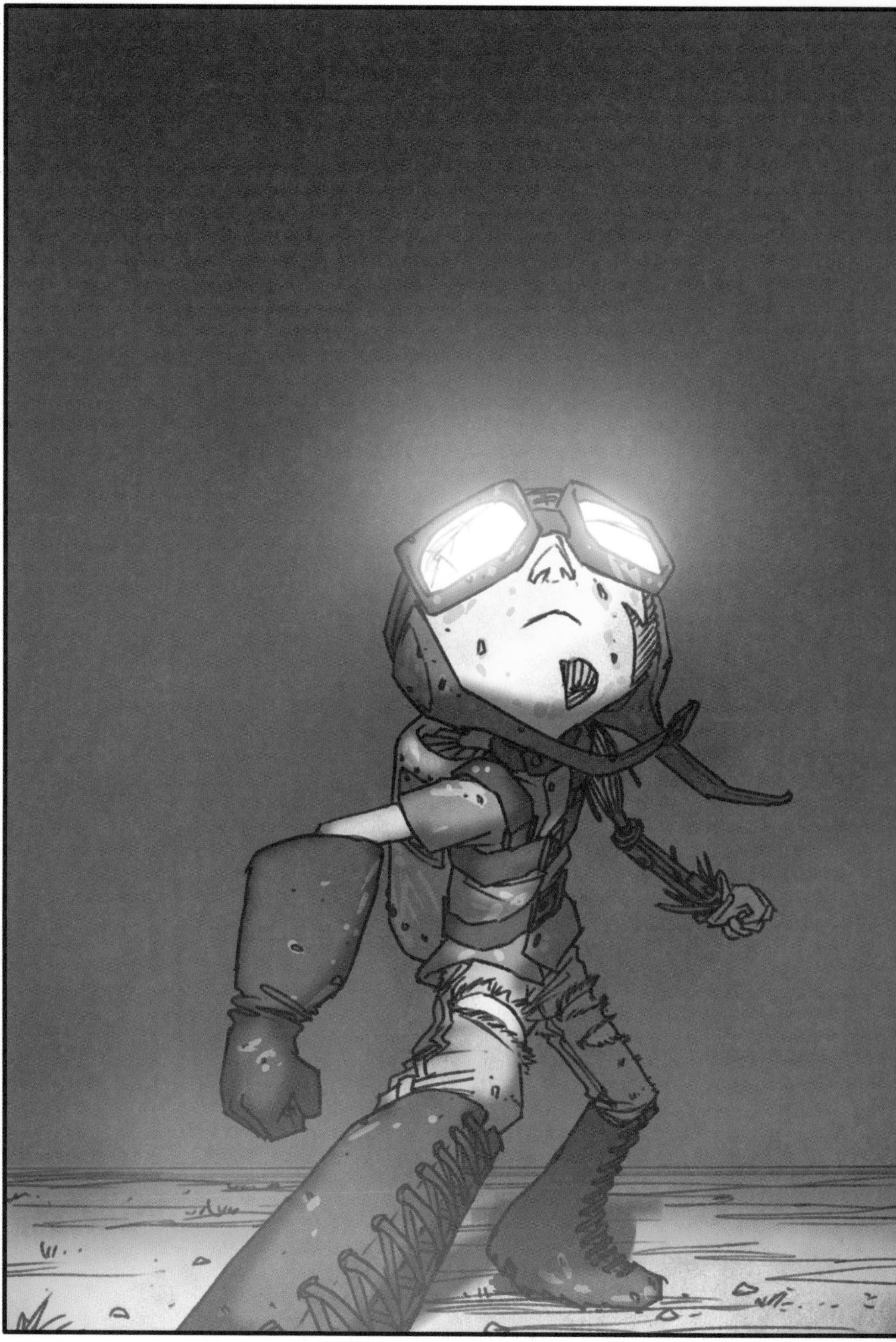

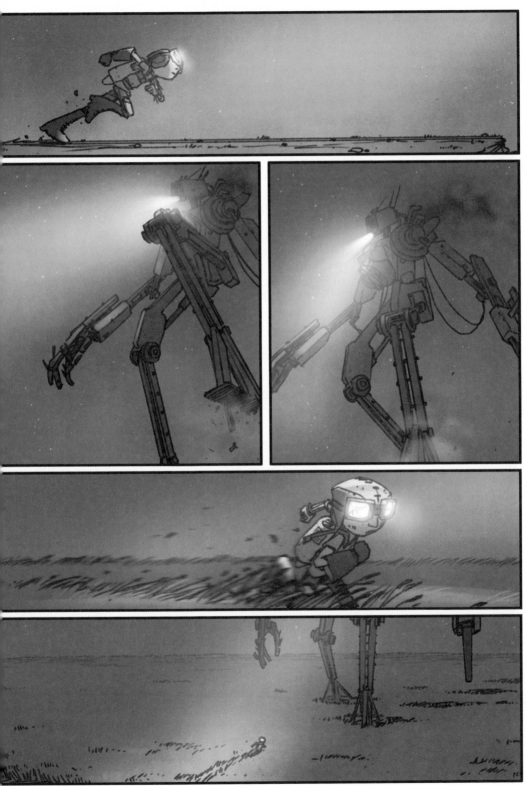

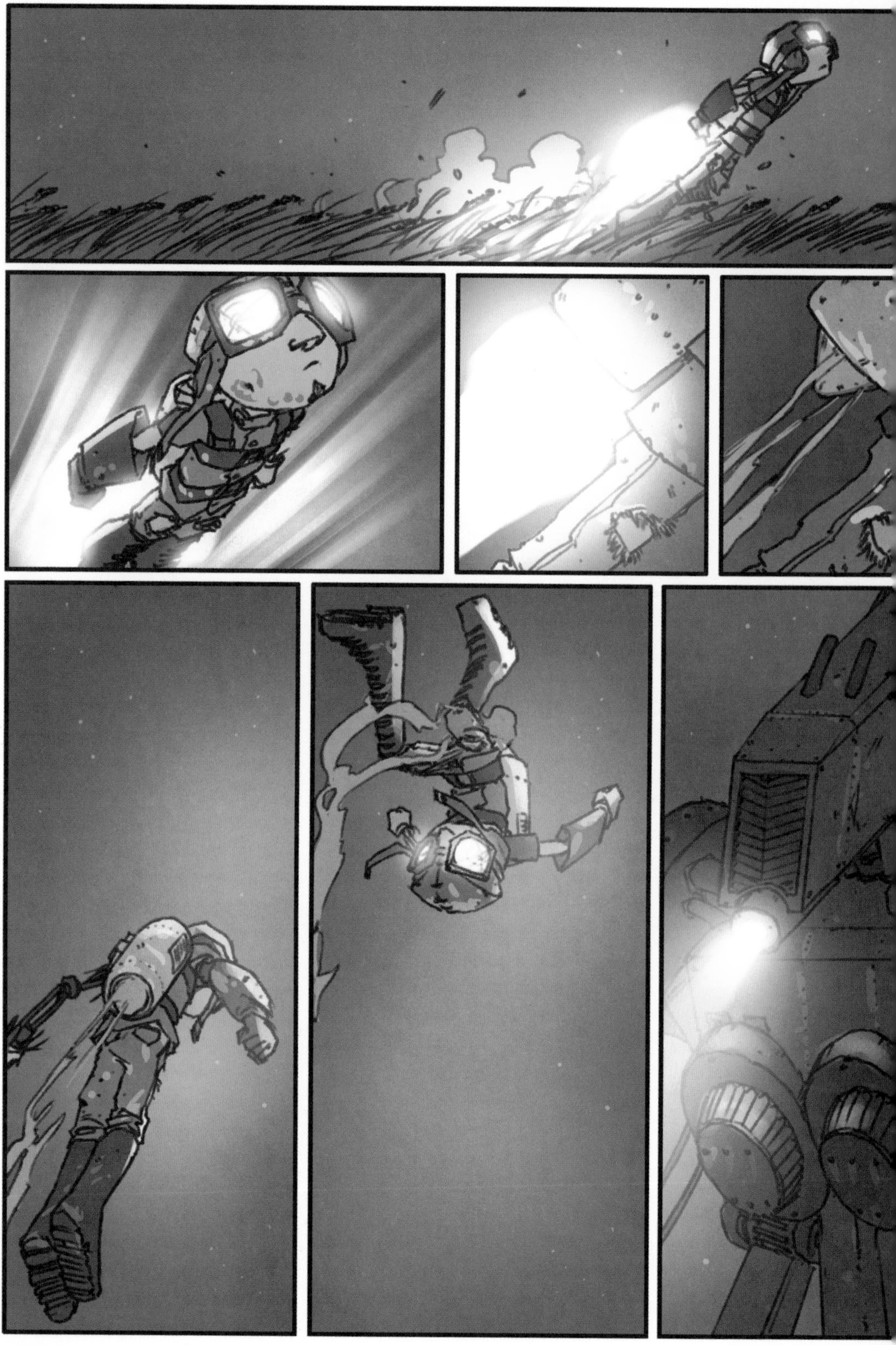

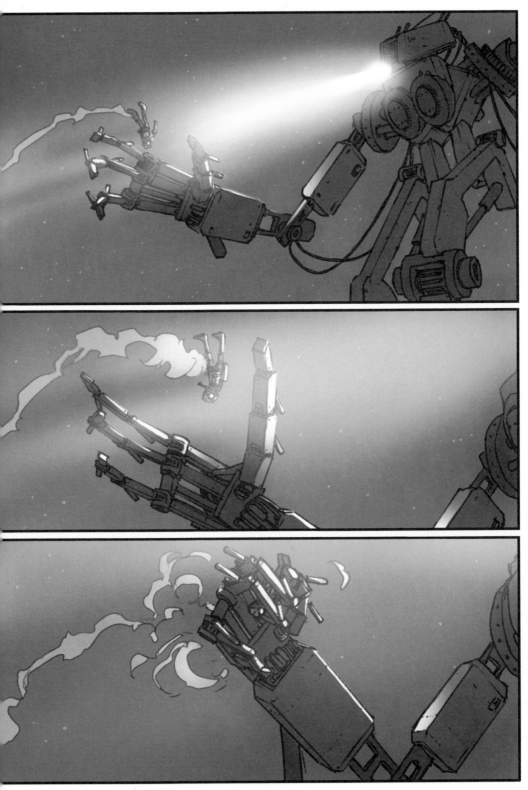

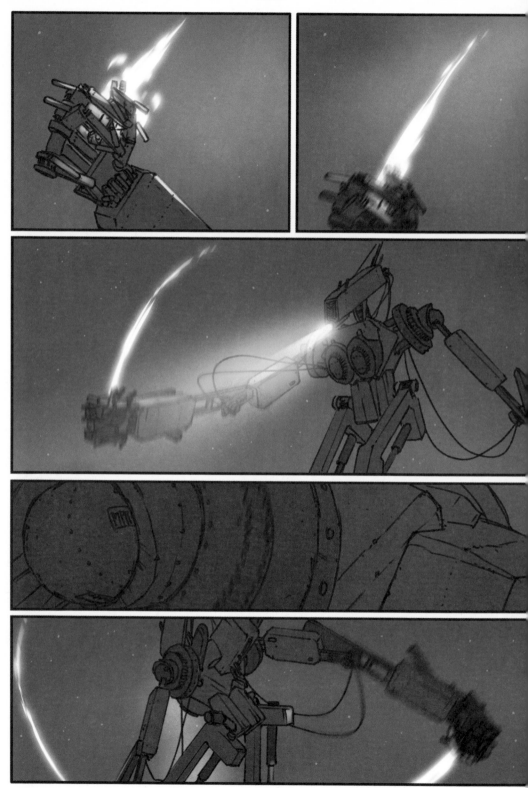

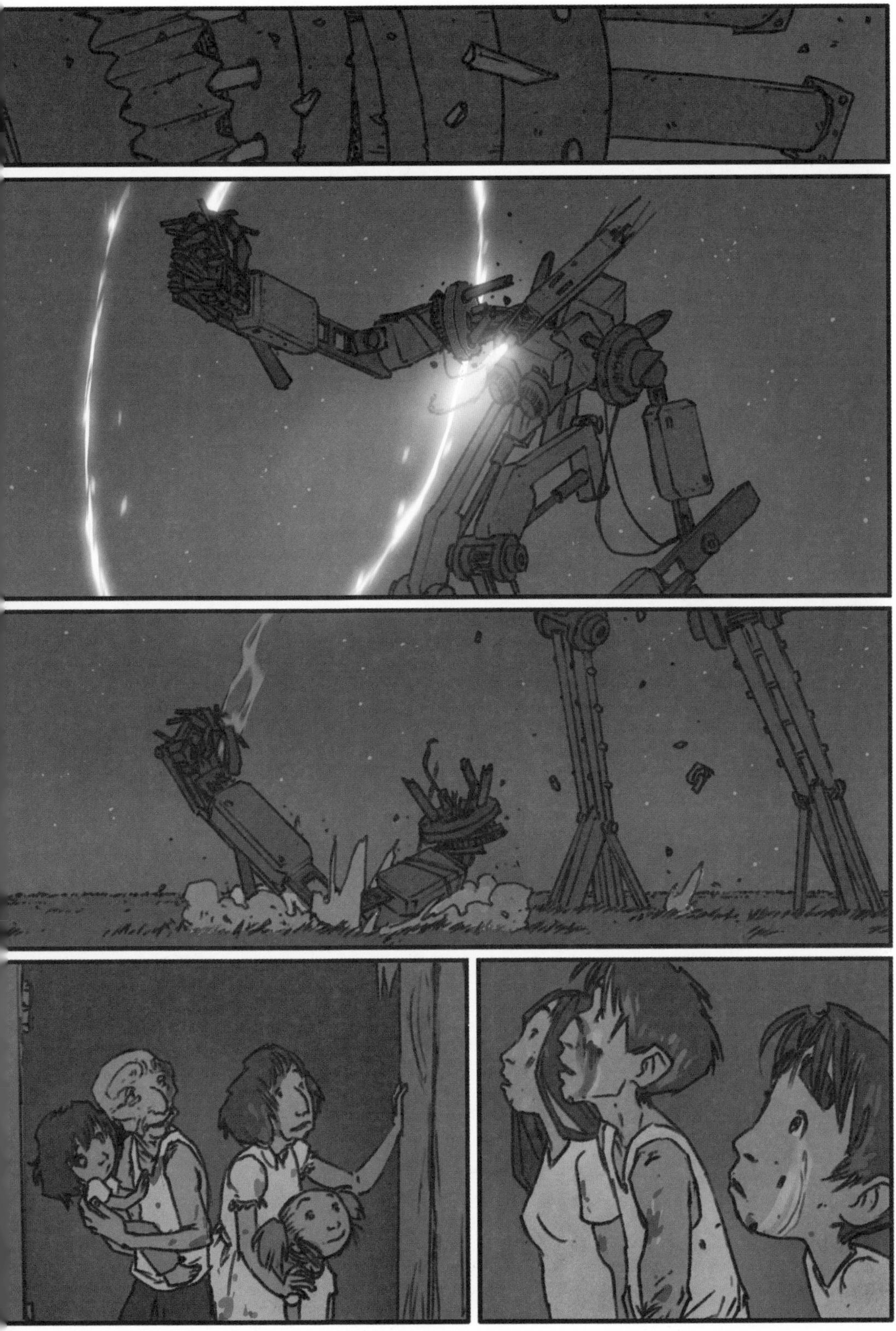

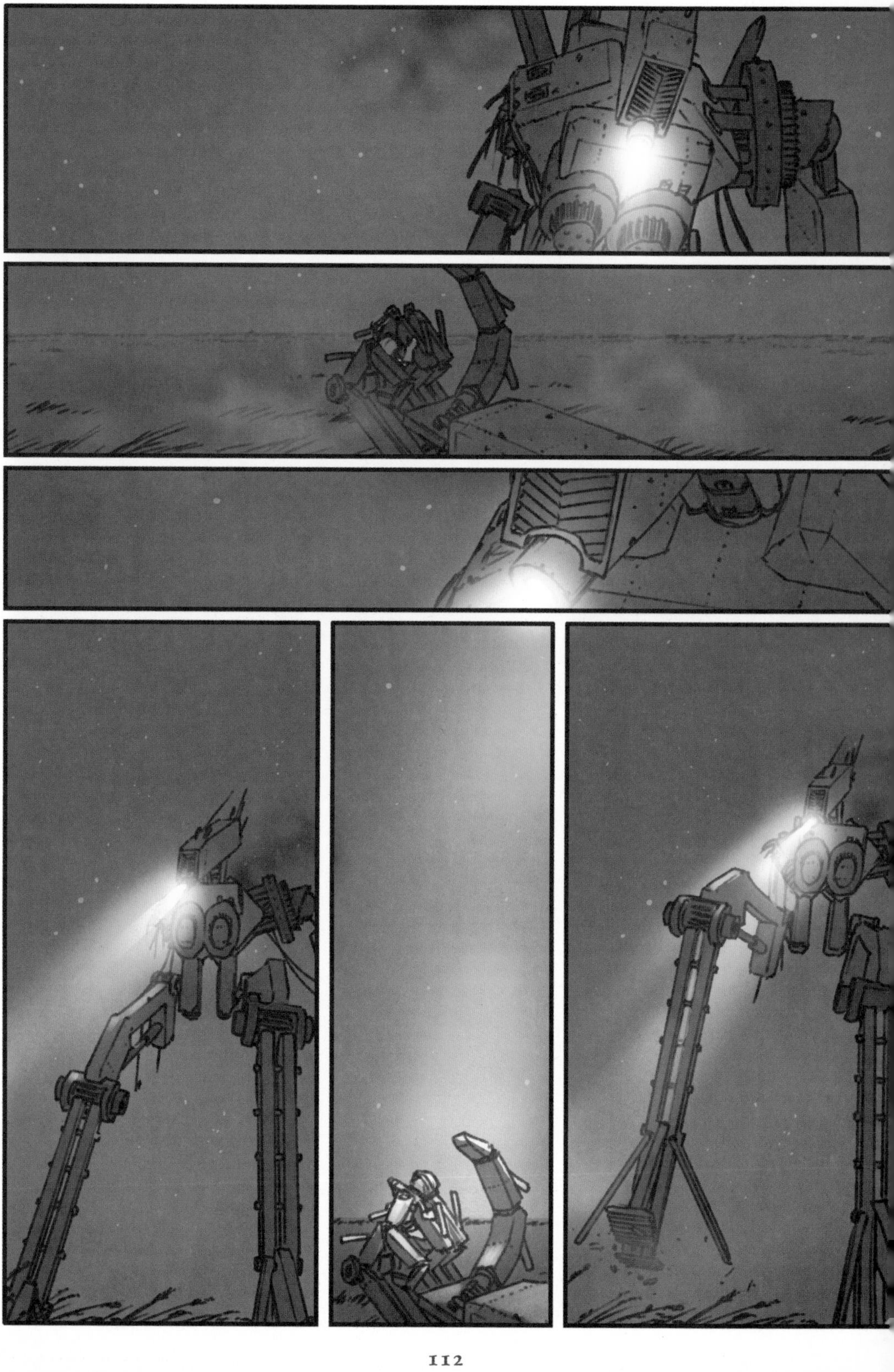

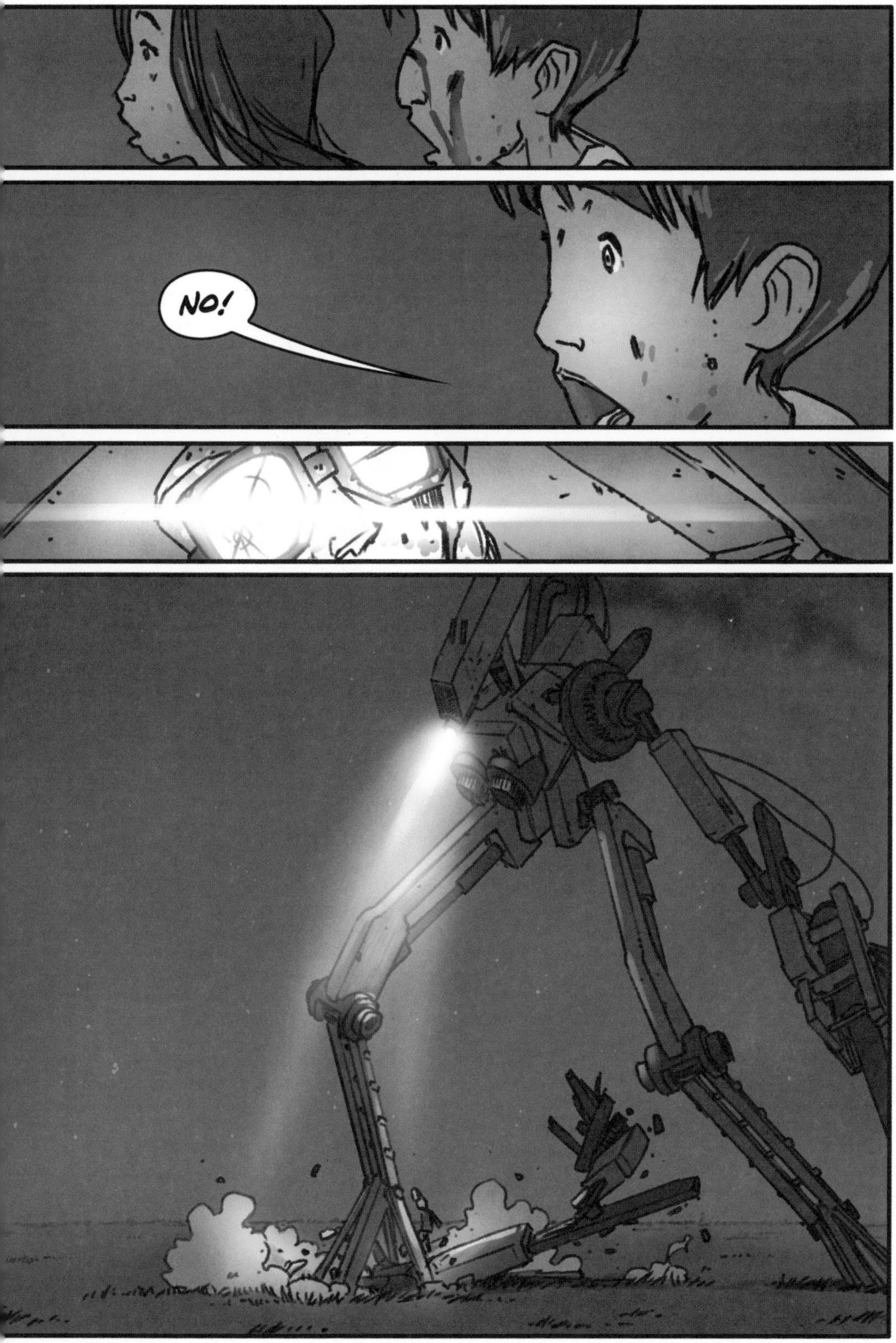
NO!

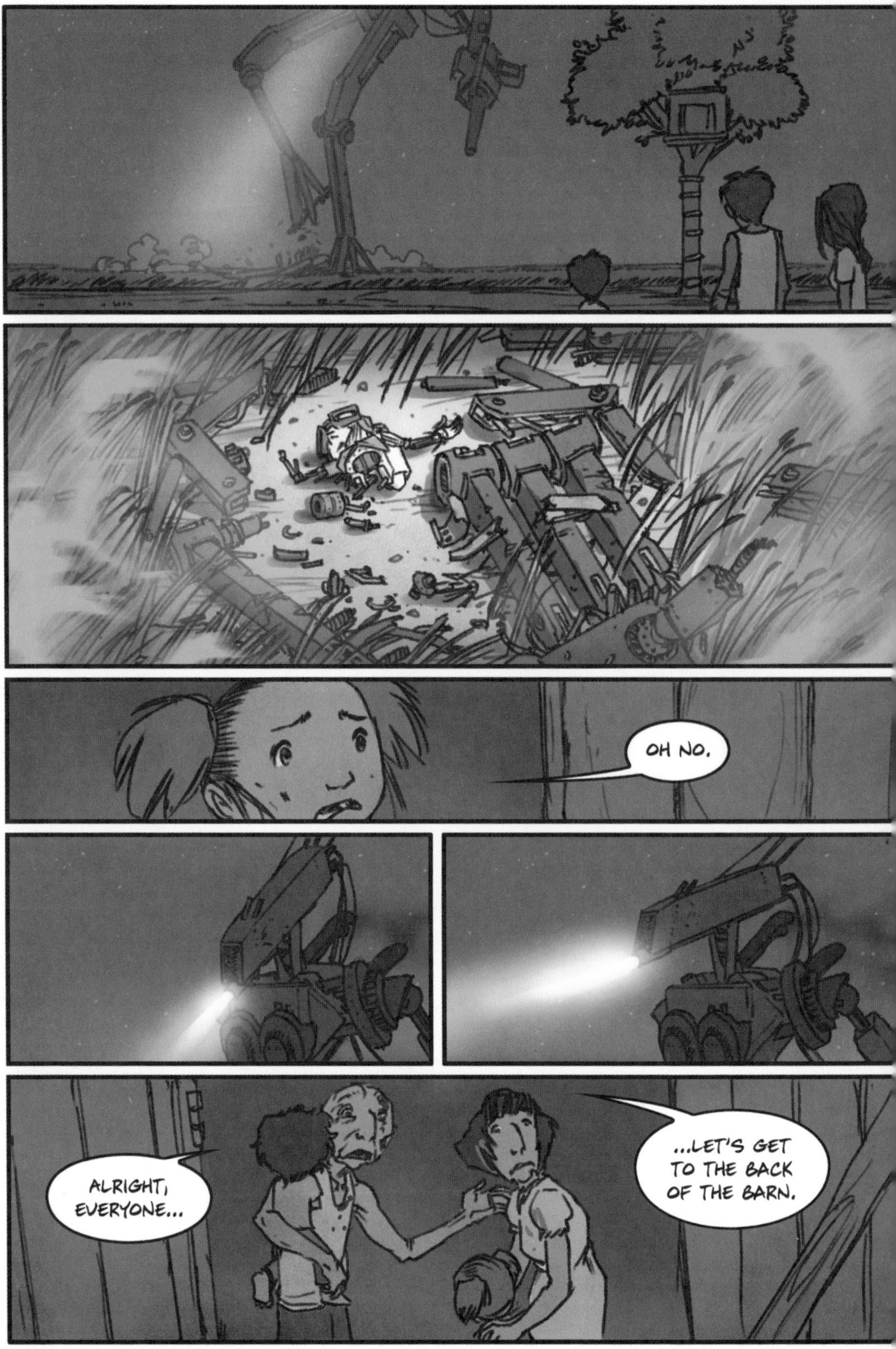
OH NO.
ALRIGHT, EVERYONE...
...LET'S GET TO THE BACK OF THE BARN.

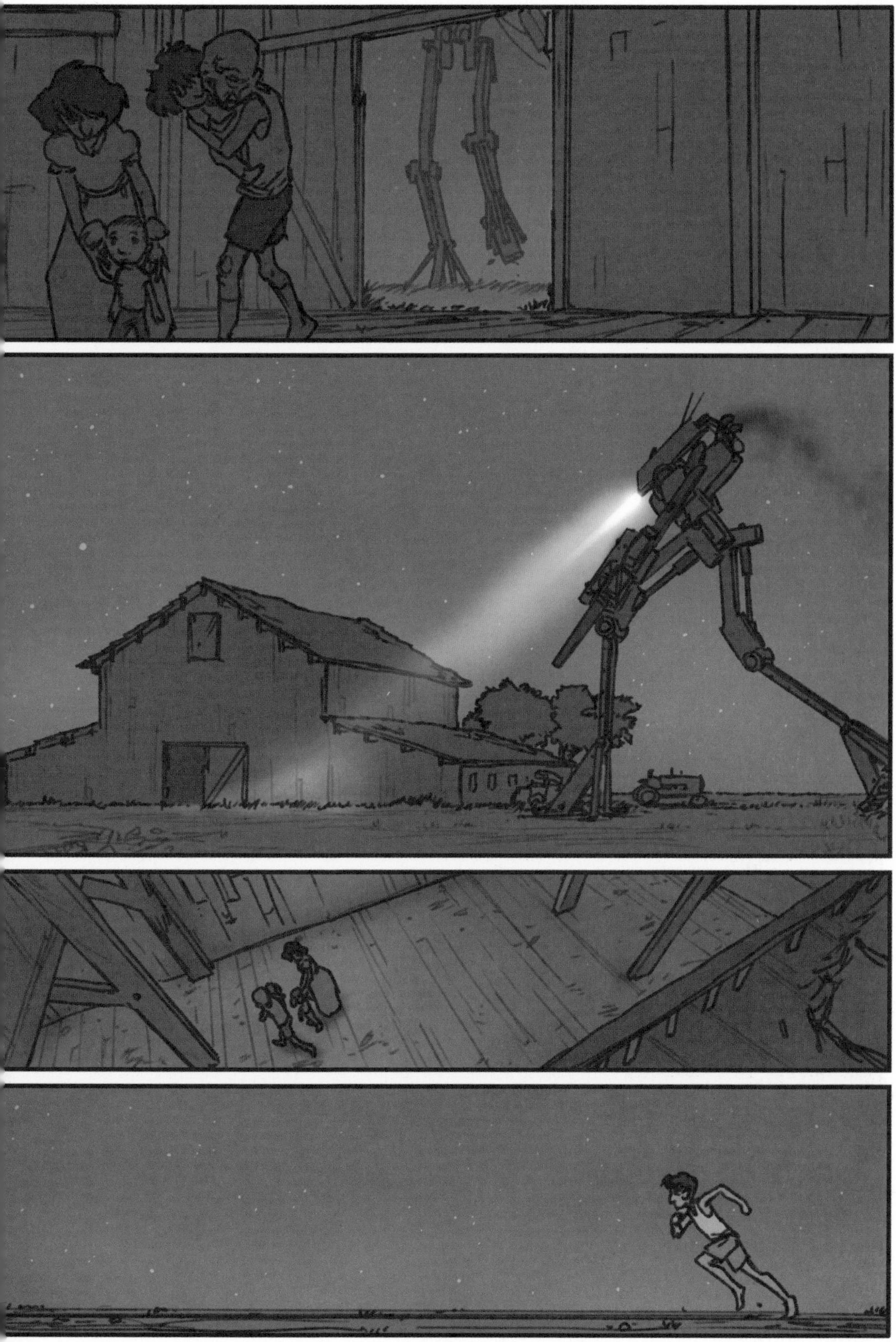

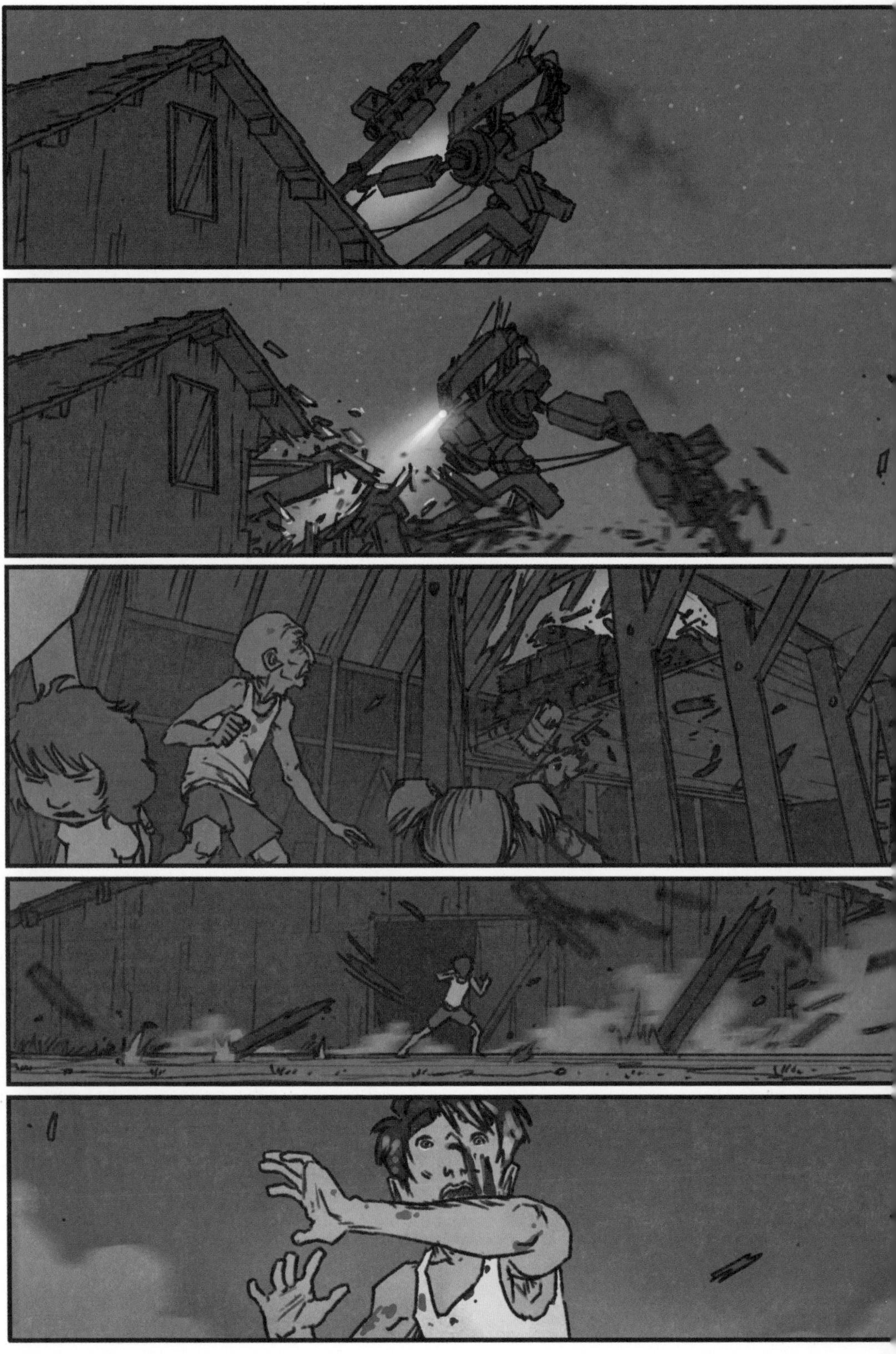

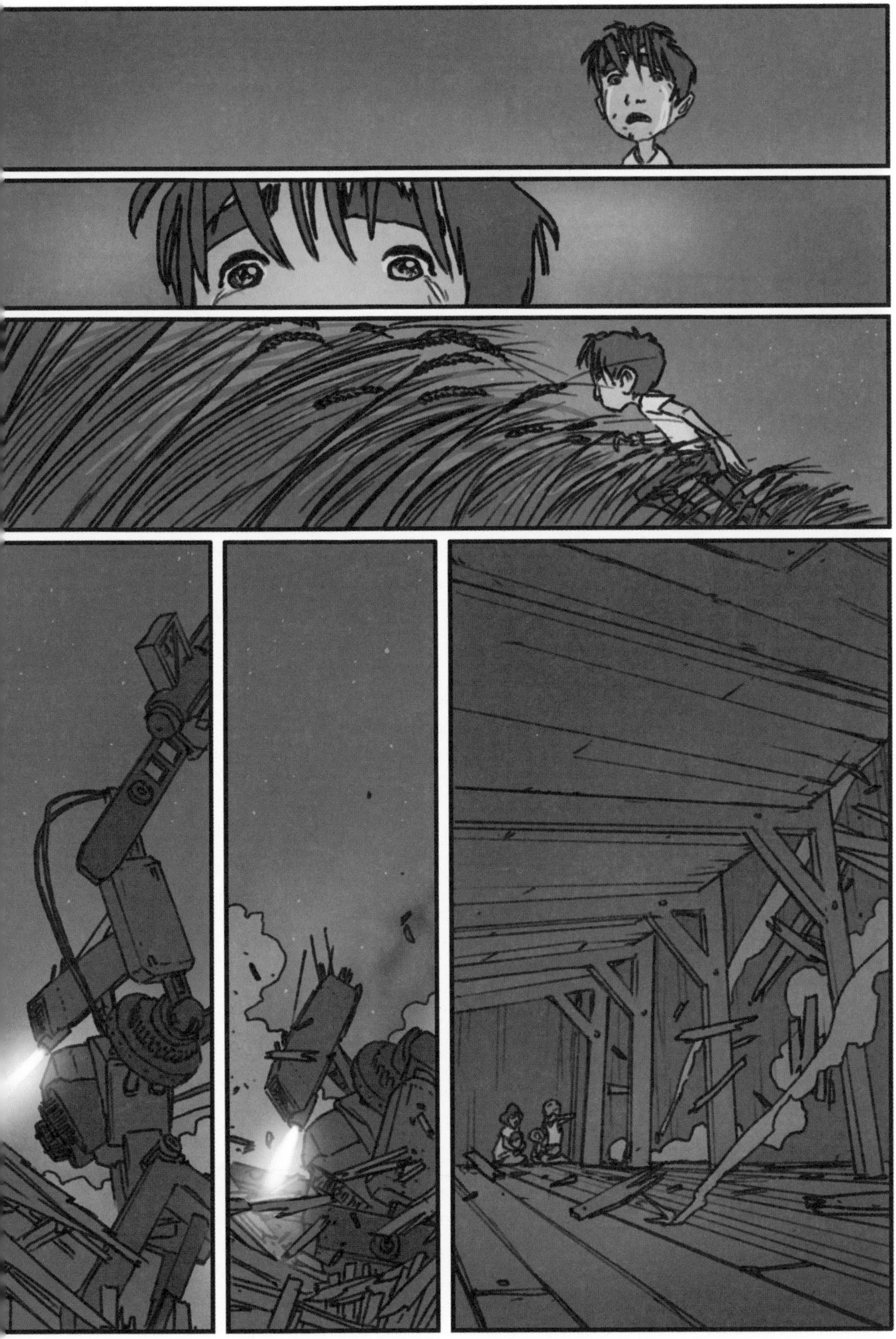

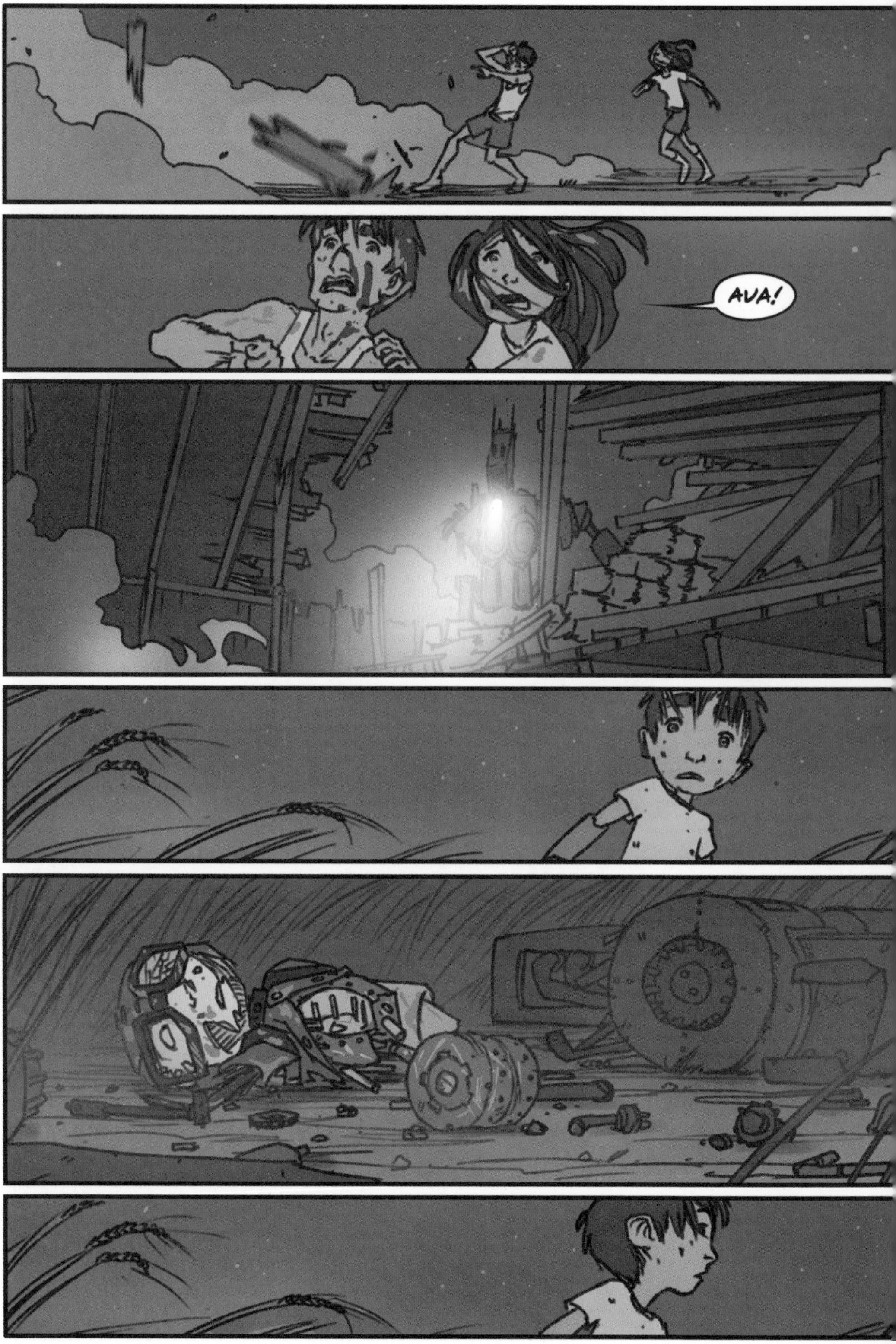
AVA!

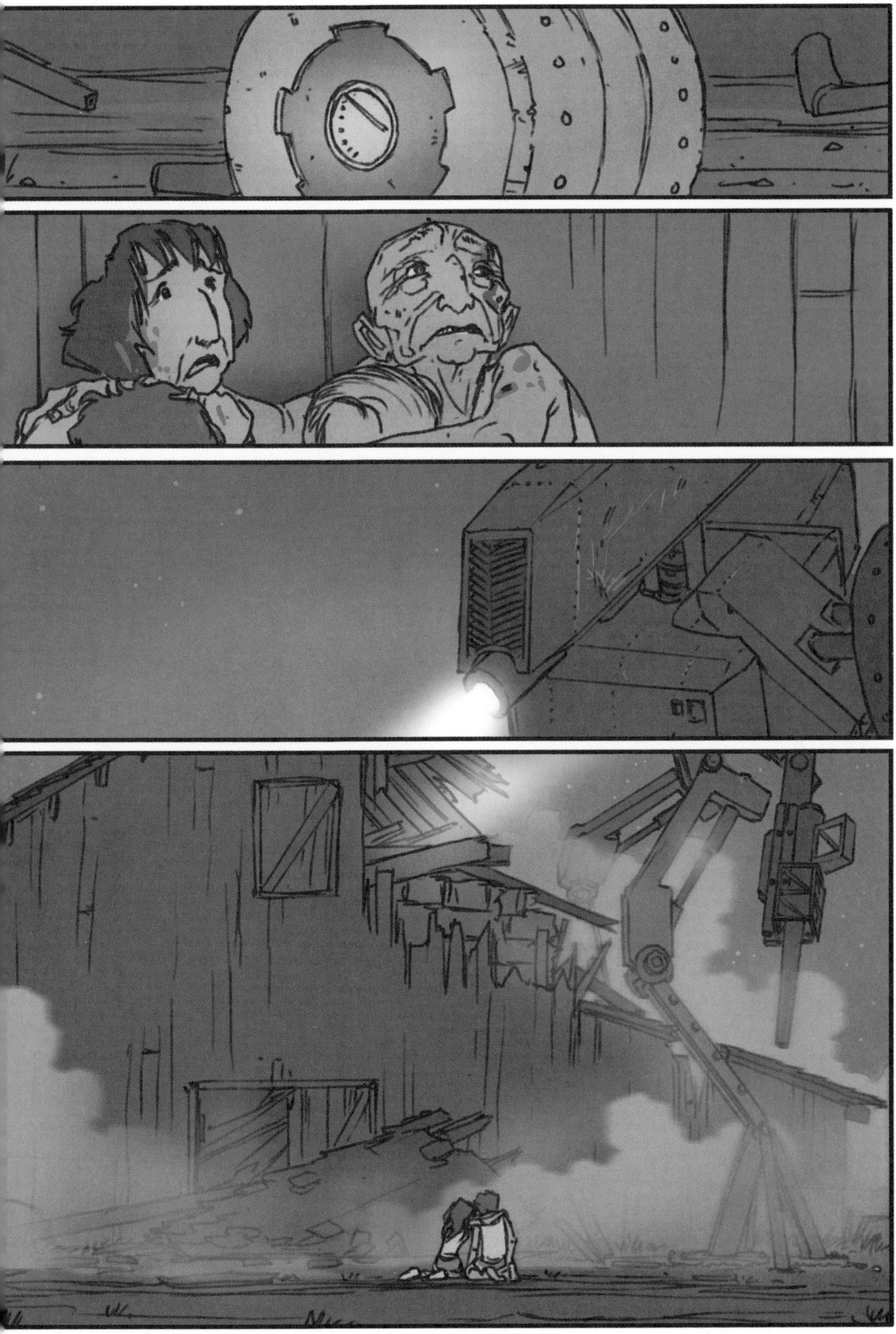

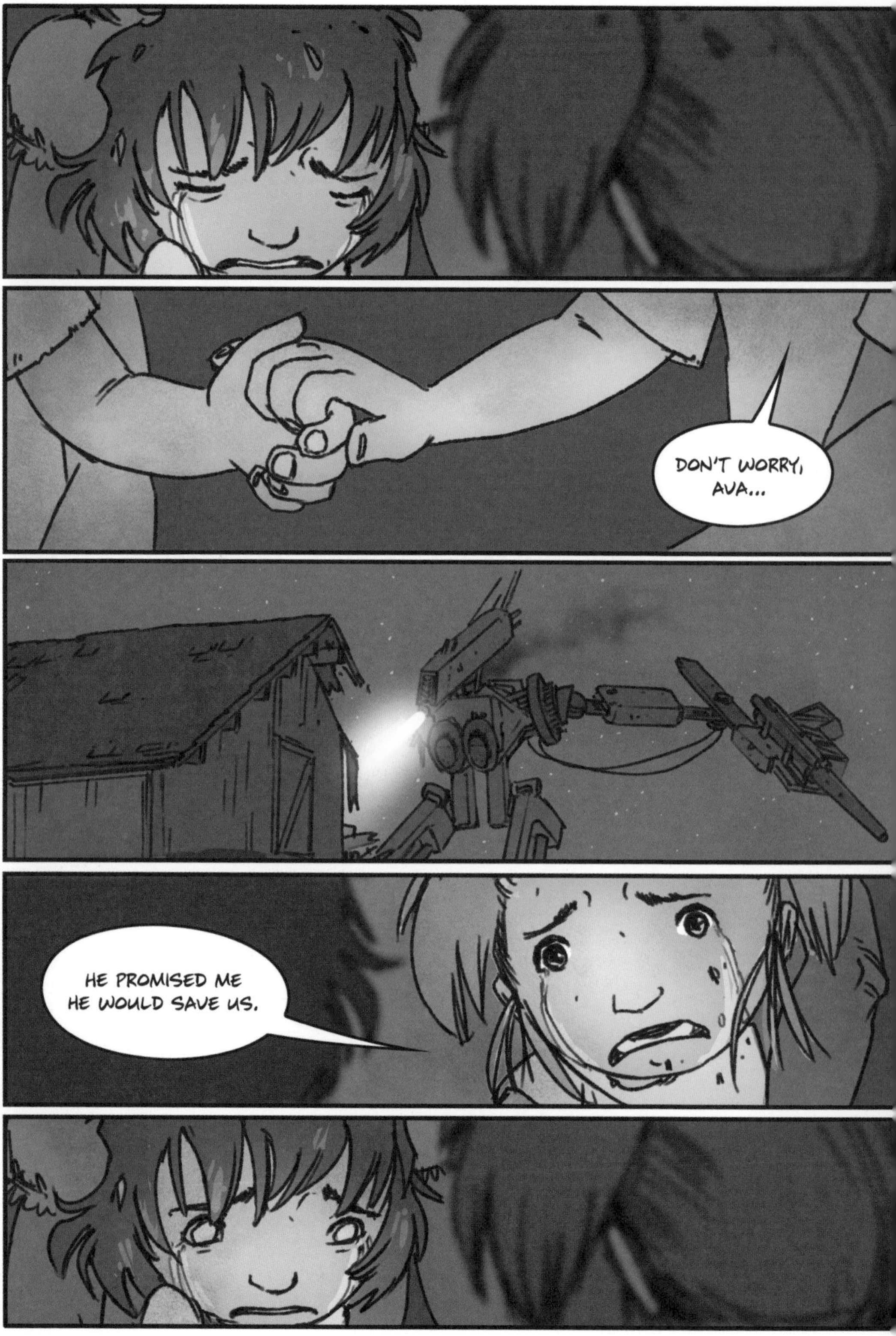
DON'T WORRY, AVA...
HE PROMISED ME HE WOULD SAVE US.

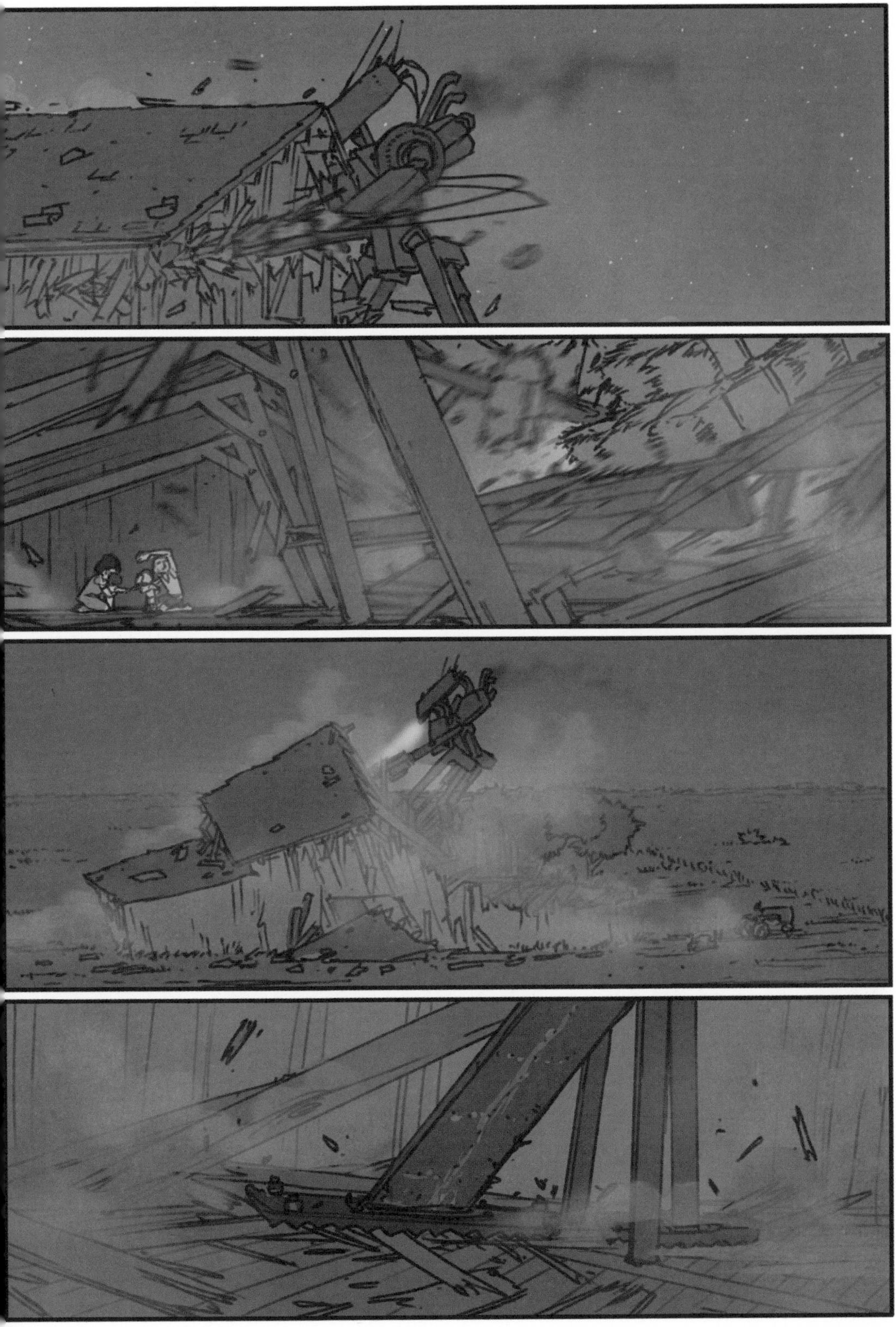

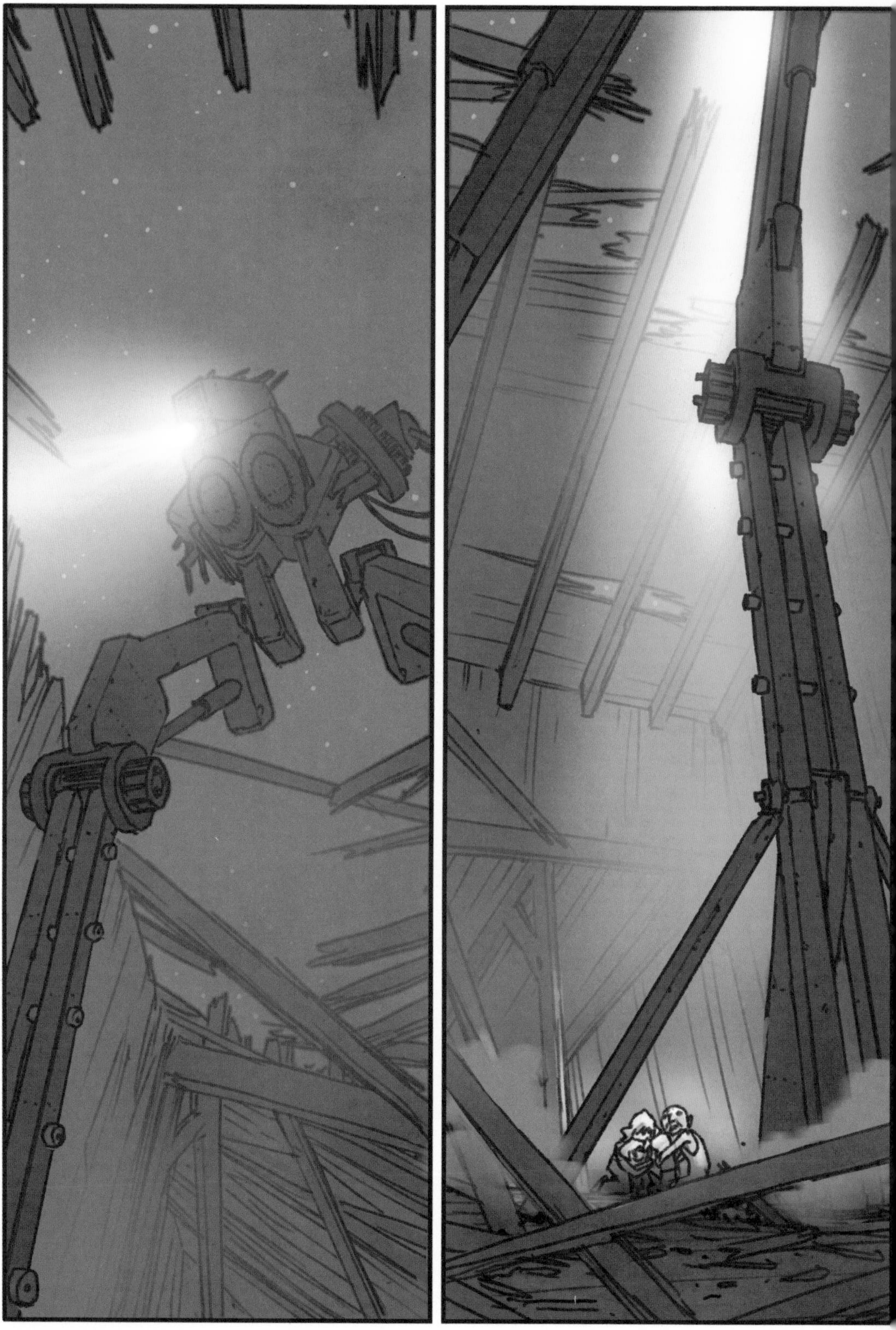

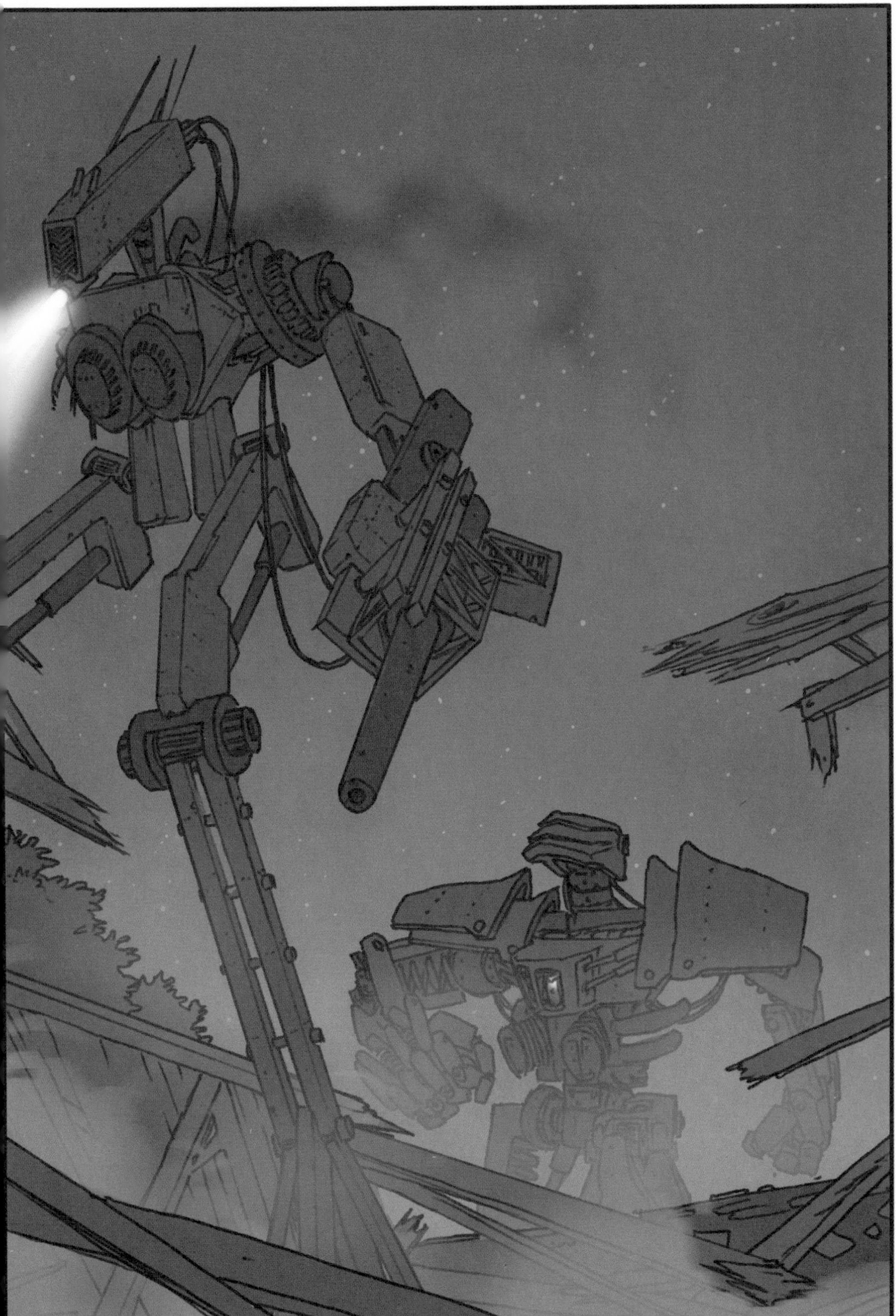

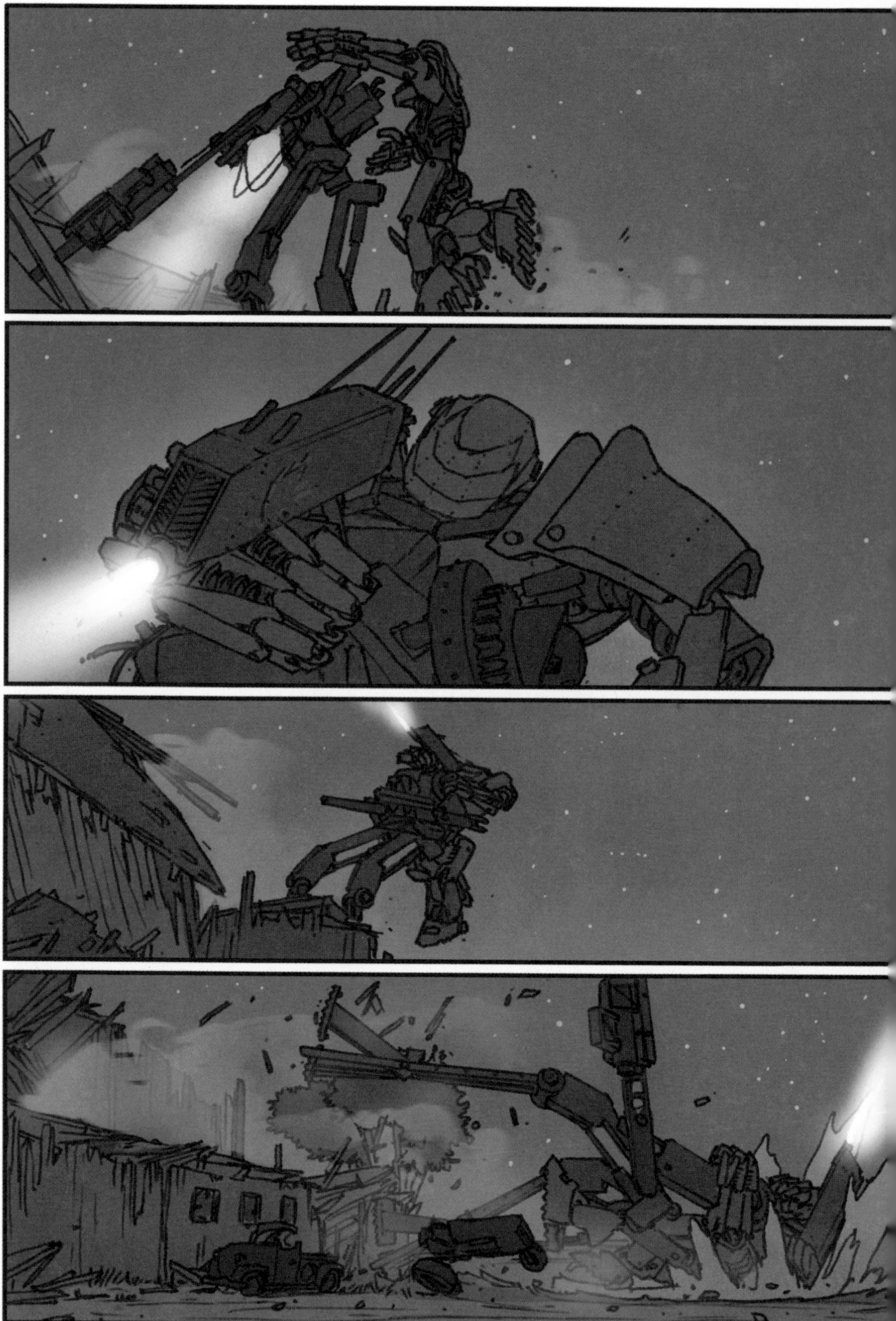

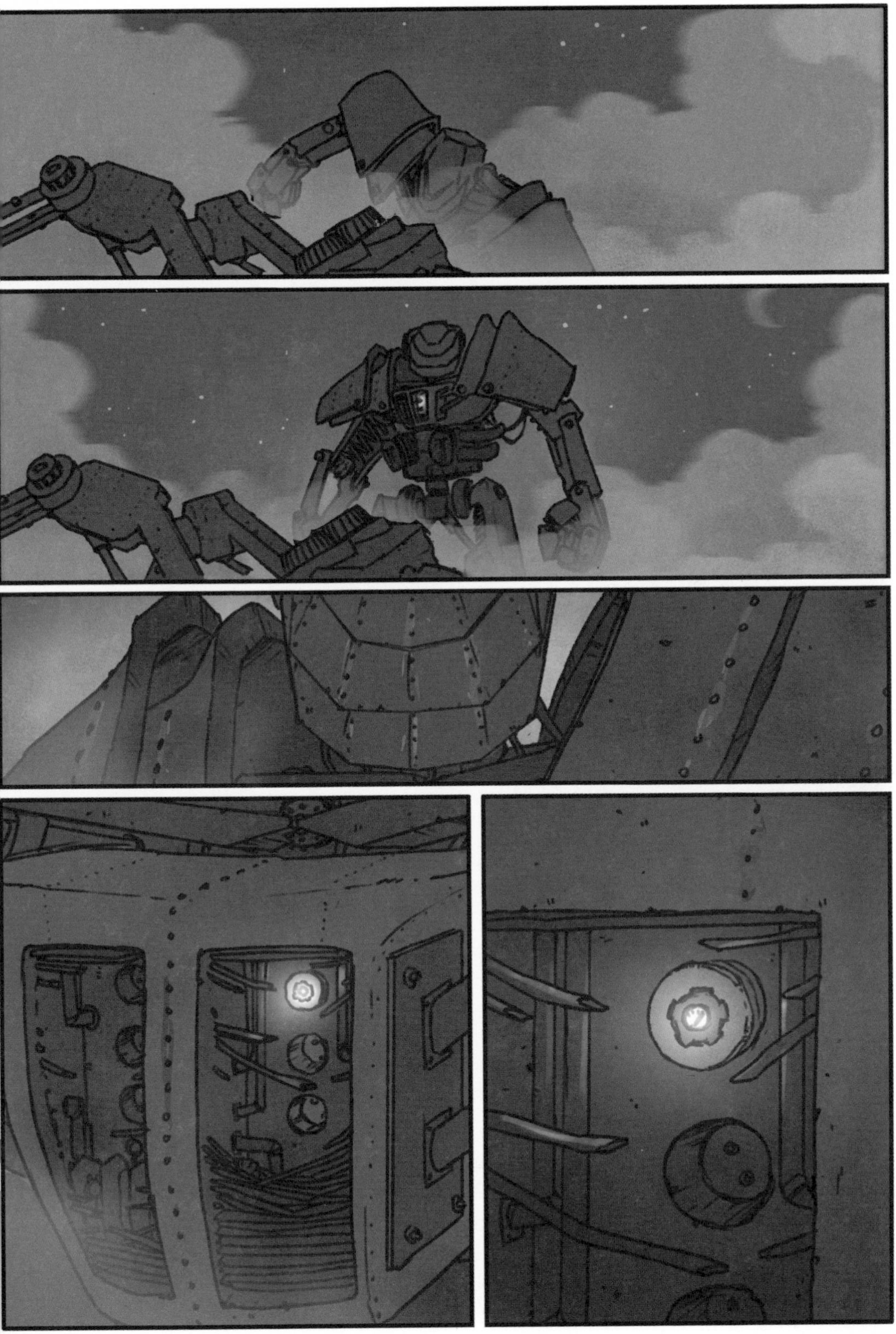

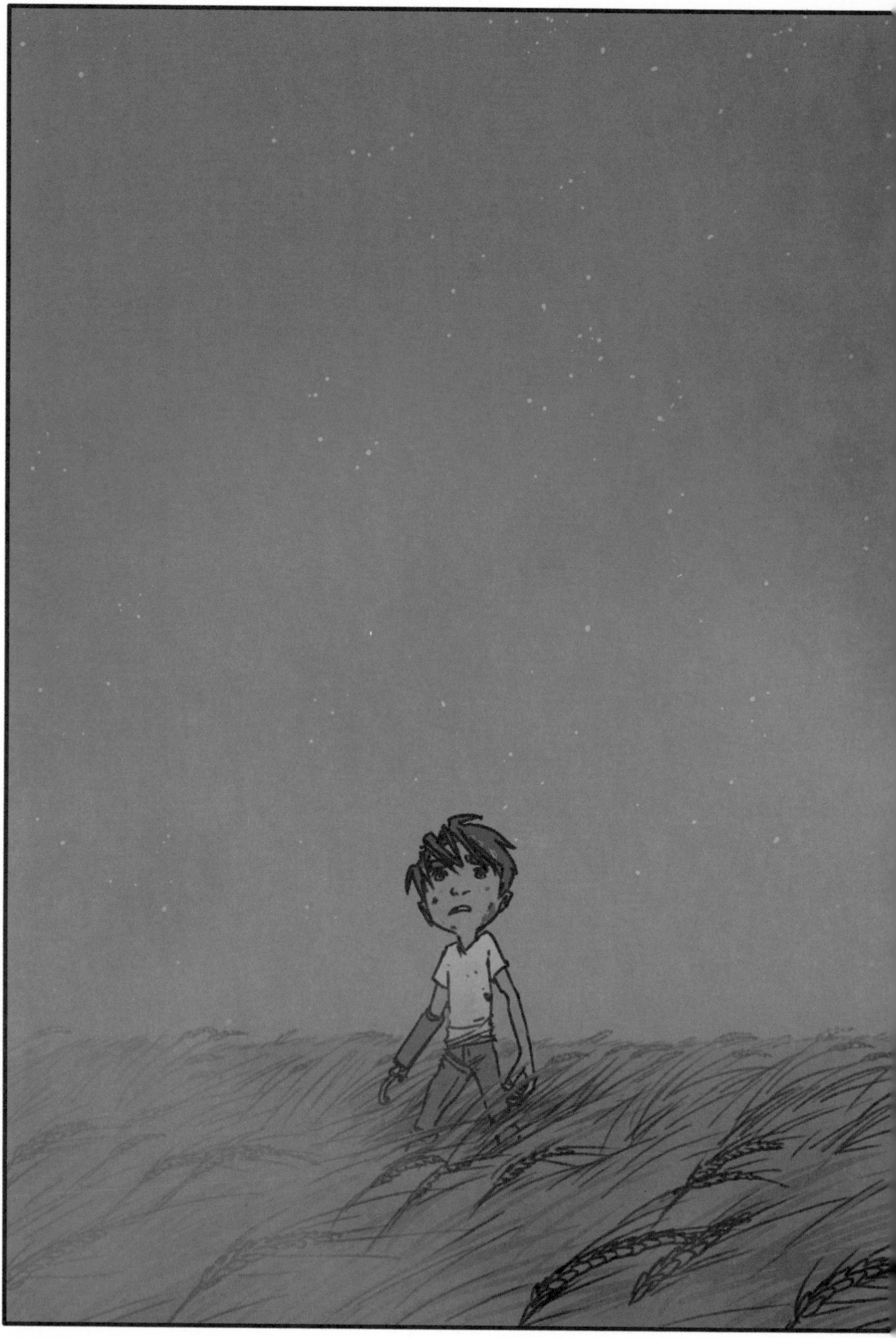

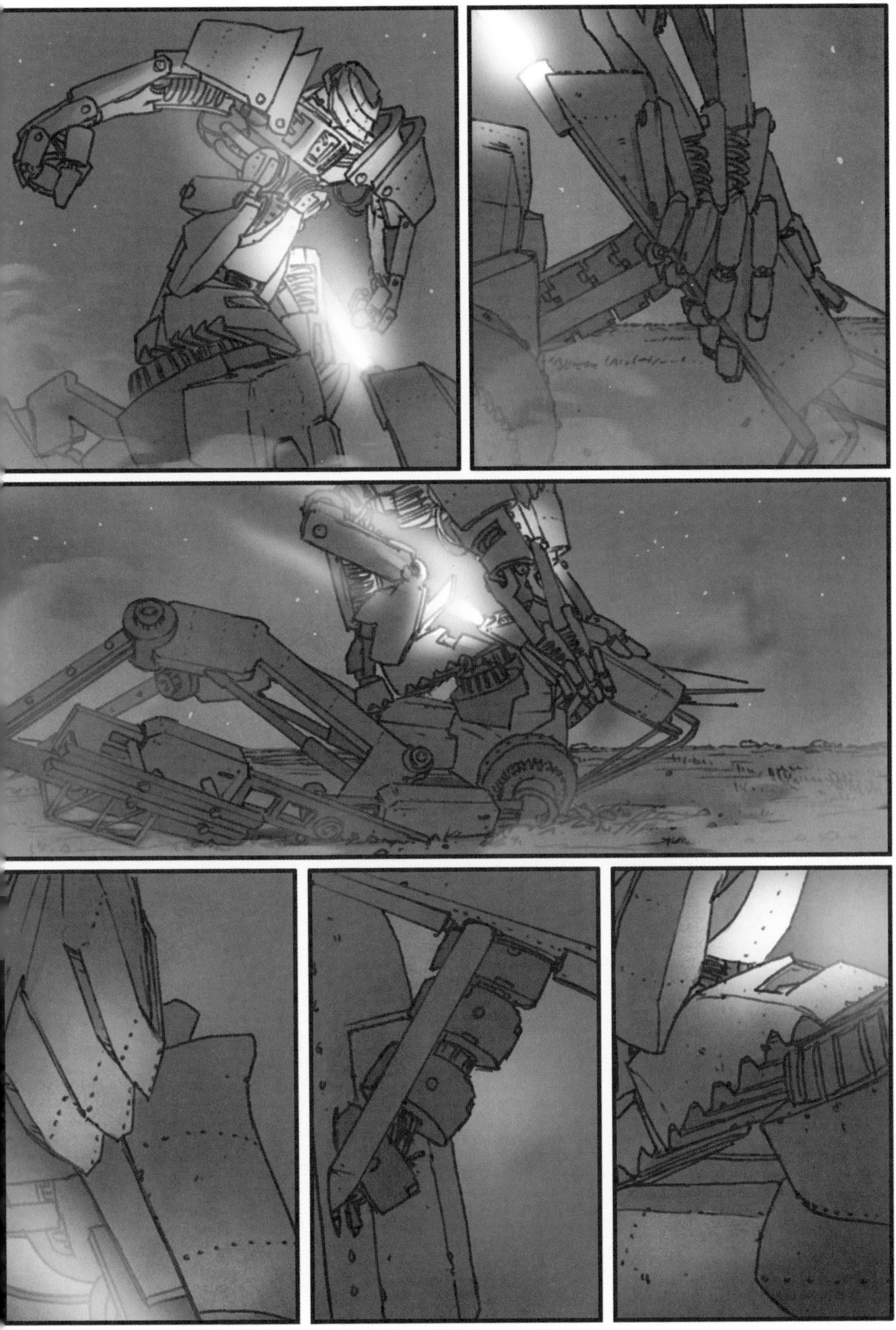

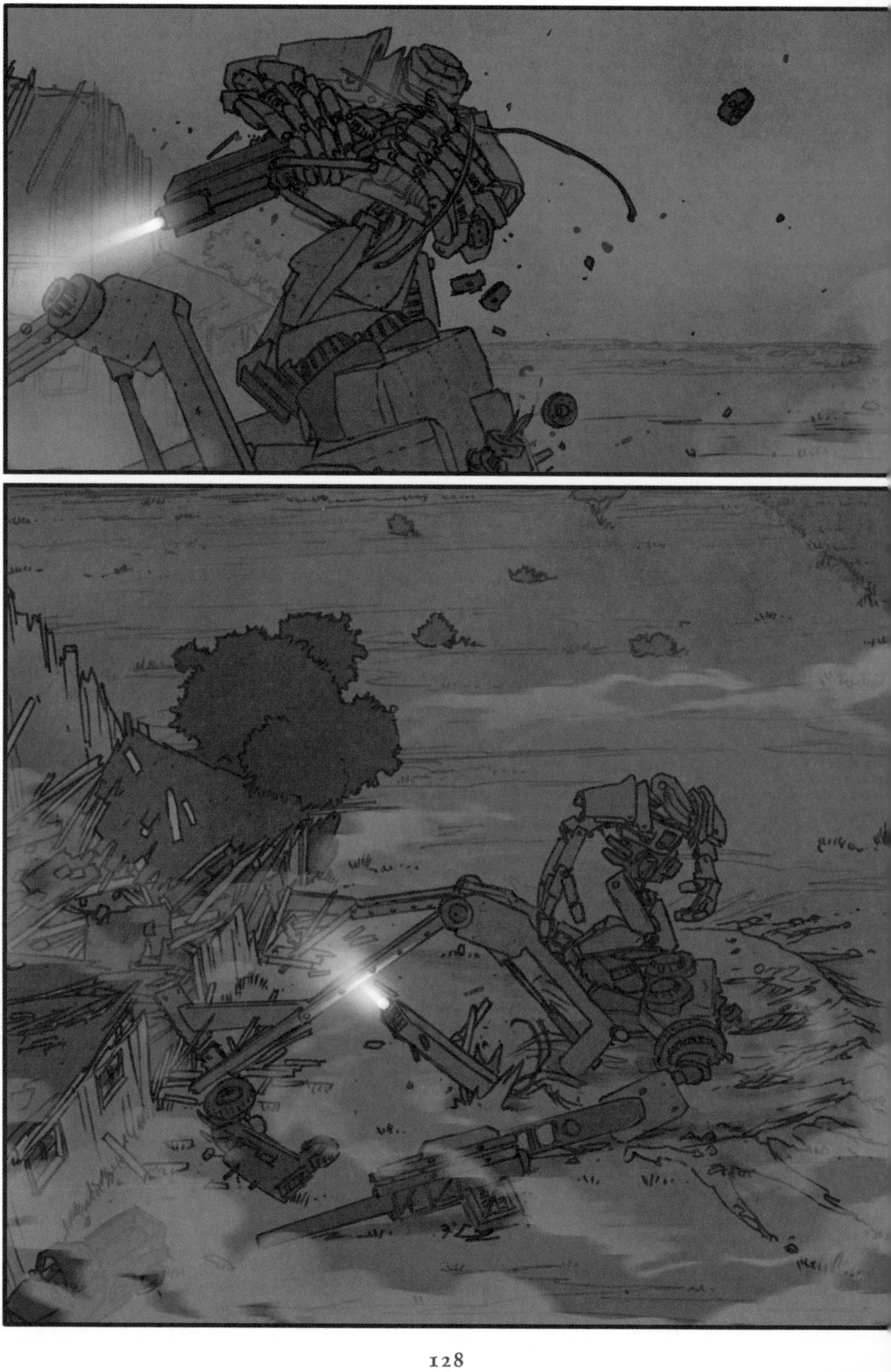

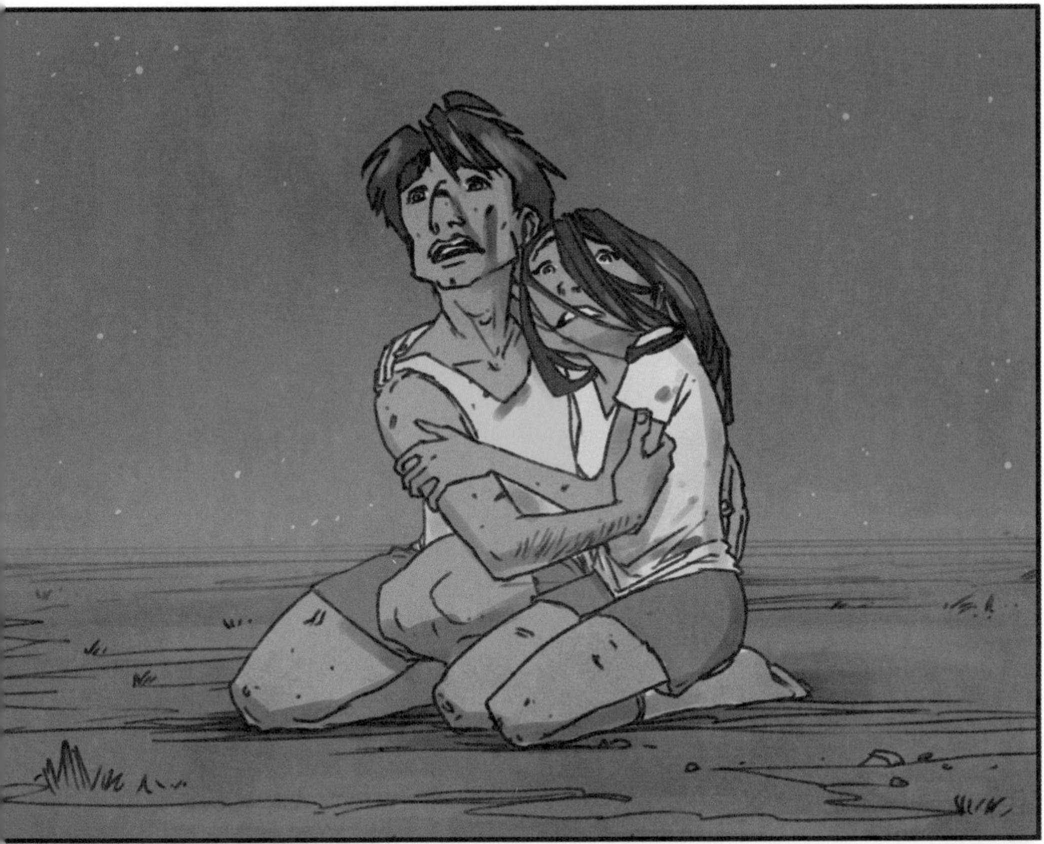

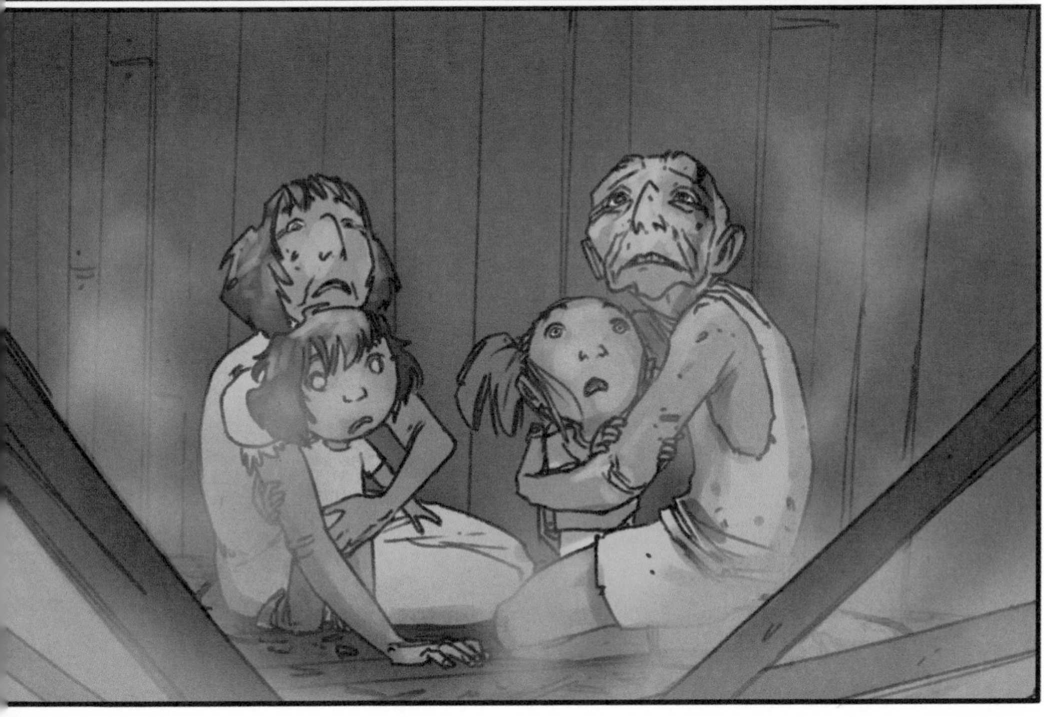

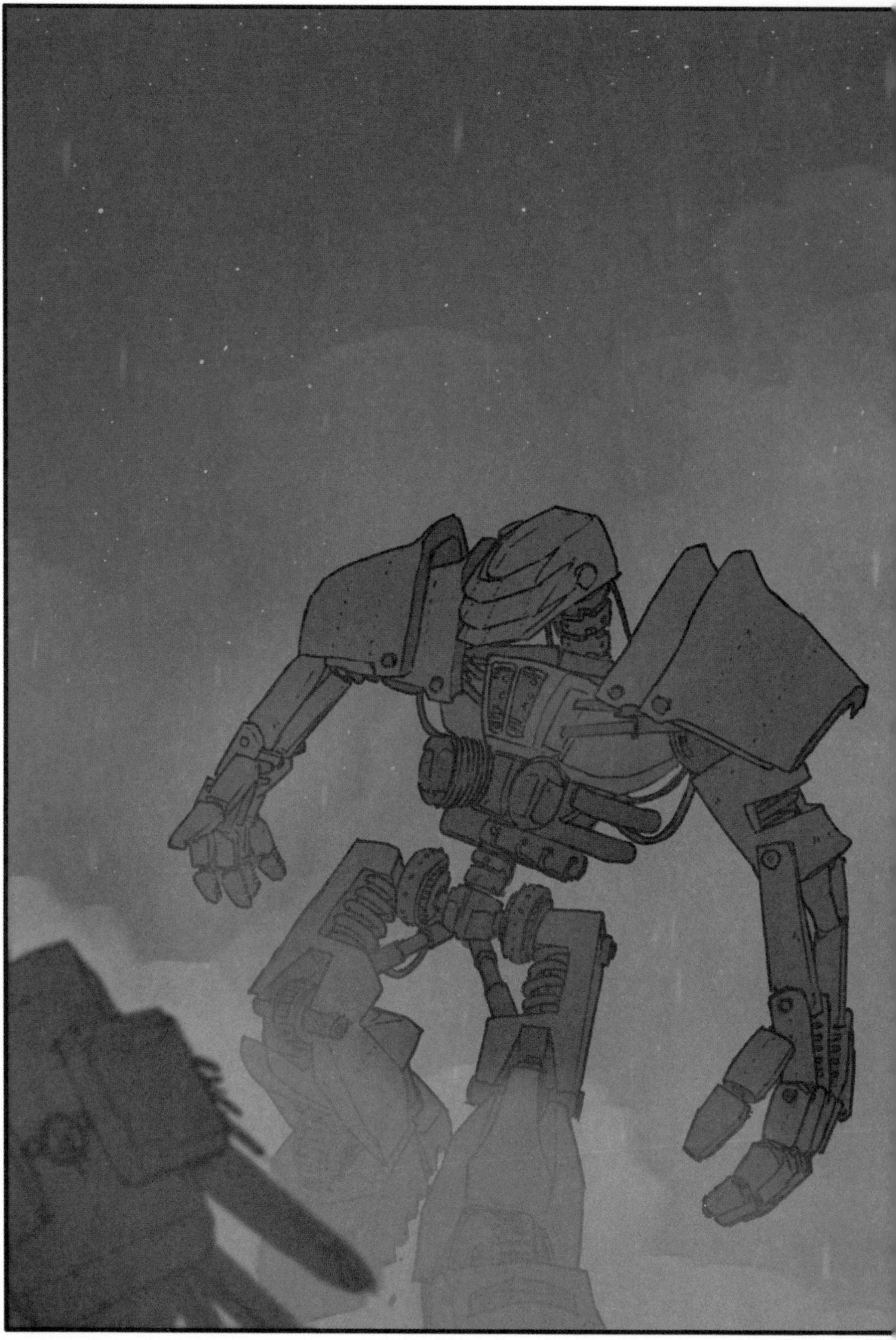

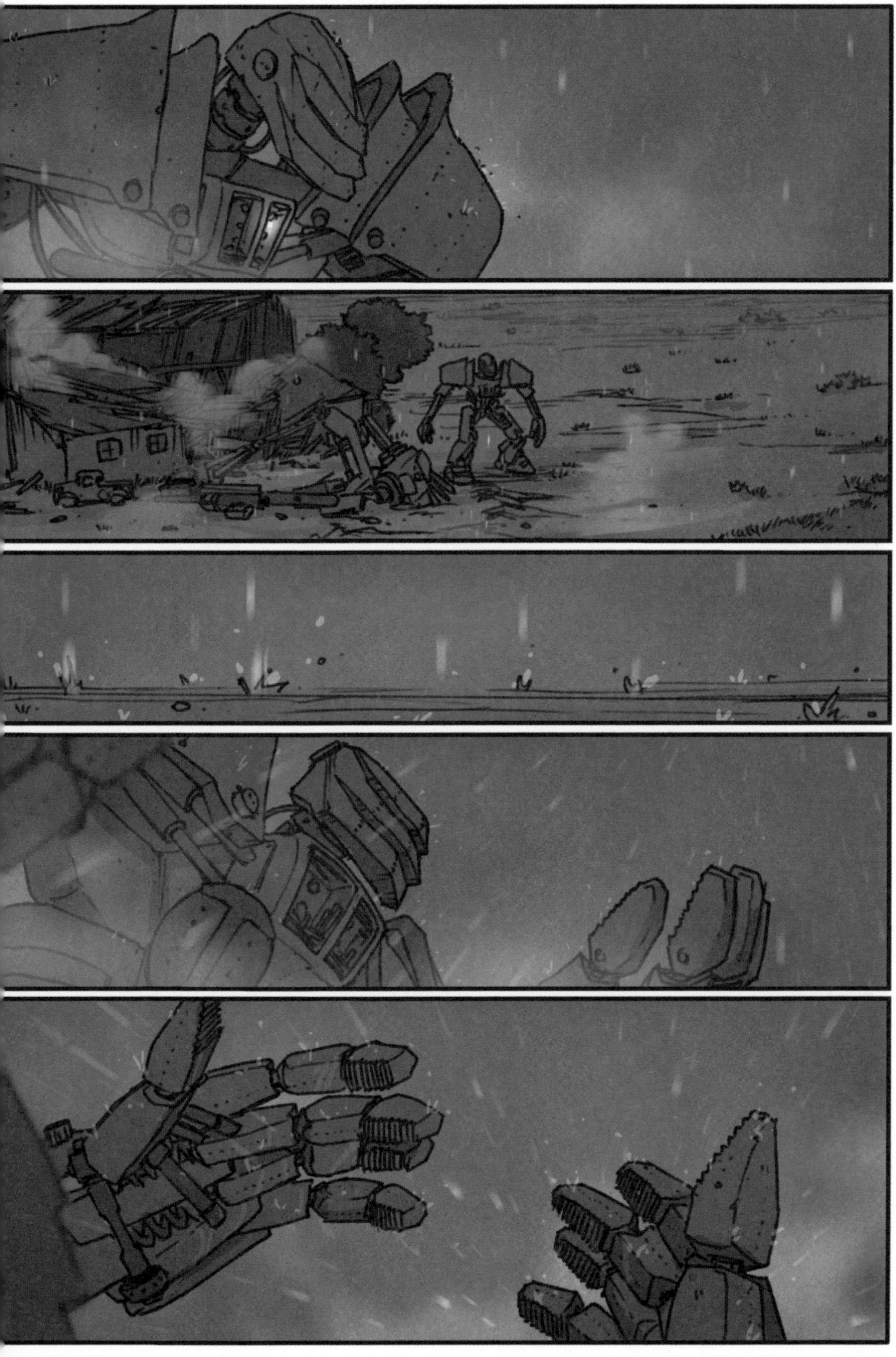

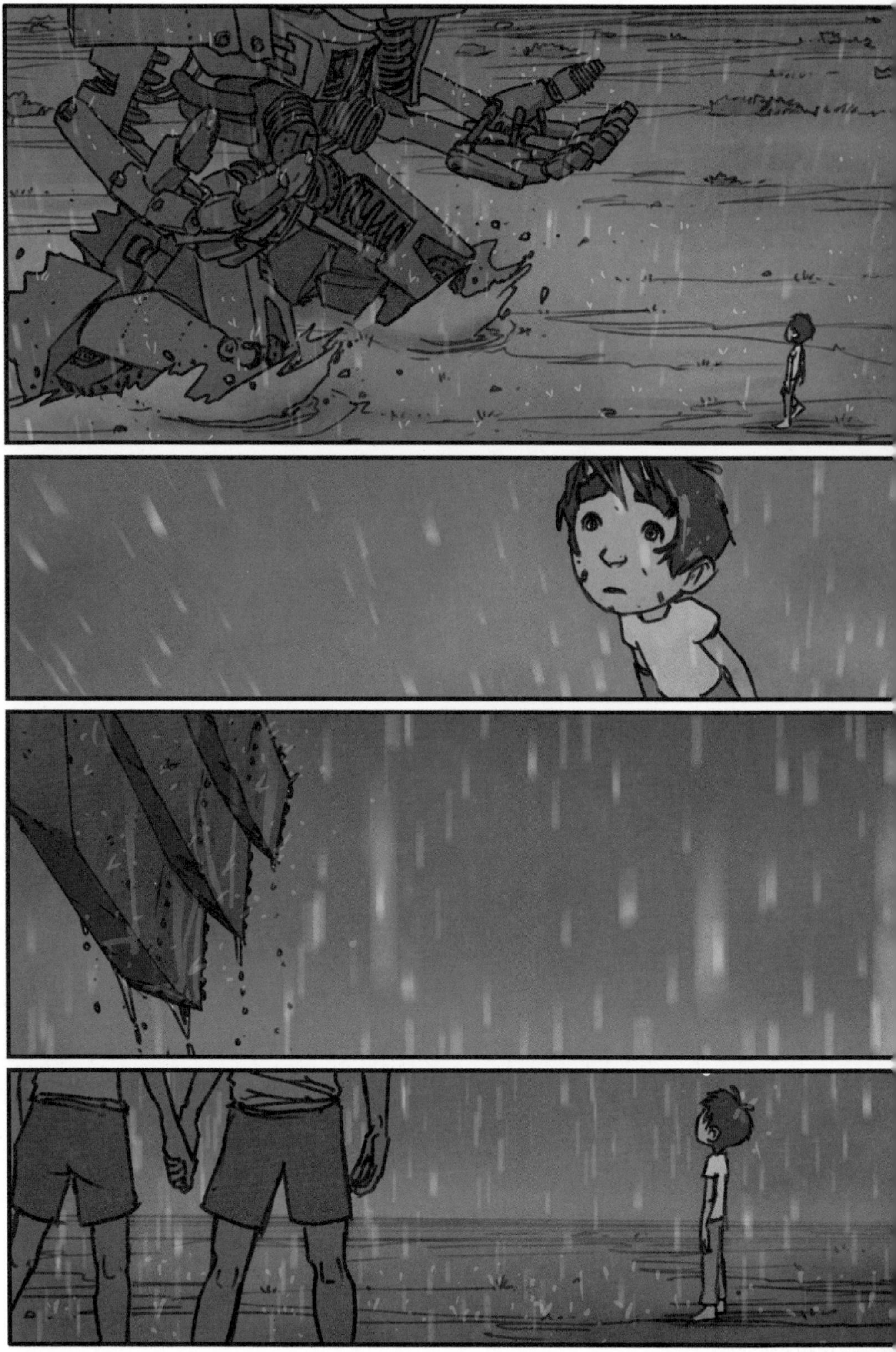

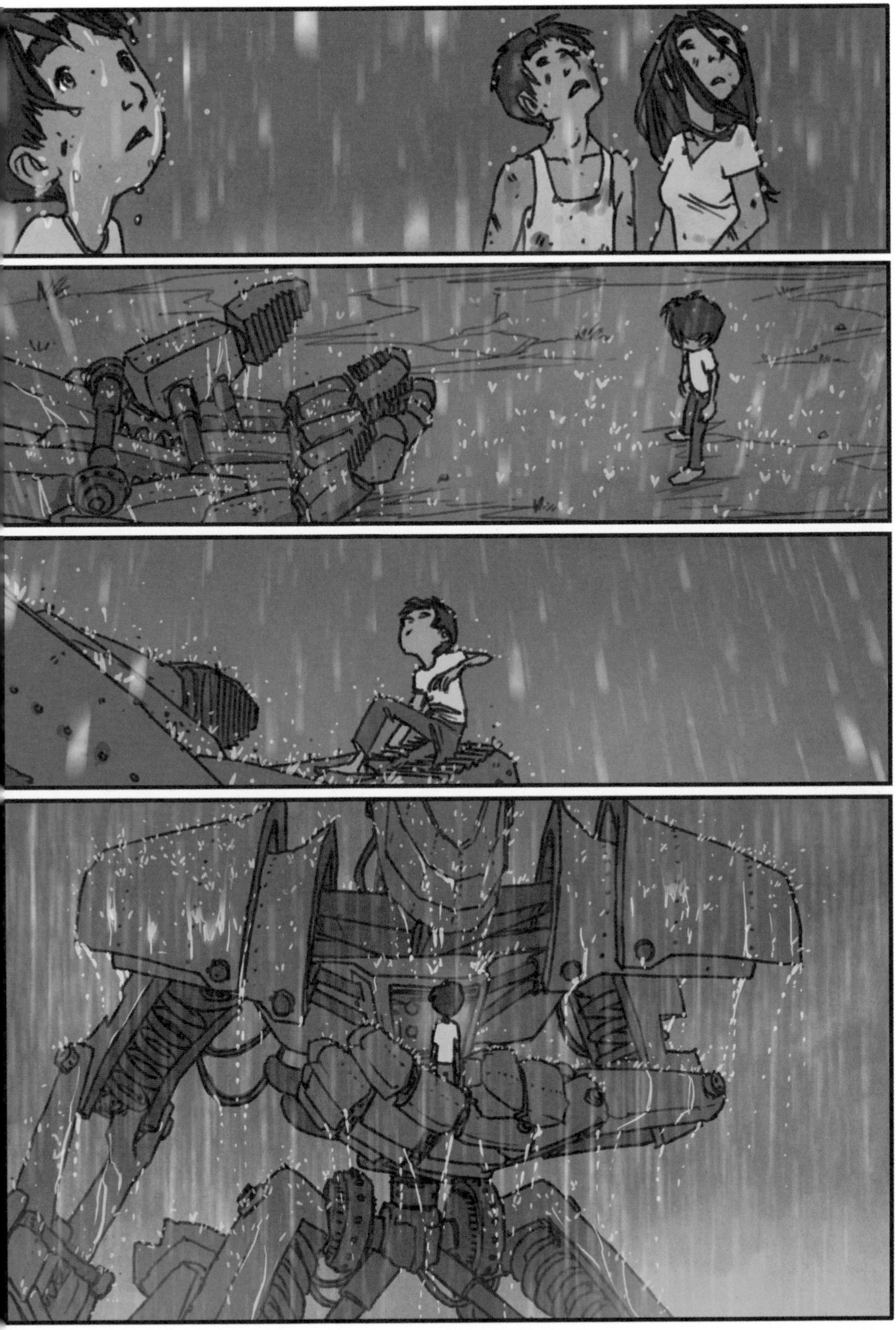

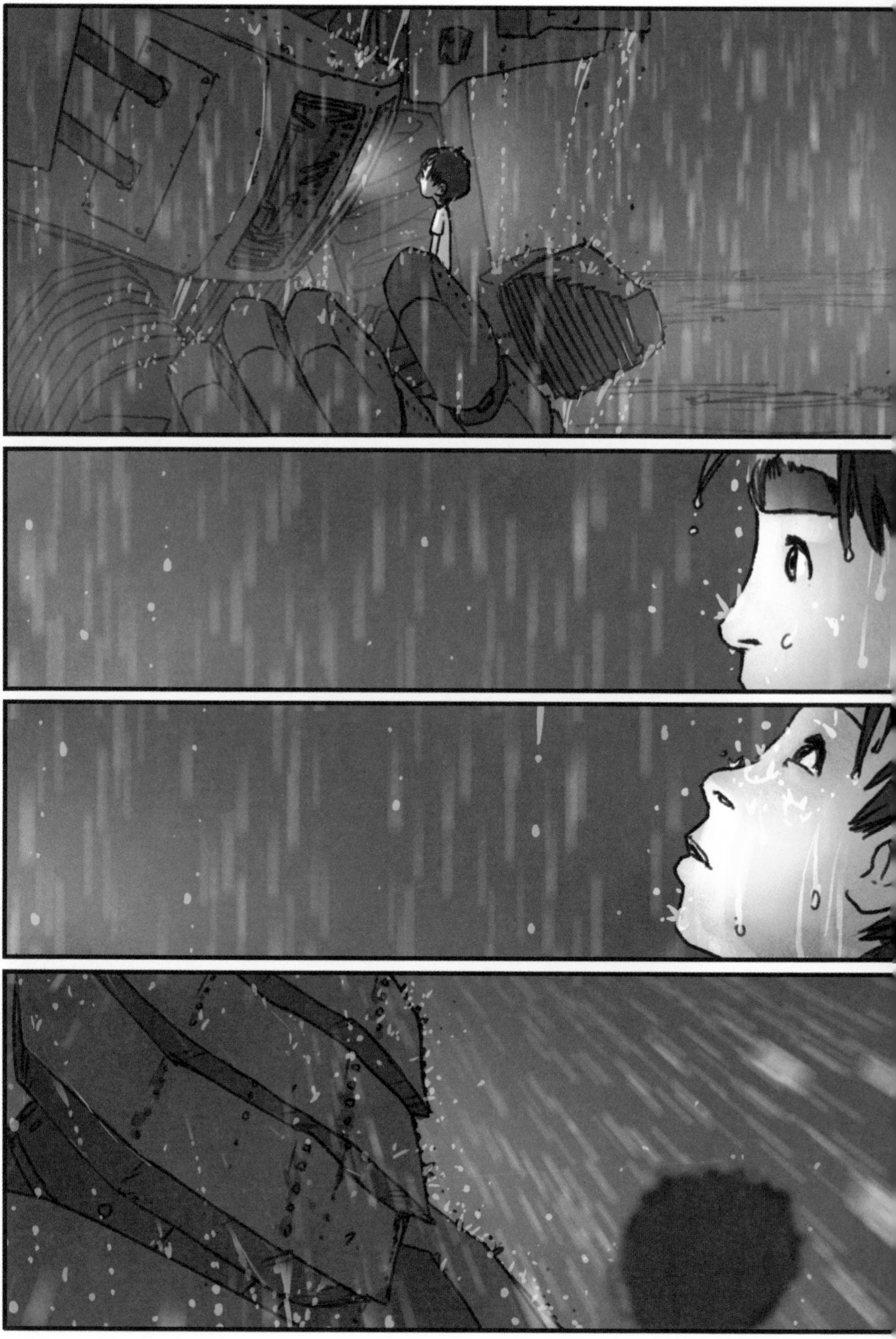

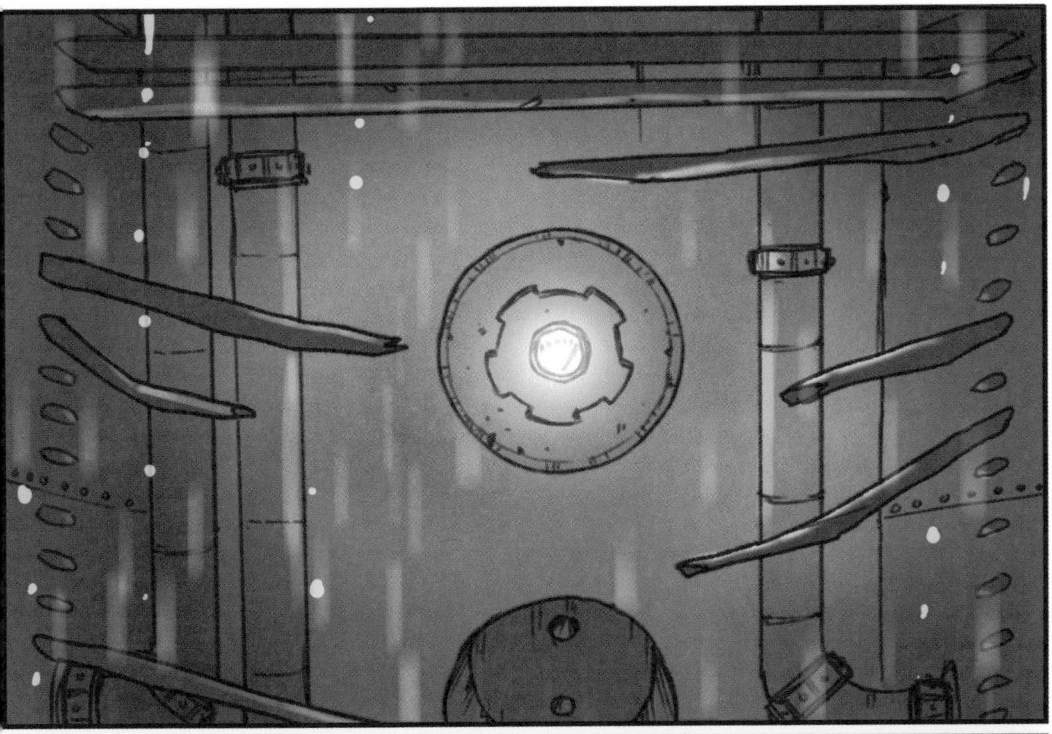

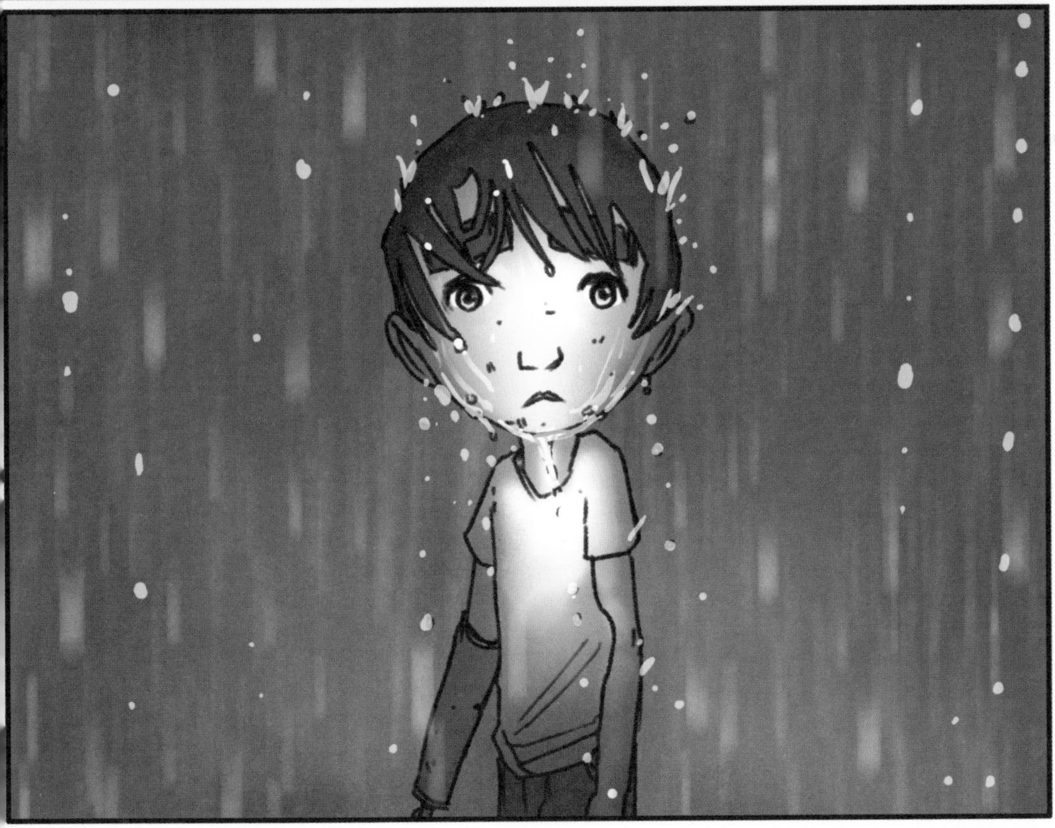

Dear Dad,

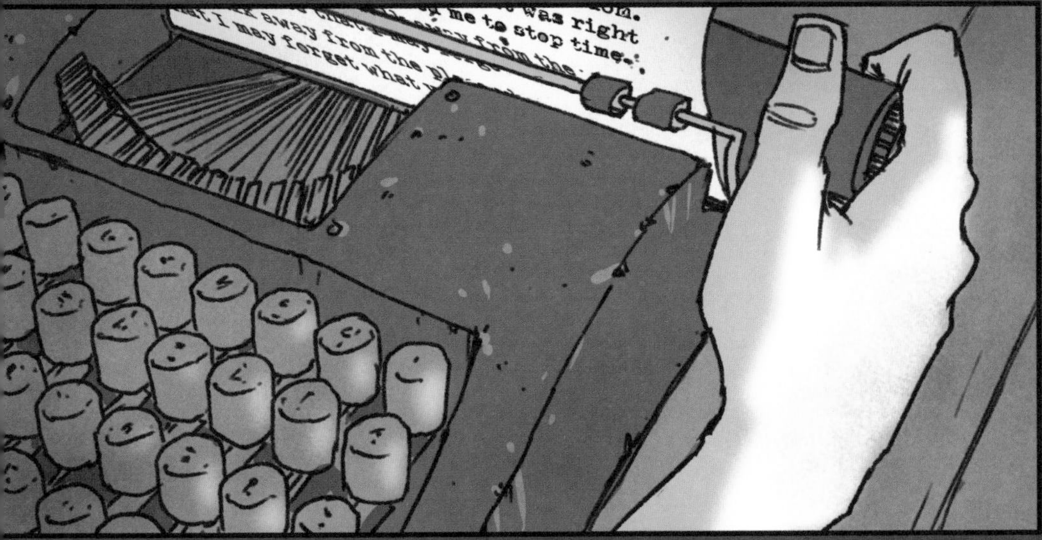
was right
me to stop time.
away from the
I may forget what

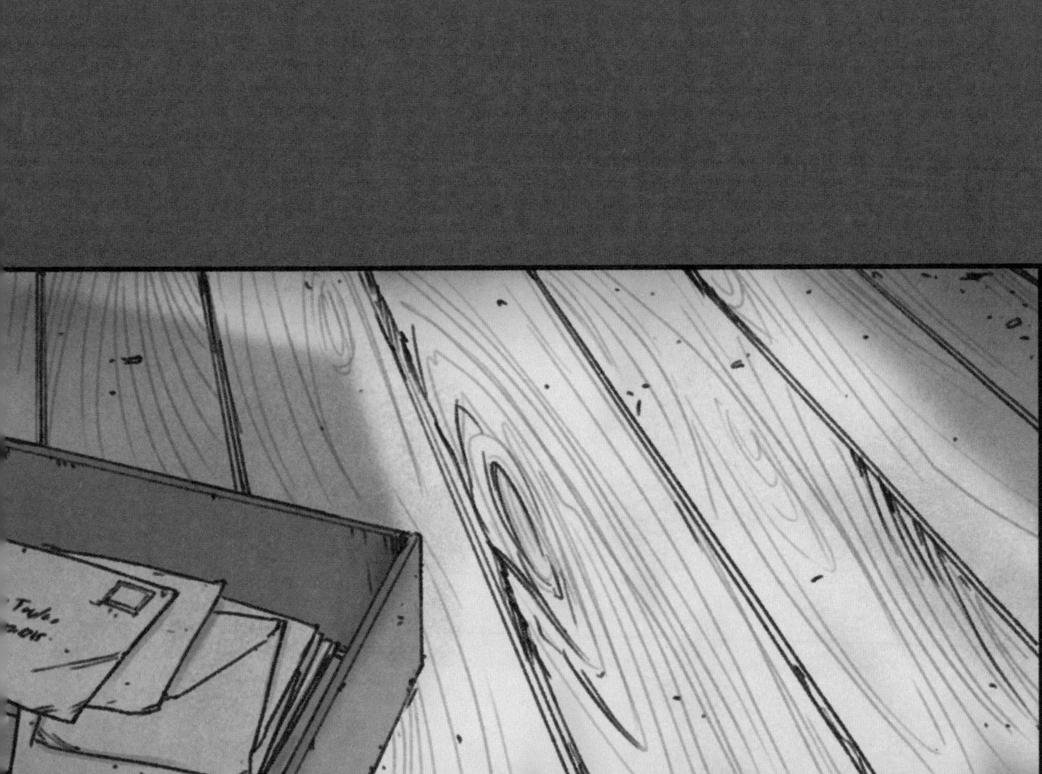

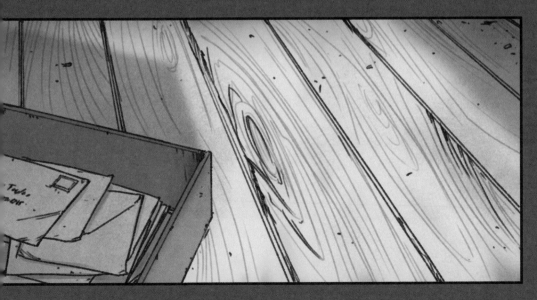

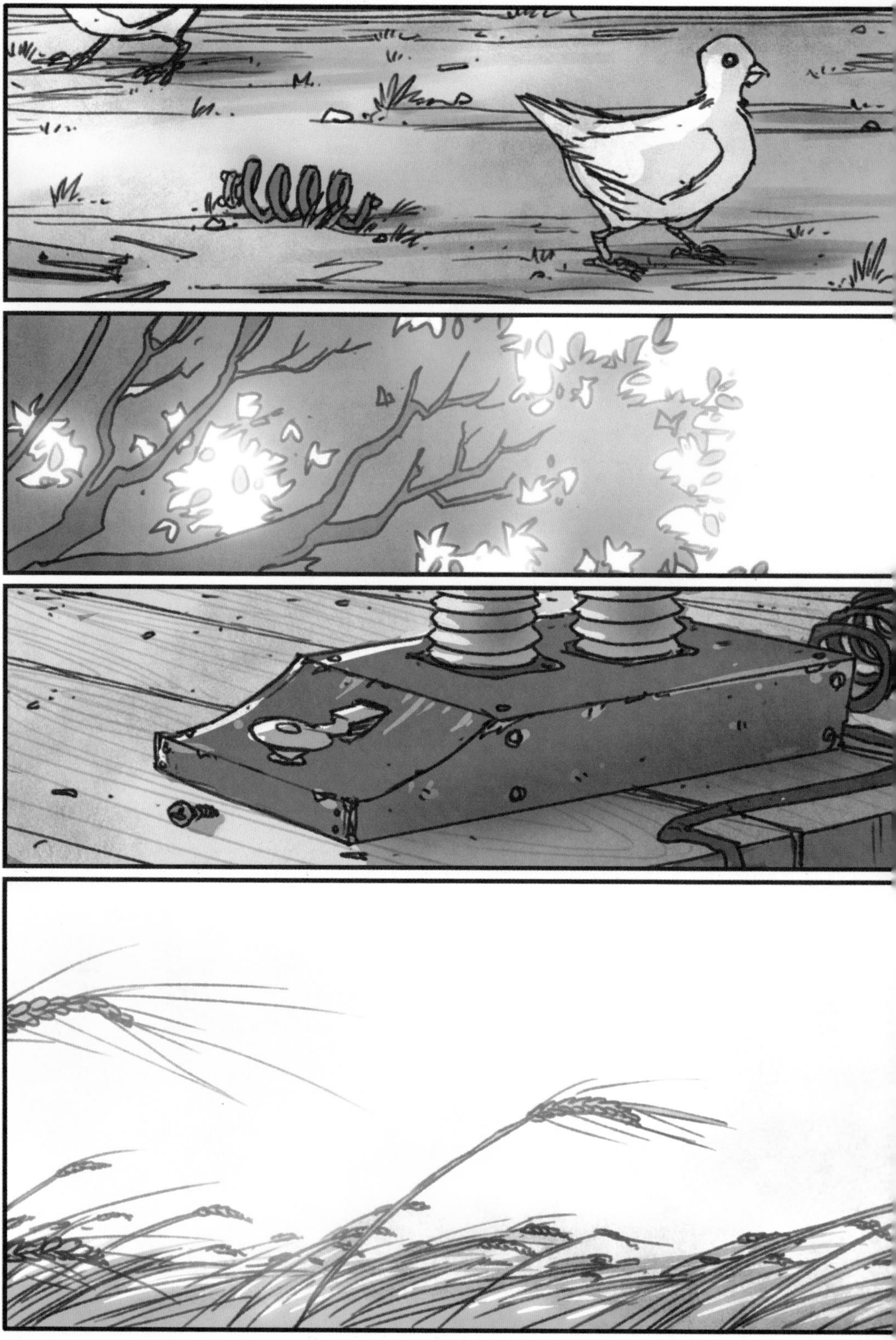

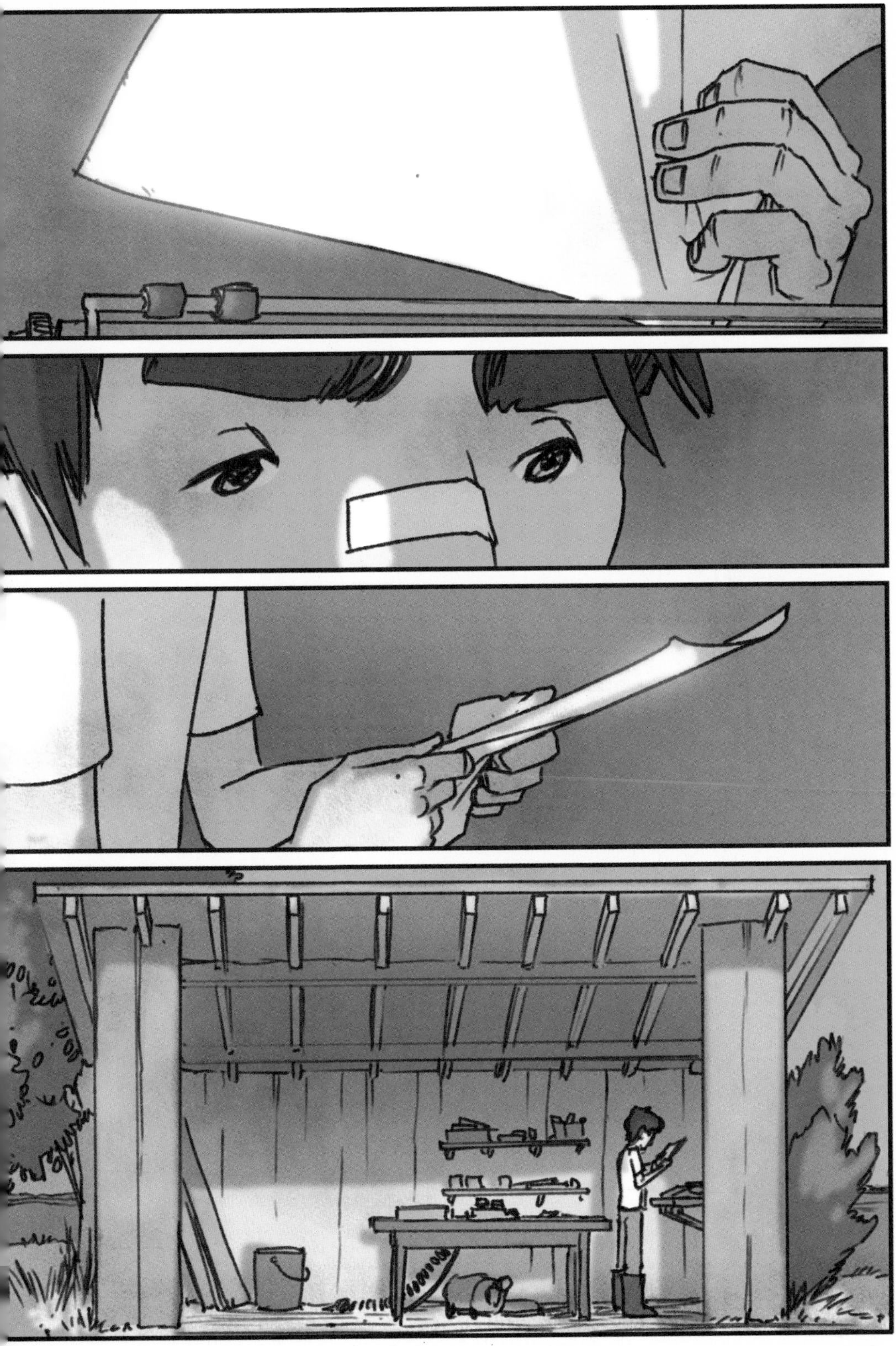

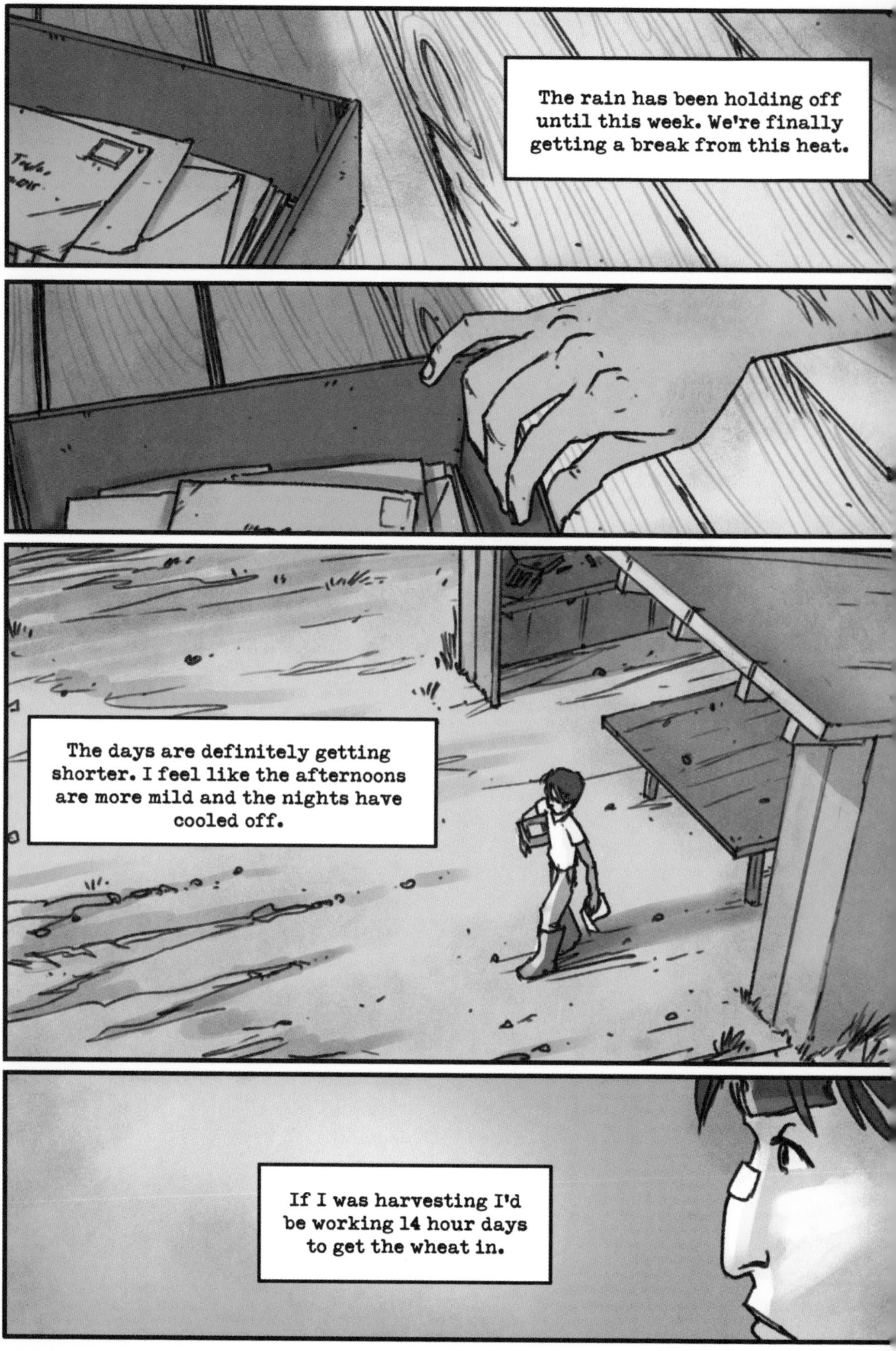
The rain has been holding off until this week. We're finally getting a break from this heat.
The days are definitely getting shorter. I feel like the afternoons are more mild and the nights have cooled off.
If I was harvesting I'd be working 14 hour days to get the wheat in.

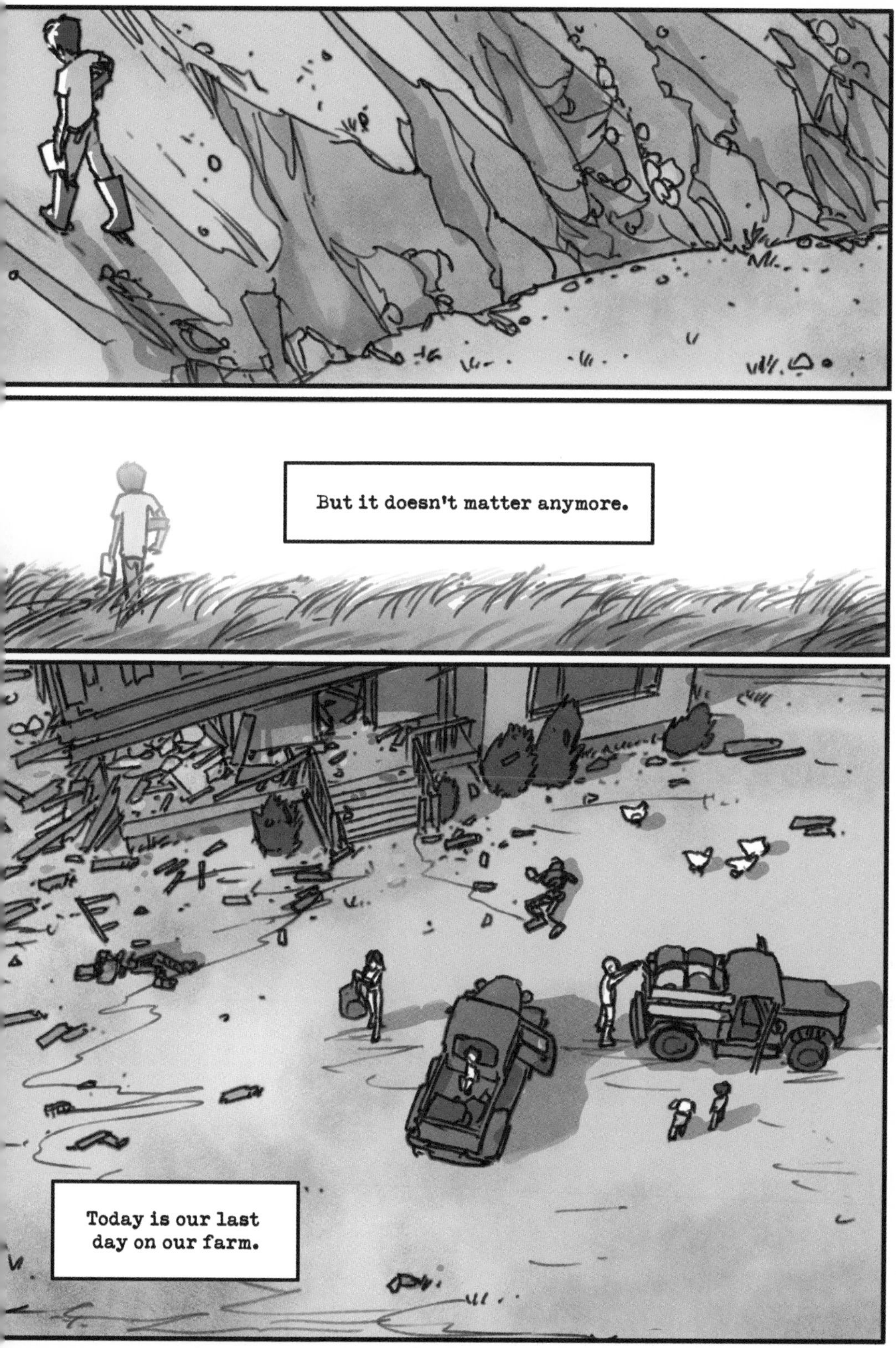
But it doesn't matter anymore.
Today is our last day on our farm.

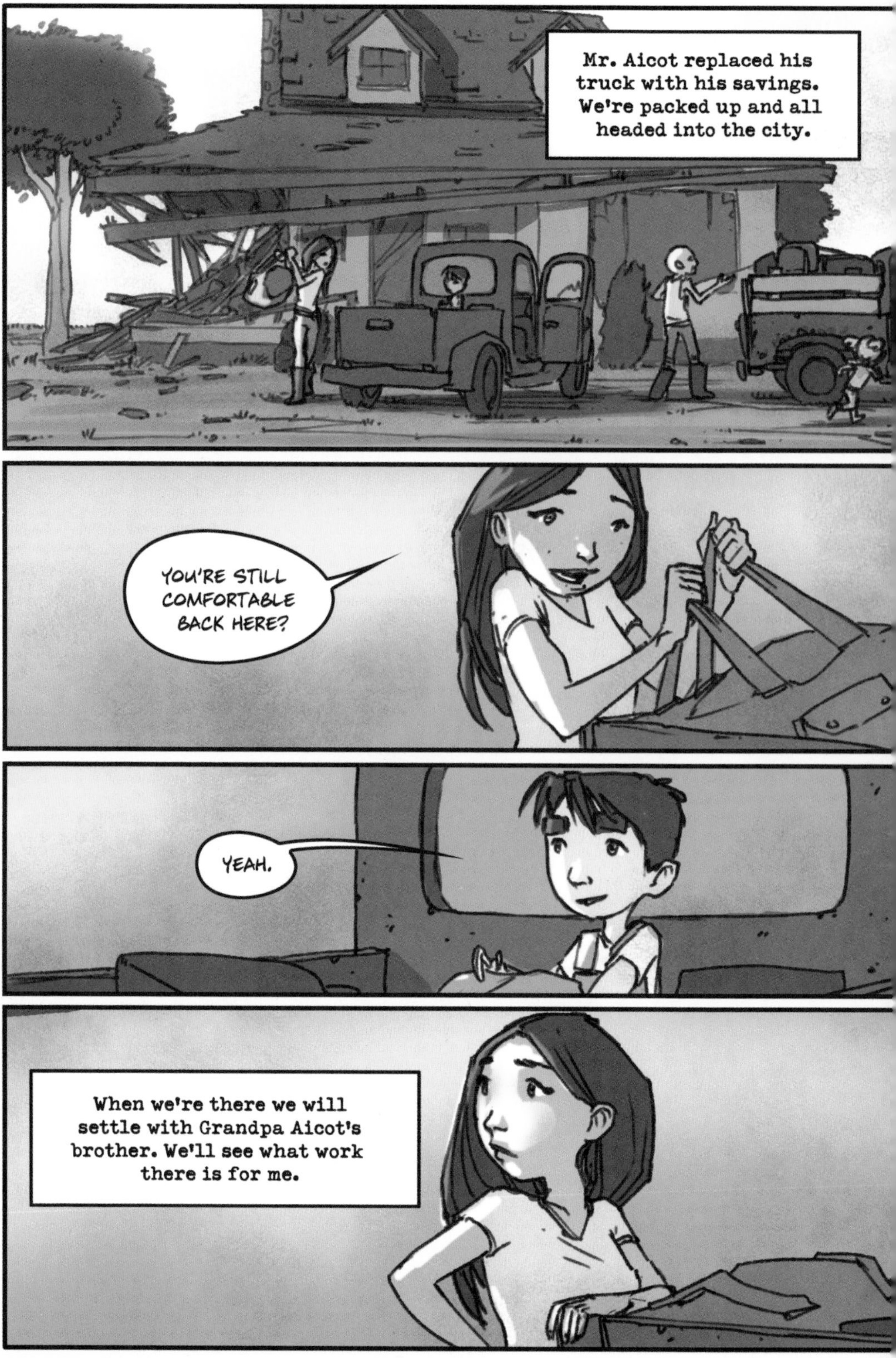
Mr. Aicot replaced his truck with his savings. We're packed up and all headed into the city.
YOU'RE STILL COMFORTABLE BACK HERE?
YEAH.
When we're there we will settle with Grandpa Aicot's brother. We'll see what work there is for me.

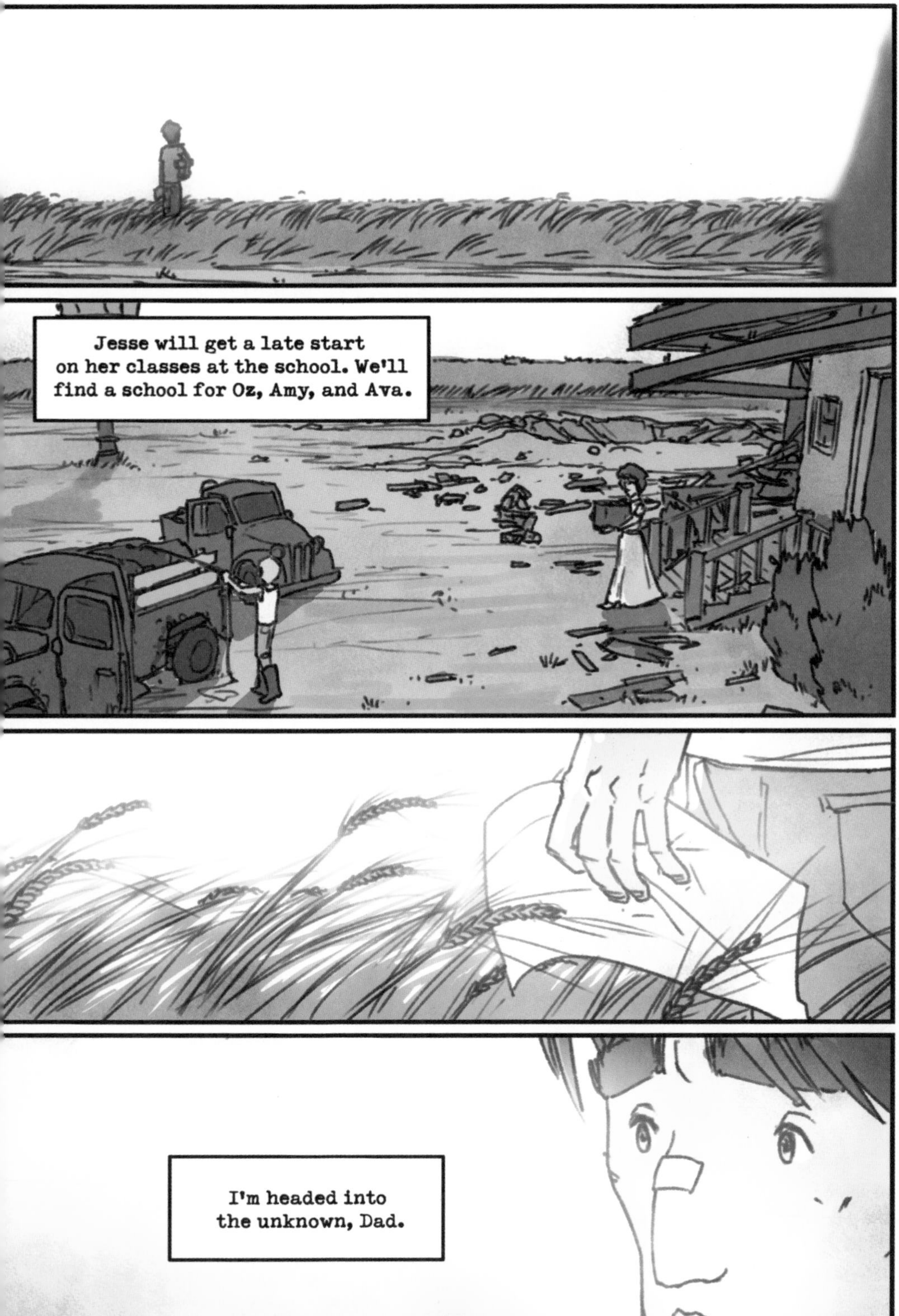
Jesse will get a late start on her classes at the school. We'll find a school for Oz, Amy, and Ava.
I'm headed into the unknown, Dad.

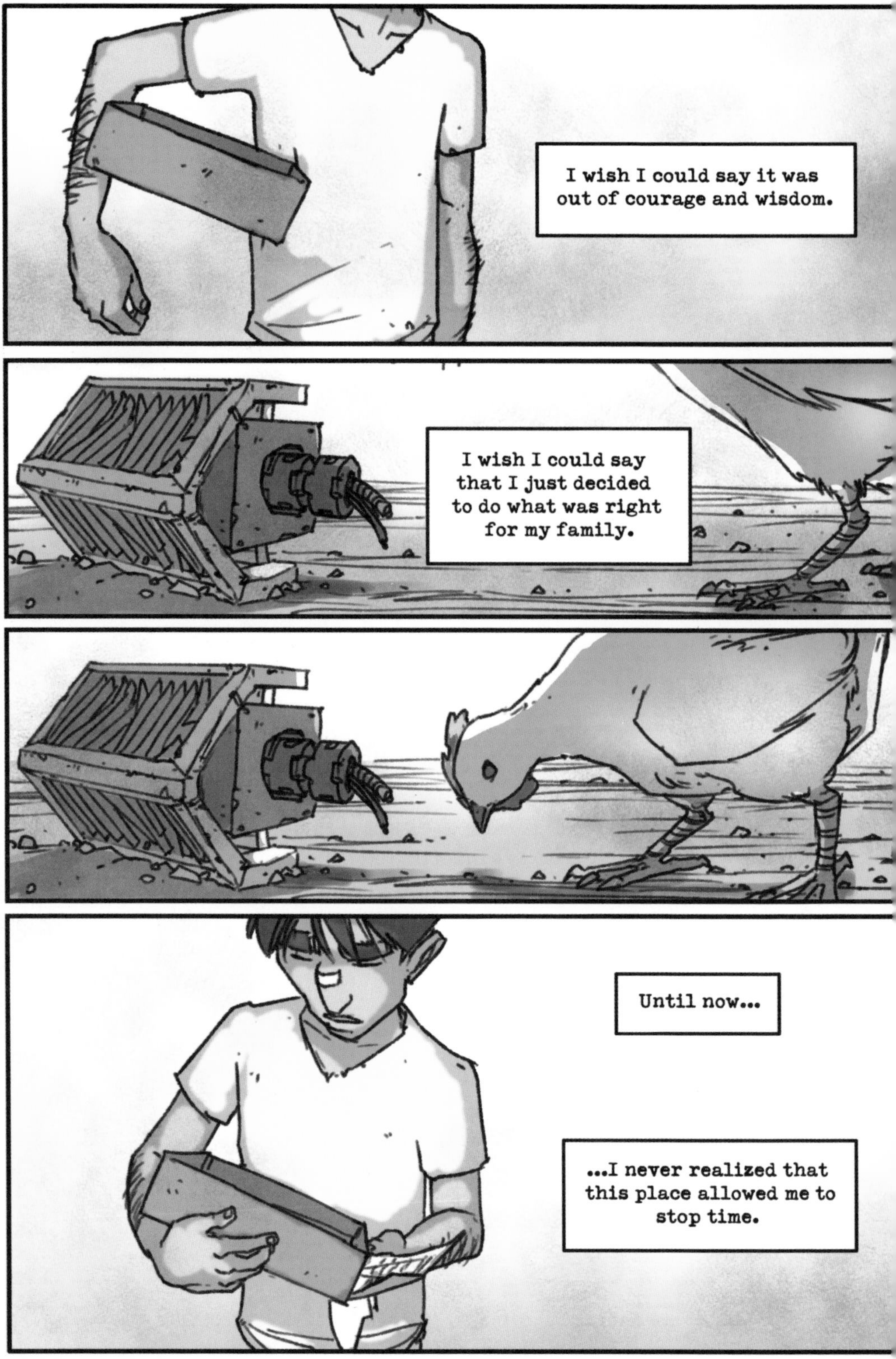
I wish I could say it was out of courage and wisdom.
I wish I could say that I just decided to do what was right for my family.
Until now...
...I never realized that this place allowed me to stop time.

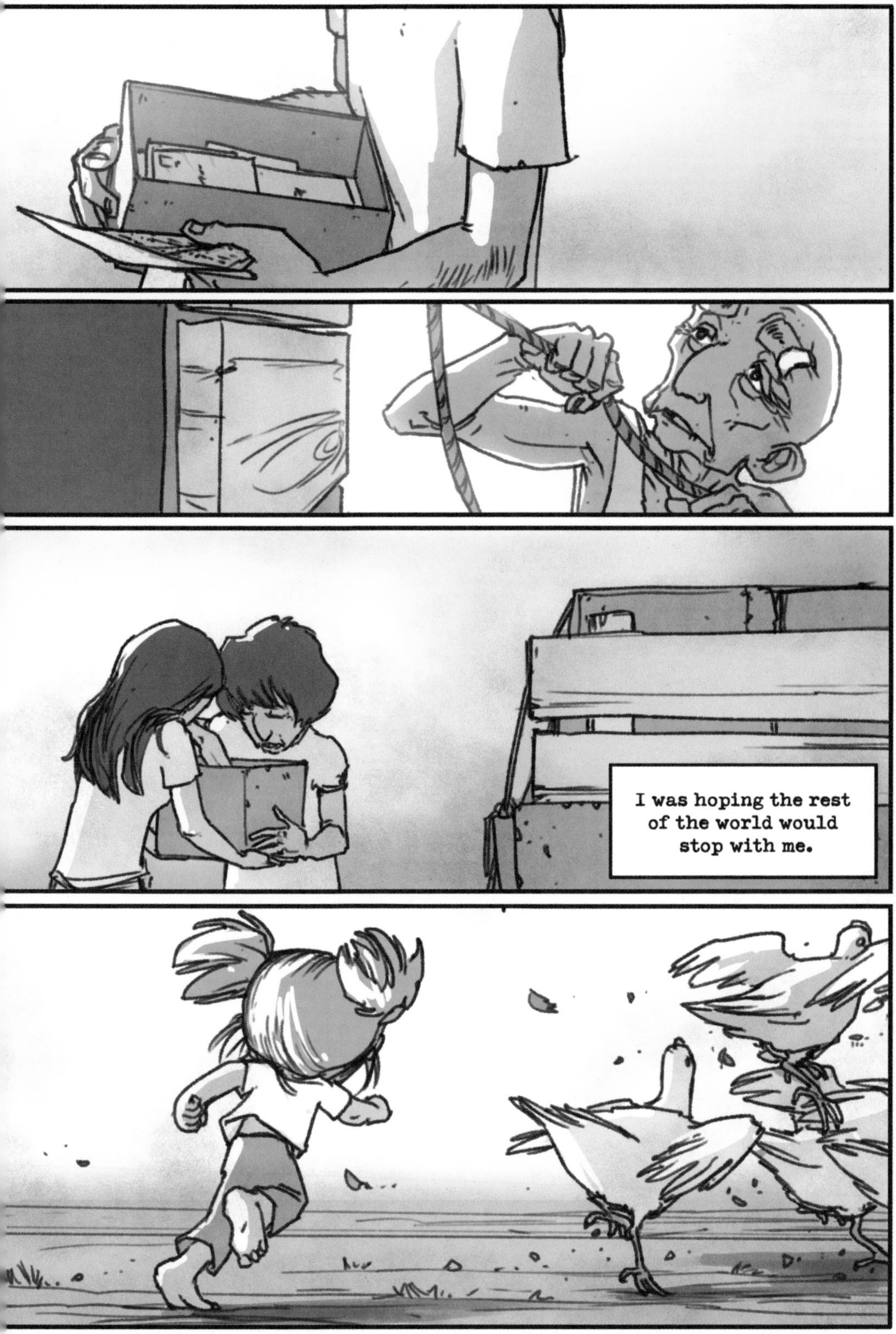
I was hoping the rest
of the world would
stop with me.

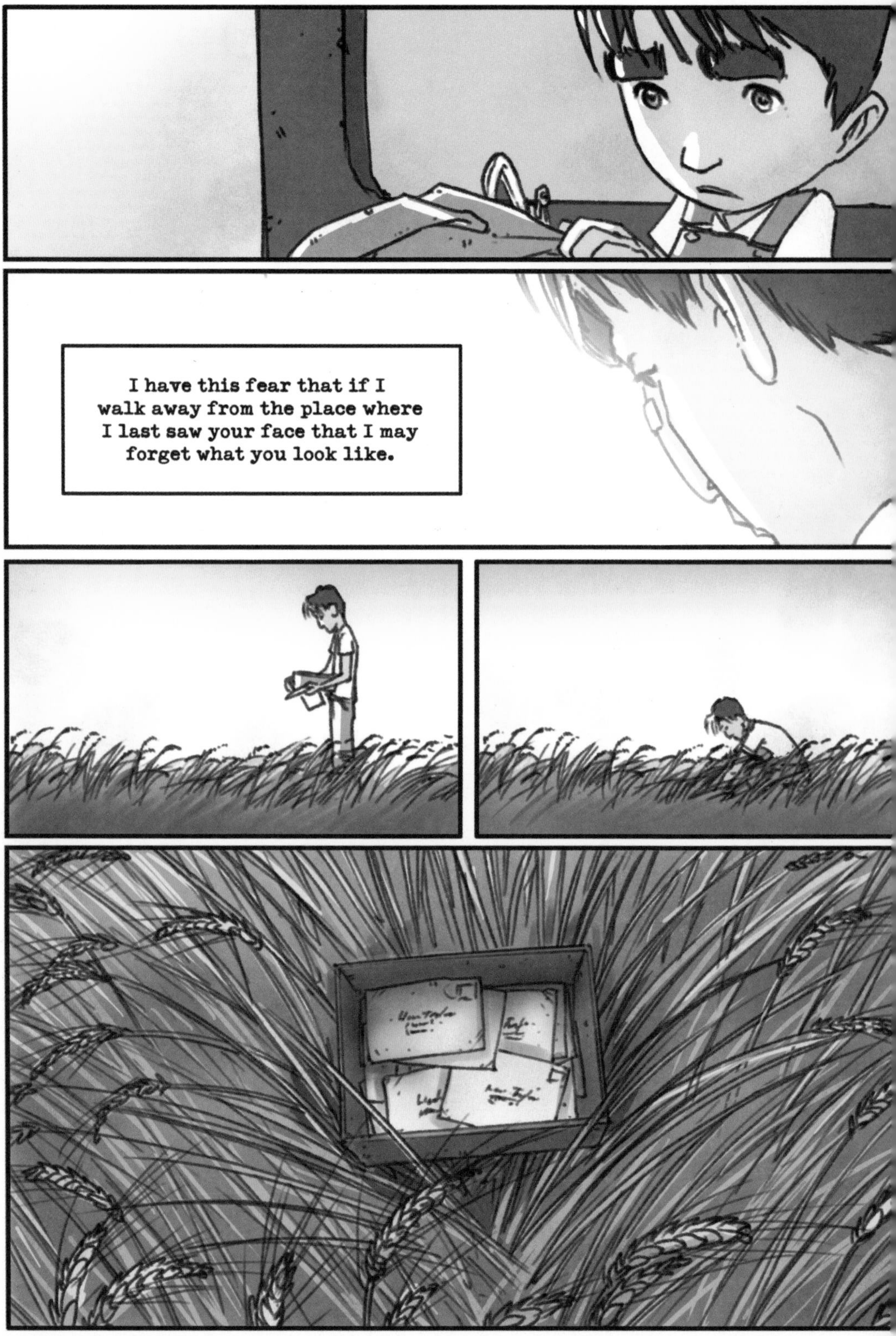
I have this fear that if I walk away from the place where I last saw your face that I may forget what you look like.

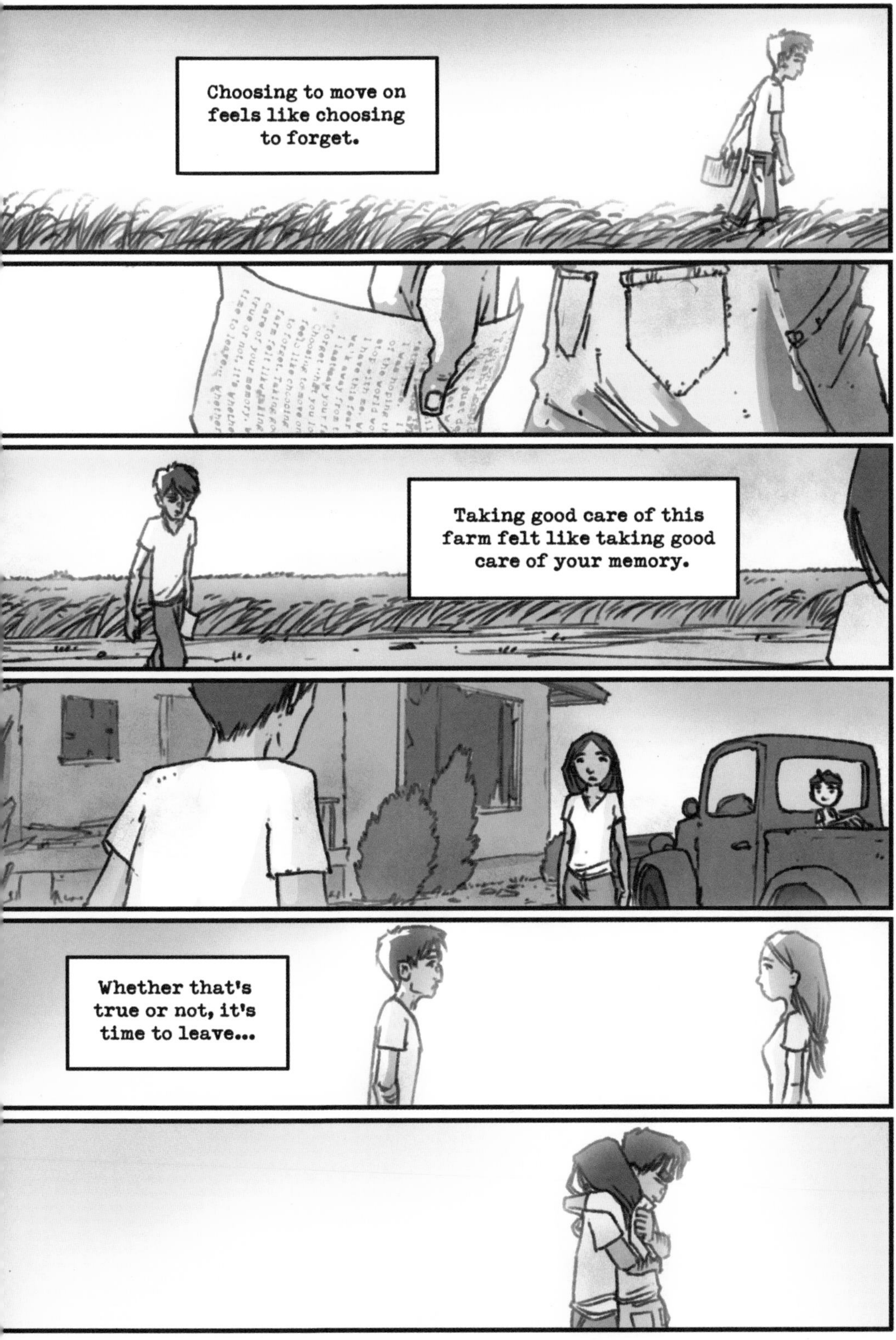
Choosing to move on feels like choosing to forget.
Taking good care of this farm felt like taking good care of your memory.
Whether that's true or not, it's time to leave...

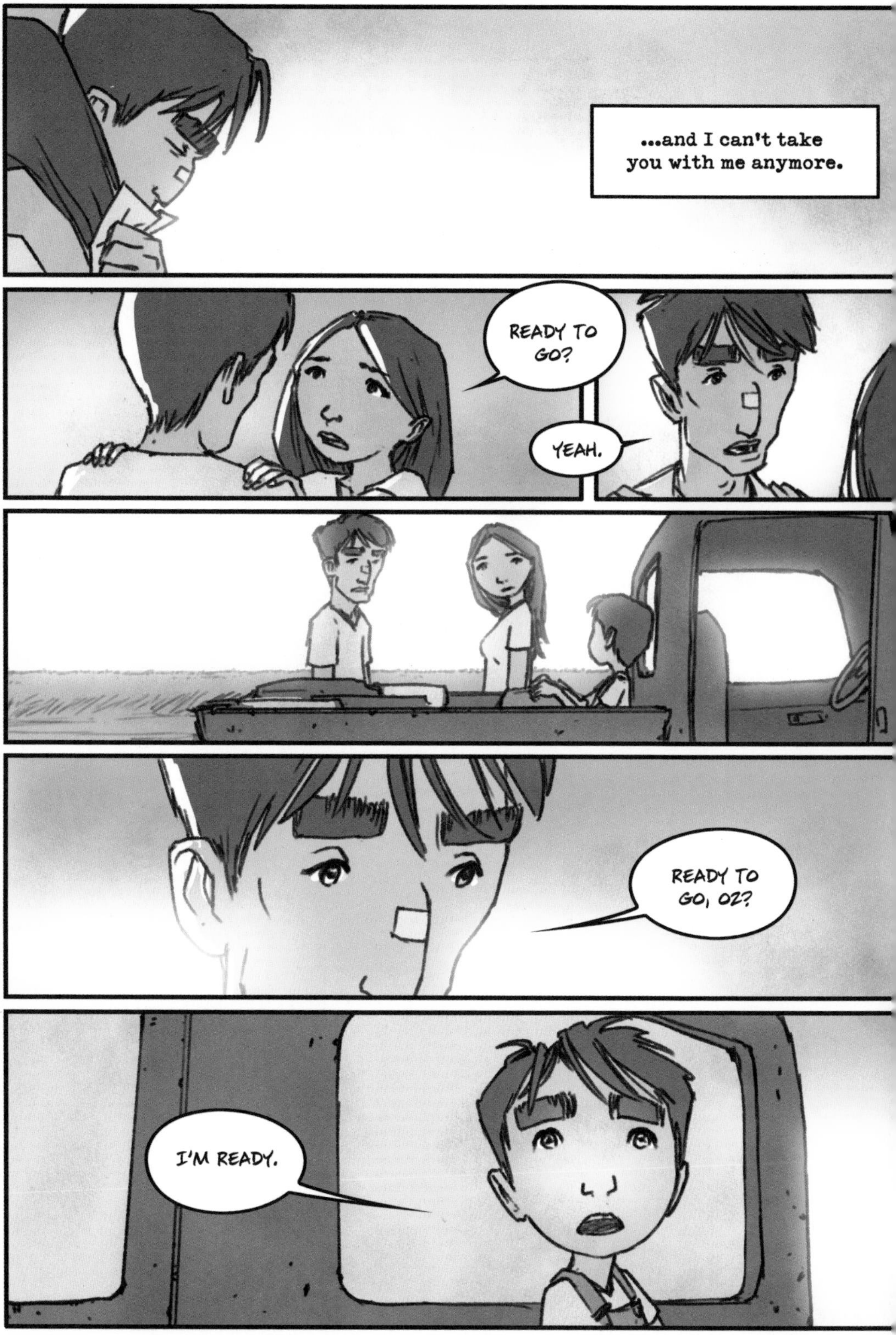
...and I can't take you with me anymore.
READY TO GO?
YEAH.
READY TO GO, OZ?
I'M READY.

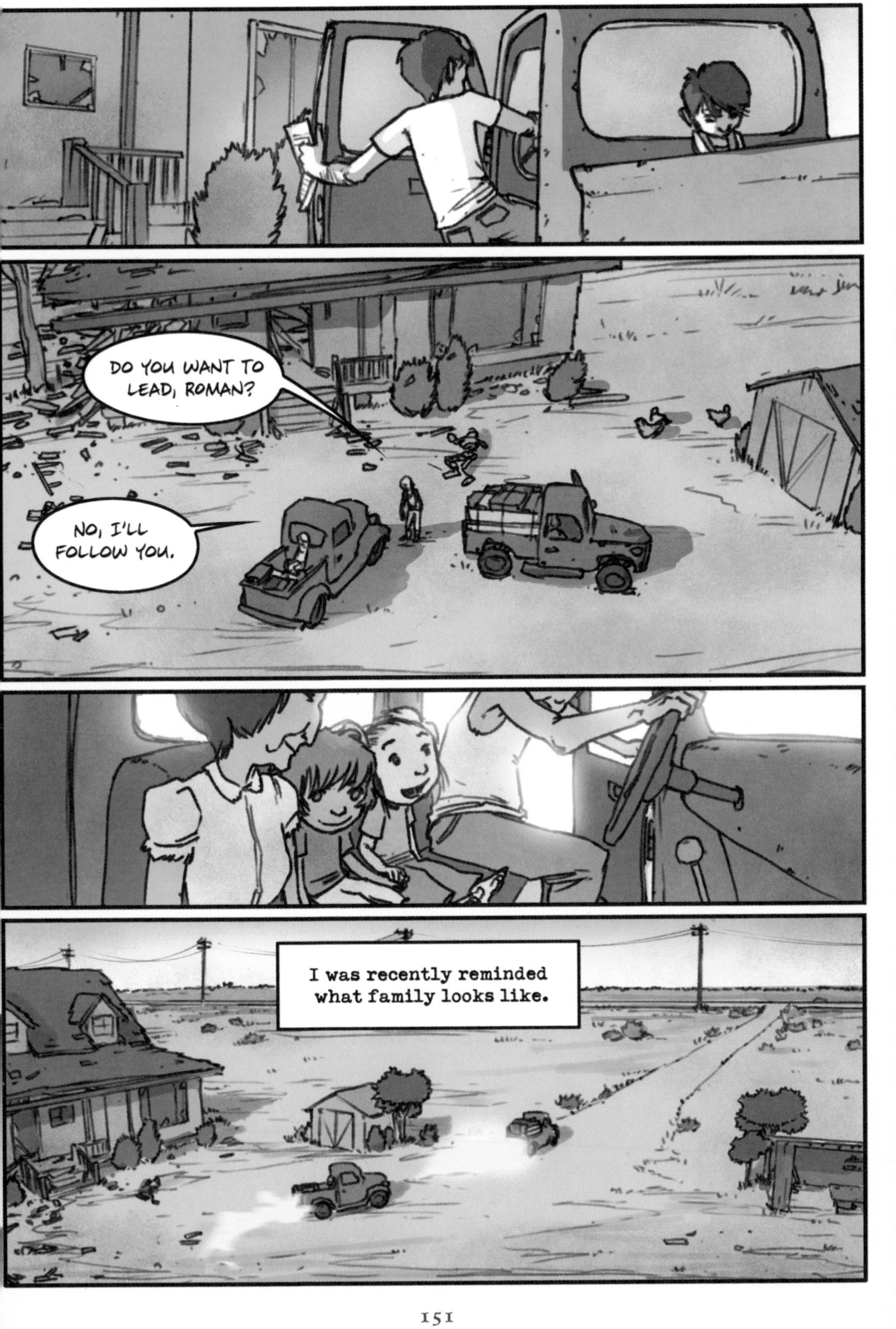
DO YOU WANT TO LEAD, ROMAN?
NO, I'LL FOLLOW YOU.
I was recently reminded what family looks like.

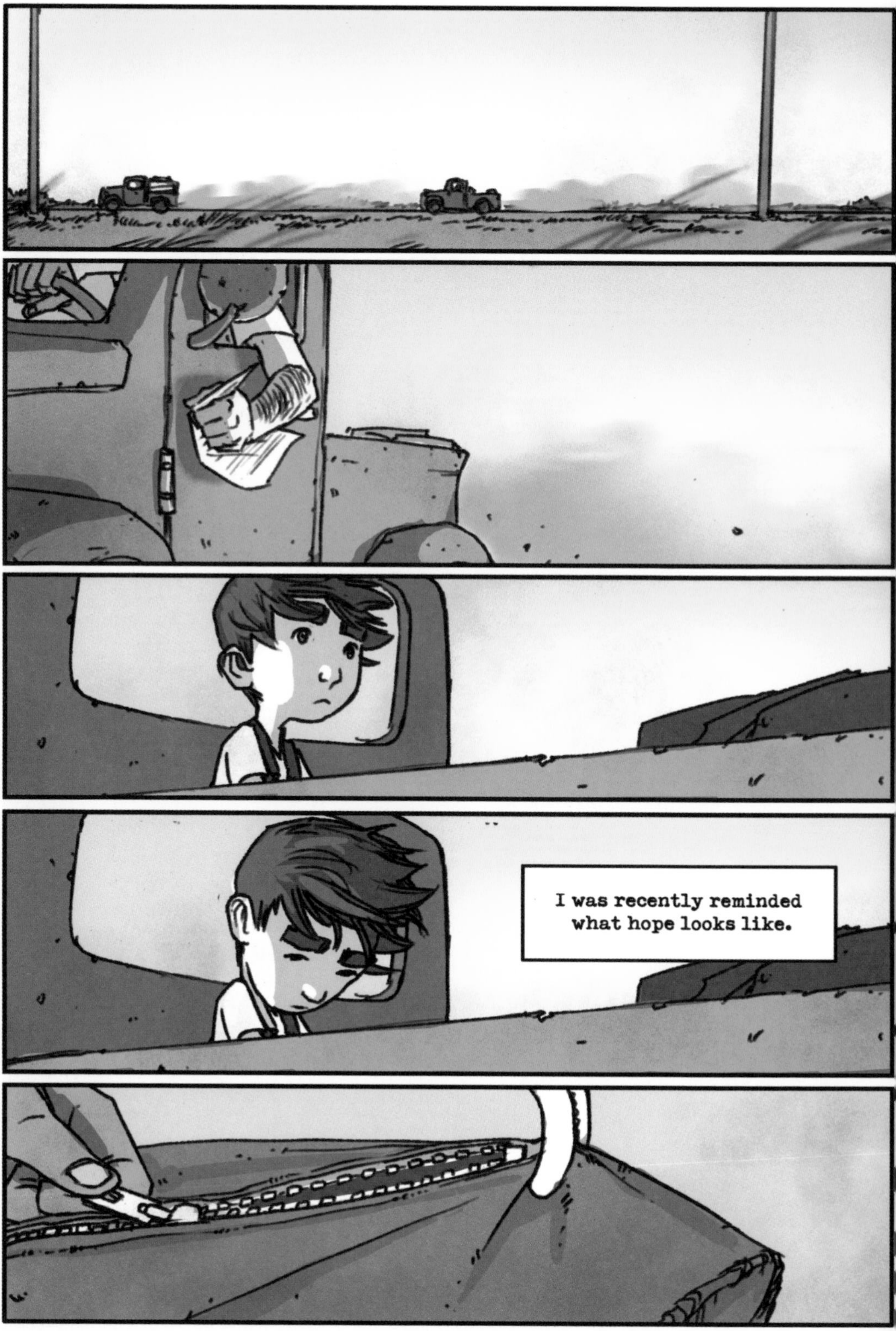
I was recently reminded
what hope looks like.

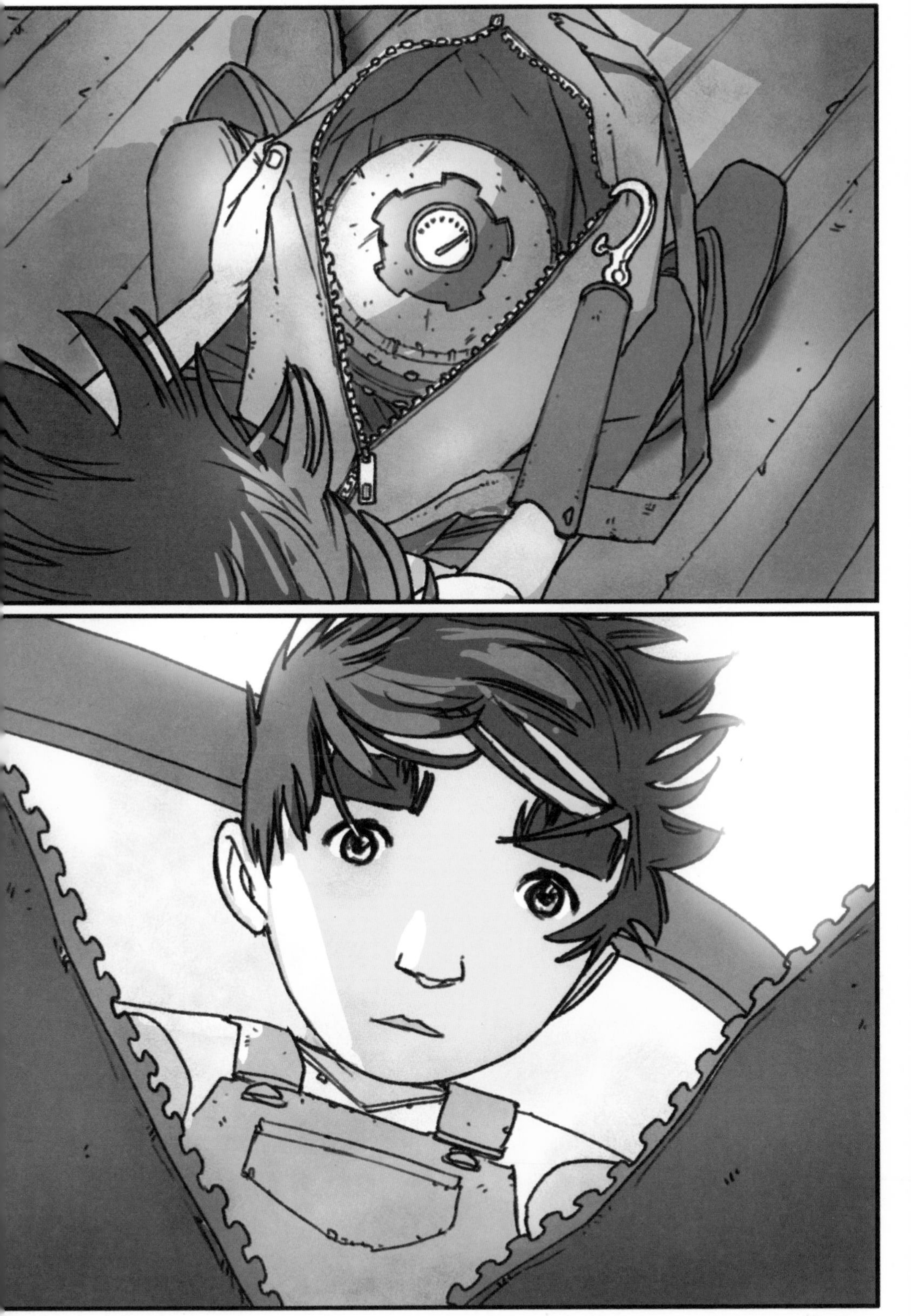

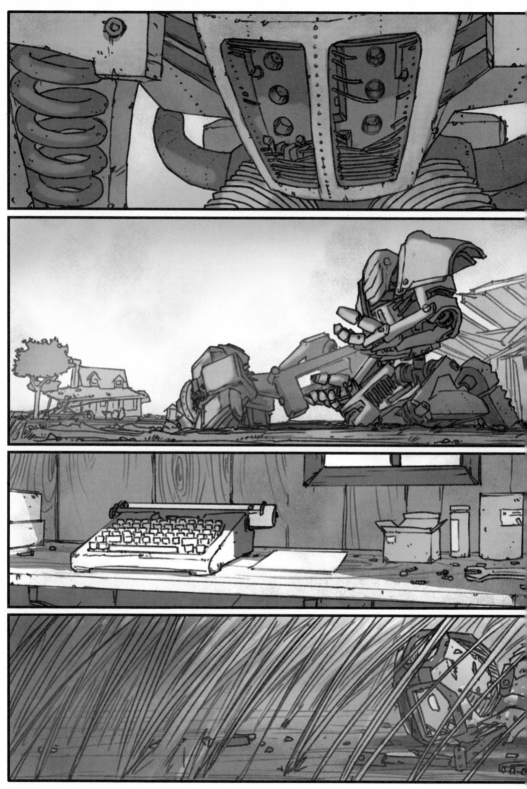

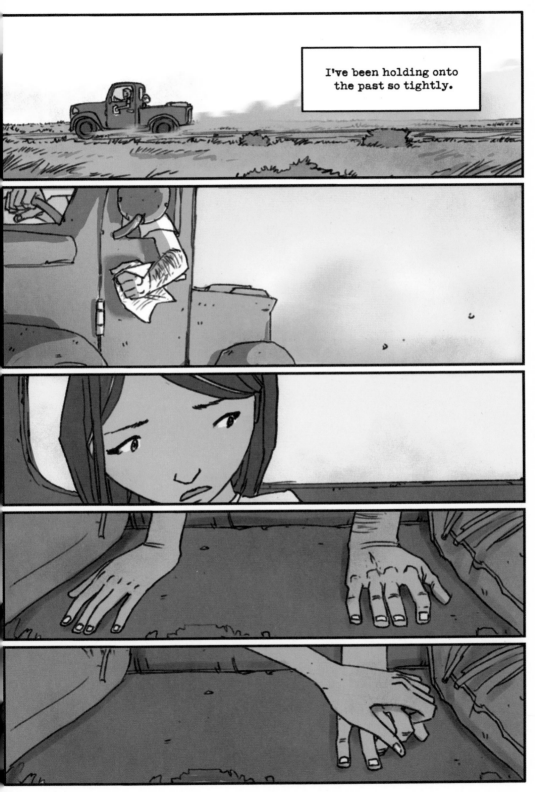

I've been holding onto the past so tightly.

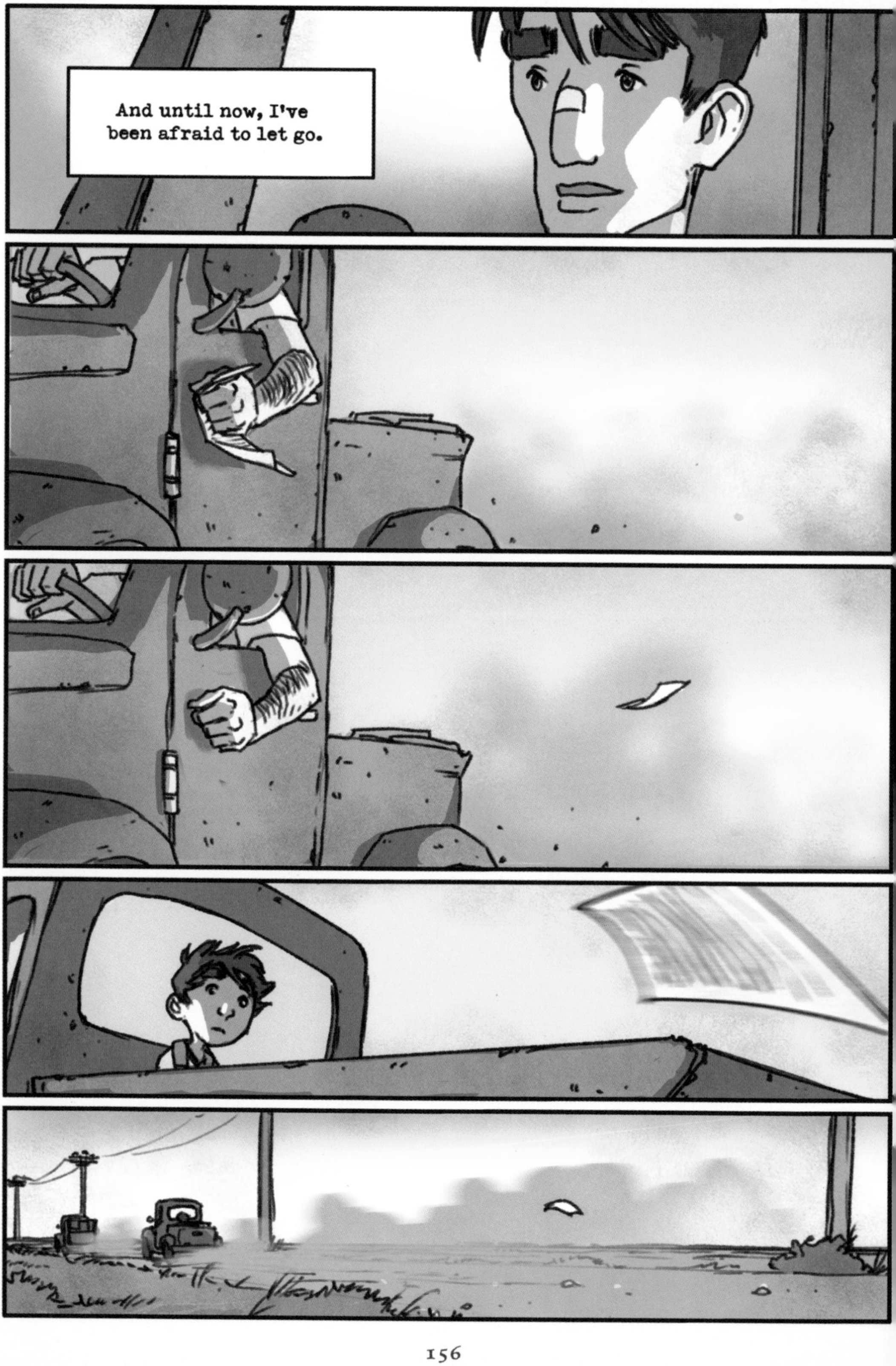
And until now, I've
been afraid to let go.

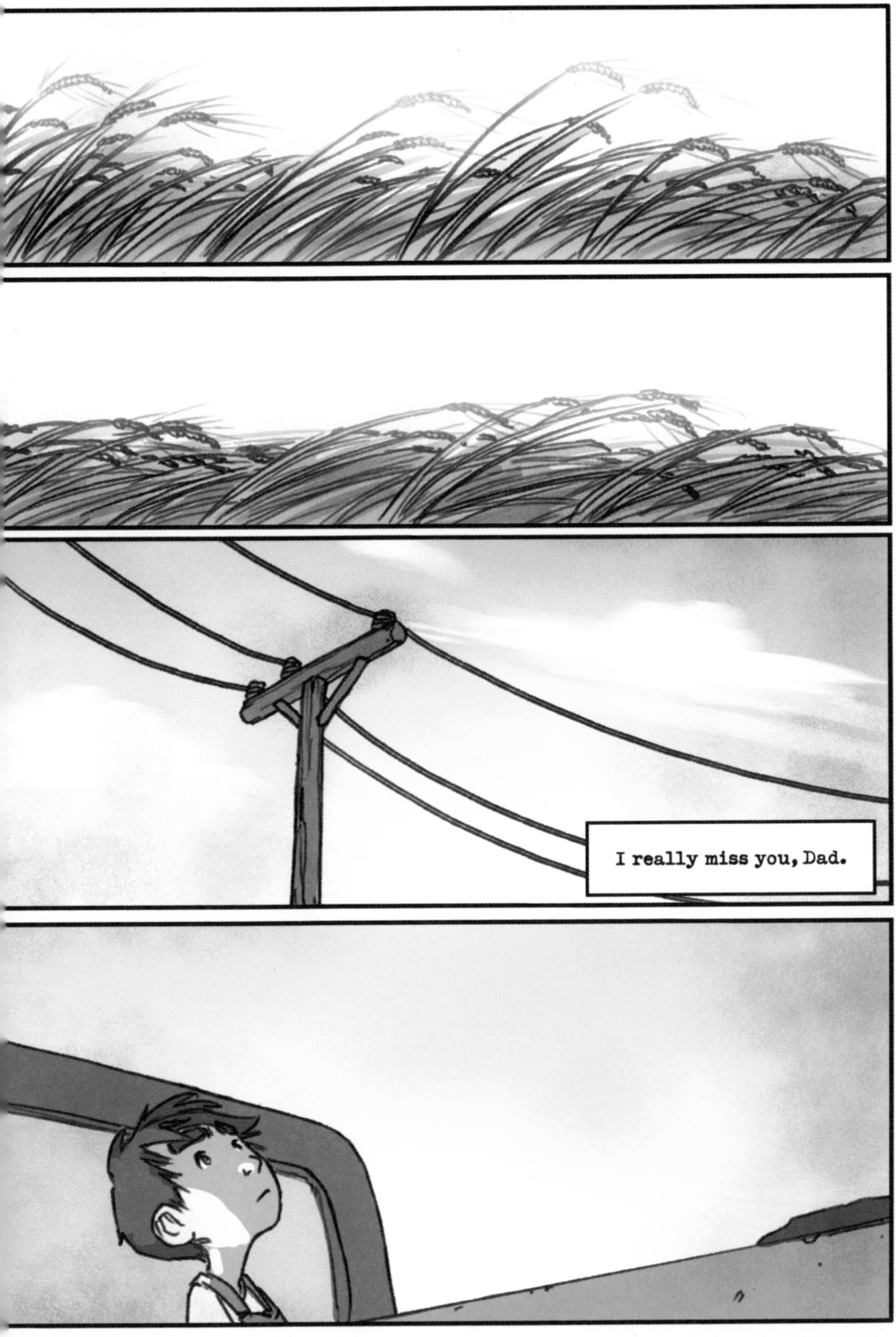
I really miss you, Dad.

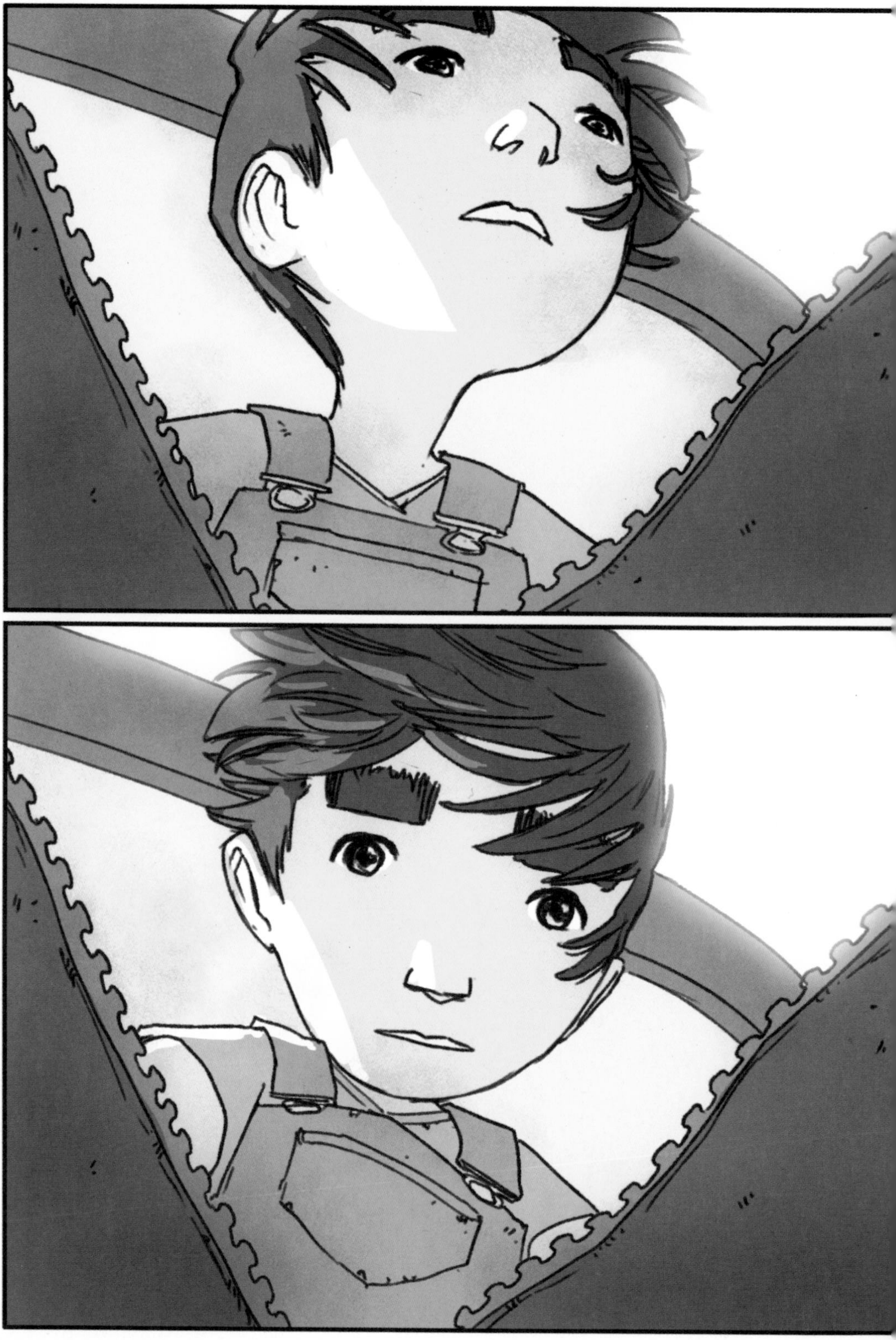

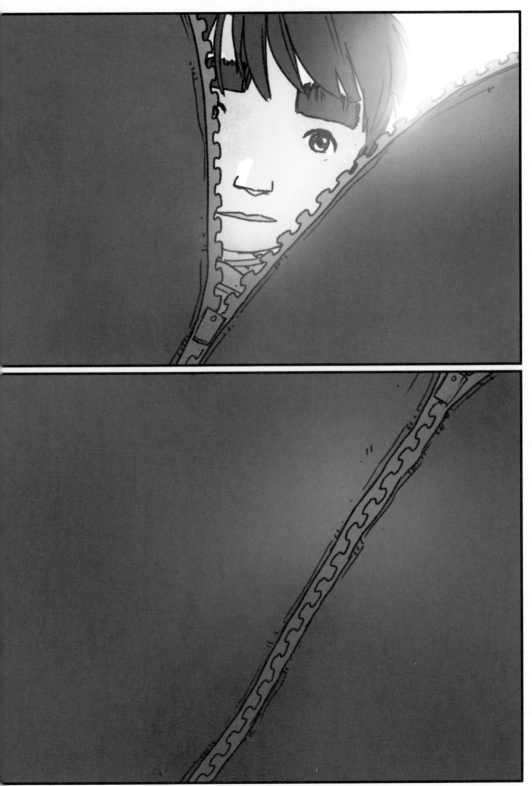

END.

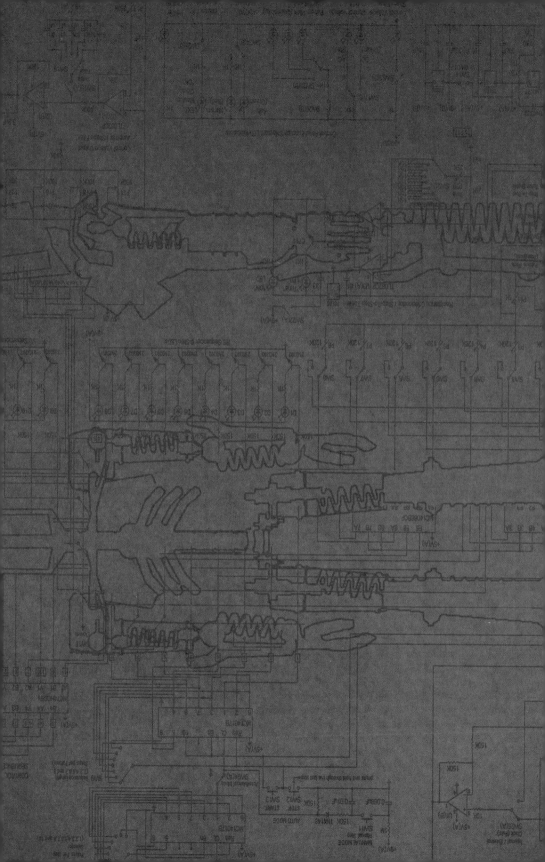

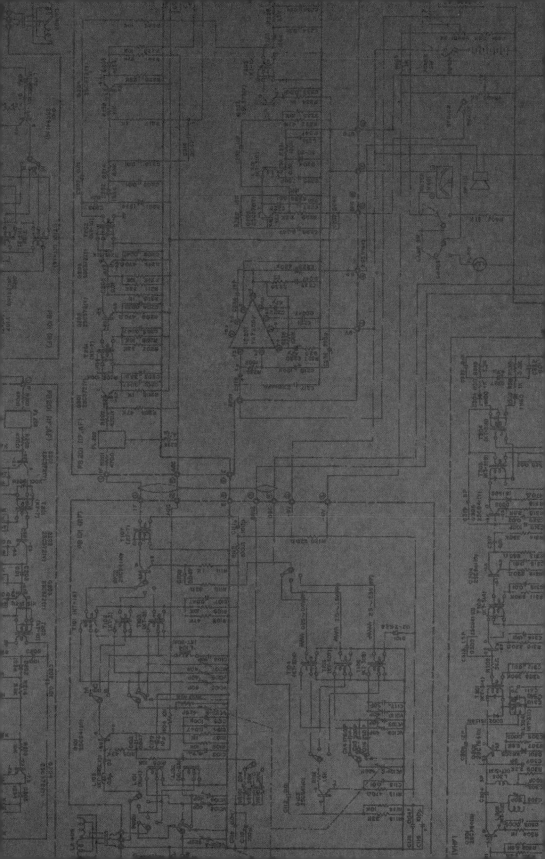

DAY 23

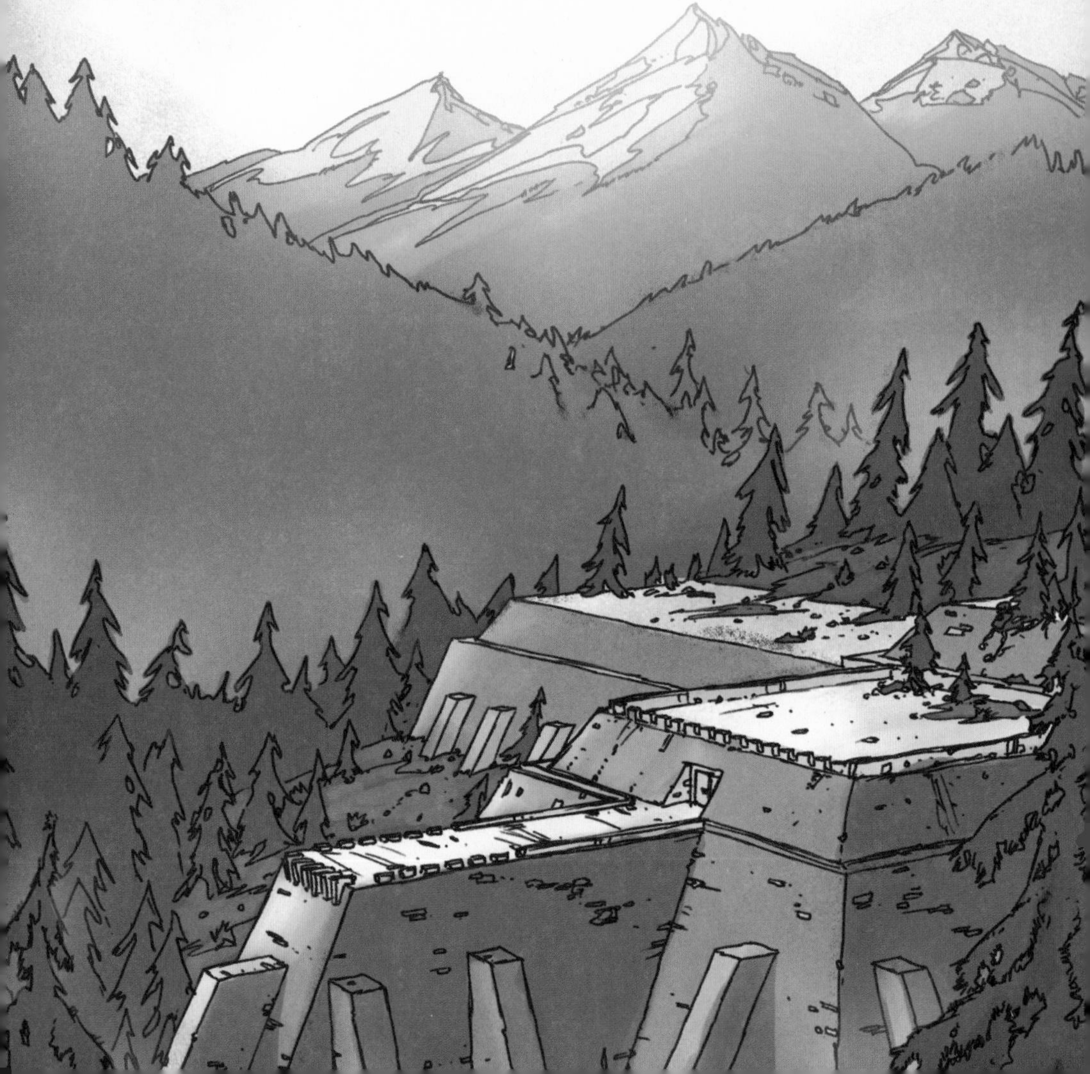

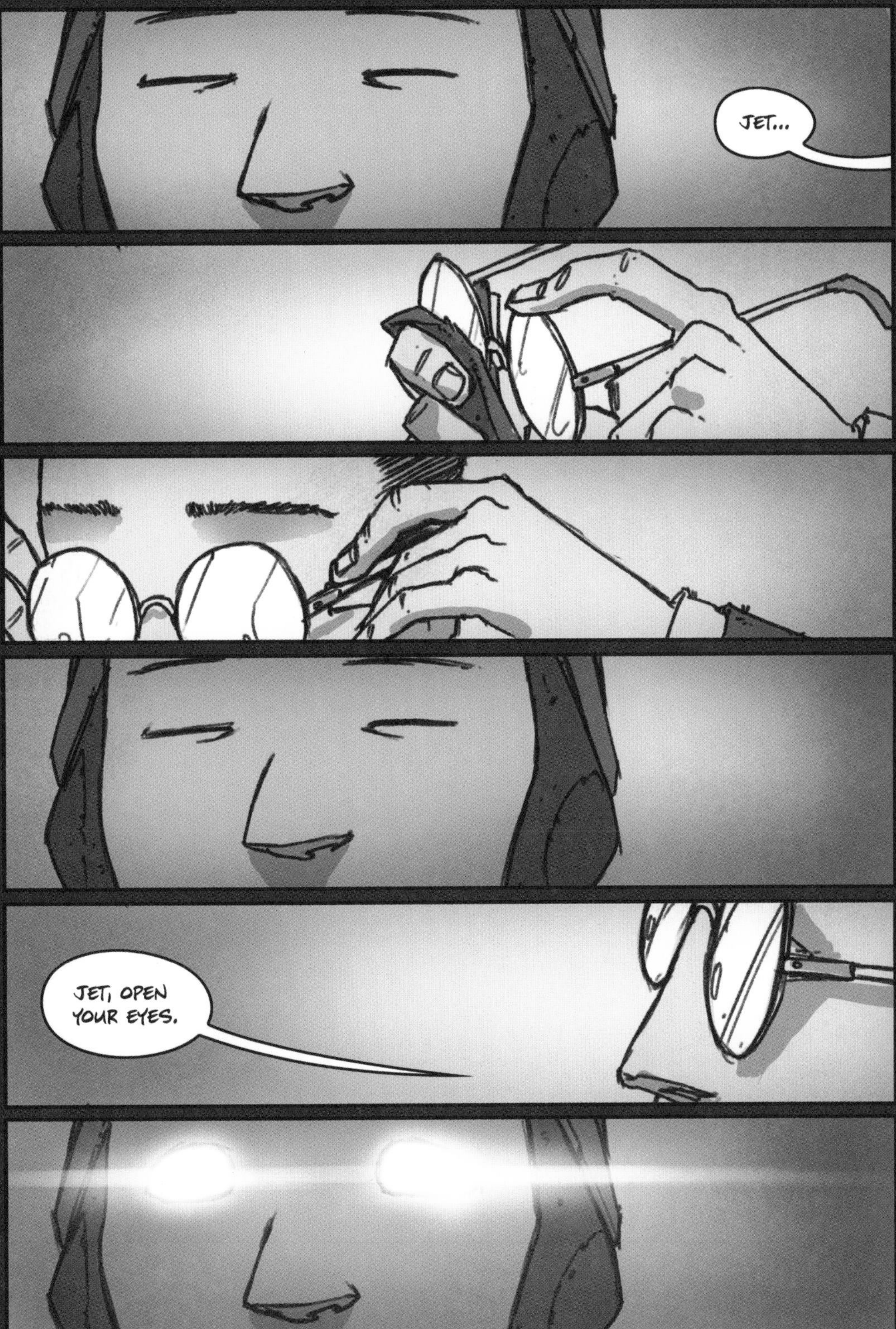
JET...
JET, OPEN YOUR EYES.

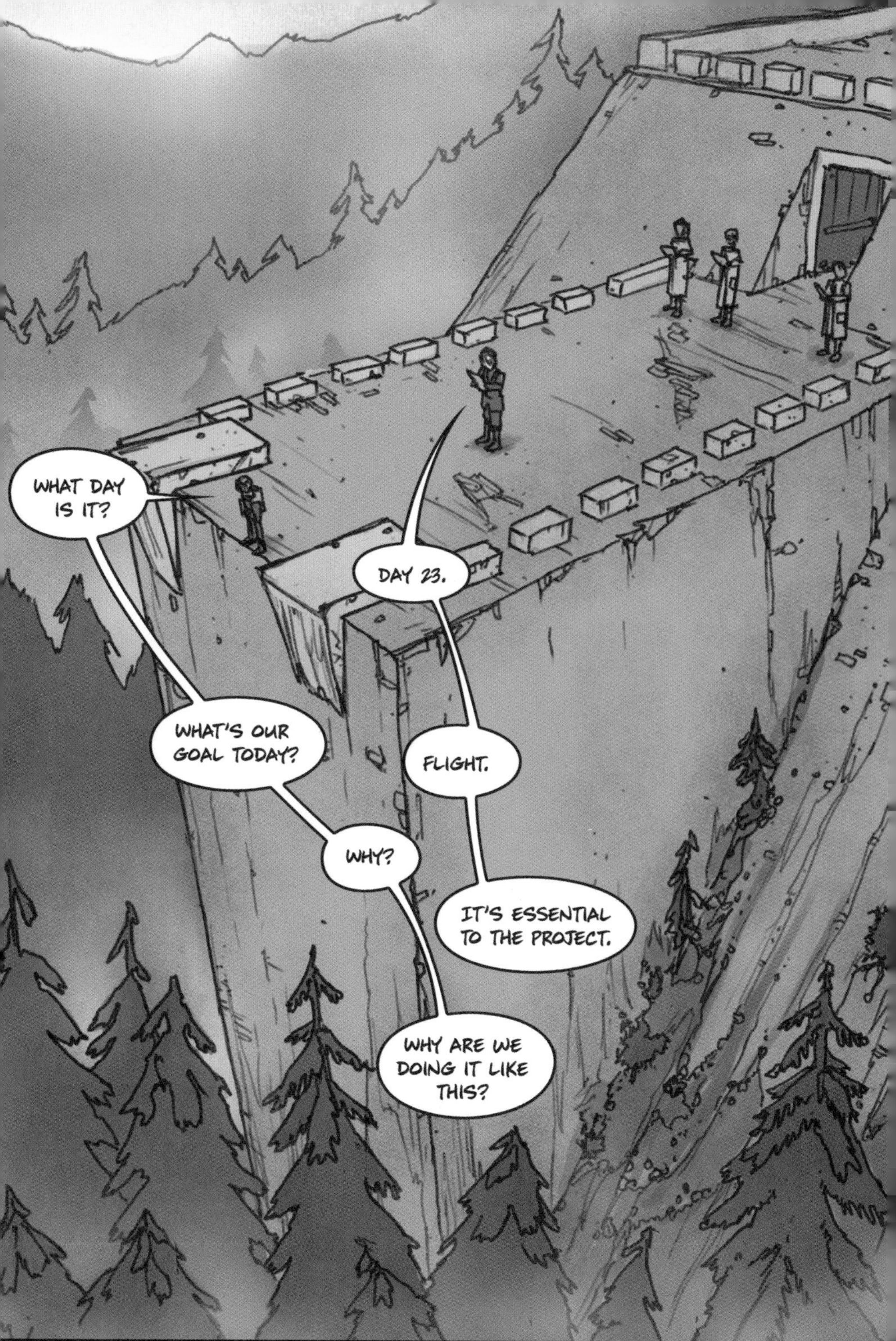
WHAT DAY IS IT?
DAY 23.
WHAT'S OUR GOAL TODAY?
FLIGHT.
WHY?
IT'S ESSENTIAL TO THE PROJECT.
WHY ARE WE DOING IT LIKE THIS?

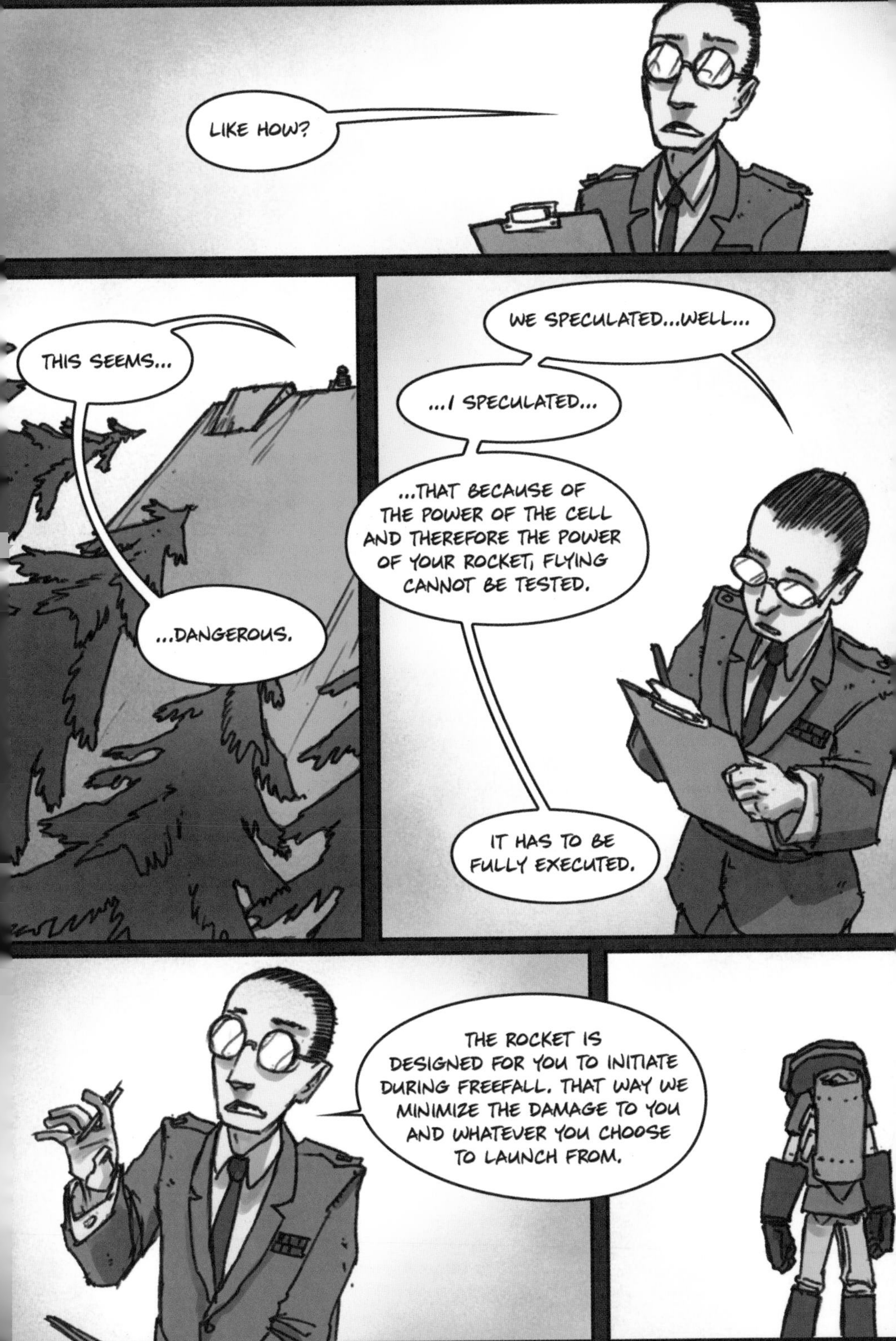
LIKE HOW?
THIS SEEMS...
...DANGEROUS.
WE SPECULATED...WELL...
...I SPECULATED...
...THAT BECAUSE OF THE POWER OF THE CELL AND THEREFORE THE POWER OF YOUR ROCKET, FLYING CANNOT BE TESTED.
IT HAS TO BE FULLY EXECUTED.
THE ROCKET IS DESIGNED FOR YOU TO INITIATE DURING FREEFALL. THAT WAY WE MINIMIZE THE DAMAGE TO YOU AND WHATEVER YOU CHOOSE TO LAUNCH FROM.

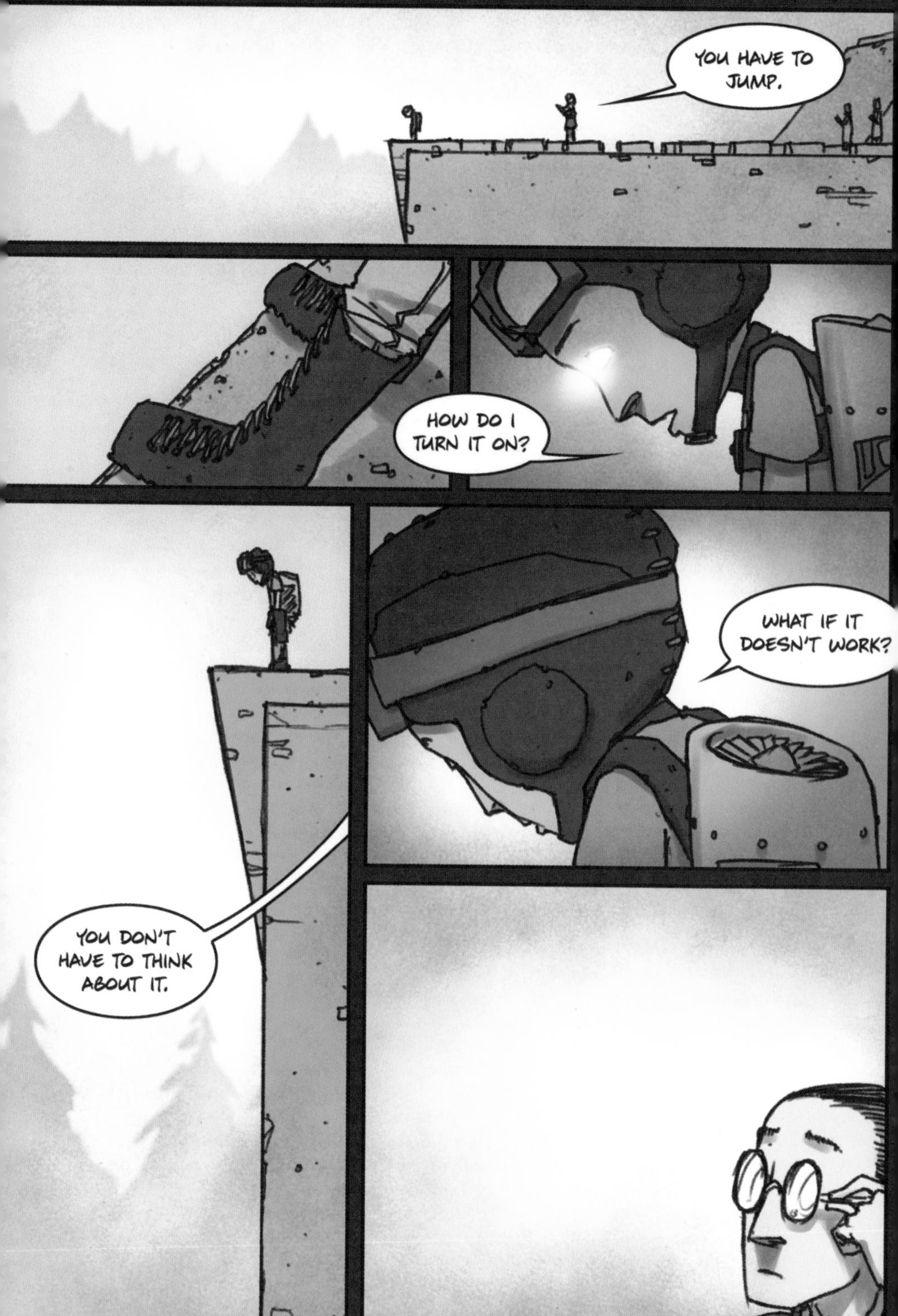
YOU HAVE TO JUMP.
HOW DO I TURN IT ON?
WHAT IF IT DOESN'T WORK?
YOU DON'T HAVE TO THINK ABOUT IT.

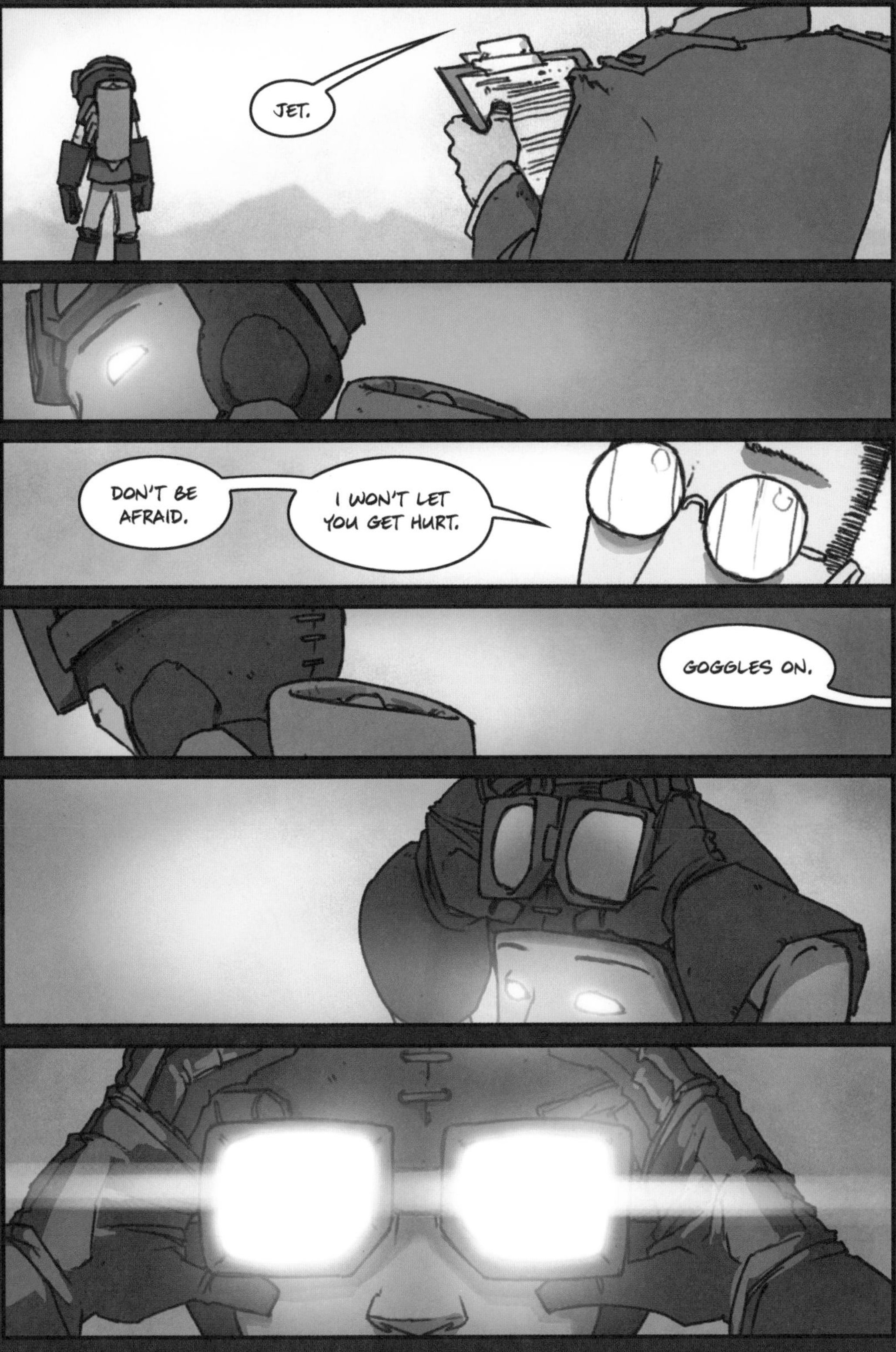
JET.
DON'T BE AFRAID.
I WON'T LET YOU GET HURT.
GOGGLES ON.

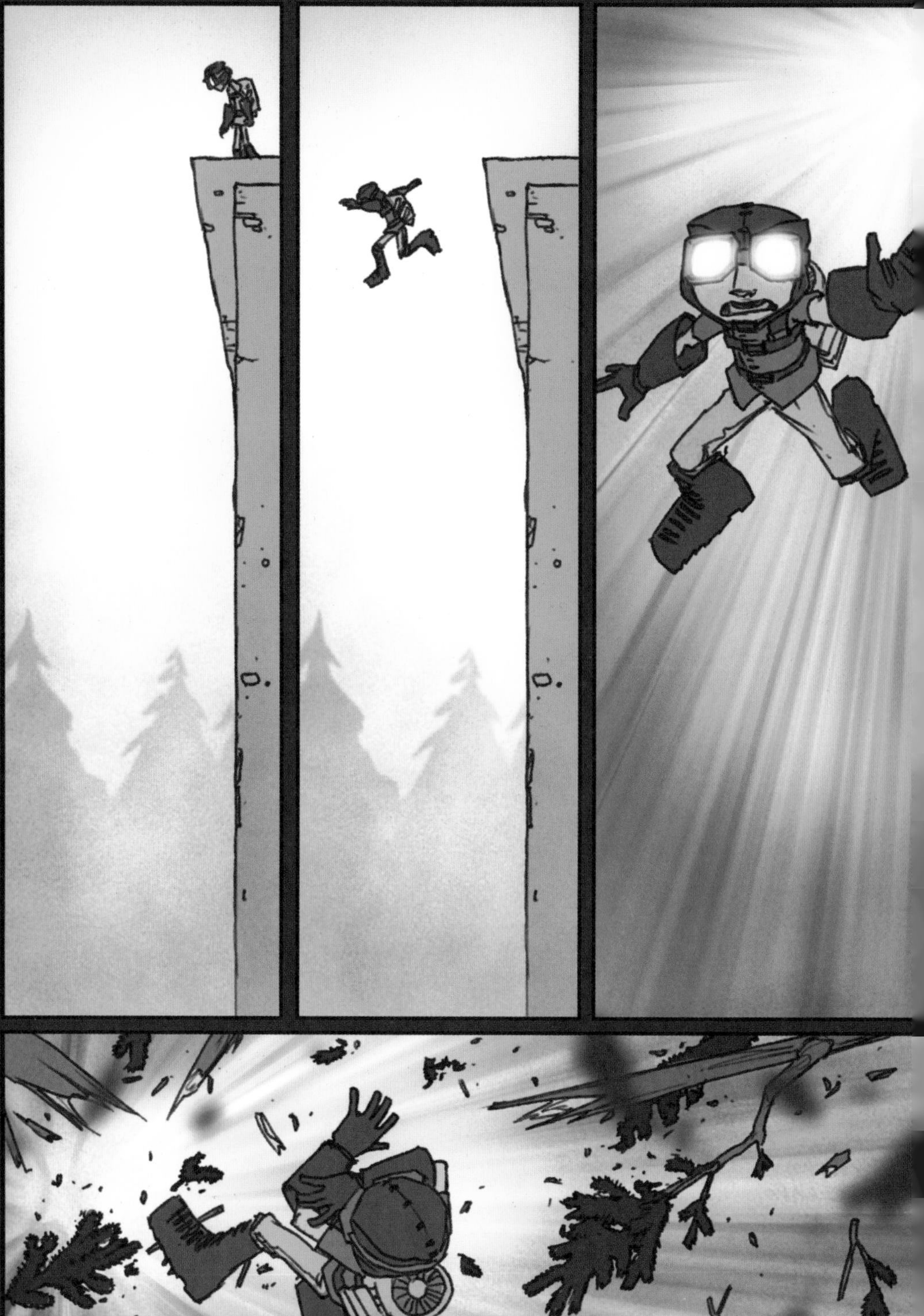

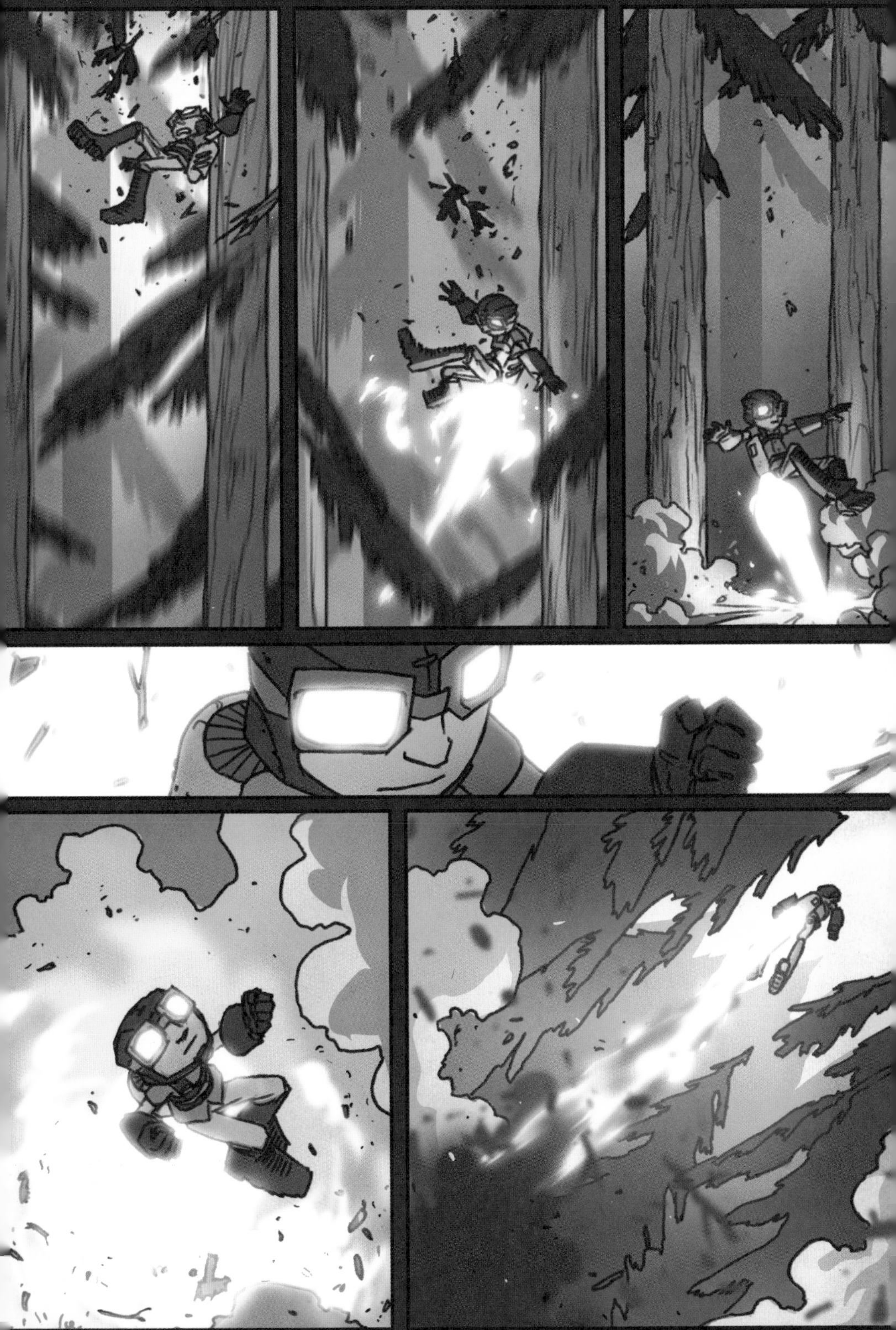

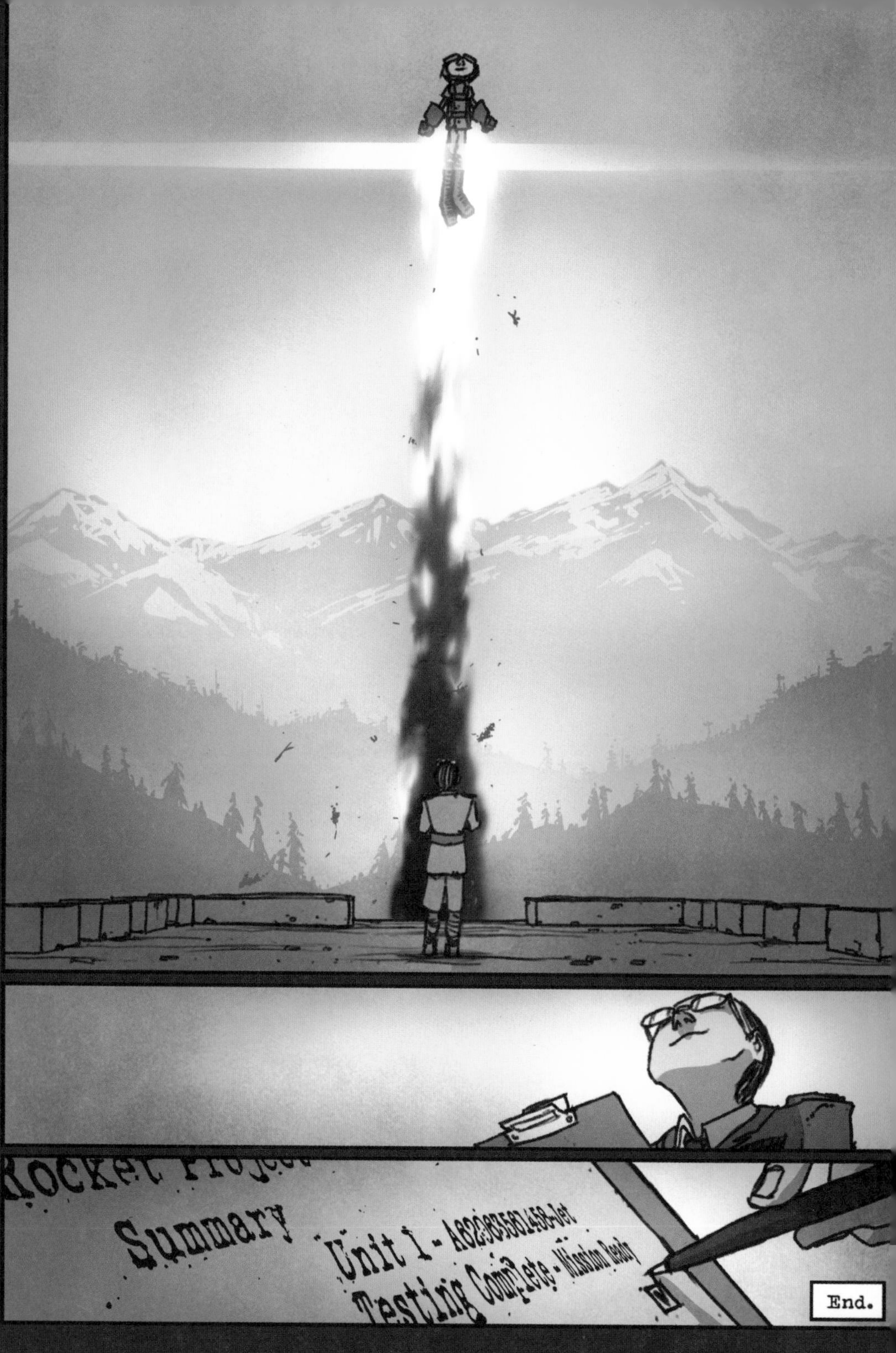
Summary
Unit 1 -
Testing Complete - Mission Ready
End.

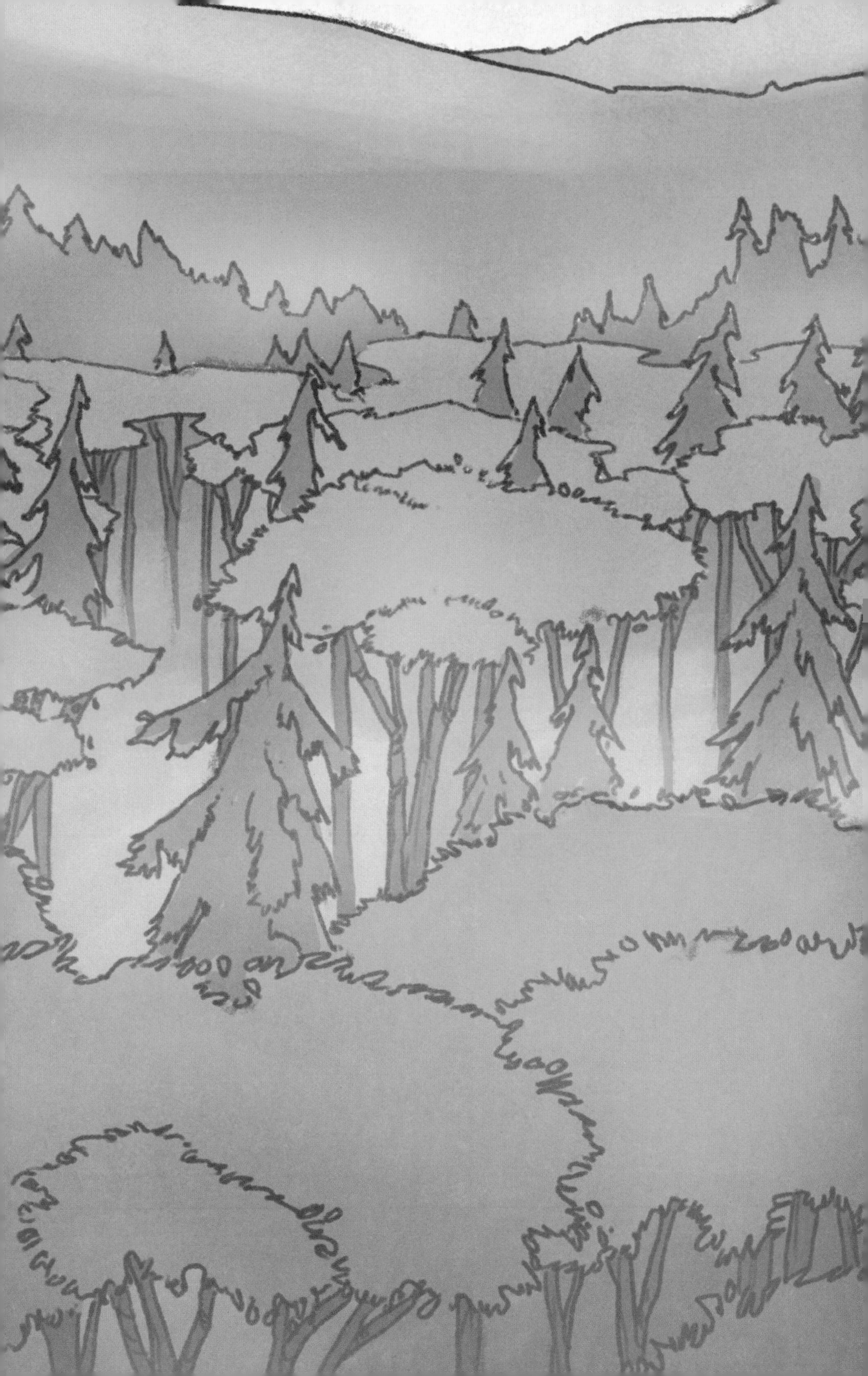

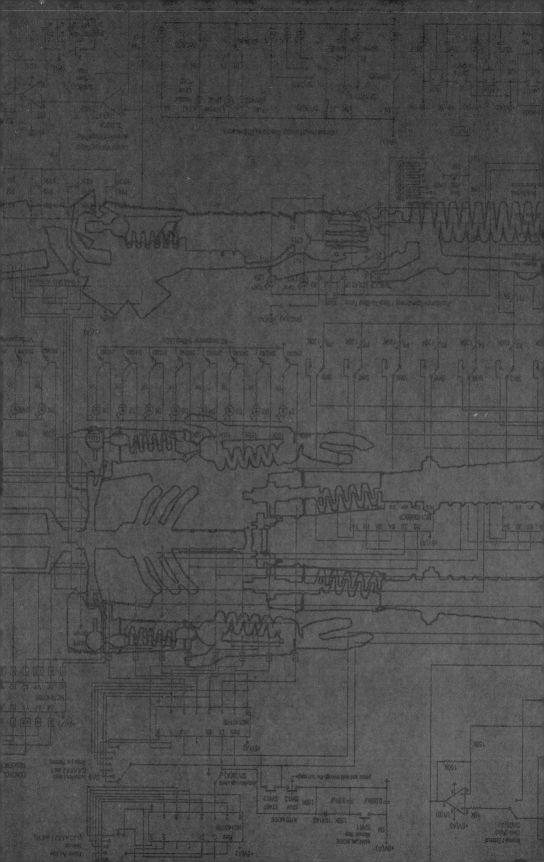